NEW
HORIZONS

To Molly
with best wishes
from

Maisie Stone.

Published under licence by Brown Dog Books and
The Self-Publishing Partnership Ltd, 10b Greenway Farm, Bath Rd,
Wick, nr. Bath BS30 5RL

www.selfpublishingpartnership.co.uk

ISBN printed book: 978-1-83952-661-9
ISBN e-book: 978-1-83952-662-6

Cover design by Kevin Rylands
Internal design by Andrew Easton

Printed and bound in the UK

This book is printed on FSC® certified paper

Sequel to 'Annie-Violet'

NEW HORIZONS

The First World War is looming, as Avie starts her adventures

Maisie Stone

BROWN
DOG BOOKS

Dedication

This book is dedicated to my dear late husband, David, who always encouraged me in my writing. I have happy memories of many lovely holidays together and these places are mentioned in the novel.

A big Thank You to my tech-savvy sons, Tim and Marty, without whose interest and support this book would not have been written.

Chapter 1

Pelham Hall, Chilham, Kent
January, 1913

Annie-Violet sat at her dressing-table and gazed at herself in the mirror. Her unruly auburn curls had been tamed by her mother's maid, Emma. They were now swept back into a soft chignon, with a few tendrils framing her oval-shaped face. A pink ribbon was woven into the chignon. Her blue eyes stared back at her and she gave a petulant sigh. Her mother had won again. She had insisted that Annie had her hair styled off her face, now she was turning eighteen. Annie had wanted to have it loose with an Alice band, but Harriet had made quite a fuss about it. She said very decidedly that all young girls had their hair put up, once they reached eighteen.

But she had allowed her daughter to choose the dress she was going to wear at the big party tonight.

Annie-Violet looked across at the beautiful silk dress hanging against the wardrobe. And she couldn't resist going over to it and fingering the delicate pale pink fabric. It fell in soft folds from the waist and the extravagant puff sleeves were decorated with lace, and satin ribbons. It was divine, quite divine.

Her mother had taken her to London and they had visited all the top department stores, Harrods, Liberty, Selfridges and Debenhams, but couldn't seem to find anything suitable. And just when Harriet had said that perhaps they should go after all to her dressmaker in Canterbury, Annie spotted it, in the window of a small boutique in Oxford Street. It was the only dress in the window, accompanied by a bouquet of flowers and a stylish gold chair, with a lady's picture hat hanging on it. Annie was immediately drawn to it.

'That's it!' she cried. 'I have to go in and try it on, it's gorgeous...'

Harriet had gasped at the price when she saw the ticket, but was assured it had come that very morning from Paris and was definitely à la mode, so agreed immediately.

'So, this is the special dress, eh?' Her father's voice interrupted her reverie as he appeared in the doorway. He came over to Annie and hugged her warmly. 'How are you, my darling child, excited?'

Annie's eyes lit up as she responded to Jeremy's hug. 'Oh yes, I forgot you haven't seen it before, do you like it?' She held the dress up against herself. 'It's just so beautiful, I can't wait to wear it.'

Jeremy nodded approvingly, 'It's lovely. Now Avie,' her father used his special pet name for his daughter, from the initials of 'Annie-Violet'. 'I have to tell you, darling, your mother is becoming a tiny bit overwrought downstairs...'

Avie nodded. 'I can imagine, there's a lot to sort out. Did the flowers arrive?'

Jeremy perched on the end of the bed and grimaced. 'Yes, but now she doesn't think she ordered enough. She wants you to come and see what you think. And then little Matthew decided to have a tantrum and says he won't go to bed.'

'I'll go and see to him,' Avie said, replacing her dress against the wardrobe. 'And I suppose Robert wants to stay up for the party, does he?' she said, chuckling to herself. Robert was Jeremy's child from his first marriage and was now five years of age. He and Avie got on just fine. She was so good with children and they adored her.

Jeremy smiled, as they both left the room and made their way down the elegant staircase of the Tudor mansion. 'We have told him he can stay up and see everyone arrive and hear a little of the music, then he has to go to bed like a good boy.'

Avie's eyes crinkled up in amusement. 'I seem to remember I promised him a little dance, so I will have to keep to that.' She turned to Jeremy. 'He is such a dear child, I do love him!'

'And he loves you. Remember the first Christmas we spent together?' Jeremy put his arm around his daughter's shoulders.

Avie nodded. 'Tobogganing down the hill? Having snowball fights? It was great.'

Jeremy was a solicitor with his own practice in Canterbury and he and Avie had a close bond, always laughing and joking together.

They reached the entrance hall and made their way to the Great Hall where much activity was taking place.

Kitchen staff and footmen were decorating the huge, panelled room with strings of fairy lights and streamers. Members of the local band were just arriving on the dais, unloading their instruments, laughing and joking. Footmen were setting up flowers and candlesticks on small side tables. A long banner was being erected over the dais proclaiming: 18 TODAY! HIP HIP HOORAY! Tubs and vases of flowers adorned every corner of the room. They could see Harriet's statuesque figure, directing the maids with different tasks. Robert was having fun, charging about the Great Hall with a box over his head.

Harriet turned, looking rather harassed, as they entered the room, little Matthew, now two, clinging on to her skirts and howling.

'Don't want to go to bed, not going! Staying up for the party like Robert.' More howls.

'He's overtired.' Harriet gave Jeremy a desperate look. 'I sent Nanny off on an errand ages ago and she still hasn't returned. We could do with her now, right now.'

Mother isn't coping like she did, thought Avie, *that's what comes of having another baby in your forties…* Lady Harriet had decided to dispense with her title on her marriage to Jeremy, but she was still the dignified woman she had always been.

'Don't worry, darling, Avie is here. She'll sort him out.' Jeremy put his arm round Harriet's shoulders comfortingly.

'What do you think, darling?' Harriet turned to Avie. 'Have we got enough floral displays? There seems to be a gap over there… Anyway, I've got all the maids to go and pick some more greenery – any greenery – so that we can perhaps space the flowers out. Do you think that will do?'

Avie nodded. 'It looks fine to me, don't you think, dad? But yes, a good idea to add a bit more greenery.' She crouched beside her brother. 'Now, young man, I've got an idea. Can you come and help me with something? I've heard that your teddy bear is a bit lonely up there in the nursery and he's lost his ribbon. Shall we go and try to find it?'

Matthew sniffed and wiped his nose with his hand. He still

looked truculent. 'All right, but want one of those special biscuits first, Nanny said I could...'

Avie winked at Jeremy and Harriet. 'I think that could be arranged, Matthew.' She held out her hand. 'Let's go!'

As she left the room, Jeremy called out after her. 'When is your young man arriving from Paris?'

Avie looked at her wristwatch, her heart beating faster at the very mention of her special friend. Nearly six p.m. 'In about an hour, I think. He's travelling with Pierre and Sylvie. They've been over there for Christmas and New Year.'

'I shall have to brush up on my French,' smiled Jeremy.

'He speaks excellent English as I'm sure you remember, Dad.' It had been several months since they had met. William was always in her thoughts, and she was desperate to become engaged to him. But her parents had said she was too young. Avie remembered his twinkling blue eyes scanning her face and the feel of his lips on hers, as he stole a kiss when the chaperone wasn't looking.

Her young man, Guillaume (known as William while in England) was an architect and they had met three years ago, while Guillaume was visiting his brother Pierre in England. So, it was a rather difficult relationship, slow to develop because of the distance between them. But they managed to see each other two or three times a year and wrote to each other frequently.

Avie took little Matthew up to the nursery and had a short game with him looking for Teddy's ribbon. She then persuaded him to go to bed, once he had had his milk and biscuit. She sat with him for a while, stroking his head and singing a lullaby to him, to make sure he was fast asleep.

At that point Nanny Rosie appeared and said she would take over. She had been back to their house in Canterbury to fetch some forgotten items.

'Nanny Rosie, are we pleased to see you! Matthew has been playing up like crazy. Mother was at her wits' end with him...'

Nanny Rosie looked at the angelic face of the two-year-old, now fast asleep clutching his teddy, thumb in his mouth. 'Never think that to look at him now...' she laughed. Nanny was very capable. Avie had never seen her angry or upset. She was always very calm.

Avie hurried from the room. *At last!* she thought. I *can get myself ready...*

Half an hour later she stood in front of the long mirror and studied herself with a critical eye. *Yes, it really is totally divine, I love it.*

The pale pink silk of the dress contrasted with her rich auburn hair, and her silver sandals complemented the outfit. She had applied just a little lipstick and a touch of rouge to her cheeks, but was so excited by the occasion that not much was required.

She looked at her watch. A quarter to seven. William would be here soon. Her heart pounded at the very thought.

Avie ran down the stairs and saw James, her uncle and Amelia, his wife, waiting in the hall with their children, Thomas, Paul and Benjamin. They greeted her warmly, but James had news for Avie about the cross-Channel steamers.

'I rang the Dover port authorities, Avie, and, sorry to say, because of the rough weather the boat was delayed setting off. So it will be arriving at least an hour late. It's really choppy in the Channel tonight apparently. Sorry to give you bad news.'

Avie's face fell, but she managed a brave smile. 'As long as they are still coming, that's all that matters. I'm sure they will get here as quickly as they can. And are Grandma and Grandpa all right tonight? They are still fit to come down?'

James was the heir to the title of Earl of Sandwich, and as his parents were now in their dotage, he was responsible for the running of Pelham Hall, after Harriet's departure to Canterbury following her marriage to Jeremy. James had made many changes to the Hall since he had taken charge. The old Tudor building was now completely electrified, and many more bathrooms had been installed. The beautiful crystal chandelier in the Great Hall had been converted to electricity and more modern equipment installed in the kitchen and the dairy.

The restoration in the east wing was now nearly complete. James had made a feature of the many valuable artworks in the Hall, by creating a picture gallery down one of the main corridors.

Avie had been born to Harriet out of wedlock and then been adopted, but they had been reunited, when Harriet and Jeremy met up again and married three years ago.

'Yes, the grandparents are fit and well, they are coming down soon. The guests are arriving at about eight o'clock I believe.'

The guests began to arrive, bringing cards and presents, and shouts of 'Happy Birthday' echoed round the hall. But although Avie was delighted to see her friends, she was anxious about William's delayed crossing and felt she couldn't relax until he arrived. She greeted her many local friends and the girls she knew from her Suffragette days, as well as old schoolfriends and acquaintances. Her adoptive parents, Herbie and Betsy, were next to arrive, and sister, Janey, with warm hugs and kisses all round. Then her beloved Aunt Florrie, who was very special to her, and her husband, Stan. The band started playing popular tunes and Robert kept pestering her for a dance, which she knew she had to give him before he went to bed.

She took to the floor with him for a waltz, which was decidedly off beat and gangly, but the child seemed to enjoy it. Avie had fun sweeping him around the floor, to the amusement of the other guests. After that, Robert was persuaded that he had to go to bed, even though he protested. But he was a good boy and obeyed his father, when he insisted that the time had come to go Up the Wooden Hill to Bedfordshire. He kissed his father and Harriet goodnight, and Avie and the grandparents.

But as he went through the door there was a slight commotion, as who should arrive at the same time, but William.

Avie's eyes lit up as she saw him and she hurried over to greet him, along with his brother, Pierre and his fiancée, Sylvie.

They all hugged each other and Avie couldn't take her eyes off her boyfriend. His tall figure was clad in a smart dinner jacket and bow tie and his face dissolved into a rapturous smile when he saw her. He gave her a brief kiss and hug. 'Darling, at last – I thought we'd never get 'ere…'

'Was it a terrible crossing?' Everyone nodded, shaking their heads. 'Really bad, a lot of passengers, they were sick, but we were fine most of the time,' said Pierre in his broken English.

'Though we couldn't eat anything,' added Sylvie. 'Too risky.'

Waiters were circulating with drinks on trays, followed by maids with canapés and snacks and they all took a glass of wine.

'To you, Avie, 'appy Birthday!' William raised his glass. 'You are looking so beautiful tonight, *ma petite*,' he murmured in her ear. 'What 'ave you done to your 'air, it looks very elegant...'

But William couldn't sit still for too long. After wolfing down a couple of sandwiches, he got to his feet. 'Come on, let's dance,' he exclaimed. And he swept her round the dance floor with an energy and style that took her breath away.

They made a handsome couple as they circulated amongst the other dancers. Avie noticed admiring glances towards William from her friends who had not met him before.

The music ended and William suddenly fished in his pocket and brought out a gaily wrapped gift box. 'But I am forgetting,' he said and led her to a secluded alcove where they could be private. He touched her on the nose with his finger. 'Mustn't forget your present.'

And he handed her the pretty gift box. ''appy Birthday, my sweet.'

Avie was all smiles, as she tore off the paper to reveal a square velvet box with the renowned name of Cartier embossed on it. She opened it up to find a dazzling pendant necklace on a white gold chain. It featured a brilliant cut sapphire surrounded by diamonds, with matching sapphire drop earrings.

She gasped, as she took them out of the box very carefully. They sparkled as she held them up and they caught the light from the chandelier.

'Oh, William. They are so beautiful. Thank you so much.'

She put her arms round his neck and kissed him on the lips. He returned the kiss, saying: 'As soon as I saw them, I knew they were for you... to match your eyes. ''ere, let me put them on, if I may.'

Avie stood up and William fastened the necklace round her neck, while she tried to fix the earrings. But her hands were shaking so much she had difficulty in doing so.

Aunt Florrie was nearby and came to her aid. 'Hey, what's this? This looks like a very special present, young lady! Here, let me help you.' And she fixed the earrings on securely, while Avie still clasped William's hand. 'There, look at you!' cried Florrie. 'My word, quite the little princess!'

'I need a mirror', said Avie and she ran over to the huge rectangular mirror on the panelled wall. She stared at herself in the mirror, the jewellery glinting and sparkling. It looked sensational and perfectly complemented her new pale pink dress. She was quite overcome, her heart beating erratically.

Harriet and Jeremy appeared behind her and admired the gift, while all her friends gathered round exclaiming excitedly about the special present.

Avie shook her head. She had never thought in a million years she would ever own such a dazzling item of jewellery. She had joined quite a poor but respectable family when she was adopted all those years ago. Jewellery was never even thought of, let alone owned.

She looked over to Betsy and Herbie sitting nearby and remembered the lovely gift they had given her only yesterday. Herbie was a skilled carpenter and he had fashioned (ironically, she thought) a fine jewellery box for her, made from rosewood, with simple, inlaid marquetry on the top and Betsy had lined it with red velvet. It was a fine present, made with their own hands and given with love. It must have taken Herbie months to complete it. It had little compartments, and niches for rings; it was perfectly made. *I shall treasure it just as much as William's fine jewellery*, she thought. She loved her adoptive parents. They had brought her up so well, along with her sister, Janey. Money had been tight, but they were such a loving family, it didn't seem to matter.

Avie suddenly felt very torn – she loved all these people who came from such different backgrounds, but she hoped that they didn't feel jealous of William's rather extravagant gift. She had noticed that even her parents had been somewhat cool about the Cartier jewellery. Maybe they felt it put their own present of an (albeit very expensive) dressing-table set in the shade…? She felt a little uncomfortable at the thought and wished she hadn't opened William's present in such a public manner.

But her troubled thoughts were suddenly interrupted by the arrival of Mrs. Cherry, the Pelham Hall cook. She was beaming as she wheeled in a trolley bearing a huge cake topped with candles. And the band struck up 'Happy Birthday to You' to everyone's delight.

Jeremy steered Avie towards the table. 'Come, darling, it's time for you to blow out the candles!'

And everyone started singing 'Happy Birthday to You' and she was blowing the candles out. The magnificent iced cake was then taken away to be cut up by the kitchen staff. Footmen began to distribute glasses of champagne around the room. Avie went over to Mrs. Cherry and hugged her. She had known her for many years and although Avie didn't realise it, she was the apple of the cook's eye. Mrs. Cherry had always had a soft spot for Annie-Violet, who had helped in the kitchen when she was younger.

'Thank you for the lovely cake, it's marvellous – how did you do those tiny roses? You are clever!'

Mrs. Cherry gave a chuckle. 'I waved a magic wand, that's what I did! No, a lot of people helped to make it, but as long as it tastes good, then that's all right with me...'

Avie suddenly spotted Isabel, her friend from the Suffragettes, sitting on her own, and went over to her for a chat. They hugged each other and Avie sat down. Isabel began to comment on her jewellery, but Avie brushed it aside. 'Are you still working for the Cause?' she asked, changing the subject.

Avie had given her time a few years ago, making the special Suffragette ribbons of green, white and violet, as she was keen to support the Cause of Women's Suffrage. The colours stood for Give Women the Vote. They also had significance. Green was for hope, White represented purity and Violet was for dignity. But her parents had forbidden her from joining in the marches or in any way condoning the violent expressions of protest, that were taking place. She was only fifteen at the time, so she confined herself to helping in the office or making tea for the protestors when they returned from a march. Some of the protests were indeed quite violent, as the protestors wanted to get publicity for their Cause. They had burned down a cricket pavilion at Tunbridge Wells, and they had set fire to the Tea Room in Kew Gardens. And a lot of them were sent to prison for their actions. Some of them went on hunger strikes and then were forcibly fed in prison; a horrendous procedure, Avie had heard.

'Oh yes, I am, but not so much these days,' Isabel said. 'I've got a job now in London. I'm just working in this office doing typing and filing, but it's great being in the city, you feel you're in the centre of things.' Isabel squeezed Avie's hand. 'Lovely party!' she nudged Avie with a twinkle in her eye. 'Like your bloke, where did you find him?'

Avie smiled happily. 'Funnily enough, I met him here. His brother was working as a chauffeur and William came to visit from Paris...'

'Oh, he's French – ooh la la!' laughed Isabel. 'Do you speak much French?'

'I'm learning, and we write to each other quite a bit, as we can't get to see each other that often. He's an architect in Paris, so it's great when I can go with my parents and see him there, wonderful city. But I'm going away soon,' Avie admitted, waving to William across the room, who was beckoning to her.

'Oh? Where are you off to?' Isabel asked.

'Switzerland,' replied Avie, hardly believing it as she said it. 'I'm going to a finishing school in Montreux, in about a month's time.'

'Well, have fun – being finished off!' laughed Isabel. 'Oh, here comes the cake, lovely...'

Trolleys were being wheeled in and maids began to distribute slices of the delicious birthday cake. A footman with a tray of champagne offered a glass to Isabel and Avie and they both accepted readily.

Avie rose, raising her glass. 'Cheers! Nice to see you, Isabel, best of luck with everything. Give my love to all the girls.'

'I will, and enjoy yourself in Switzerland, don't fall down a mountain!'

Avie joined William talking to a group of guests. The Master of Ceremonies then announced the next dance would be the Veleta, to which everyone clapped, except William.

'What is this Veleta? I don't know it, is it like the Foxtrot?' he asked, looking puzzled.

'Oh no, it's a progressive dance – it's great fun! You form a circle and do some steps, then move on to the next partner...'

William looked straight-faced. 'Oh, so I'm not going to dance with my favourite girl?' His face was quite petulant.

'You'll enjoy it, you'll see!' smiled Avie, shaking her head.

The music started and several circles had been formed around the room. Everyone was laughing as they performed the steps and then moved on to the next person. Much merriment was occurring as they changed partners, feet were trodden on and apologies blurted out.

The evening passed quickly and Avie managed to speak to a lot of friends. She spotted Clara, whom she had known at the Mother and Baby home when she was there. Avie had been engaged as a nanny to the baby daughter of Katherine, a young widow whose husband had died in a shooting accident. And Harriet had suggested that it might be good for Avie to spend some time at the local Mother and Baby home; she could gain some experience with babies and young children, before she started the job.

Avie had enjoyed her time there and made friends with several of the poor young girls, who were caring for their babies, before they were adopted. Many of them were in tears when they had to give them up. And Avie gained valuable experience in dealing with babies, bathing them, feeding them, changing their nappies and learning how to hold them in a special way if they developed colic.

She also took a basic First Aid course which was useful.

She felt at the end of the month that she was well equipped to look after little Gwendoline, Katherine's baby. It had given her confidence to deal with most situations, added to the fact she was a sensible young girl anyway and loved children.

'Hallo Clara, and how are you?' Avie went up to the young woman who had been the manager of the Mother and Baby home in Chilham when she was there. 'Are you still there, or have you spread your wings?'

Clara hugged Avie and they both admired each other's outfits. 'No, I left about six months ago. I'm now working as a nanny to a family in Maidstone.'

'Oh, nice family? How many children?'

'Nice overall, though the mother's very critical. You have to watch your step all the time. The children are good most of the time – there are two boys and a girl, eight, six and four. And you, what are you up to these days?'

'Well, I'm off to Europe soon, they're packing me off to a finishing school in Montreux for six months.' Avie looked a bit glum, as the truth dawned on her that yes, she would be off to Switzerland very soon.

Clara's eyes widened. 'Hey, that's great – or is it? I sense you're not entirely in favour of it…?'

'I'm a bit nervous about it, to tell you the truth. But I'm sure once I get there I'll be fine.' Avie knew she could be frank with Clara, who was a close friend.

'Well, everyone will be in the same boat, won't they?' Clara said, ever the sensible one. 'You'll all be starting out together. I'm sure you will make friends, knowing you…' she added with a laugh. 'Best of luck to you!'

'Excuse me interrupting,' Harriet appeared by their side suddenly. 'I need to take Avie away from you, Clara. The photographer has arrived and wants all the family to gather together.'

Jeremy had hired a professional photographer to take photos of the family and several of Avie on her own. It was essential that such a milestone as an eighteenth birthday was properly recorded. He set up the camera in front of the dais. 'Now, first, a few of you on your own, miss, if I may...'

And Avie dutifully posed by a pedestal adorned with a bouquet of flowers, and smiled until she thought her face would break.

Then a big family group was taken, with her parents, grandparents, aunt and uncle and cousins. Next came one with her adoptive parents, Betsy and Herbert and sister, Janey, Florrie and Stan.

Avie also wanted a photograph taken of herself and William. But Harriet was a little reluctant, as he was not in fact her fiancé yet. But after some insistent pleas from Avie, Harriet relented and the couple stood together holding hands and smiling at each other, happiness radiating from them.

'I'm sure '*Tatler*' will like that one', said Jeremy, referring to the socialite magazine which regularly reported on the lives of aristocratic young women. They did indeed make a handsome couple.

'I think we are just about finished, madam,' said the photographer and he began to pack up his equipment.

The clock struck midnight and the band began playing the music for Sir Roger de Coverley, the traditional final dance at parties. Everyone took to the floor and began singing and dancing. The waiters were soon clearing away glasses and plates from the tables. All the guests began to drift away, murmuring thanks and goodnights.

It had been a wonderful party and, as Avie clasped William's hand, she gazed up at him adoringly. She had loved him from the moment they met and felt a powerful desire for him coursing through her body.

They reached the corridor where Avie's bedroom was situated. And William held her close.

'You know what I am going to say, *ma petite*, don't you? I love you, Avie, and I want to express my love for you – please don't deny me tonight of all nights. You are driving me crazy! Let me come to your room later.'

But Avie knew she had to say no to him once again, even though her heart was desperate to say yes.

And she could only watch in dismay, as he turned away and strode down the corridor, head down.

Chapter 2

Montreux, Switzerland

The Institut Villa Pierre Philippe
EARLY MARCH 1913

Avie Spicer drew back the curtains in her room and gazed out at the view before her. She gasped as she took in the panoramic scene, with Lake Geneva sparkling in the distance in the early morning sunshine. The Institut was set high in the mountains, and she could see distantly the ancient Chateau de Chillon in the morning mist bordering the lake. The houses and buildings of the small town clustered around the long promenade.

She had arrived late last night after an exhausting journey of several days. The boat train had reached Calais after a rough Channel crossing, and after stops at Lille, Stuttgart and Zurich, it had finally pulled into Geneva, where Avie gave a sigh of relief. Jeremy had arranged the help of two friends of his, who by chance were also travelling on the same train. So she had some companions on the long journey, a very pleasant married couple, Mr. and Mrs. Edward Dupont. They were very helpful, particularly as they both spoke fluent French. It was rather confusing for Avie, not having travelled so far before. She began to realise what a sheltered life she had led previously.

A car with 'Institut Villa Pierre Philippe' emblazoned on the side awaited her at Geneva station, to convey her to the school. And the driver in his smart uniform and peaked cap took her luggage, with a gabble of French and a big smile.

When she arrived at the school, it was nine p.m., and the big mansion was deserted. But then suddenly a door was pushed open, and a small lady emerged into the hall and hurried up to her. She was wearing a blue uniform and there was kindness in her eyes as she approached.

'Oh, you must be Annie-Violet Spicer, *oui*?' She thrust her hand out, smiling broadly.

'I am Marguerite, the 'ousekeeper 'ere. Welcome to the Institut! I 'ope your journey it was good? Now I'm sure you are tired, so we 'ave prepared tea and sandwiches for you in the lounge and then I'm sure you will want to go to your room, *oui*?'

Avie murmured and nodded, feeling in a daze with all the events of the last few days, as she shook hands.

Marguerite pointed to a small bell on a table nearby. 'So, when you are ready to go up, just ring that little bell and I will escort you. Your luggage, it 'as already been taken up there. You are on the second floor.'

Avie had fallen into bed, after pulling off her clothes, and was asleep as soon as her head hit the pillow. She was exhausted but also excited as she drifted off to sleep. The prospect of spending the next few months here in this magical place was exhilarating, albeit tinged with a degree of apprehension.

Pelham Hall and her home in Canterbury seemed a long way away...

Avie was brought back to the present by a note being pushed under the door. She ran and picked it up and began reading it. Fortunately, it was in English, as she had heard that mainly French was spoken at the school, which filled her with alarm. Her French was still rather basic, but no doubt she would learn through grim experience.

'Miss Spicer, the Principal, Madame Corbeau, will see you in her office at 10 a.m.'

Avie grimaced. It sounded like a command, not a request. But as she was still in her dressing-gown and it was now eight o'clock, Avie reckoned she should get washed and dressed *tout de suite*, so that she was respectable to appear before the Principal.

Nobody had said anything about breakfast, but once dressed Avie made her way down the stairs and found the dining room. It was a bright and airy room at the back of the house towards the snow-capped mountains, which towered up quite close by. And it seemed to be a help-yourself arrangement. A few young women were gathering by a huge mahogany sideboard, where various meats, cheeses, fruit and bread were laid out, along with pots of coffee and jugs of milk. One or two of them looked at her curiously at first, then a tall girl with blonde hair smiled at her and waved an arm towards two silver domes alongside the other food.

'*Il y a la nourriture chaude ici, aussi, si vous voulez...des oeufs, des saucisses...*' There is hot food here as well if you wish, eggs, sausages...

'*Merci*,' murmured Avie. *This is going to be harder than I imagined. I should have learnt more French*, she thought.

'*Parlez-vous Anglais?*' she enquired, her cheeks reddening. '*Je parle le Française un peu...*'

The tall girl laughed and put out her hand. 'Oh, you are English! Welcome to the School! My name is Claire Carruthers.' She had long fair hair tied back with a ribbon and wore a grey dress with a lace collar.

Avie grasped her hand and shook it, smiling and feeling relieved to hear English being spoken.

'My name is Annie-Violet Spicer, but I'm known as Avie – for obvious reasons.'

Avie had helped herself to some fruit and bread and poured herself a cup of coffee. And the two girls went to the dining table, where other young women were already tucking into breakfast.

Claire waved an arm towards the other girls. 'Girls, we have another new recruit, Avie Spicer.' All the girls smiled and waved. She turned to Avie as she munched a croissant. 'So how was your journey?'

Avie pulled a face. 'Very tiring. But also very interesting, amazing scenery. This is a beautiful area – the view from my bedroom is incredible!'

'So you have an appointment with Madame Corbeau, I imagine?' said Claire.

Avie glanced at her wristwatch. 'Yes, at ten a.m.' It was now 9.20 a.m.

'Don't be late, whatever you do', advised Claire. 'She's a bit of a stickler for punctuality.'

Avie nodded as she peeled a banana. 'So, how long have you been here?' she asked Claire.

'Oh, only a day or so. We're all new here, we're the new intake as it were.' She turned to the other girls, laughing. 'So we're all in this together, aren't we, girls?' She began cutting up a peach as she said: 'I'm sure we're all going to have a lot of fun together!'

Avie was surprised. Claire had seemed so super-confident, she had imagined she was on the staff perhaps. And Avie looked around at the other girls at the table and was glad. She was glad they were all new here – they were all in the same boat, whatever their background. It would be great getting to know them and learning new things together.

At five to ten, Avie left her room and went downstairs. She had tidied herself up and brushed her hair again. But she suddenly realised she didn't actually know where the Principal's office was. After enquiring at the reception desk, she was directed to an office along a corridor nearby, and knocked on the door.

'Come!' A stentorian voice came from within, and nervously, Avie pushed open the door and entered the Principal's office.

Madame Corbeau was seated at a desk in the centre of the room. She rose when Avie entered and came forward offering her hand. She was a tall spare woman, with an iron-grey bob, immaculately coiffed. She was dressed in a tailored navy suit, with a white blouse and commanded instant respect by her appearance alone.

'You must be Annie-Violet Spicer, I presume? Please sit down.'

Her face was unsmiling and her tone rather clipped. So it was with some trepidation that Avie sat down on a chair near the desk, suddenly feeling unsure of herself and lacking in confidence.

She wondered, not for the first time, whether Madame Corbeau had been told her full history by her parents, when they arranged this course at the finishing school. Was she aware that Avie had spent most of her childhood in a very modest home and went to the village school? Did she know she had been abandoned at birth by her mother, a titled lady, and then adopted by village folk? She suddenly wished she had asked her parents what exactly they had told Madame Corbeau. As she gazed into the pale blue eyes of the Principal, she felt at a distinct disadvantage.

A lot of the other girls there she knew came from wealthy backgrounds, had attended private school and their confidence was sky-high. They had numerous accomplishments, went abroad on holidays, and spoke French fluently. They were no doubt used to mixing with educated people. Since being reunited with Harriet, Avie had gradually been introduced into a more genteel way of life and Harriet had employed an elocution teacher to improve Avie's rather rough Kentish accent. She had also taught her some basic French. Yet Avie still felt she had a long way to go. *But then* – she suddenly thought fiercely – *that's what I am here for. I can do it, I know I can! I can do it as well as anyone else.*

A shadow of a smile crossed Madame Corbeau's face. 'Welcome to the Institut! I 'ope you will be very 'appy here. As you probably know, the aim of this school is to give a well-rounded course, to enable our students to face the world with confidence and to cope with any situation they are presented with. We do tend to concentrate on social occasions and 'ow to behave – also 'ow to entertain in your own home, with the emphasis on correct procedure for laying a table for a formal dinner, for instance. Also the guidelines for polite conversation amongst acquaintances and, yes, even royalty, should you ever be in that fortunate position.'

Avie didn't like to tell her that she knew how to lay a table backwards, from her days as a parlourmaid at Craven Manor. But she wisely kept quiet.

And Madame Corbeau continued:

'But we also try to improve each individual girl and her accomplishments. Do you paint or sew?' Avie shook her head. 'Play a musical instrument?' Again the shake of the head. 'But I believe you have a little French, yes?'

'Yes, madam, I am learning at the moment, but I'm not fluent and I'm afraid I don't have a good grounding in grammar and verbs, like some people do...'

Madame Corbeau widened her hands expressively. 'At least you're honest. But we won't worry too much about that now. We will concentrate on the spoken word. And I think you will find that the more you try to speak it, the easier it will become. French is spoken 'ere most of the time, but all the tutors and staff speak excellent English, so don't be afraid to admit if you don't understand something, is that clear?'

Avie felt quite relieved at that news. Although Madame Corbeau had a rather strict manner, Avie thought she was quite kind underneath - at least she hoped so.

'Now, you are permitted to go into the town over the next few days to acquaint yourself with the locality. Montreux is a pleasant town with some interesting shops and cafes. Also, an excellent museum. And there are steamer trips on the lake in the summer, if you wish to venture further afield. Watch how you behave in public, as never forget, you are representing the school whenever you are in the town. So, make sure you are well-dressed and always wear a hat and gloves, of course. Marguerite will find a school hat and coat for you, with a blazer for the summer. You may wear your own dresses. But you must always be back for dinner, is that clear? Dinner is at seven p.m. sharp, so don't be late. And we always dress for dinner. The course will start next Monday at nine a.m. *précisément* in the board room, so don't make any personal arrangements for next week. I shall expect you to be present at all the lessons, is that clear? Your parents are paying a considerable sum for you to attend this course, and your behaviour will be watched, believe me.'

Madame Corbeau rose from her chair, indicating the talk was coming to an end. She went to the door and opened it, giving another frosty smile. 'Oh, if you need your English pounds changed into Swiss francs, please see Mr. Webster, our business manager, in the office. I believe it's quite a good exchange rate at the moment.' This was something that had never entered Avie's head. The Principal put her hand out again.

'Very nice to have met you, Annie, and I hope you will enjoy it here. Good morning!'

Avie found herself in the corridor, her mind in a whirl of information and advice. She was glad they had a few days of freedom, before they started the course. She was looking forward to exploring the town of Montreux and hoped that some of the other girls would accompany her. As she began to climb the stairs, she met Claire coming down, who stopped and pulled a face at her.

'How was the interview with the dragon?'

Avie gave a grimace. 'Bit of a grilling, to be honest.'

Claire nodded. 'She's got a rather stern manner, but she's fair. Now, some of us are going down to the town later after lunch, are you coming?'

Avie's eyes lit up. 'That would be great. I have to unpack my steamer trunk first. What happens about lunch?' Avie's stomach was already rumbling, and she wished she'd eaten more at breakfast.

'It's very casual. We just all go down to the kitchen and make ourselves a sandwich or have some soup. And I don't know whether she mentioned it, but we must do our own ironing, groan, groan. So that's down there just off the kitchen, all right? I'm sure your clothes will be *so creased* like mine were, nightmare!' Claire had a way of emphasising certain words when she spoke, Avie noticed.

'How do we get down to the town?' Avie asked, as she remembered the journey was a fair way up the mountain road.

' Oh, Albert takes us, you know, the driver who met you last night? He usually gives us a few hours down there, then picks us up at about five o'clock.' Claire started down the stairs again, then turned back. 'Have you changed your money yet?'

'No, but I believe there is a Mr. Webster?'

'Yes, in the office near Reception. All right? It's a lot to take in, I know. I was in a flat spin when I first arrived. So anyway, see you about two o'clock in the foyer, yes?'

'Thanks, Claire, see you later.' Avie continued up the stairs, feeling excited about going down to the town with the girls. Now to unpack her trunk…

*   *   *

The school limousine was waiting outside, as the girls left the building after lunch. Albert, the chauffeur, in his smart maroon uniform and peaked cap, was standing by the car. He joked as the young ladies began appearing.

'ope you 'ave plenty of money with you, ladies, the shops 'ere they are *so expensive...*'

'Take no notice of him, he's joking. We know where to find some cheaper places, don't we, girls?' smiled Claire.

Once in the car they started out down the mountain road. It took a skilful driver to negotiate the sharp hair-pin bends on the perilous road, with its vertiginous drops, scene of many an accident. Claire did some introductions. There were only four of them and Avie was introduced to Poppy and Amy, who came from London. Poppy was of slight build and quiet, whereas Amy had a more solid frame and was smiling and more sociable. They all exclaimed at the view, as they descended to the lakeside.

'It's just so scenic, I love it,' cried Amy, as Albert turned into the main boulevard by the lake and parked the car. They all tumbled out and Avie looked around. She took in the great expanse of the sparkling blue Lake Geneva and the little towns and mountains bordering it. It really was breath-taking.

Several small shops and cafés lined the broad street, which was busy with traffic, both motorised and horse drawn. Impressive stone buildings and mansions faced the lake. Statues and sculptures were displayed along the promenade gardens, which were immaculately kept.

Claire pulled on her gloves. 'Now, girls, let's take a meander down the promenade and show Avie the sights.'

The four girls began to saunter down the esplanade bordering the lake. The air was fresh and clear and Avie was glad to have her thick wool coat on and a scarf knotted round her neck, as the early spring temperature was hovering around 50 degrees. The breeze blowing off the lake was decidedly chilly.

They could see the Chateau de Chillon further along the shore, a magnificent sight with its turrets and battlements. 'When does it date back to?' asked Avie. 'It's really rather splendid.'

'Twelfth century, I think', murmured Poppy, 'but I'm a bit vague about dates…'

'We could go there another day and look round it, perhaps,' put in Amy.

'Yes, not today, I want to show Avie my favourite dress shop,' Claire said. 'We could cross the road here perhaps, it's over there.'

When Avie had unpacked her trunk, she began to realise that she had not brought enough clothes with her. The girls seemed to dress very smartly, and she felt a bit of a country cousin in her blouse, jumper and skirt.

But she was a bit nervous about this dress shop Claire was heading for. *I'm sure it will be expensive*, she thought. She had brought a considerable sum of money with her, and Jeremy had assured her she only had to say if she wanted further funds. But she didn't want to splurge it all on the first day, obviously.

To her surprise, when they turned up a side alley and reached the shop, it was quite a small building. As they began to inspect the clothes displayed inside, Avie was amazed that the prices seemed modest. The owner of the shop had greeted Claire like a long-lost friend and ushered them into the shop in a very welcoming manner. Avie was impressed by Claire's fluent French, when she replied to the shop-owner.

'She speaks such good French,' she murmured to Amy.

'No wonder,' Amy replied. 'Head Girl at Cheltenham Ladies

College. Natural leader, born to rule and all that.'

'Crikey!' Avie had heard that the prestigious boarding school was the best in the country.

'Prices are much cheaper off the main boulevard,' Claire remarked, and she selected a long woollen dress with decorative embroidery on the shoulders and sleeves. She held it up against Avie. It was a lovely sage-green colour, which suited Avie's auburn hair. 'I bet that would fit you, why don't you try it on?' she urged. 'Not a bad price either.'

Avie realised that if they had to dress for dinner every night, she was going to need quite a few more dresses and obviously couldn't always wear her best finery. She had packed her lovely Parisian dress, but would keep that for special occasions. She looked again at the dress and decided to try it on.

Avie emerged from the fitting room. 'What do you think?'

'Hey, that looks just the ticket,' cried Amy, 'I like it, it fits you very well...'

'Yes, the colour suits you so well with your flaming hair,' murmured Claire.

Avie decided to buy the dress, but then had another look round to see if there was anything else she fancied. The prices seemed so reasonable, it was a good opportunity.

So, she ended up buying two dresses and a long skirt and as the girls left the shop, Avie suddenly thought how nice it was to shop for clothes with young friends for a change, instead of her mother.

'Let's go and have some tea now, shall we, girls?' Claire said, as they walked along the street.

'Can we go to Madame Theresa's again?' asked Poppy, tossing her plaits back. And they made their way along the main boulevard to the delightful *Salle de Thé*, a small tea-room, where they all devoured some delicious madeleines with their tea. It was a popular spot and crowded with ladies and gentlemen enjoying some mid-afternoon refreshment.

As they came outside again, it began to sleet, and the wind off the lake was freshening. They all turned up their coat collars. 'Let's have a quick peek at the Museum,' suggested Claire. 'Oh, here comes a bus, that's handy!'

And they climbed on board the bus, which took them to the other end of the promenade and the Museum, a splendid Belle Époque building.

'I'm just closing up, ladies,' the official grumbled as they entered the *Musée*. But he agreed they could have a quick look round, before he finally closed the building. The gentleman probably realised the girls had come in to escape the bad weather, rather than being keen on history.

It was fascinating, although Avie found it difficult with all the signs and notices in French. But Claire and Amy explained a lot of the exhibits to her, as their French was decidedly better than hers. Avie began to worry about the lessons on Monday.

Once outside again, they realised that time had flown by, and it was now ten to five and starting to get dark. But at least the sleet had stopped, and the lights of the little town were starting to appear in the shops and cafés. They could see the lights from other towns around the lake and the dark shapes of the mountains behind them, as light began to fade.

'We'd better get a move on, girls,' said Claire. 'Albert will be at the rendezvous soon. Let's run there quick smart!'

And they all hurried along the promenade, pulling their

coats and scarves around them against the cold.

To their relief Albert was already there with the limousine. He had arrived in good time, anticipating an early pick-up, due to the worsening weather.

Once back at the school, Avie said 'Au revoir' to her new friends, until they met later for dinner. She had seen the town of Montreux and bought a few clothes. What fun she was going to have here in these new surroundings! And as she went back to her room, she began to feel quite relaxed, thoughts of home receding into the background.

* * *

'So, are all the students here now?' Avie enquired, when the girls met up for coffee the next day in the lounge. It was Saturday and the course was starting on Monday, at nine a.m. sharp, as Madame Corbeau kept reminding everyone.

The lounge was a pleasant room overlooking the front of the house and they could see a snow-storm raging outside, as they sat near the roaring fire toasting their toes. No-one wanted to go out today.

'I believe there's just one more girl to arrive,' said Claire, as she nibbled on a biscuit. Fifteen girls had arrived from their various destinations in Europe, but were mainly from England. They were all a similar age, some as young as sixteen, but most were seventeen and eighteen.

'I believe she is arriving tonight – and we are in exalted company, I'm told…'

The girls looked up questioningly. 'Oh?'

Claire lowered her voice. 'I'm not normally one to gossip, but Marguerite let it slip the other day. She is a titled lady no less…'

'M'm. One wonders why a titled lady needs to go to a finishing school!' Amy said, frowning.

'Well said, Amy. Her name is Lady Ruby Manners, from Kent. Anyone heard of her?'

Inexplicably Avie felt a slight feeling of dread in her stomach. She had known a Ruby when working at Craven Manor and that was in Kent. But she certainly wasn't a Lady. She was a rather bumptious kitchen maid, who had crossed swords with her. She had been dismissed when she was found to be consorting with the male servants. No, it couldn't possibly be her. It was quite a common name. So she kept quiet.

'Well, we will see tomorrow morning, won't we?' smiled Claire. 'Anyone for more coffee?'

The girls shook their heads and Amy stretched her arms and stood up. 'I'm getting too hot here. How about a game of ping-pong, anyone?'

'I'll take you on,' smiled Avie and the two girls left the lounge to go to the games room down the hall.

Avie had enjoyed playing ping-pong at the local youth club when she had moved to Canterbury with Harriet. Then she had heard about the Suffragette movement and seemed to spend more time there helping the Cause.

The girls had an energetic couple of games and then decided to part company until dinner, once they had done the washing-up, that is. The students were expected to help in several ways and not be waited on hand and foot. Avie had found the ironing room and ironed some of her clothes earlier that day. As Claire predicted, they were dreadfully creased. It made Avie realise how lucky she was at home to have all her clothes laundered by the housekeeper. It was hard work, damping down the fabric and getting all the creases out. You had to be quick, in case someone else was waiting to use the iron. *At least now,* she thought, *we have electric irons – unlike the days at Craven Manor when the iron had to be heated on the range, a real chore.*

Avie was glad she had bought a few more clothes, as the other girls seemed to have an endless supply of different frocks, though jewellery was kept to a minimum. Avie had decided not to bring the beautiful Cartier jewellery given to her by William. Jeremy had said it was too valuable to risk taking it. It was stowed away in the safe at The Laurels, their home in Canterbury. But she had brought her beautiful pink silk dress from her eighteenth birthday party, hoping that there might be a special occasion for her to wear it. Claire had mentioned at dinner that occasionally they went to functions, which young men from the local Montreux College also attended. A Summer Ball was mentioned and an outing and steamer trip on the lake during the warmer weather.

Also, most of the girls joined the Montreux Tennis Club during the summer and they had social functions where boys and girls mixed. It was going to be a lot of fun. At the mention of boys, Avie suddenly realised she hadn't even thought about William for a couple of days. She did miss him, but had been so busy and involved settling into the school, there had been no time to mope or have regrets. But she did miss her parents and her room at The Laurels overlooking the North Downs.

She had brought her new silver-backed dressing-table set

in its leather case and, as she laid the brushes and mirror out on the dressing-table, it reminded her of her parents. Avie had also packed the jewellery box given to her by Herbie and Betsy. She had filled it with the few items of jewellery she had brought with her. The lovely seed-pearl necklace given by Jeremy on her fifteenth birthday, a fine gold chain from Harriet on another birthday and some pearl stud earrings which had been a gift from Florrie and Stan. Also, Florrie's gift for her eighteenth birthday was so pretty and useful – two mother-of-pearl hair slides. It was special jewellery, special to her, but discreet enough to be suitable to wear at dinners at the school. She noticed that none of the girls wore anything too flashy or swanky. Most of them were well-bred and well-educated young women. They knew the value of elegant but understated jewellery and clothes.

'There!' Avie stood back and looked with satisfaction at her glass-topped dressing table with its triple mirrors, now furnished with her own personal items.

She placed the photograph taken with her parents on her eighteenth birthday on one side and on the other the photo of herself and William at the same occasion. What a lovely celebration that was!

She began to dress for dinner and as she did so, heard the limousine arriving outside and went to the window and peered out. Must be bringing the new arrival. She remembered how she had felt, excited but nervous at the prospect of the new venture. But the snow had now turned to sleet. All she could see in the darkness was Albert holding a large umbrella over the figure of a young woman, as she stepped out of the car, muffled up with a long coat and scarf. They then hurried towards the house, so Avie's vision was restricted.

Meet her in the morning, she thought, as she brushed her hair and fixed her earrings. Now for dinner. And she suddenly realised how hungry she felt.

* * *

Next morning at breakfast all the girls gathered in the dining room and started helping themselves to food, chattering away. No-one had met the new arrival yet, as she had opted to have dinner in her room, obviously exhausted from the journey. So, the girls were tucking into their breakfast, when the double doors were pushed open rather forcibly. The sturdy figure of a young woman appeared in the doorway. She was very smartly dressed and heavily made up. Her dark hair was carefully coiffed, and she appeared to be overloaded with chunky jewellery. All the girls looked up, surprised. Someone even gave a snigger.

Avie gave a gasp, as she recognised her. Yes, the new girl was indeed the Ruby she had known all those years ago. She was astounded. She couldn't understand what Ruby was doing in Switzerland or how on earth she had now become a titled lady. The last time she had seen her she had been a lowly kitchen maid, always giving cheek and being rude to people and certainly not a popular member of staff.

Now she was amazingly transformed into a smart young woman, well dressed and wearing fashionable shoes.

Indeed, Lady Ruby Manners appeared supremely confident and gazed at the assembled company, with a smug smile on her face. And when she recognised Avie, she nodded her head and laughed. 'Oh, cripes, it's little Miss Blue Eyes – are they trying to make a lady of you?'

Avie was furious and felt highly embarrassed in front of her new friends, who had been so kind to her. But all she could stutter out was: 'What on earth are *you* doing here?'

Chapter 3

What indeed? Only two years before Ruby had joined a domestic agency and was sent to Fairfield Hall, a Georgian pile in North Kent. It had been the ancestral home of the Manners family for two centuries. Ruby had lied about her previous employment and produced falsified references attesting to her capabilities.

The master of Fairfield Hall was Sir Roland Manners, a childless widower in his fifties. Known as Roly because of his corpulent figure, he soon became aware of the new kitchen maid, with her winsome smile and pleasing curves. Before long the two were secretly engaging in some serious hanky-panky, an activity very familiar to Ruby from her Craven Manor days.

When Ruby came to him and tearfully revealed she was expecting, he had at first been mildly annoyed and thought of paying her off like the others. But then on reflection Roly began to think it could work to his advantage. Here he was, leading a lonely existence in the faded splendour of the Hall and desperate for an heir to his vast estate. He hated the cousin to whom the estate would pass, should he not produce an heir. He decided he would marry the girl to spite his cousin and hoped fervently the child would be a boy. Ruby seemed a pleasant enough girl and was certainly a good bed-fellow.

Ruby, of course, was over the moon and thought all her Christmases had come at once. She went round swanking to all and sundry in the alehouse that she was going to be the Lady of the Manor. But most local folk shook their heads and sniggered behind her back – 'Never in a month of Sundays!'

However, once married and after the birth (by the grace of God) of a son, Toby, Sir Roly found life with Ruby decidedly difficult. The girl seemed to be completely illiterate. She didn't even seem to know who was on the throne and had never heard of Shakespeare. Her table manners were atrocious. It was impossible to take her out in decent society. In short, she was a total embarrassment.

He began to realise he had made a dreadful mistake. Then a friend suggested sending her to a finishing school and engaging a live-in nanny for the child for six months. Alleluia! It seemed to be the perfect answer to Roly's prayers and, moreover, he would be rid of her for six months. And hopefully she would return to him as a more genteel version of her former self - God willing…

* * *

But of course, all these facts were unknown to those in the dining room. The two women were still glaring at each other, and Claire could foresee a row brewing. So she took charge. She went up to Ruby and introduced herself. 'Hallo there, you must be the new arrival. I'm Claire Carruthers, how was your journey?' And she gave a broad smile and shook hands with Ruby.

Ruby seemed slightly taken aback and gave an uncertain smile as she shook hands. 'Lady Ruby Manners. Pleased to meet you', she muttered in her broad Kentish accent.

'You will find we don't use titles here, just Christian names,' smiled Claire. 'We're a happy bunch, so if you would like to help yourself to some breakfast, then sit wherever you like. There is hot food under the domes, eggs, sausages, mushrooms, whatever you fancy…'

Ruby gazed at the extensive spread and wrinkled up her nose. 'Is there any porridge? That's what I usually have…'

'I'm afraid not, there is some muesli there, if you want some cereal, and coffee or tea. We all help ourselves.' Ruby began to serve herself some food, while Claire went over to Avie.

Avie was fuming inside, but was determined to keep her dignity and not make a scene in front of the other girls.

'I didn't realise you two knew each other,' murmured Claire, as she began buttering some toast. 'You should have said.'

Avie shook her head, still mystified by Ruby's arrival. She was the last person on earth she expected to see at this Swiss school and could foresee a lot of trouble ahead in the coming weeks.

'I knew her years ago,' she explained, 'when we were both working in the kitchen of a Big House. She was a right little bitch, excuse my French. And how she has become a titled lady and ended up here, I'm completely foxed.'

Claire put her arm round Avie's shoulders. She could see she was shaken by the encounter and wanted to help her. 'It might be best,' she said slowly, 'if you could swallow your pride and try to befriend her. I know that might be difficult, if you have had crosses in the past. But I think, frankly, that she is completely out of her depth here. You might find she warms to you if you're friendly, you never know… I should warn you that the school will not tolerate any bad behaviour between girls. It would be instant expulsion.'

Avie was still doubtful – the last thing she wanted to do was to befriend that common girl, who had been so unkind and rude to her in the past and had now insulted her in front of her friends. But perhaps Claire was right. Ruby must be feeling so alienated by this school, the well-to-do girls with their cut-glass accents and the whole foreign situation, with the language problem. If Avie steeled herself and tried to present a friendly image, Ruby might be more approachable.

Avie gritted her teeth, as she peeled a banana. *Maybe that might be the best option*, she thought, as she wrestled with her mixed emotions. *We certainly don't want to be at each other's throats in this rarefied atmosphere. Madame Corbeau is bound to hear about it. I would never live it down with Harriet and Jeremy if I was expelled. I must keep the peace, even though it will be really difficult.*

She looked over to Claire, now engaged in conversation with Amy. What a special person she is, she thought. That was such wise counsel, to suggest that. Not many people would have come up with that advice. No wonder she was Head Girl.

So after breakfast, Avie went over to Ruby, sitting on her own at the end of the long table, and had a heart-to-heart with her. With her ultra-smart frock and rather garish jewellery, she looked oddly out of place amongst the other girls, who were all avoiding her, after her dramatic entrance. Avie had summoned up all her inner reserves and was determined to crack Ruby's hostile façade. But she could see the wary look in her eyes as she approached.

'Come on, Ruby, what's going on? What on earth are you doing here?' She shook her head, mystified. 'I'm amazed, to be honest. Have you had a change of fortune or something?'

Ruby looked at her suspiciously. 'You could say that. You know I got married, don't ya?' she said gruffly. 'And I've got a little baby, Toby, he's three months old now...'

Avie was surprised. 'No, I hadn't heard, oh lovely! And where is it you live then?'

'In North Kent, Higham, near there. God-forsaken spot it is an' all, near the marshes. No shops, no nothing.'

'So when did you get married? I didn't hear,' pressed Avie. 'Must have been a titled gentleman I presume?' Knowing Ruby as she did, she could imagine the circumstances only too well.

'Yeah, Sir Roly Manners, nice gent, a widower. So, fell on me feet really. Nice big 'ouse, servants, you name it...'

'Quite a change then,' prompted Avie, 'from when you were at Craven Manor, eh? Remember Mrs Bury, she was a right termagant, wasn't she?'

This elicited a reluctant smile from Ruby. 'Not 'alf, she got me sacked, did you 'ear? Silly old bag.'

Avie had heard, but replied in the negative.

'Well, I took a fancy to one of the gardeners, didn't I? Alf 'e was called. Lovely chap, but so randy – you 'ad to let 'im 'ave 'is way, 'is wife didn't understand 'im, y'see. But I got found out, more's the pity.' Ruby gave a suggestive nod to Avie. ''ow about that chauffeur, then? He's a bit of orl right...' Her bold eyes glistened at the thought.

Avie shook her head, horrified. 'Don't even think about it, Ruby - out of bounds. He's walking out with one of the tutors' daughters... and anyway, you're married, remember?'

Ruby shrugged and wiped her nose with her hand, obviously

beginning to relax now in Avie's company. ''ow about yourself, you married yet?'

Avie thought of William in Paris. 'No, not yet, but I've got a boyfriend. Trouble is, he's in Paris, so we can't see each other much. Have you got a picture of your baby? I'd love to see it...'

Ruby fished about in her bag and produced a small photograph. 'There 'e is, dear little chap, Toby. He's me pride and joy, love 'im I do, really love 'im. Miss 'im I do.' Tears came to her eyes. 'We've got a nanny lookin' after 'im, while I'm 'ere.' Ruby nodded and gave a coarse laugh. 'Yeah, they're trying to improve me manners – Lady Manners, improve your manners – they'll 'ave a job! So, what's it like 'ere then, looks a bit posh for the likes of us...' Her eyes were cautious and she frowned nervously as she spoke.

'Yeah, it is a bit posh, but they're such nice people. I think you'll like it once you get used to it. We're all in it together, eh? Anyway,' Avie smiled, 'give it a try, eh? Oh, how did you get on with Madame Corbeau? Bit of a dragon!'

Ruby grimaced. 'Not 'alf, never cracked 'er face once!'

'That's what I thought about her', Avie laughed, 'but Claire says she's pretty fair with everyone. She's just got a rather stern manner.'

'Say that again! But she said she's going to get me special 'ellycution' lessons, whatever they are.'

'Oh, that'll be good. I had some of those, they're not bad...'

At that point, Marguerite appeared at the door and called out to them. 'Some of the girls, they are going on a mountain walk – just the lower slopes – either of you want to join them?'

Avie looked at Ruby conspiratorially. 'Shall we? Might be fun. We can always turn back if we get too tired...'

'Yeah, let's do it – but I'll 'ave to change me clothes…'

Marguerite nodded. 'Oh good, Rachel said to meet outside at ten o'clock, all right, girls? But wrap up warm, it's still cold out there. We can find some boots for you.'

And Marguerite hurried out, the girls following her. Avie felt relieved. The ploy had worked, she had managed to get Ruby onside and smooth things over. At least they were being civil to one another now.

As she passed through the hall, on her way back to her room, Charlotte at the reception desk called out to her, 'Oh, Miss Spicer! There's a telephone call for you. It's your mother calling from England. You can take the call in the office here…'

Avie was surprised but delighted. She hurried to the office and picked up the telephone.

'Hallo, mother? Avie here, how are you?'

'Hallo, Avie, can you hear me? It's a poor line. How are you, darling, we've been wondering how you've been getting on. Did you have a good journey?' Her mother's voice sounded very far away and distant. Avie could imagine her sitting in the hall at The Laurels, where the telephone was situated.

'Yes, fine, Mother, absolutely fine. I'm enjoying it here. I had a good journey, though it was very tiring. But the Duponts were good company, and it was helpful to have them there. And how are you all? And the children?'

'Yes, they're just as mischievous as ever. But I was ringing to mention something, darling. We heard after you had gone that another young lady from Kent will be staying at the school. A Lady Manners, Ruby Manners. We don't know the family, but I just thought I would mention it, might be a nice companion for you…'

Avie gave a chuckle. 'Yes, we've already met, Mother – and I knew her from my days at Craven Manor, amazing coincidence...' She didn't think she would elaborate, as the phone call must be so expensive.

The Swiss cuckoo clock in the hall started chirruping for ten o'clock and Avie realised she must ring off as she hadn't yet changed her clothes.

'Sorry, Mother, but I've got to ring off now, we're going out on a mountain walk. Yes, it's been snowing here but it's better today, so we're getting some exercise. Thanks for ringing, Mother and give my love to dad and the children. I'll write you a letter once a week, promise. Oh, and can you send me some more smart clothes? Bye!'

And she replaced the receiver. *Lovely to speak to Mother,* she though. *No doubt she thinks Lady Manners is an aristocratic lady – well, what a surprise she would have, if only she knew...* She loved her mother and had long since forgiven her for her decision at her birth, which she knew Harriet now regretted.

In the foyer, Avie bumped into Ruby, who was pulling on some boots from a pile nearby, as Avie came up. 'I've just been delayed by a phone call from England. Can you ask them all to wait for me? I'll be as quick as I can!'

Phew! Avie felt as if she had survived a marathon. A walk in the fresh mountain air was just what she needed, to blow away those cobwebs and get a bit of exercise.

* * *

It was Monday at nine a.m. and the girls had gathered somewhat nervously in the board room. The room was panelled in dark oak and had portraits on the wall of previous governors and principals. Also featured in a prominent position over the fireplace was the school coat of arms. The school motto – *'Unité et Courage'* was in gold lettering, above a figure of a young woman holding a flaming torch, against a backdrop of mountains. Alongside this was a portrait in oils of Pierre Philippe, the school's Founder.

The room was rather austerely furnished with a large mahogany table and eight matching chairs, with other smaller chairs stacked up in a corner.

They were talking amongst themselves when the door opened and their tutor entered, clutching a briefcase under one arm. They all rose respectfully as she came in.

She was dressed in a blouse, jumper and tailored skirt and seemed very businesslike, as she smiled at the girls and asked them to bring some more chairs up to the table. Her eyes were sparkling, as she faced the group, and she was brisk and efficient.

'Good morning, girls', she said cheerfully in her broken English. 'My name is Madame Allain. I 'ope you 'ave all 'ad a chance to assimilate yourselves with the school and the area by now. And so we can begin today to start our course.

As Madame Corbeau will have told you, the aim of this course is to prepare all of you for the busy social lives which you will no doubt be engaging in – and 'opefully we can give you some advice which will make your lives 'appier and easier. We will concentrate on giving a formal dinner party initially. You will learn 'ow to set the table properly, 'ow to arrange flowers for the table, the art of conversation and etiquette, your own personal deportment and 'ow to serve wine correctly, not forgetting 'ow to 'old a wine glass. We will 'old formal dinners which will be cooked by you, and students will be assigned various roles, as guests, as 'osts or as servants. In about a month's time, there will be a final exam during which you will 'ave to prepare and 'ost a formal dinner for the staff.'

All the girls groaned and exchanged horrified glances.

'So,' Madame Allain smiled as she looked round at the students' expectant faces, 'I'm sure we're going to have a lot of fun together. I am speaking in English today, as I believe there are a few of you whose French is not exactly fluent. So, I 'ope that suits everybody. Please let me know if there is anything you don't understand – I am not an ogre!'

Avie was so relieved that the tutor was speaking in English. She had been worrying about today and not being able to understand the lesson, if it had been in French. Most of the students were English, so she felt she wasn't the only one who was glad about it.

Madame Allain delved into her briefcase and began handing out exercise books and pens to everyone and she went through everyone's names on her list as she did so.

'Now, if a few of you could go to that cupboard over there and take out all the china, glassware and cutlery that you see there, also there are table mats. 'andle them with extreme care, as the glasses, they are crystal and the china, it is fine porcelain. And we will begin by learning 'ow to set a table for a formal dinner party.'

The girls brought all the things carefully over to the table and Madame Allain began to show them the correct procedure for the placement of cutlery and wine glasses. And she told them when serving food, one must always serve from the left. This was nothing new for Avie, though Ruby had only been a kitchen maid, so didn't know the drill.

After the tutor had demonstrated the correct cutlery placement, she jumbled it all up again and each girl had to set a place herself, along with the wine glasses. One girl tried to be smart and asked: 'But what if someone is left-handed?'

At this Mme. Allain looked a trifle irritated and replied with a sigh that obviously one didn't know that in advance. The person concerned would have to change it themselves. She gave the girl an exasperated look.

This was all useful advice and the girls had been making notes in their exercise books as they listened. As the class ended Avie felt quite relieved. She had survived the first lesson. Alleluia!

*　*　*

The girls had enjoyed their walk on Sunday and been exhilarated by the fresh mountain air and the astounding views over the lake and the town, as they ascended the slopes. They had seen signs of spring here and there, even though it was early in the season. A few Alpine crocuses were poking their heads up bravely through the frozen earth, along with snowdrops. Avie looked around at the craggy peaks above. Every blade of grass, every bush was glinting and sparkling with a pristine layer of snow. It was quite magical. There had been some weak sunshine trying to penetrate the clouds, and the weather had remained dry and clear. And though their legs ached, the girls had really found the walk energising.

They were passed by a group of intrepid mountaineers, who hailed them cheerfully. They were wearing coils of rope round their necks and carrying their long wooden skis. But ski-ing was generally considered a risky sport and certainly not one for young girls. On the way back they had suddenly heard the melodious chimes of the church bells, coming through the clear air, from the Anglican church of St. John in the town. Some of the girls had been worshipping there that morning. It was such a beautiful moment, one to savour.

Once back at the school they all had coffee in the lounge. They could hear Mozart being played expertly in the adjoining room on the grand piano, and the pure sounds of a violin coming from another. There was a convivial atmosphere in the grand mansion, formerly the home of a Swiss industrialist. Most of the girls knew each other now and so socialised together quite easily, as they followed their individual pursuits. There were many rooms, affording spectacular views of the mountainous countryside known as Glion. The mansion had certainly been built in a prominent position.

'Oh, here comes Madame LeLoup!' Rachel said, as the school cook bustled into the room, a big smile on her face. She was carrying a plate of small cakes, which she offered around to all the girls. Madame LeLoup was a popular figure and she and her team produced some tasty meals every evening for the girls. There was no choice, but you could always let the kitchen know in advance if you really disliked something, as the meals for the week were posted on the notice board in the common room.

* * *

The students were nervously anticipating the day they had to prepare and cook dinner for all the staff. This was set for about a month's time. Some of them had already been looking up recipes and they had to decide on the menu. Once they had come to a decision, they would draw up a list of ingredients to be purchased. They had been given a budget, which they had to adhere to, and a sum of money was allocated from Mr. Webster in the office.

The staff were friendly and efficient at the school. There was a resident matron who was always on hand giving advice and support, if there were any health problems, and a resident fitness coach, who held regular classes once a week. She also cut the girls' hair, being a former hairdresser. Matron was a capable, motherly figure and was a shoulder to cry on, should any of the girls suffer from homesickness. Several of them had never left home before and really missed their families. A few of them who were eighteen had been due to be presented at Court as debutantes in May, but had deferred this until next year.

Avie had found herself sitting next to Rachel during the class, the girl who had organised the walk, and in conversation had mentioned that she had a boyfriend in Paris. Rachel's ears had pricked up at this news, and she had made a suggestion to Avie.

'I've got a brother in Paris and I'm going to see him at Easter. Would you care to come with me, and you could see your boyfriend perhaps? You could stay with me at my brother's place, he's got a roomy house in central Paris. Where does your friend live?'

'Central Paris, near the Champs Elysées. That's so kind of you,' Avie answered and already her mind was whirring with ideas. It would be so marvellous to see William again. She would have to contact him and arrange it. But then she began to think it would be more fun to surprise him, but find out if he was going to be there first, without committing herself.

So, when the class was over, Avie went back to her room and wrote William a letter. He knew she was in Switzerland, of course, and so she couched the suggestion in vague terms. She might be in Paris at Easter, not sure yet, but would let him know. Would he be at home?

William still lived at home with his mother, a rather formidable figure who had inspected Avie as if she was a servant, the first time she had met her. She had maintained a frosty demeanour the only other time she had met her last year. So Avie was dubious about another meeting with her. She had to hope that perhaps she would be going to their villa in Menton in the South of France for the Easter break.

Oh, how exciting, Avie thought, as she went back to her room after lunch. *Paris in the spring!* That would be divine. She gazed at the photograph of William on her dressing-table and gave it a kiss. She couldn't wait until Easter came, only three weeks to go now…

Chapter 4

Central Paris, Easter 1913

Well, here she was in Paris and staying in Rachel's brother's house in Rue d'Eglise near the Arc de Triomphe. The girls had arrived last night, having travelled from Geneva by train, a long, tiring journey of twelve hours. The steam train had frequent stops, as it had to take on water. They chatted on the journey and talked about their families and the school. The views were stupendous, as they crossed the snow-capped Swiss Alps.

Marguerite had kindly provided them with a small hamper full of goodies for the journey, to allay their pangs of hunger, along with a stone bottle of lemonade, cups, plates and serviettes. She had thought of everything, sandwiches, fruit and biscuits. They particularly enjoyed the delicious Swiss chocolate!

Rachel's brother, Tom, was a hotel manager and he was interested to hear about the girls' sojourn in Montreux. He had attended a college there a few years ago, where he had obtained a degree in hotel management. They had a lot to talk about and he was able to inform them about various places of interest to visit nearby. During his time there he had been aware of the Institut at Glion and had often seen the girls in the town, with their distinctive red blazers.

Tom had married an English girl three years ago, but when they came to live in Paris, Emily, his wife, had not settled very well. Once their child, Nancy, was born, she decided to return to England, sadly.

'Yes, I'm rattling around in this big house,' he said with a shrug. 'So it's delightful to have some company – welcome to Paris!'

'Very kind of you to have me, Tom,' Avie murmured, as she finished her *petit dejeuner* and drank some orange juice. 'It's lovely to be back in Paris. I was here last year with my parents, but that was in the summer – it's great to see it in the spring. I must visit the Bois de Boulogne, I'm sure it will be spectacular at this time.'

'Now, let me give you directions to your friend's house, the Avenue de Montaigne, I believe you said… m'm, nice area.'

And so half an hour later Avie found herself walking up the very same road, lined with impressive stone and brick mansions and historic terraces. She felt excited, yet nervous at the same time. Now she was here, she began to wonder whether she should have let William know. Perhaps he wouldn't appreciate her surprising him. She shrugged; it was too late now. She recognised the striking detached stone house with its painted shutters and urns of flowers either side of the entrance door, the steps immaculately scrubbed, the polished brass knocker.

She rang the doorbell. The entrance door opened and a maidservant appeared in a smart black dress and white cap. '*Oui, madame? Puis-je vous aider?*' Can I help you, madame?

Avie wracked her brains for the right phrase. '*Monsieur Guillaume, est-ce-qu'il est a la maison?*' Is Mr. Guillaume at home?

The maid bobbed. '*Oui, madame, entrez, et le nom?*' Come in, and the name?

Avie followed the maid in and was shown into the sitting-room at the front of the house. The maid then disappeared and after a lengthy pause, the door was flung open and William appeared. He did not look happy and appeared dishevelled and untidily dressed. He expressed surprise at seeing her and only gave her a perfunctory hug on greeting.

'Oh, Avie, I didn't expect you. I thought you were going to let me know if you came to Paris?'

Avie was heartbroken at his response. 'I thought you would be pleased to see me,' she said in a small voice.

At that point there was the sound of hurried footsteps on the stairs, a gabble of French, followed by the slam of the front door. And Avie could clearly see through the window a young woman running away down the street, looking decidedly upset.

Avie gave a gasp. It was clear to her that she had interrupted a liaison between the couple and even clearer that she was not wanted in this house. William seemed ill at ease and distracted and Avie knew she had to leave at once.

'I shouldn't have come, it was a bad idea,' she faltered and turned to leave the room.

She couldn't get out fast enough. Pushing open the door, she ran down the hall. William called out to her. 'Avie, it's not what you think, come back...' Tears welling in her eyes, Avie opened the front door and almost fell down the steps, in her haste to get away.

Her romance with William was over. She could never forgive him for this.

Avie returned to Tom's house heartbroken and upset. She had been looking forward to seeing William. To be treated so badly by him like this was surprising and perplexing. But she tried to compose herself when the door was opened by Rachel.

'Oh, Avie, what happened? Wasn't he there? Come in, we're just having a cup of coffee...'

Avie wasn't a good liar, so she had to confess that yes, William was there, but he was – otherwise engaged, shall we say?'

'Oh, was he busy with something?' Rachel asked innocently.

'Yes, he was very busy with something, but she seemed to be rather upset when I turned up...' Avie gave a bitter laugh.

Rachel put her hand to her mouth and her eyes were shocked. 'Oh, my goodness, you don't mean – he wasn't with another woman?!'

'Fraid so...' Avie still felt distraught inside and wished she could be alone with her thoughts. She blinked away the tears and sniffed hard.

Rachel put her arm round Avie's shoulders. 'Oh, Avie, don't get upset about it – but I'm afraid a lot of Frenchmen are the same. They are notorious womanisers. But I'm sure he still loves you.' She noticed Avie's eyes were suspiciously moist. 'Oh, you poor girl, you need a strong cup of coffee. Sit down here and I'll fetch it.'

Tom was sitting reading a newspaper and he glanced at Avie sympathetically. 'When you mentioned you were going to surprise your boyfriend, I did wonder... Not always a good idea...'

He went over to the bureau in the corner and took something from it. 'Rachel and I were thinking of going to an art exhibition this morning. Would you care to join us?' He waved the leaflet at her.

Avie smiled at him as she sipped her coffee. 'That sounds lovely.'

'It's not a big exhibition, just a collection of works from a local art society, no big names, but there is a lot of talent locally, especially from the Left Bank.'

And so the three friends set off to the Halle de Victoire nearby, where they spent an enjoyable hour or so perusing the many exhibits on display. Various subjects were covered, from portraiture to landscapes and still life. Avie was interested in the paintings, some of which were oils, others watercolours.

Afterwards they went for a simple lunch at a local bistro where they all enjoyed a glass of *vin ordinaire* and a simple *salade niçoise* with some crusty baguettes.

Then they walked round the covered market nearby, full of bric-a-brac and treasures. Tom announced then he had to get back, as he was seeing someone. Avie was sorry to see him go. He and his sister had been so kind to her.

It was now a pleasantly warm spring afternoon and Rachel and Avie had a stroll through the pretty Parc Monceau which was close by. It was often frequented by families and nannies with their charges. The sun was warm on their faces, as they admired flower beds bright with daffodils and jonquils. Pale pink magnolia trees were out in bloom, with their delicate petals, such a lovely sight. They saw the huge Rotunda at the entrance and the many statues of artists, musicians and writers in the park.

After a while they decided to go and look at some fashion boutiques. Avie was tempted to buy one or two of the outfits she saw, but decided against, as she wasn't really in the right frame of mind. She still felt moody and unsettled after the brush with William. The visit to Paris had been spoilt.

* * *

Back at the school after Easter, Avie was immediately drawn into lessons with their tutor, Madame Allain. The students were now engaged in flower arranging and learning how to present a feature for the table. This should not be too large or too small. It should embellish the table, along with the silver candlesticks.

It was quite tricky, Avie found, as she wrestled with flowers and greenery, to achieve just the right size, without the guests having to peer over the floral arrangement to see one another. Also, it shouldn't be too small, as then it wouldn't be noticed.

Avie found herself sitting next to Ruby, who was curious about Avie's visit to Paris.

'So you saw your boyfriend then?' she said, nudging Avie with her elbow. 'What's 'e like in bed then?' Her eyes were so bold, as she scanned Avie's face. She was obviously itching to know the intimate details.

Avie was shocked to the core and her blue eyes flashed, as she replied impulsively: 'We're not all little tarts, you know!'

Ruby had annoyed her, thinking that all girls had the same morals as her. It had been well known at Craven Manor that Ruby was associating with several male staff members. Most decent young girls kept themselves pure, until they had met their one true love and tied the knot.

'Oh, excuse me, I'm sure!' Ruby's face darkened. 'Being a Frenchman I was sure 'e would 'ave bedded you by now…' She stuck some flowers in a vase and as she flounced off tossed in a final insult. 'But perhaps 'e don't fancy you, with your red 'air...'

Avie was furious. She was fuming inside. This girl was impossible. She had gone out of her way to swallow her pride and be pleasant to her, even though it was a real effort at times. Now Ruby had tossed all that aside and gone back to her old self. She thought of the old saying: 'You can't make a silk purse out of a sow's ear.' Never a truer word.

Claire appeared at Avie's side and put her hand on her shoulder. 'I heard some of that. Don't take any notice of her. She thinks everyone is tarred with the same brush...'

'She is so infuriating. I've tried to be friendly, but she's basically still a common kitchen maid, I'm afraid, despite her title.'

'Anyway', Claire smiled, 'changing the subject, did you enjoy Paris? Such a lovely city.'

'Yes, I had an enjoyable time. Rachel and I stayed with her brother who works there. Paris was looking beautiful. But in fact', Avie thought she would confide in Claire, who she knew would be discreet. 'I've broken with my boyfriend – I won't bore you with the details, but he upset me and so I won't be seeing him again.'

'Oh, I'm sorry – but plenty more fish in the sea, eh?' Claire said, as she cut some greenery for her vase.

Avie felt relieved to have told her friend her news, which still smarted. She looked at her with gratitude and warmth. Claire was so diplomatic and sensitive to everyone's feelings. No prying into private matters with her. She was a lady through and through and it showed.

Avie had been having some private French lessons with one of the tutors and she felt she was improving a tiny bit. 'You must try and speak French as often as you can', advised the tutor, Madame Benoit, 'even if you aren't certain of the correct word or phrase. Go into the shops in town and ask for something. It will give you confidence.'

This advice had had laughable consequences, however, as the next time the girls went into town, Avie ventured into the *boulangerie* and, pointing to one of the cakes on display, said in French, '*Je voudrais acheter une piscine, s'il vous plait*,' at which everyone in the shop burst into laughter.

Poor Avie was most embarrassed and went bright red, when the shop attendant informed her she had just asked for a swimming pool! She had meant to say *patisserie,* but it had come out wrong. Another time when it was broad daylight, she had gone into a shop and greeted the shop attendant with '*Bonsoir*' (Good evening) instead of '*Bonjour*' (Good morning).

All the girls laughed when she told them about it and said similar misunderstandings had happened with them when they first arrived.

Avie had returned from the outing and was in her room, intending to write to her parents. But there was a knock at the door, and it was Charlotte, the receptionist, who handed her a letter. 'This came for you earlier, so I thought I would bring it up to you...' It was post-marked Paris and Avie recognised William's handwriting. She was tempted to throw it in the bin unread, but out of curiosity decided to open it.

'*Darling Avie*', she read, 'I'm *writing to beg your forgiveness for what occurred at Easter, when you came to see me. I do apologise most sincerely.*

I had been conversing with my cousin, Amelie, just before you arrived, and we had had a disagreement. It was concerning the will of my uncle, her father, who sadly passed away a few months ago.

My Uncle Gilles had bequeathed to me in his will an apartment just outside Paris, very generous of him and most unexpected. Amelie was expecting to inherit this apartment herself and she accused me of pandering to my dying uncle to influence his decision – an entirely wrong assumption, I can assure you.

So tempers were raised that morning and I was not in the best of moods when my maid announced that you had arrived unexpectedly. And Amelie ran off in a huff when I said I had to see you.

So I do apologise once again and can assure you that it was entirely a family disagreement which caused my bad behaviour and do hope you will forgive my rudeness.

I value our friendship and wish it to continue. I love you, ma petite, and hope we can still be friends. Please find it in your heart to forgive me.

Your devoted
William'

Avie was now thoroughly confused. She sat on her bed, clutching William's letter, and so many thoughts were racing through her head. He sounded very sincere – and why, if he *was* having a dalliance with his French ladyfriend, would he want to resume their friendship, which he seemed keen to do?

She had to admit to herself that the family will problem certainly seemed to be a genuine explanation. But he could have invented the whole scenario, to hide his association with this Amelie. She really didn't know what to think.

She wished – oh, how she wished – that she was at home in England. Harriet would be there to give her advice, or Florrie, her beloved aunt, to whom she had run, when she discovered she was a Foundling all those years ago. She was wise beyond her years. Avie really missed her. And then there were her friends, Isabel and Clara. The list was endless.

But here in Switzerland, who could she turn to? Avie thought initially of Claire, but then realised she hardly knew her, even though she admired her immensely.

It was then she remembered Matron. She was very popular with the girls and seemed to have a strength and stability about her that would weather any storm. At six foot tall, she was built like a bull. She looked so professional and efficient in her blue uniform, with the elasticated black belt. Her disposition was cheerful and practical and she was always smiling. Matron was forever saying that if anyone had any problems, however small, they should come and see her. Her door was always open, she said, and it was, literally. She was very calm and had a comforting manner about her, that was reassuring and stabilising. Moreover, she was English, so there were no language problems.

Poppy had confessed that when she first arrived, she was incredibly homesick, but had gone to Matron on the advice of Marguerite and found her to be a tower of strength. She had suggested that keeping busy and active was the best way to forget her troubles. She had put Poppy in charge of writing up the dinner menus every week, as she had heard her handwriting was excellent. Matron had also appointed her to be a mentor to a young girl of only sixteen, Daisy, who was also suffering from pangs of homesickness. And so between them they had comforted each other and gained strength by helping one another. They *were* now the best of friends.

But of course Avie had to make up her own mind about William first. Did she still love him? Did she trust him? And did she want to resume a relationship with him, after this horrible misunderstanding, if that is what it was?

She decided to sleep on it and think it over during the next few days. If she was still undecided, perhaps only then would she go and see Matron.

Her tormented thoughts were suddenly interrupted by a knock on the door. Opening it, Avie found tousled-haired Amy standing there and she looked a tiny bit rattled.

'Come in, Amy, what's up?'

'Sorry to barge in like this...', Amy began as she walked into the room. But then stopped in her tracks, staring out of the window. 'Oh, what a splendid view you have!' she cried. 'Better than mine. I'm on the side and I find the mountains a bit intimidating at times. Yes, what I've come about, I've just heard that tomorrow night's dinner is going to be a do-it-yourself affair. They said that was going to happen next week, but now apparently Madame LeLoup has been taken ill. So they've decided in their wisdom that we must cook the dinner tomorrow night for ourselves, and do the role-playing Madame Allain mentioned. Someone will be the host, other people the guests and others will be servants...'

'Crikey, rather short notice,' said Avie, 'but we can have access to the kitchen and the food they had planned, can we?'

Amy shrugged. 'S'pose so, it's all been sprung on us rather...'

'Anyway,' Avie smiled, 'I'm sure we'll manage. Who's going to decide who does what -Madame Allain?'

'Who knows?' Amy rolled her eyes. 'It all seems a bit disorganised. Apparently the rest of the kitchen staff have been given two nights off. They think it's this influenza outbreak going around, and they don't want them all to catch it... but hopefully we'll be told at breakfast tomorrow what our roles are and what the drill is.' She shook her head. 'Hope to God I'm a guest, that's all I can say. Then I can just sit there and have a nice glass of wine and eat my dinner. I'm having enough problems with this dinner for the staff. A lot of girls are sort of backing out, you know, they said they would do it, now they're not so sure...'

'Well, I'm willing to do anything,' Avie said, 'I'm not the best cook in the world, but I can cut up a bit of meat and prepare some vegetables...' She remembered slaving away at Craven Manor, preparing vegetables in the scullery for sixteen people. 'And I can set a table blindfold...'

'Well, it's not the end of the world if it's a disaster, is it?' said Amy. 'It's only for us girls. We can put on a brave face and say it's delicious, even if it isn't, can't we?'

'Yes, as long as the food and the table look presentable to Madame Allain.'

Amy turned to go and opened the door. 'Sorry to be the bearer of bad news, but I thought I should let you know. Claire's telling a few other people and so hopefully we'll all be *au fait* by tomorrow. Nuisance though, I was hoping to go into Geneva tomorrow to meet someone. Heigh ho! *C'est la vie!*'

'Well, let's hope there are a couple of chickens in the refrigerator we can roast and then we just have to do the vegetables,' put in Avie. 'Thanks for letting me know, Amy, and if there's anything I can help you with, give me a shout. Oh, by the way...' Avie stared at Amy as light dawned, 'what's going to happen with *tonight's* dinner, does anyone know?'

Amy chuckled, as she backed away down the corridor. 'I think we'll be lucky to get soup and scrambled eggs somehow! Bye, see you later.'

Avie shook her head once Amy had gone and gave a whimsical smile. Somehow, this little in-house drama had helped to settle her. She was with a good bunch of girls and they could all have a giggle and a laugh together, whatever happened in this great mansion. It seemed to put things in perspective for her and gave her some sorely needed comfort.

* * *

Chapter 5

It was the night of the role-playing dinner, and the girls were in the kitchen. And it was chaotic. Madame Allain hadn't yet appeared, nor had she been at breakfast. So they were going ahead cooking the dinner as best they could. There had been no chickens in the refrigerator and the stewing steak due to be delivered by the butcher hadn't arrived, despite several phone calls.

Apparently cook had been intending to serve stew and dumplings, to remind them of home. So the girls were frantically searching through the big refrigerator for meat – any meat – that they could turn into a tasty stew.

No-one had any idea how to make dumplings and none of the Swiss cookery books even mentioned them. But Avie vaguely remembered Mrs. Cherry, the cook at Pelham Hall, tossing together some flour and water and forming it into balls. She started doing that with gusto. She reckoned on two dumplings each, so was ploughing through the flour and water to make thirty dumplings. They looked a bit weird and misshapen, but she hoped they would form a better shape once they were tossed into the stew.

'What on earth can we do for a starter?' wailed Rachel, as she struggled to roll out some pastry for an apple pie. 'Ugh! This dratted pastry won't seem to roll out..'

'Just one thing,' Ruby said, searching in the store-room, 'we don't seem to have any cooking apples...'

'Well, we've got plenty of eating apples, we'll have to have those,' put in Amy and she started peeling them with enthusiasm, not noticing they were turning brown as they piled up in the dish.

'Perhaps we could just have some tins of soup?' someone suggested. 'It would be a lot easier...'

'I don't think Madame Allain would think much of that,' one of the girls said darkly.

Poppy and Daisy were bravely peeling a mountain of carrots and parsnips and cutting up onions, which was reducing them to tears. Other girls were rapidly peeling potatoes and looking for pans in the cupboards.

The only triumph of the day had been the dining table. It looked magnificent, the silver cutlery was gleaming, the crystal wine glasses were sparkling, and Claire had achieved perfection in the floral display. Some early spring flowers had been arranged in a crystal vase, with some greenery filched from the garden. They had found some bottles of wine in the butler's pantry, and these were chilling nicely in the fridge, even the red wine. Someone had spied the table napkins and rings in a drawer, and these had been placed on the table, along with the table mats. The silver candelabra had been polished to perfection and had pride of place in the centre of the dining table. The silver condiment sets were positioned nicely in two places on the table.

'Halleluia!' A shout went up from Victoria as she discovered a large bag of meat at the back of the fridge. 'It's beef, so we're saved, girls! Yes,' she sniffed it, 'it smells all right. Here, who's good at chopping meat? Where's a sharp knife?' Two of the girls volunteered to cut up the meat and others were searching the cupboards for some tasty spices or stock cubes to enhance the flavour.

Olivia from rural France suddenly found several tins of sardines at the back of the cupboard. 'I seem to remember an old recipe my mother used to make years ago – I think it was sardines with lemon juice and port. That would make a good starter. Yes, we could dress it up a bit and garnish it with some salad and a slice of lemon on top, serve it with some crusty baguettes and some butter pats.'

Amy gave a cheer. 'I think we're getting there, girls.' She came over to Olivia who was landing what looked like a hefty catch of sardines. 'Yes, that looks good, that'll do. If it looks impressive, it doesn't matter what it tastes like. I'll find some port for you and some nice dishes.' She started towards the butler's pantry.

At that point the door opened and Claire came in. Her face was serious and a worried frown was creasing her brow. She clapped her hands and the girls all looked towards her expectantly.

'Bad news, I'm afraid, girls. Madame Allain has gone down with the flu and guess who's taking her place?'

The girls held their breath. Then someone said in a horrified voice. 'Not the old dragon?'

Claire nodded grimly. 'The very same. I've just seen her and she said it was her duty to take Madame Allain's place. She didn't want to deny us the pleasure of cooking this special meal. She will be coming to inspect it at eight p.m. *précisément*.' Everyone groaned and clutched their heads.

'Oh my God, what a turn-up! I don't believe it,' cried Amy, looking distraught.

'We just have to hope', Claire said, fingers crossed behind her back, 'that she doesn't want to taste it. No offence, girls, but you know what I mean...'

In the absence of Madame Allain, Claire said she would decide who would be the hostess, guests and servants. She looked at them keenly. 'And I don't want any arguments, all right? Someone has to make a decision, so whatever I say goes, understood?' This was the Head Girl of Cheltenham Ladies College speaking and you didn't argue with her.

'So,' Claire stood facing them and announced that Rachel would be the hostess for the evening and that Bertha from Spain would play the part of the host. The servants would be Clemmie as butler, Primrose as wine waiter, Olivia playing the part of a footman, and Ruby as the parlourmaid.

'If I could have two volunteers to transfer the food into serving dishes in the kitchen and bring it up here on the trolley?' Two hands shot up. All the other girls would be guests. Amy heaved a sigh of relief. She would get her wish and just enjoy herself, thank God for that. Claire knew she was already having challenges organising the staff dinner party, so felt she deserved it.

'Just one other thing, girls, once you are seated at the table and eating the meal. Whatever it tastes like, you will declare it delicious, all right? You have done a good job with the table, it looks magnificent, so once it's all cooking, go and tart yourselves up in your finest frocks, and let's have a good evening together. You have done so well and hopefully Madame Corbeau will approve.'

There was a frantic moment just before they all went to dress. They realised they'd completely forgotten to write the menu. Indeed, several menus were required. But Poppy offered at once. She was a quick and accurate writer and produced six copies in forty minutes in beautiful calligraphy. They came up with some fancy French names for the dishes and once it was finished it looked quite impressive.

MENU

Entrée
Fruits de Mer en porto avec citron et salade

Plat de Resistance
Ragoût de boeuf en cocotte avec les légumes divers

Dessert
Tarte aux Pommes Anglaise

Once Rachel was dressed in her finery, she wandered down to the kitchen to check on the stew and the apple pie. As she was the hostess, she had taken care with her appearance and was wearing her smartest dinner dress and jewellery. All was going well with the food, and she was about to leave, when there was a loud hammering on the back door.

She was surprised, as it was after seven o'clock and night had fallen. But she opened the door to be hailed by Jacques, the school handyman. He greeted her in French, asking for Madame LeLoup, and then gabbled on about something else, which she couldn't understand.

'*Je ne comprends pas,*' she muttered. 'I don't understand.'

He spoke a little English and then said slowly 'Meat for dog – have come to take – for Bonzo.' Bonzo, his collie dog, was often seen around the school with Jacques and was very popular with the girls.

Rachel shook her head. 'Don't know about that.' But as she said it, a horrible realisation began to dawn on her. The parcel of meat at the back of the fridge– could that be what he meant?

She went to the refrigerator. It was a Domelfre – Madame LeLoup's pride and joy and only recently purchased. She made a pretence of looking for the meat, but knowing in her heart that Bonzo's meat was now bubbling away nicely in the range oven, along with succulent vegetables and gravy.

A feeling of horror descended on her. But she tried to put on a brave face to Jacques and again shook her head. '*Désolée, le viande n'est pas ici. Madame LeLoup est malade, elle a oublié…*' Sorry, no meat here, Madame LeLoup is ill, she has forgotten.

Jacques' face dropped, he looked very forlorn. '*Merci m'selle, bonsoir.*' Thank you, miss and goodnight.

And he departed none too happily, slamming the door behind him.

Rachel stood stock still, breathing heavily and holding onto a chair for support. How on earth was she going to tell everyone? *They would be eating* dog's meat, *dressed up to the nines, in the splendour of the* dining room, she thought, *what a farce!*

At that moment Avie came in and saw Rachel standing there, looking shocked. 'Hey, what's up? You look like you've seen a ghost!'

'You're never going to believe this,' she began and explained the situation to Avie. To her surprise she thought it was funny and began to laugh hilariously.

'How are we going to tell them all?' Rachel stuttered, looking utterly grief-stricken.

Avie put her hand on her friend's shoulder. 'We're not,' she said. 'It's our little secret. Tell you what, we'll put a couple more stock cubes in the stew, that'll perk it up.'

And she went to the cupboard and picked up two more stock cubes, crumbled them into the huge casserole dish and stirred it around. 'M'm, smells good.' She turned to Rachel with a grin on her face. 'It's not poisonous you know. It's just a low-quality cut of meat and rather fatty. Probably shin of beef, very tasty.' She remembered Betsy cooking stews and casseroles with this meat, which was cheaper than other cuts. 'It won't kill us!'

Rachel shook her head. 'Yes, but Madame Corbeau might, if she ever finds out…'

*   *   *

The stage was set. It was five to eight and the girls, miraculously transformed into smart young ladies, were sitting bolt upright at the dining table, waiting for Madame Corbeau to appear. The candles had been lit and the long velvet curtains drawn, and everyone agreed that the table was looking splendid. All the girls had made a special effort with their dress and hair and were wearing their best jewellery. Avie had managed to arrange her hair into a soft chignon, adorned with the lovely hair slides given to her by Florrie and Stan for her birthday. She had decided to wear a black figured dress with long sleeves, which fitted her perfectly.

Claire was looking very elegant in a cream brocade dress, and she too had put her fair hair up into a soft bun at the back. As usual her jewellery was very understated, just a single string of pearls with matching stud earrings.

Ruby was acting true to form and wearing a low-cut dress, revealing her ample bosom, and lots of sparkly jewellery. Claire had circulated with the sherry decanter while they waited, a very welcome move.

'She's coming, she's coming!' said one of the kitchen girls in a stage whisper, keeping watch at the door. Then to her horror, Rachel noticed a grubby tea-towel had been left on the trolley and hastily grabbed it and stuffed it behind the curtain. Just in time…

Madame Corbeau entered the room and for once she was smiling. She surveyed the scene in the dining room, taking in every detail, her keen eyes sweeping over the table, the candelabra with its tall candles illuminating the room, the twinkling crystal wine glasses, the girls in their finery and the floral display in the centre. She nodded and gave a little clap of her hands. 'Well done, girls, you have done so well. It all looks perfectly splendid.' She approached the table and Rachel offered her a menu. 'Here is the menu, Madame. The girls have done quite well I think at this difficult time, but may I offer you a drink perhaps? I am the hostess for the evening.'

Madame Corbeau declined, to the relief of most of the girls. She then perused the menu and nodded. 'It sounds an interesting menu I must say, and fine calligraphy. Who is responsible for that?'

Poppy blushed and gave a little smile, as she raised her hand. She was wearing her plaits up on top of her head this evening and looked very grown-up.

Then the Principal spotted the huge casserole dish weighing down the trolley. 'I will sample a little of the main course, if I may?' All the girls held their breath.

Rachel's heart sank. She had been dreading this would happen and raised her eyebrows at Claire. Please God, let it be edible, that's all I ask, let it be edible, she prayed. 'I will be a good girl, promise...'

Rachel offered the Principal a fork, plate and napkin and lifted the lid of the dish. And Madame Corbeau dipped her fork into the stew and tasted it. Rachel and Avie exchanged glances and Avie gave her a wink. This was the moment of truth. What would the verdict of the Principal be?

Madame Corbeau gave a slight cough, after she had swallowed the mouthful. Then she smiled, a ghost of a smile, but it was a smile. 'An unusual flavour,' she commented, 'but, um, very tasty, I must admit...' She tried to stifle another cough unsuccessfully.

Rachel stepped forward, forcing a smile to her lips. 'We tried some new spices, didn't we, girls? I'm glad it meets with your approval, Madame.'

Madame Corbeau put the fork down and wiped her mouth with the napkin. She looked at all the girls, as they sat expectantly at the table on their best behaviour. 'You all look so smart tonight, I must say. We must do this more often. Indeed, I'm looking forward to the staff dinner in a few weeks' time.' She turned to Rachel as the hostess. 'Your role-playing has gone well?' Rachel smiled and nodded. 'Well, thank you, all of you and I hope you enjoy the evening. You have excelled yourselves tonight without doubt. *Bonsoir!*'

And she swept out in regal fashion to her lonely room, giving a wave to everyone at the table.

Phew! Everyone relaxed and gave a sigh of relief. And a buzz of excited chatter began to fill the room. Now at last they could enjoy themselves.

Olivia and Primrose were quick to re-fill the girls' wine glasses. It really was a superb wine, they agreed, and they were soon all becoming very merry and loquacious. The waiting staff had begun to realise that if they kept up this charade, they were not going to eat tonight. It was decided that everyone would squeeze around the table, and all eat together. Clemmie as the butler delegated Ruby to fetch more chairs from the corner and they all began to tuck into the first course. It was found to be quite piquant and certainly colourful.

The *pièce de résistance* was found to be too heavy to lift. So it was agreed that everyone should help themselves from the trolley and fill their plates, as much as they wanted. Avie and Rachel took a cautious forkful of the dish, holding their breath and watching everyone's faces as they began to eat.

It was rather over-seasoned, but had a certain *je ne sais quoi* about it, they agreed. But Avie's dumplings were declared a disaster, as they were small, hard and inedible. They realised afterwards she had used plain flour instead of self-raising, and no fat. Halfway through the meal, Rachel suddenly clutched her head and cried out: 'The apple pie, we've forgotten the apple pie!'

Amy and Poppy ran to the kitchen to rescue it. It had been left on a low heat. But although the pastry was slightly burnt and hard, it was declared just about edible – though the apples were rather tasteless, not having the sharp flavour of cooking apples. They forgot the cream, but who cares, when you are enjoying yourself?

For a final toast, as the grandfather clock struck eleven, Avie suddenly stood up rather unsteadily and Rachel feared she was going to spill the beans. But no, she announced à propos of nothing, that she had happened to see Jacques the handyman that evening, walking his lovely dog, Bonzo. 'We all love Bonzo, don't we, girls?'

'Yes, we love Bonzo, we love Bonzo,' the tipsy girls chanted, banging the table excitedly with their fists. 'We love Bonzo, we love Bonzo!'

And so Avie declared a toast to Bonzo the dog, who had influenced their dinner more than most of them realised. She winked at Rachel, who dissolved into helpless giggles. 'To Bonzo!'

'To Bonzo!' they all echoed.

Chapter 6

Mr Paul Webster was a quiet sort of chap. He lived simply on his own in a small flat in Montreux, with only his tabby cat for company. Occasionally Peter, the churchwarden, would join him for a game of chess, and he visited his brother in England about once a year. But on the whole, he disliked community life and was very reserved. He had worked at the school in Glion now for three years and it suited him very well. He did his job to the best of his ability and then he went home. He was rather shy with women, so was slightly amazed that he had ended up as business manager in a Ladies' College. But he had limited contact with the students and mainly only saw them when they first arrived and wanted to change their money.

'Just as well,' he thought sourly. Most of the girls seemed very young and silly. He would hear them chattering and giggling, as they passed his office. And he thanked God that he had no children. So, Mr. Webster enjoyed his own company and took pleasure in cooking himself an *omelette aux fines herbes* with some crusty bread or a simple fish dish. But most of all he loved a glass of wine. He took pride in his knowledge of wines and regarded himself as a connoisseur, having worked in the office of a local vineyard for several years. And the School Principal seemed impressed by his expertise and often asked his advice on selecting special wines.

And so Mr. Webster happened to visit the butler's pantry that very morning. He noticed at once that several bottles of vintage wine kept for special occasions were missing from the shelves. He was horrified. He knew exactly how many bottles had been there, gathering dust since the Coronation of George V in 1911: sherry, port, claret and hock. He had catalogued them himself. Mr. Webster was puzzled at first and thought perhaps they had been taken back to the wine cellar.

But in conversation with Marguerite, he then discovered that the girls had held their special dinner the previous night. And it was further established that because of the illness of Mme LeLoup, they had been given free rein in the kitchen, with no staff supervision. His suspicions were confirmed.

His anger began to grow. The thought of all those spoilt young women tossing back these special vintage wines with gay abandon was too much to bear. He thought he should report it to Mme. Corbeau at once, as a flagrant breach of etiquette.

But on speaking further with Marguerite, he was persuaded to confine his critical remarks to Claire, who, as the daughter of the Earl of Lansdowne who owned half of Sussex, would perhaps understand his anger and outrage, coming as she did from a prestigious background. Hopefully she could then relay to the girls their horrendous mistake and learn from it.

Mr. Webster still felt hot under the collar about it. And suffered a further indignity. He went outside the kitchen back door and found several of the precious bottles tossed into the rubbish bin, lying forlornly amongst the potato peelings and sardine cans.

He could have wept and retrieved one as a souvenir; he washed it until it was spotless. *Oh, the scandalous shame of it! Did they have no discernment, these girls?*

But when later they sought out Claire, alas, she was found to be at the dentist in Vevey.

And so it was that Rachel was called in to see Marguerite. And she fully expected to be gated for giving Bonzo's meat to the girls. But no, that thankfully remained a secret. Instead, Mr. Webster appeared from a side room, to Rachel's surprise. What was *he* doing here? He seemed to be trembling with rage, as he pointed out that the wine the girls had drunk last night was vintage wine dating back two years. Wine, moreover, served at George V's Coronation in 1911.

'Did no-one inspect these wines, to see what year they were?' he spluttered. 'I'm just amazed that someone could just grab these bottles willy-nilly without identifying them first…'

Rachel was shocked when she realised that a grave error had been committed. She knew she must apologise on behalf of all the girls, even though she had played no part in it. She couldn't quite remember who had fetched the wine. It might have been Primrose as the wine waiter. But Rachel had still been reeling from the Bonzo debacle at the time and wine was the last thing on her mind.

She spoke up bravely. 'I do apologise for this. But we were in a difficult situation and trying to produce a meal of sorts, without any help or guidance from anyone. We were concentrating on the food; our thoughts were not about the wine at all. It was quite a trying procedure, without Madame Allain there to help us. I will let Claire know about this and make sure it never happens again.'

But then she looked at Mr. Webster and Marguerite directly, lifting her chin.

'Though I must say I am somewhat surprised that such special vintage wines were so readily on hand in the butler's pantry. Surely, they should have been in the wine cellar?'

Mr. Webster had the decency to look rather embarrassed. 'I don't know about that, miss', he mumbled. 'The wine was brought up for a special dinner, I believe, which was then cancelled.'

Rachel held her ground. 'Well, I think it might be a good idea to make sure they are always kept in the wine cellar, don't you agree, Marguerite?'

Marguerite had to agree with her and they then decided the matter was closed.

And as Rachel returned to her room, she felt she had escaped quite lightly. Things might have been different, had they known about Bonzo.

* * *

Avie had at last written to William. She had decided she didn't need to consult Matron, as it was a very personal issue and one she had to resolve herself. It might be better, she thought, if they had a break from one another, particularly as she was so involved here at the school. So she phrased these thoughts as tactfully as she could, when she put pen to paper, and kept it quite short.

She shrugged. William could make of it what he wished. Avie still felt upset about the incident in Paris. She had gone there especially to see him and had been rejected. But perhaps once she was back in England in the autumn, they could see how they both felt and get in touch again. Avie sighed: *'The course of true love never did run smooth.'*

It was now June and the weather was improving every day. Warm temperatures and blue skies greeted them most days and so the girls' thoughts began to turn to outdoor activities.

A gentleman from Montreux Tennis Club had come to the school last week, to enquire whether anyone was interested in joining the club. As he was tall, dark and well-built, with a flashing smile, a lot of the girls were *very* interested. He was wearing immaculately pressed white trousers and his shirt, emblazoned with the words 'Guy Petier, Tennis Coach', emphasised his broad shoulders. He stressed there were three levels of play at the club. Beginners, those with some experience and expert players.

But he encouraged those girls who were complete beginners to join, as the club gave weekly group tuition classes and even personal tuition for an extra fee. With another flashing smile and a wave, Guy was gone. But his visit had caused much excitement amongst the girls and several of them were keen to join, including Avie and Rachel. The coach had left a bundle of forms to be filled in, which were then dealt with by Mr. Webster, who had delivered them to the Tennis Club, situated near the lakeside.

It was half term now, so the girls had a welcome break from their studies. But they were due to hear the results of the Staff Dinner today, which had taken place recently. Amy had managed to organise the event without too many worries. She and Claire had decided on a menu which was impressive, but easy to prepare. They were much better organised this time. The Bonzo meal (which everyone now knew about and was the cause of much hilarity) had given them valuable experience. So, this time they had planned every stage of this special meal meticulously.

They had decided to keep it simple, but were pleased with the Menu.

MENU

Le Melon à la gingembre

Le Poisson Sole en la sauce asperges avec les légumes divers

Les Fraises fraîche avec la glace, faite à la maison

Melon with a touch of ginger for entrée, a Sole fish dish with an asparagus sauce, for the main course, garnished with grapes, and accompanied by broccoli and new potatoes, and then for dessert fresh strawberries with home-made ice-cream.

The only disaster was the ice-cream. Although it had been prepared perfectly well, with fresh cream and vanilla extract, someone (who would remain nameless) had forgotten to remove it from the icebox in time. So, there was cream instead of ice-cream. But none of the staff seemed to notice the difference thankfully, due maybe to the Campari in which the fruit had been soaked! And maybe also due in no small part to the vintage wine, which (this time) they were able to serve with official permission.

The girls had taken great care in setting the table and were very happy with it. The crystal glasses were twinkling, the cutlery was set perfectly, and starched linen napkins were on every side plate. The silver candelabra was in the centre of the polished table, with its tall white candles.

Claire had again agreed to take on the flower arrangement and she made an artistic display. She had used some sprigs from the pink Alpenrose shrub, a few yellow globe flowers and a sheaf of blue bugles, gathered from the lush meadows near the school. It looked so pretty and fresh.

So the girls were anxious to know how they had fared, for this was a final test for them. It had been quite an unnerving experience to cook and serve a formal dinner for these tutors, who had been teaching them for several months now.

They were gathered in the common room having coffee, when Madame Allain appeared in the doorway. And immediately there was a hush in the room and everyone looked up expectantly. All eyes were on the tutor.

But she was smiling and waved some papers at them, reports by several tutors and the Principal, as to the success or otherwise of the dinner.

'I 'ave 'ere, girls, the report on the Staff Dinner which you organised recently. And I am pleased to say that you 'ave scored top marks, eighteen out of twenty. The general standard was excellent, the table setting was extremely well done, and the menu selection and standard of the food served was judged to be first class.' She paused. 'If anything, the one thing which could 'ave been improved was the waiting service.

'One tutor, for instance, stated in her report that her wine glass was empty for ten minutes before it was replenished. That is a minor faux pas, but one that should be addressed next time.

'It is very important to look after every guest and make sure their needs are met. Now, all these marks 'ave been given to you as a group. No one person 'as been singled out for praise or criticism, as indeed, the event was a team effort. I offer my congratulations to you all, you 'ave done so well – it was very well organised, I must say, and thoroughly enjoyable.

'To show our appreciation, we will be 'olding a Champagne Reception in the Ballroom next week on Friday. So, I 'ope you will all be there in your finest attire.' Madame Allain gave a beaming smile to everyone. All the girls gave a gasp and clapped their hands.

'Summer is beginning 'ere in Montreux, so let's enjoy it! Oh,' and the tutor's eyes twinkled as she spoke, 'and by the way, there might be a surprise for you at the Reception, that's all I will say'.

All the girls were intrigued and looked at each other, puzzled. 'What could it be, how mysterious!' But Madame Allain was giving nothing away. And she gave a final wave and left the room.

The girls chattered excitedly, as they exchanged ideas about what to wear for the Reception and what the surprise could be. Avie thought she would at last wear her lovely pale pink silk dress, bought for her eighteenth birthday, as she hadn't worn it since. And she was hoping there might perhaps be another occasion in the summer when she could wear it again.

But she was completely mystified as to what the secret could be…

*   *   *

It was the night of the Champagne Reception in the ballroom, and it was a beautiful evening.

The French doors had been flung open to the terrace, with its spectacular view of the lake and the town of Montreux below. It had been a hot day and was still pleasantly warm. The girls were gathering in the magnificent ballroom, with its panelled walls, elegant furniture and stunning crystal chandelier.

When they arrived they noticed a small band was ensconced on the dais, playing popular medleys. Was this the surprise? And there was much murmuring as the girls all admired each other's smart dresses. Waiters were circulating with trays of aperitifs and canapés and there was an atmosphere of fun and anticipation, as the girls relaxed and began to enjoy themselves.

Avie's hair was shining and loose, with a sparkly pink Alice band to match her gorgeous silk dress. It was so good to wear it again. She felt like a princess. She had Jeremy's pretty seed-pearl necklace round her neck and was feeling happy and confident.

The Principal entered and the music stopped, as if by a signal. Madame Corbeau joined the group of tutors gathered near the dais and then stepped forward. She was very elegant in a black dress and black patent shoes.

She clapped her hands and was all smiles as she spoke. 'Good evening, young ladies, and I must say you are all looking so smart tonight. I 'ope you will enjoy the evening. Well, we thought you would appreciate some different company, so we are delighted that some of the young gentlemen from Montreux College can join us tonight. I would like you to give them all a warm welcome...' And the Principal began clapping, which then became louder as everyone joined in.

An audible gasp ran through the assembled company and the girls looked with interest as a group of young men entered the room. They looked extremely smart in dinner jackets and bow ties. Some of them appeared rather embarrassed, while others were confidently striding into the ballroom, looking around at the huge room, decorated with tubs of flowers and exotic plants in pots.

The tutors immediately went up to the gentlemen and engaged them in some welcoming chit-chat. But before long the young men began to cast their eyes around the room, gazing with interest at the young ladies in their finery. The music resumed and the waiters immediately offered the students drinks and canapés. These were gobbled up very quickly, as the boys laughed and joked with their friends.

Some of the tutors then took it upon themselves to introduce the male students to the girls, as several of them appeared rather shy. Madame Allain came forward to Avie's group of friends accompanied by a tall, fair-haired boy who was smiling somewhat diffidently.

'Avie, may I introduce Roberto, who is from Italy – Roberto, this is Avie…'

Avie had spotted the fair-haired lad, as he had entered the room, and liked his appearance. But she was surprised to hear he came from Italy. She always thought Italians were dark-haired.

Some people had now started dancing and the sprung floor of the ballroom was perfect for this. So Roberto immediately offered his hand and suggested they should join them. The band was playing a waltz and several other people were starting to venture onto the dance floor.

'My English is not good, but I will try…' he smiled, as they began to dance together.

Avie grinned back at him. 'Well, I don't speak any Italian, I'm afraid, just a little French, but I'm sure we'll get by.'

'So, 'ow long 'ave you been at the College?' Roberto asked, as they became more adventurous and he swung her around.

'A few months. And you? What are you doing at the College?'

'I am doing a business course; it lasts a year...'

'...enjoying it?' asked Avie.

He shrugged. 'It's good, yes. A lot of 'ard work, but I love it 'ere. Montreux is such a beautiful place.'

'Shall we get a drink?' Avie suggested. 'It's quite hot in here.'

'Yes, of course.' And they returned to Avie's seat, grabbing a cool drink from a waiter on the way back. They sat down together and Avie glanced shyly at her new companion, liking his manner and his looks. His brown eyes were warm and friendly, and he had a ready smile.

'Do you play tennis by any chance?' asked Avie, suddenly thinking it might be a possibility.

'I do,' he laughed. 'Perhaps we might meet up at the Tennis Club? I'm playing there next week.'

'I'm just a beginner,' Avie admitted. 'So do you play much?'

'Oh, yes, I play quite a bit at 'ome. I belong to a club.'

'So where is home, may I ask?'

'Northern Italy,' Roberto replied. 'Lake Como, near Menaggio.' He looked at her keenly. 'It's so lovely there, 'ave you ever visited?'

Avie shook her head. 'No, my home is in England, in Kent.'

The waiters were now circulating with champagne and so this was accepted with alacrity. There was a real buzz in the room, as the girls engaged in laughter and chat with the boys or were dancing together.

He smiled at her shyly and raised his glass. ''ere's to you, Avie from Kent. *Salute!*'

Two of his friends came up to him at that point and called him away to meet someone. Roberto gave an apologetic wave as he disappeared, saying, 'See you again.'

Avie was sorry to see him go, but almost immediately another boy came up and asked her to dance, so she was busily engaged. This boy was English, so it was easier to have a conversation. His name was Michael and he came from London. He too was doing a business course at the College.

'And are you a tennis player?' she enquired, but he shook his head. 'No, I'm keener on mountaineering and rock-climbing,' he said.

'And do you do skiing in the winter?' Avie asked and Michael nodded enthusiastically. 'Yes, I love it. It's best to start as young as possible,' he said. 'My family brought me here on holiday when I was six, with my brother. We used to go on the nursery slopes. But I took to it right away. So where do you live in England?' he asked.

'In Kent, Canterbury, it's pretty there in the summer...' And as Avie said that an image of The Laurels with its tree-lined driveway and lovely garden appeared in her mind's eye. She suddenly felt rather homesick. And she thought of Pelham Hall, where she'd met William, and her loving adoptive family nearby, in their small cottage at Hampton Copse. She must send another postcard to Betsy, Herbie and Janey and tell them all her news. They were very dear to her.

But then she realised that Michael had asked her a question and she'd been miles away. 'Sorry, what was that?' she asked, as they danced the Fox-trot together.

An irritated look crossed the boy's face, as he repeated his question. 'I said, where did you go to school?'

She shrugged, flicking her blue eyes up at him levelly. 'Just a local school'. She could never tell this boy she had been to the village school and had been a scullery maid in a Big House. He would never understand.

Michael fell silent at this news and when the music ended, they parted company rather coolly.

The evening passed quickly, with more champagne and canapés on offer, and some progressive dances, which were hilarious fun. But by midnight the final dance of Sir Roger de Coverley was held, with everyone joining in enthusiastically. And the girls knew that, sadly, the evening was drawing to a close. Madame Corbeau appeared on the dais and thanked everyone for coming, and hoped they had all enjoyed themselves. Then she bid everyone goodnight and the little band began to pack up their instruments.

As people began to drift away, Avie spotted the tall figure of Roberto as he left with his friends. Their coach had arrived to take them back to their college. She gave him a wave and he waved back.

Let's hope we meet again, Avie thought. *Nice boy, I must try to learn some Italian...*

All the girls were exhilarated by the unexpected social event. There was a buzz of excited conversation between them as they made their way back to their rooms. What an evening they'd had!

Chapter 7

Avie and the girls were down by the lakeside, exploring some of the shops in the back streets. It was a fine summer's day and the lake presented a sparkling image, with the ferry boats criss-crossing to and from Lausanne. The town was busy with visitors and traffic as the girls wandered along.

They had found a small *brocante* sandwiched between two other shops. The girls were having fun, rummaging amongst the junk items and second-hand goods on display.

'Oh, look at this', exclaimed Rachel as she picked up a prettily decorated box with inlaid marquetry on the top. She held it up. 'I like that, it would be good for jewellery or gloves or anything, really...'

She looked at the price ticket. 'M'm, not a bad price, it's a beautifully made item.'

Claire was holding a china trinket box and inspecting it. 'This would be ideal for earrings', she mused. 'I haven't brought many things like that with me...'

But Avie had found a stuffed lion, sitting solemnly on a child's chair. She liked the expression on the lion's face. It would be ideal to take back for little Matthew, she thought.

'He's got a bear, but I don't think he's got a lion'. The soft toy was in good condition, and she was sure he would love it.

She missed the children so much. She had been away from home some four months now and was often overcome by bad feelings of homesickness. She loved it here in Montreux, but sometimes felt desperate to be back amongst all the people she knew so well and loved so dearly.

So Avie bought the lion for Matthew, but Robert was more difficult to buy for, as he was older. She would have to think about that and keep her eyes open for a suitable gift for him. But as she cast her eyes about the small shop, she suddenly spotted a cuckoo clock.

It was hanging on the wall, so she went closer to look at it. It was beautifully carved with a bird design, in the tradition of the Swiss clocks, and decorated with *edelweiss* flowers in bright colours. She nodded. '*Yes, Robert would love that in his room*', she thought. The shop-keeper took it off the wall and allowed her to hear the cuckoo striking the hour, before he wrapped it up.

'Well, that was fun, girls, wasn't it?' Claire said as they left the shop with their parcels and walked down to the lakeside area again. 'Now, do we want some tea or...'

But Avie interrupted her. She had just caught a glimpse of a sign over a large Belle Époque building nearby. 'Hey, look, Montreux Tennis Club!' she cried. '*Ecole de Tennis*.' How about we look in there and see what it's like, before our lesson tomorrow?'

Rachel and Avie were due to have their first tennis lesson the next day and were intrigued to find out about the club. It looked an impressive building and had a sign on the front, stating 'All welcome – all ages from 4-20. Tuition given.'

Claire was already an experienced player, as they had a court at home, but Avie and Rachel were novices, never having played before. They made their way into the building and Claire spoke to someone in fluent French. She had been here before and played on the courts quite recently.

A smiling lady waved an arm towards the nearby grass courts, which had seats outside so that one could watch the matches being played. 'Please take a look, it's fairly quiet at the moment...'

The girls went over to a court where some young men were playing and sat down on one of the seats. There was a doubles match in progress and suddenly Avie noticed that one of the players was Roberto. She was thrilled and started to watch with added interest.

As she watched, she also saw that Roberto had been very modest, when he spoke about his tennis. He seemed to be a very good player. There was much hilarity between the young men, and they all seemed very fit and active. They chased after balls and slammed shots down with energetic jumps.

The game finished and the young men gathered up their racquets and balls and left the court. But Roberto had spotted Avie outside and at once came over to the girls, with a grin on his sun-tanned face.

'Hallo there again, how are you today? Welcome to the Club!'

Avie introduced him to Rachel and Claire, who surprised everyone by speaking Italian to Roberto, to his delight. 'Did you enjoy that? You are an excellent player...' Avie murmured. But Roberto was anxious to offer them some hospitality.

'We're just going to have a drink in the clubhouse – would you like to join us?'

Claire looked at her wrist-watch. Albert was picking them up very soon along the promenade, but she reckoned they might just have time for a quick drink.

'That would be very nice', they agreed and followed the boys into the clubhouse. It was a very comfortable and traditional room, with leather arm-chairs and tables near the bar, which was stacked with bottles of every description.

They were soon sipping a very welcome *citron pressée,* a lemon squash, while the boys had a beer. Avie felt very relaxed as she sat next to Roberto, admiring his mop of fair hair and easy manner.

'So you're having your first lesson tomorrow?' asked Roberto.

Avie nodded. 'I'm looking forward to it.'

'It will take a while before you can play a proper game,' warned Roberto. 'You 'ave to get used to 'andling the racquet and knowing 'ow to play different strokes. Also, learn 'ow to score, in French. But I'm sure you will love it!'

'So will we have Guy Petier as our coach?' asked Rachel. The girls had all been enamoured by Mr. Petier when he came to the school, and thought him very charming.

Roberto looked doubtful. 'There are quite a few coaches,' he admitted, 'so you may not be allocated Guy first time. But all the coaches are excellent, they will teach you so much. You will soon be 'itting the ball over the net, *bellissimo!*' And his brown eyes met Avie's blue eyes, as he laughed uproariously, and she knew she liked this boy, liked him a lot.

At that point Claire looked at her watch and finished her drink. 'It's time to go, girls, sorry to break it up, boys…'

The girls stood up and reluctantly said farewell to Roberto

and his friends. 'Thanks a lot, boys, see you again!' And they all left the clubhouse, with smiles and waves and went to meet up with Albert along the prom.

*   *   *

Avie was in her room, practising her French figures before the tennis lesson later that morning. She had been rather shocked to learn they had to score the tennis game in French. So, after speaking to Claire, who seemed to know everything, she was now concentrating on learning fifteen (quinze), thirty (trente) and forty (quarante). 'Love' was 'zero' and Advantage was 'avantage', while 'thirty all' would be 'trente partout'. The only one she wasn't sure about was 'deuce'.

'Help!' She looked at her watch. Nearly ten, must get changed. She quickly put on her tennis dress and brand-new plimsolls. Then she thought back to yesterday and seeing Roberto at the Tennis Club. Avie had taken a liking to this Italian boy, and it had been wonderful to see him and his friends playing such an energetic game at the club. But she realised she had a lot to learn. It would be quite a while before she was able to play with such style and panache. 'It will be good, Avie, just to get the ball over the net', she lectured herself, as she tied her shoelaces.

As she fastened the buttons on her dress and looked at herself in the mirror, there was a knock at the door. *Must be Rachel,* she thought, and ran to open the door.

But no, it wasn't Rachel, but Ruby. What a surprise! And Ruby was looking quite distressed, as she stood there, staring at Avie.

'Have you got a minute?' she blurted out. Avie could see her eyes were red-rimmed and there were tear-stains on her cheeks.

'Of course, come in,' Avie smiled, opening the door wider. 'What is it, you look upset. Sit down here, now what's the matter?'

Ruby entered the room and sat down in the nearest chair. 'I feel silly, now I've come. But it's my little Toby, I'm missing him so much, I want to go home…' And tears began coursing down her cheeks. She reached for a handkerchief and began to mop her eyes.

Avie came over to the girl and put her arms around her. Past misdemeanours were completely forgotten, when she felt Ruby's shoulders heaving, as she sobbed her heart out.

'I'm so sorry, Ruby, but I quite understand. It must be awful for you to have a small baby and then have to leave him behind. But tell me, do you speak to your husband much on the telephone? Does he tell you about little Toby?'

'He hasn't telephoned once, the devil. He does write occasionally, but you know what men are like, he never tells me much about the little one. It's all about his golf and his charity do's and his dinner parties.' She sniffed hard. 'I wish I'd never come here, I'm that homesick for little Toby.'

Avie sat down next to Ruby. 'Now, have you spoken to Matron at all? She's very good when girls are home-sick. She did wonders for Poppy, did you know that? Poppy was feeling very down, and Matron had a good chat with her and now she's fine…'

'I expect she's busy seeing to the girls and such, she won't want to listen to my moans, I'm sure'. Ruby looked decidedly doubtful.

'Well, that's where you're wrong, Ruby, because she's only too glad to listen to people's problems. Would you like me to come down with you? We can see if she's available and if not, I'm sure she would find a time to see you later.'

'P'rhaps', she said. But she still looked rather dubious.

'I'll come with you now if you like', said Avie, 'only I'm going out soon – we're having a tennis lesson down in Montreux, Rachel and some of the others. Let's go now, eh?' And Avie gave Ruby an encouraging smile, as the two girls left the room and went down the stairs.

And as Avie accompanied her friend, she suddenly realised that Ruby was speaking much better English now. She knew she had been having elocution lessons from one of the tutors. After a few initial clashes, it seemed that Ruby was indeed now trying to cut out the swear words and improve her accent.

As usual, when they went along the corridor near the foyer, Avie could see that Matron's door was indeed open and after knocking timidly, her hearty voice boomed out 'Come in, come in!' and Matron's statuesque figure appeared in the doorway, with her usual smile.

Avie just stayed briefly to explain to Matron that Ruby had a problem and then left. She felt it would be better for the girl to explain herself how she felt. She crossed her fingers as she walked away. Let's hope she can help her, she thought. Poor Ruby, she seems in a bad way.'

Even though she wasn't exactly her best friend, Avie felt enormous compassion for her. Here she was, a young girl, living in a foreign land, so far from her baby son and married to a man who didn't seem to care about her.

She looked at her watch, as she went back up to her room. Ten twenty. The girls were being taken by Albert to the Tennis

Club in twenty minutes' time. They were being loaned racquets by the Club, until they had had a few lessons – they could buy their own racquets, once they had decided whether they liked the game or not.

But Avie had already decided. Seeing Roberto leaping above the net and slamming down shots at his opponents had convinced her it was the game for her. And Harriet and Jeremy would be so delighted when she told them, as they loved the game too. Also, the thought of maybe actually playing a game with Roberto one day filled her with excitement – what a thrill that would be!

The first tennis lesson at the Club went well. Their coach was a gentleman called Pierre, he wasn't as dashing as Guy Petier, but he spoke good English and was very patient. He quickly showed each girl how to hold a racquet and how to change the grip from the forehand to the backhand. He also mentioned the footwork, saying how important it was for your body to be balanced before you made the stroke. The students were shown all the different strokes and also lobs, drop-shots and volleys – Avie found this quite difficult. A lot of balls ended up in the net.

Then they did some gentle batting of the ball over the net to each other, which was fun. He touched on serving for a short time, but then said it might be best to leave this until next week. This was the hardest thing to learn and the most important in a tennis match.

To Avie's disappointment, after all her hard work, Pierre did not once mention scoring. When she asked him, he said he would leave that until they were able to play a proper game.

Well, at least I will know how to do it when we can play a game, Avie thought petulantly, and she shoved the racquet back in its press rather forcefully.

She had enjoyed their first lesson and as the girls were sipping a very welcome cool squash drink outside the clubhouse, she thought of Harriet and Jeremy. They would be thrilled to know she had started playing tennis. She must write to them that very day. The post was quite good between the two countries. Harriet had sent the parcel of clothes for Avie and that had taken longer to reach her than a letter, about a month. There were a couple of new dresses, which were very welcome, two blouses and a skirt. It was nice to have more choice now. And yes, she loved her tennis dress, though the new plimsolls were pinching a bit after all that exercise!

Once back at the school, Avie bumped into Ruby in the foyer and she seemed much happier, indeed almost radiant.

'So how did it go with Matron?' Avie asked and Ruby nodded happily.

'Very well, she is so nice.' Matron had immediately contacted Mme. Corbeau, who telephoned Ruby's husband, Sir Roland Manners, and was on the phone to him for nearly twenty minutes. 'One of the maids overheard her speaking', Ruby said, 'and said she sounded very frosty and angry. She heard her say: I will not 'ave one of my girls upset like this. Ruby is quite depressed about it all. So please arrange to come as soon as possible, sir, your wife needs to see you and your child. So do I 'ave your assurance on this, Sir Roland?'

'Oh good, so what's happening then?' Avie asked.

Ruby's face was wreathed in smiles. 'They're coming here', she said excitedly. 'I had a telegram, never had one before! They're coming here next week and bringing my Toby with a nanny!' She turned to Avie. 'Isn't that wonderful? They're going to stay a whole week, in the guest apartment.'

Avie hugged her friend, whose delight was plain to see. 'Oh, that's amazing news, you must be so thrilled! You can see little Toby again, how marvellous that will be! And we can all see him too, wonderful!'

Avie began to move away, then turned back. 'Have you heard, we've got another class on Friday...?' Ruby shook her head. 'It's at ten thirty in the board room with Mme Allain, it's about table etiquette and conversation, things like that, how to hold a wine glass.' She gave a grin and nudged Ruby. 'Next week your little Toby will be here – and I'm sure it will be good to see your husband again?'

And as she returned to her room, Avie felt a pang of envy. For a tiny moment, she wished – oh, how she wished – that her parents and family were coming next week, for she was missing them so much. But she had to be strong. She was enjoying this course and it would soon be July. She would be back in England in September, so not long.

* * *

It was Friday and the girls were gathered in the board room. Mme Allain entered the room and the girls all stood up respectfully.

'Firstly, I must mention acceptable conversation at a dinner party. I would like to emphasise,' she began, 'that one must never speak of certain subjects: religion, politics or personal matters. It would spoil the evening if there was a clash of views. By all means mention if you 'ave been on your Grand Tour of Europe and 'ad some interesting experiences, but nothing too upsetting or bizarre.

'Now another point I wish to make is that you should always pace yourself with the 'ost and 'ostess when eating. You must not finish eating before your 'ost, understood?

'Now to the wine glasses.' She fetched more glasses of different sizes from the cupboard.

'Now, of course, different wines necessitate different glasses. So, we 'ave this one for white wine, this one 'ere for red and these much smaller glasses for port, sherry or martini. Also, there are these tot glasses for whisky and these pretty ones for cocktails.

'For champagne of course we 'ave the flute glass, as I'm sure you know.'

She moved back to her seat and then took some booklets from her briefcase and began distributing them.

'I just wanted to touch on Art Appreciation for a while today. It won't be as lengthy or detailed as I would wish, but it will give you some idea of 'ow art 'as changed and developed over the last century. These little booklets contain a lot of useful information about The Impressionists and include some particularly good reproductions of their most famous works.

During the Renaissance period we 'ad the traditional artists known as the Old Masters – Rembrandt, Rubens, El Greco, Michelangelo and Leonardo da Vinci, Joshua Reynolds, Delacroix.

But then in the latter 'alf of the nineteenth century a 'breakaway' movement began in Paris. These artists became known as The Impressionists, due to the radical change of style that they introduced. They often painted in the open air and used bright, clean colours, and they were drawn to the special light of the South of France.

They were treated with suspicion at first by the Musée des Beaux Arts, but after a while the public began to take an interest and appreciate the new style of painting more fully. These artists include Van Gogh, Renoir, Monet, Gauguin, Cezanne and Seurat in France and Sisley, Constable and Turner in England. They would often meet in Montmartre, discussing ideas and the finer points of their work.'

The girls started looking through their booklets, perusing them with keen interest.

At that point Mme Allain stood up and gave a beaming smile. 'Now, girls, don't groan, but I am going to set you some 'omework. I would like you all to write an essay on any one of the Impressionist painters, their lives, their work. Keep it fairly brief, say 600 words and submit it to me by Thursday of next week – all right?'

She looked along the table. 'And I would add that the assessment of this essay will be added to your overall performance score at the school, when you leave at the end of August, so bear that in mind. So do your best and do some research – there are plenty of books in the library as you know, as well as these booklets.'

Mme Allain began to collect her brief-case and papers together. 'So girls, I will now bid you au revoir and wish you good luck with the 'omework.'

And she left the room. 'Thank you, madame,' they all echoed.

The girls all began talking amongst themselves and then

Ruby muttered grumpily to no one in particular: 'Well, this is the first time we've had bloomin' homework!'

To which Claire replied promptly: 'Well, it *is* July, so I think we've done pretty well.'

* * *

Avie had woken up in the night with a toothache. It was a nagging pain and seemed to be getting worse. She stumbled out of bed half asleep and took some aspirins from the bedside cupboard. She tossed them back, before trying to get back to sleep. But in the morning, she could hardly eat anything, and the hot tea didn't help. Time for action.

'What's the name of your dentist, Claire?' she asked as her friend joined the table for breakfast.

'Dr. Schiller', replied Claire and enquired about Avie's problem. 'He's very good and quite kind. Go and see Mr. Webster', she advised. 'He will make an appointment for you and arrange for Albert to take you down there. It's in Vevey, so quite nearby.'

So, three hours later, Avie found herself dropped outside the building set in a row of terraced houses off the main square. Albert gave his usual wide grin. '*Bonne chance, m'selle!* Good luck. 'ope 'e doesn't 'urt you too much. Let me know when you wish me to collect you. *Au revoir!*'

Avie winced and pushed open the door of the dental practice nervously. She was ushered into the waiting room, where two other people were sitting, reading magazines or staring at the wall. One of the patients was called in and it was then that Avie began to notice the young woman sitting opposite her. She immediately thought how very smart she looked.

She was wearing a tailored brown uniform with a matching hat and gloves and highly polished brown shoes. Her hair was arranged into a neat bun and her complexion was healthy and flawless.

Avie wondered about the uniform and just had to ask. '*Excusez-moi,*' she began. But the young lady smiled and immediately said: 'You're English, aren't you? Well, I am too!' She put out her hand and introduced herself.

'Penelope Cartwright. I recognised your red blazer – are you at the School in Glion?'

Avie was somewhat taken aback, but nodded and smiled as she replied. 'How do you do? I'm Avie Spicer and yes, I am at the school. But I'm curious about your uniform – it's so smart!'

Penelope came and sat next to Avie. 'I'm a Norland Nanny – see, here's the badge.' And she pointed to the shiny badge on her dress.

Avie had vaguely heard about Norland Nannies. She knew they were trained to look after children of wealthy families, even royalty, and they became part of the family. She felt slightly overwhelmed by this confident young lady, but she seemed so friendly and so she responded in kind. 'Oh yes, I've heard of them. Do you like your post?' she asked, intrigued to know more.

'Yes, I love it', Penelope replied. 'But of course, it depends on the family and the children.'

She gave a laugh. 'Sometimes they can be little horrors!' she admitted, shaking her head.

'What's the family like where you are now?' asked Avie.

'They're pretty good. I get on with the mother – which is

very important, and the two children are quite well behaved most of the time. I don't see much of the father, of course, as he's frightfully busy with his business.' Penelope smiled again, showing white even teeth. 'And what are *you* hoping to do when you finish at the school?'

Avie put her head on one side, her toothache forgotten. 'I'm not sure yet, but I have had dealings with children, and I love them...'

Penelope interrupted, her brown eyes shining with enthusiasm. 'Then you should become a Norland Nanny,' she said decidedly. 'You would love it, I know. It's great fun and you get to go abroad with the family on holiday.' She opened her handbag and pulled out a card. 'Here, this is who you should call if you're interested, or your parents of course. Head Office is in London.'

At that point the nurse in her starched uniform entered the room and Penelope was called into the surgery. She gave a wave. 'Bye! Nice to have met you, Avie. *Bonne chance!*'

Good luck!

And Avie sat on the hard chair, her mind spinning with different thoughts. What a lovely girl! And what an amazing prospect that would be – to be a Norland Nanny! She gave a relieved sigh. Suddenly, she knew what she was going to do in her life. And she began to imagine herself in one of those smart uniforms, shepherding a gaggle of children through the park.

Chapter 8

When Avie returned from the dentist at Vevey, her mouth was still feeling uncomfortable from the treatment. But she didn't care a jot about that. She was so thrilled to have met Penelope Cartwright. Her mind was still whirling with thoughts of becoming a Norland Nanny. And she knew she had to ring her parents right away and let them know the good news. Avie went to Reception and asked to make a telephone call to England. The girls were allowed a free call to their parents once a week and could speak for fifteen minutes or pay for extra time.

'Hallo, is that you, Dad? Avie here...'

'Hallo darling – you sound a little strange – are you all right?'

Avie sighed impatiently. 'Yes, I'm fine, Dad. I've just been to the dentist – so my mouth is still a bit painful. No, what I'm ringing about, I met the most amazing girl there – at the dentist – and she told me all about her post – the most amazing post – so now I know what I want to do!'

Jeremy sounded rather bewildered. 'You're not making a lot of sense, darling. So what does this amazing young woman do then? You sound so excited and a bit garbled. Slow down, speak more slowly...'

'I had to ring you, Dad. She thinks I would be absolutely

ideal for the position. She's a Norland Nanny – have you heard of them?'

'Oh yes,' Jeremy admitted, 'I've heard of them – one sees them about quite a bit in London, taking their charges to the park and all that. Why, is that what you'd like to do?'

'Yes, yes', shouted Avie down the phone, 'she gave me a card and I would like you to find out all about it for me. I've got a telephone number here...'

'Hold on, hold on, Avie. Let's wait till you get home, shall we? One thing at a time, eh?'

'But I want to start enquiring straight away,' Avie insisted, 'you know how I adore children. It would be ideal.'

'Look, I'll have a word with your mother, she's not here at the moment. She's at a garden party. But I'm sure she will agree with me, not to rush into this. You should consider other things. And anyway, we don't want you dashing away again as soon as you get back. We've missed you, darling. Let's spend a few months together and then perhaps after Christmas...'

'...after Christmas!?' Avie cried incredulously. It seemed aeons away.

But Jeremy continued. 'Yes, in the New Year perhaps we could think about getting in touch with someone and making some enquiries.'

Avie felt deflated by Jeremy's stolid, sensible attitude. She was so excited about this post and wanted to find out more about it now, now this minute.

But when she thought about it, she had to agree it would be lovely to spend some time at home, before she took on a proper paid situation. Perhaps it would be best to cool her enthusiasm somewhat and concentrate on the last few weeks at the school. Jeremy was usually right about things, even though Avie didn't always agree with him.

'All right then, I s'pose it would be best not to go into it too hastily', she reluctantly agreed.

And as she came off the phone, Avie was happy. She had told them her news and set the wheels in motion. What an amazing chance she had met Penelope! Jeremy had remembered they knew someone who had employed a Norland Nanny. They would speak to them, he said, and find out some details, which sounded promising.

As Avie went through the foyer, she bumped into Claire hurrying along. 'Coming to the class?' she asked, raising her eyebrows.

Avie clapped her hand to her mouth. 'Crikey!' In all the excitement she had forgotten about the deportment class.

'In the common room in five minutes', called Claire moving away, but then she turned back. 'Oh, how did you get on at the dentist?'

Avie smiled a crooked smile. 'Yes, fine, I had a filling. But I met someone there, a lovely lady – I'll tell you about it later. See you in a minute.'

***

The deportment class was in full swing. Their tutor was lively and pretty and was called Mlle. Le Brun. She went round asking their names and seemed to remember them all straight away. The students were asked to walk round the room with a book on their head, keeping their head and shoulders erect. Then they had to do it again without the book, with the tutor watching them keenly. 'Shoulders back, girls! Heads erect!'

And they were taught how to sit elegantly, always keeping their knees together and not to cross their ankles, which was bad for the circulation; how to get in and out of a car in one easy motion and how to rise from a low chair. They were shown how to curtsey, should they ever be introduced to royalty. This they all found quite difficult and there was a lot of laughter at initial efforts.

Mlle Le Brun gave them a radiant smile, as they rested for a few minutes. 'Now, girls, you have all done so well today. But I do hope you are all eating healthily? Not too many cakes and buns, but lots of salads, and try to get some exercise every day and drink plenty of water. I know most of you attend the Keep Fit class once a week and I have heard that some of you have started playing tennis, which is great. Keep it up, particularly during this lovely summer weather we are having now. Now, any questions?'

To Avie's surprise Ruby put her hand up. 'Can you give me a diet to follow, only I'm trying to lose weight but finding it difficult...'

Mlle Le Brun beamed. 'Certainly, Ruby. I'll have a chat with you at the end of the class and give you a diet sheet. Well done for trying to lose weight. You won't regret it. Now, girls, let's all do another stint of walking with a book on your head...'

The girls giggled and once more tried to walk about the common room with perfect posture. It was quite hard.

Avie was impressed with Ruby's attitude and admired her for speaking up and admitting she was trying to lose weight. Not an easy thing to do in front of your peers. Some girls could be quite catty. She had heard that Ruby had been given a personal crash course in current affairs and history, which would improve her general knowledge. It would also be so helpful to her, when mixing with her husband's friends at social occasions. And her accent had improved since she had been having elocution lessons. Her husband would be most surprised. Mme Corbeau had asked to see Sir Roland when he arrived next week, and she would no doubt talk to him in her usual stern manner. She needed to tell him a few home truths about dealing with Ruby. Avie felt the poor girl should be offered more support and encouragement from her husband. He should be told to ring her up more often and give her some news about little Toby. But it was so good to hear that he was coming to the school soon and bringing the baby. Ruby would be overjoyed to see them both.

The class was over and Mlle Le Brun was preparing to depart, after speaking privately to Ruby. Avie was about to leave when Ruby came running after her.

'Can I have a word, Avie? I wanted to thank you for your help the other day...'

Avie shrugged and smiled. 'That's all right. So glad to hear your husband is coming and bringing the baby with him, that's great! When do they arrive?'

'On Wednesday', Ruby's face broke into a grin at the thought. 'It will be marvellous to see them both.' She hesitated. 'But there's something else I wanted to speak to you about. You know Mme Allain has set us to do an essay on those painters?'

Avie nodded. 'Yes? Which one will you choose, do you think? Have you looked through the booklet yet?'

'I've read through it but haven't written anything yet. I'm

going to do it this weekend, it's my only chance before they come.' She looked rather doubtful as she spoke. Poor Ruby had probably never written an essay in her life before. She had left school at thirteen and wasn't exactly literary. She had only ever read cheap novelettes, written in basic language. She was from a poor background. Her father was a cowman and her mother was illiterate. She certainly had no idea how to write an essay on art, that was evident.

Ruby produced the booklet out of her pocket and pointed to the two paintings by Renoir,

'Dancing in the Town' and 'Dancing in the Country'.

'I like this one – how do you pronounce it? Renwa. And I love those pictures. But I'm not certain what I should say...' she ventured timidly.

Avie saw her dilemma and decided to keep it simple. 'If I were you, I'd just quote it word for word from the booklet. Say where he was born and all that, then mention his early life and where he learnt to paint, etc. Here', she took the booklet from Ruby. 'I'll underline a few phrases and you can quote them. Then mention his most famous works listed here, all right?'

Avie went through the booklet and underlined some key points. This was no time to be lecturing her on the finer points of essay-writing, she thought. It would be a miracle if Ruby could produce an article of any kind, so it would be best to simplify things. She continued. 'Say what it is you like about the paintings, why they appeal to you, the colours, the light, anything like that, all right? And if you've got time to go to the library and find a book on Renoir, you might be able to quote something from that.'

Avie smiled at Ruby as she handed back the booklet. 'Best of luck with it! I haven't decided which one I'm doing yet – maybe Monet, not sure...'

'Thanks, Avie, you're a pal.' Ruby grasped Avie's hand. 'You've been a real chum to me since I've been here – and I'm sorry if I've not returned the favour at times...'

'That's all right, Ruby...' It was an apology of sorts and quite an effort for her.

The two girls began to climb the stairs to their rooms. 'Well, I hope to meet your husband next week and your little one. See you soon, bye!'

* * *

'Now I want you to have a little rally, four at a time, all right? Two pairs of girls on each court.' Pierre went to each girl and made sure she was holding the racquet correctly. 'See 'ow long you can keep it up before you miss it, eh?' he laughed.

Avie was down at the Tennis Club the next week and she had been paired with Rachel. It was another fine day and good to feel the sun on her limbs. She found she enjoyed doing this rallying and managed to keep on hitting the ball for eight shots before she missed it. She felt quite pleased with herself.

Pierre was watching the students keenly and he kept up a running commentary of advice and instructions as they played.

Once they had all done a stint of rallying, Pierre began teaching them the rudiments of serving. It was difficult at first. A lot of girls entirely missed the ball or failed to serve it over the net. So, there was plenty of frustration, as the students tried again and again to perfect the action. But Pierre was very patient. 'Don't despair, young ladies. The more you practise, the easier it will become.'

Phew! Avie was feeling quite hot and breathless after all the running about and unfamiliar actions. But she was loving it. She found after numerous attempts that she could just about serve a decent shot into the service area. Rachel was finding it harder, as she was left-handed.

Pierre was quick to praise the girls once they had (almost) mastered the action and so they carried on practising serving for another fifteen minutes. He was a quiet man, but took a keen interest in his students. He worked hard to ensure each girl was given his dedicated tuition and that she improved while in his care.

As the girls relaxed with a cool drink afterwards and Albert arrived to take them back, Avie reflected on the morning she had spent. She had loved the tennis lesson and couldn't think why she had never been keen to learn before. Harriet had tried to teach her years ago. But at the time when she was younger, she hadn't been interested. Her life was very different then. *Perhaps it's the new company here*, she thought, *and the new surroundings.* She looked around – a glimpse of sparkling Lake Geneva, with the backdrop of the impressive Swiss Alps – the manicured grass courts and Pierre, the friendly and patient coach. How could she *not* like it here?

Albert gave a honk on the horn of the vehicle he was driving. He had to accommodate quite a crowd of them today. The girls all ran towards the small bus and began piling in chattering and laughing. But then another car pulled into the car park and four boys from Montreux College jumped out. Roberto spotted Avie and came towards her, his face wreathed in smiles. 'Hallo there, Avie, how are you?'

His fair hair was ruffled, and she could see his sun-burnt chest, where his shirt was open. Avie was quite overcome to see him so unexpectedly and blushed as she spoke. 'Been having a lesson – it was great.'

Roberto stared at her, still smiling. 'I'm glad I've seen you. Are you coming to the Summer Ball?'

She nodded eagerly. She didn't know when it was or where it was, but she was coming.

'Will you come as my partner?' urged Roberto. 'It's in a couple of weeks.'

Avie nodded again, lost for words and dazzled by his close proximity. 'I'd love to', she murmured.

'That's a promise then!' Roberto smiled and clasped her hand briefly, as she climbed into the bus. '*Magnifico!*' he cried and waved as they drove away.

Avie was on Cloud Nine...

* * *

Avie was nearly at the end of her essay on Claude Monet. She had taken a lot of information from the booklet, but also been to the library and gathered other useful facts about the painter. She had discovered he had been poorly educated, poverty-stricken and unwell, when a young man. But with the support of fellow artists such as Manet, Sisley and Renoir, his output was prolific, though with very little financial reward. They would all meet in the cafés of Montmartre, arguing vociferously and discussing techniques for hours. Many of the Impressionist painters adored the Cote d'Azur for its amazing light and they loved to paint *en plein air*. Monet even bought a boat to use as a floating studio. He was devastated by the death of his wife, Camille in 1879. She had supported him through desperate poverty in their early years.

His well-known landscapes included 'Wild Poppies', many studies of water lilies from his home at Giverny and several different studies of haystacks at different times of day, not to mention his amazing paintings of sunrise over Westminster Bridge, when he was living in London. Also, a series of pictures of Rouen Cathedral and The Gare St. Lazare in Paris.

She wrote the final line and had quite enjoyed doing it. Finding out about the painter's life and admiring the merging undefined brushstrokes and colours in the works. She placed her essay in an envelope and submitted it to Mme Allain, crossing her fingers as she did so.

Avie had just met Sir Roland Manners, Ruby's husband, in the corridor, after he had been speaking to Mme Corbeau. He emerged looking suitably chastened. When Ruby introduced him to Avie, he put his arm around his wife, shaking his head: 'She is a changed woman, quite amazing, I'm very proud of her.'

Ruby seemed very happy to see her husband again. Avie had to hope that this episode at the Swiss school had been a turning point in their marriage.

'Come and see my little Toby!' Ruby led Avie into the common room where Mrs. Thomson, the smiling nanny, was looking after baby Toby. 'Here's the little pet! He's grown so much!' Several of the girls were surrounding the baby and admiring his ready smile and happy nature.

Toby was six months old now, with quite a thatch of dark hair, and sitting up nicely in his perambulator. As soon as he saw his parents, he clapped his chubby little hands and crowed delightedly. It was a joy to see the family so happy together.

But Avie's thoughts were constantly on the Summer Ball, only two weeks away, after her unexpected meeting with Roberto. It was to be held at Montreux College and included a light supper first in the dining hall overlooking the gardens. The college was in a prominent position in Montreux near the lakeside and was a Belle Époque stone mansion, formerly an hotel. It was an occasion to look forward to and all the girls were in a state of high excitement, as the date approached. 'Now, shall I wear my pink silk dress again or shall I buy something new?' She was in a quandary.

Mme Allain had organised another outing for the girls – they were to be given a tour of the Chateau de Chillon and a picnic in one of the parks. She also said if there was time they might be able to go on a steamer trip across the lake to Lausanne. So, the girls felt delightfully free now their studies were over, and they had done their final essay. Now they could really enjoy themselves and see something of Montreux before they left. Avie would be sad to leave Montreux, but she was also looking forward to going back home. It would be so good to see everyone again and be in her familiar surroundings.

A few days later the girls were gazing up at the vast stone walls of the Castle of Chillon by the lake. Up close it was even more impressive. The ancient castle was a prominent landmark in the area, with its fairy-tale setting, and the mountains rising behind it. They learnt that in the thirteenth century it became a summer residence, the underground vaults later being used as a prison and a weapons store. Restored in the nineteenth century, the castle then became a venue for cultural concerts and events. In the chapel, the girls admired the fourteenth-century murals and frescoes, faded but still intact. The views from the ramparts over the lake and surrounding area were amazing. Some of the girls remembered studying Lord Byron's iconic poem 'The Prisoner of Chillon', which certainly had more relevance, now they had seen the castle.

Chapter 9

It was the night of the Summer Ball. The day had been hot and humid, but now the temperature had dropped. There was a cooler breeze blowing off the lake, as the girls arrived at Montreux College. It was an impressive stone building, with a fine marble staircase sweeping down to the wide foyer, with its parquet flooring.

The girls were ushered into the splendid Great Hall with its magnificent chandelier, where a local band was already playing popular melodies on the dais. An atmosphere of conviviality greeted them. A group of smartly dressed young men immediately came forward and began claiming their partners. Avie spotted Roberto approaching. Her heart skipped a beat. He looked so handsome in his evening attire, and she greeted him warmly, when he reached her side.

'*Ciao, bella!*' Hallo, beautiful!' There was admiration in his dark eyes as he scanned her appearance and took her hand. Avie was wearing a new dress, quite a bold emerald green taffeta with a gold lurex thread on the bodice and shoulders. The colour suited her well and contrasted with her shining auburn hair, which had been swept back into a soft chignon. Her gold jewellery was discreet and her pretty gold sandals completed the outfit.

Waiters were circulating with aperitifs and canapés, and the girls joined a group of Roberto's friends and chatted animatedly. The huge room was magnificently decorated with tubs of flowers and garlands adorning every painting and window. The French doors had been opened to the terrace, giving an amazing view of the lake beyond. Several couples were spilling outside to enjoy the warm evening air. After a while they were all invited to adjourn to the dining hall, where a light buffet supper awaited them.

Avie spotted Rachel, as they were serving themselves from the inviting spread and gave her a wave. Then the gentleman beside her also looked up and acknowledged her with a smile.

'Oh!' Avie was so surprised when she recognised Tom, Rachel's brother. He had been so kind to her in Paris. An unexpected feeling of warmth flooded her body. She just had to speak to him.

'Excuse me', she muttered to Roberto, who stared at her in dismay, as she left him suddenly.

'Hallo, Tom! I didn't know you were here in Montreux.' Avie greeted Tom with a hug and Rachel.

Tom gave a shrug. 'I had some business here, so I thought I'd combine it with a visit to see my dear sister...' He put his arms around her.

'So, when I mentioned the Ball', Rachel smiled, 'he said he would be my partner if I wished.'

'Lovely to see you', Avie responded. Tom's eyes met hers and he looked at her appraisingly.

'You're looking very elegant tonight, if I may say so', he murmured. 'Save me a dance later, all right?'

Avie nodded. 'I will, certainly. Now, excuse me, I must get

back to Roberto...' And she scurried back to Roberto, who appeared relieved to see her. 'Sorry about that', Avie apologised, 'my friend, Rachel, and her brother. I met him in Paris a few months ago.'

They took their plates, piled with scrumptious delicacies, to one of the tables, where some of Roberto's friends were sitting. The wine was flowing freely, and the group was soon laughing and joking together. But most of them were from Italy and when they began conversing in rapid Italian, Avie felt distinctly alienated. Roberto made the odd remark to her in English now and then and one of the girls tried to engage her in a halting conversation in broken English. But Avie found it quite difficult to relax, even though she had enjoyed the meal.

Then she noticed Ruby and her husband were sitting at a table on their own. She made her excuses to Roberto and went over to join them. It was nice to speak English again and they seemed delighted to see her. 'So, are you enjoying your stay here?' she asked Sir Roly.

'Having a whale of a time', Roly replied, nodding good-naturedly. 'We went over to Lausanne to-day on the paddle-steamer. It was a good trip, fine town there.'

Avie noticed how much more relaxed and happier Ruby appeared. 'Your nanny looking after little Toby tonight?' Avie asked.

Ruby nodded. 'But we won't be late back. We'll probably leave at half past ten or so. Toby will be due for another feed by then – I said I would do it. Mrs. Thomson needs to get her sleep.'

'Does he sleep through the night yet?' Avie remembered this was a milestone much anticipated by young mothers.

Ruby shook her head. 'Not yet, he still wakes at about four

a.m. But I don't mind, it's a pleasure for me!' Ruby said, smiling. 'I've missed him so much that I'm happy to do it...'

Avie nodded. They seemed good parents and happy to pull their weight with the baby's routine. Roly even admitted he had bathed Toby recently and changed his nappy, quite a coup!

Avie was suddenly interrupted by a smiling Roberto tapping her on the shoulder. The band was playing the popular tune 'You Made Me Love You, I Didn't Want to Do It' and people were crowding the dance floor. 'May I 'ave this dance, please?' he asked politely.

She rose to take the arm of handsome Roberto and he swept her off to mingle with the other dancers. He was a good dancer and they stayed on the floor for two more dances, enjoying the music. Then Roberto suggested they should wander outside to the terrace for a breath of fresh air.

It was a still, warm evening and myriad stars were twinkling overhead. The night sky looked quite dazzling. The moon was shafting a silver pathway across the lake. A scent of roses was in the air. He held her close, and their lips met in a tender kiss. Avie gazed up at him, but the magic just wasn't there, so she pulled away. 'I'm sorry,' she murmured and averted her gaze. She was perplexed. She liked Roberto and found him attractive. But somehow the connection was missing.

Roberto clasped her hand and seemed very concerned. 'Forgive me, Avie, I thought …

Do you 'ave a young man in England perhaps?' he enquired earnestly.

Avie shook her head. She hesitated. 'We have parted for a while...' She looked at Roberto directly. 'You know I'm returning to England next month – the course is finished now.'

Roberto looked aghast. 'I am sad, I shall miss you, but perhaps we could write to each other...?'

'Maybe...' Avie had a feeling that friendships conducted by post were doomed to failure, as she knew to her cost with William. 'Shall we go back inside now?' Avie could see Tom in the ballroom, craning his neck as he danced with Rachel. She thought he might be looking for her.

Once inside, Avie tried to lighten the mood. Rachel and Tom came up to them as they appeared from the terrace. 'Hallo, there, beautiful evening!'

'Now you did promise me a dance', Tom said, fixing his eyes on Avie.

'So shall we exchange partners then?' Avie said gaily. And somewhat reluctantly Roberto agreed and took Rachel's hand, leading her away.

Tom and Avie began dancing together to the music of 'When Irish Eyes Are Smiling'. Avie loved the feel of his strong arms about her, as he guided her forcefully round the room. The amused twinkle in his eyes reminded her of Jeremy and she felt very relaxed with him.

'So, how have you enjoyed the course here?' he asked.

Avie nodded. 'It's been great – a lot of fun and I think my French has improved a little,' she laughed.

'You know the French for 'Bonzo *le chien*', I believe,' joked Tom.

'Oh, you heard about that!' laughed Avie. 'It was so funny, though we didn't think so at the time.'

'And how's the tennis going?'

Avie pulled a face. 'I'm still a beginner, but I love it. It's a wonderful game.'

'And now your time in Switzerland is coming to an end...' Tom said.

'M'm, I'm sad in a way, it's been a wonderful experience. But it will be good to go back home and see my family.'

'Where do they live?'

'In Kent, Canterbury – do you know it?'

'Funnily enough, my wife is in Kent at the moment, in Tunbridge Wells with our daughter, living with her mother.'

Avie flicked her blue eyes up at him. 'You must miss them both so much...'

There was a pause and then Tom replied. 'Yes, I do, of course. But I'm so busy with the hotel in Paris.'

Avie was cautious in her reply. 'So do you see much of them?'

'Well, I've had so much on lately, I don't get back that often.'

'Oh, I'm sorry,' Avie murmured, not quite knowing what to say.

As they parted Tom gave her a brief hug and squeezed her hand. 'Who knows,' he said quietly, 'we might meet up in England...'

And when the special evening ended and she was back in her room again, it was Tom, not Roberto, who occupied Avie's thoughts, as she drifted off to sleep...

* * *

'All aboard, come this way!' The girls were down at the Quai des Fleurs and about to board the stylish paddle steamer '*La Suisse*'.

It was a long, curved vessel, flying the Swiss flag proudly, as well as coloured banners at the prow. They were going on an outing to Lausanne, and Albert and Jacques had joined them, carrying two large picnic hampers. They hurried up the gangplank and made their way to the upper deck. Two of the tutors, Mlle. Brun and Mme. Benoit, were shepherding the students, so that they could all sit together.

As they drew away from the quay and out into the centre of the lake, Avie and Rachel stood by the rail and gazed at the pretty town of Montreux huddled along the promenade and facing the sparkling, sunlit lake.

'There', said Rachel, pointing to a fine building, as they passed Vevey. 'There's the hotel where we're going on Friday with Tom.' Tom had very kindly offered to take the girls out to dinner as a final get-together before he went back to Paris.

'Crikey, it looks splendid!' cried Avie as she spotted the Grand Hotel du Lac, standing in a prominent position at the lakeside.

Rachel nodded. 'It's very top-notch, so best bibs and tuckers I think are in order.'

'Very kind of him,' murmured Avie.

'Oh, don't worry', said Rachel breezily. 'He's in the trade, so he probably gets a discount!'

Avie giggled and shook her head. 'You shouldn't say that, Rachel.' But Rachel was very down to earth, that's what Avie liked about her.

The two girls stayed on the deck and it was good to feel the cool breeze on their faces as they sailed along. 'What will you wear, your pink?' Rachel asked.

Avie nodded. 'Probably, it's my best dress, how about you?'

'My black crêpe de Chine with the beading, I think,' Rachel said.

'Yes, that's lovely, it suits you with your fair hair. Did you get it in Paris?'

Rachel nodded.

'Mine too,' Avie said, thinking back to her eighteenth birthday party. It seemed ages ago now, so much had happened since then.

Mlle le Brun came up to them. 'We're landing soon, girls,' she smiled, 'so make your way down to the lower deck – lovely ship, isn't it?'

'Beautiful, very stylish,' the girls agreed.

As they approached the town of Lausanne they couldn't fail to notice the Chateau d'Ouchy built in a prime position by the quayside. It was a striking building with red roofs and pointed turrets. 'Hey, that's a lovely building,' Avie cried. Mlle le Brun nodded. 'It has twelfth- century origins, but it was rebuilt and is now a luxury hotel.'

They were soon disembarking. It had been a pleasant journey and had only taken about twenty minutes.

They all walked in a crocodile along the pretty tree-lined promenade. 'We're going to the Parc de Mon Repos for our picnic.' Mme Benoit informed them. 'It's a fair step, but will give us all some exercise.'

'We must keep in touch,' Avie said as she and Rachel followed the others past colourful flowering shrubs and immaculate lawns. The girls were leaving Montreux in a week's time. It would be sad to leave, but they were all looking forward to seeing their families again.

'Where is it your family live?' Avie asked.

'Suffolk,' Rachel replied, 'near Clare. It's very isolated but my father is in farming, so he loves it. And you're in Kent, aren't you?'

'Yes, in Canterbury, so we're quite a way from each other, but perhaps we could meet up in London occasionally. We could go up by train.'

The girls were soon arriving at the Parc de Mon Repos. Aptly named, the park was very quiet and restful and was based on English designs, so had many seats, flower beds and open spaces, as well as beautiful trees. So, they found a shady area and spread out travel rugs on the manicured lawns. Soon Albert and Jacques were coming round with the hampers and the girls fell upon the tasty goodies eagerly. It had been a long time since breakfast! There were pitchers of lemonade and bars of delicious Swiss chocolate as a treat, as well as more substantial fare.

Afterwards they walked a short distance and were given a tour of Lausanne Cathedral with its fine spire. Dating back to the thirteenth century, the Cathedral of Notre Dame was a substantial building and quite a landmark in the area. On leaving the cathedral, they had some free time to wander in the town and explore. It was quite busy with traffic and visitors. They had to be back at the quayside by four p.m.

Rachel and Avie were strolling through the streets and stopping now and then, when they saw a fashion boutique or an interesting shop. Help! Suddenly they remembered to look at their watches and saw it was ten to four. As they ran back to the quayside, they saw that '*La Suisse*' had already moored there and several girls were already on board.

Rachel and Avie had had a wonderful day. And as the girls relaxed on the journey back to Montreux, they put their arms around each other, realising their days together were numbered.

Chapter 10

'Well done, girls! You 'ave done very well.' Mme Allain was in the common room the next day, giving them the results of their essays on The Impressionists. 'The overall standard was quite 'igh', she said, 'and I think you 'ave shown to me that you are all very interested in these artists, *oui?* who are now so popular with the public.'

She reached for some papers. 'But one essay stood out for me. And that was written by Claire, so well done again, Claire. She wrote a lovely piece, with so much detail about one of the minor Impressionist painters, Berthe Morisot. And so we 'ave awarded Claire top marks of twenty out of twenty, as I really couldn't fault it. Congratulations, Claire!'

Everyone gave a little clap. Claire was always top in everything, but she was such a friendly, superior girl that nobody begrudged her.

'And in second place', continued Mme Allain, 'scoring eighteen out of twenty, is Alicia. Alicia as some of you may know is an artist herself, so she 'as brought first-'and expertise to 'er essay on Degas. So well done to you, Alicia.'

Rachel and Avie did not know this girl very well, who was very quiet and reserved, but nevertheless they joined in the applause.

But Mme Allain continued. 'And in my Highly Commended section, I have awarded fourteen out of twenty to Avie for her piece on Claude Monet. It was very well researched and written in beautiful calligraphy. So well done to Avie! I didn't know you could do this Avie. You 'ave been 'iding your light under a bush, *oui?'*

Everyone clapped and Avie felt her cheeks turning pink. She was happy that she had received an award of some kind, as she had worked hard on the essay and knew that her parents would be proud of her.

Mme Allain gathered up her papers and picked up her briefcase. 'I should mention you will all receive an overall assessment of your time here from Mme Corbeau. This will be given to you in a sealed envelope before you leave next week. Also you will receive your essays back.

'I 'ope you 'ave enjoyed your time 'ere with us in Montreux. We 'ave certainly enjoyed meeting you all. So, I will bid you all farewell and wish you all the best of luck in everything that you do in the future. Thank you, girls.'

And she made to leave the room, but Claire stood up and said a few words on behalf of all the students, thanking her for her time and patience. 'Three cheers for Mme Allain, girls. Hip, hip, hooray!'

Mme Allain smiled and nodded before she left the room.

Rachel turned to Avie, smiling approvingly. 'Well done, old bean. You did very well. I shall have to read it.'

'Which artist did you do?'

'Van Gogh. So it was a bit sad at the end ... '

'Yes, but what amazing paintings he did, some legacy, eh?'

'So, we've got a few days off before we leave next Wednesday. Shall we go down into the town tomorrow? I need to buy some presents for the family...'

Avie clapped her hand to her mouth. 'So do I! I clean forgot, I've got quite a few more to buy as well...'

'Let's go tomorrow.'

* * *

It was Friday, and Avie and Rachel were sitting in the foyer waiting for Tom to pick them up.

The girls were in their finery, Rachel very smart in her black crêpe dress and Avie pretty in her pale pink silk frock. They had been down to the town earlier in the day and bought a few presents for their families. Avie knew they would love whatever she gave them. On the spur of the moment, she had bought a present for herself – a model Swiss chalet. It would be a nice memento of her special time here in Switzerland. There were these chalet houses dotted all over the mountainside and it would remind her of Glion and the happy months spent at the school.

A honk of the horn alerted them to Tom, just arrived outside in the taxi. And as the girls appeared he came forward to greet them.

They were soon being whisked down the mountain road and taken to Vevey nearby, and the Grand Hotel du Lac. It was an impressive building. They entered the dining room and were shown to their table, set by the window overlooking the lake, and they both marvelled at the view.

'There goes the paddle steamer!' pointed out Rachel and the girls began to regale Tom with news of their recent trip to Lausanne.

The waiter presented them with menus and Avie was glad that she now had some knowledge of French and could recognise most of the dishes. Tom selected some wine for them all and the resident pianist began playing some familiar melodies. The restaurant was only half full, but a pleasant relaxing ambiance pervaded the room, which was softly carpeted and furnished impeccably with gilt chairs and tables set with snowy linen tablecloths. Long velvet curtains with embroidered swags dressed the windows and the walls were decorated with a heavy flock wallpaper.

The service was efficient but discreet and they all raised their glasses, as Tom proposed a toast to both the girls and their futures, whatever they decided to do. He looked at Avie. 'So, what are you hoping to do when you get back to England?'

Avie's eyes twinkled. 'I'm going to be a Norland Nanny', she said decidedly. And she proceeded to tell them the story. How she had met Penelope Cartwright quite by chance and been impressed by her uniform. 'So, I'm hoping after Christmas we can get in touch with someone and apply to join. I love children', she said earnestly, 'and I've looked after a baby as a nanny and worked in a Mother and Baby home. So I feel I might have a chance.'

Tom nodded. 'Oh, good, best of luck with it.'

'And what about you, Rachel', Avie asked, 'any idea what you want to do?'

Rachel exchanged glances with her brother. 'Well, Tom seems to think he can find me a situation in his hotel...'

'We need a housekeeping manager at the moment and I'm

sure Rachel could do the job standing on her head,' Tom said confidently.

Avie was rather upset at this news. She had hoped she would keep in touch with Rachel in England, but she smiled and nodded in agreement, hiding her feelings.

The evening passed quickly, and they all enjoyed the three-course meal which was delicious fare, elegantly presented. They were just finishing their coffee and petit fours, when another party of guests arrived and were shown to their table, quite near them. Avie suddenly realised she recognised the young lady. It was Penelope Cartwright, but dressed so differently from when she had last seen her, Avie did a doubletake. *Yes, it is her,* she thought and admired her stylish clothes and immaculate hairstyle. *She must be with her employers.* A lady and gentlemen and two well-behaved children, all dressed very smartly.

Within minutes champagne corks were popping and the group began singing 'Happy Birthday!', so it was obviously a celebration. As they raised their glasses, Avie happened to catch Penelope's eye and gave her a wave and a smile. Penelope looked surprised, but then smiled in recognition and gave a wave back.

'Friends of yours?' Tom asked, out of curiosity.

Avie nodded. 'Sort of, it's the girl I mentioned from the dentist, Penelope Cartwright. She's a Norland Nanny and she's here with the family on holiday.' The thought of going on holiday to places like Switzerland, if she became a Norland Nanny, was very appealing to Avie and she felt enormously thrilled inside. She couldn't wait till she had that uniform on. The prospect was very exciting and it convinced her she was making the right decision.

* * *

The Laurels, Canterbury, One Week Later.

It was now early September and Avie was back at home in England, after a long, tiring journey on the train from Switzerland. She had travelled most of the way with Rachel, but they had parted in London and gone their separate ways. Rachel was going back to Suffolk to see her parents.

As Avie waved goodbye to her friend, she felt suddenly bereft. The girls had developed quite a rapport over the past few months. She would miss her, miss her a lot.

Jeremy was meeting her in London and taking her home by car, so Avie waited at St. Pancras station, feeling so tired after all the travelling. She couldn't wait to see her loved ones again. She was standing with her luggage outside W.H. Smith, the newsagents, on the station concourse. After fifteen minutes she began to feel a trifle impatient. But then quite suddenly she spotted her father's familiar figure approaching, amidst all the travellers scurrying past and porters wheeling trolleys loaded with luggage. She gave a wave, and he waved back. And then he was by her side, hugging and kissing her. 'My darling child, how lovely to see you at last!' he exclaimed. 'Sorry I'm a bit late, the traffic was pretty bad, well, it is rush-hour, so what did I expect?'

Avie threw her arms around her father, beaming with delight. 'Dad, so good to see you!'

'Now, do you want to go and have some tea – or shall we just get home?'

Get home, they both agreed. And they chattered all the way to the car, with Jeremy firing questions at her non-stop. But Avie had to admit to him she was feeling rather exhausted. Once they had negotiated the maze of London streets, with its trolley buses and vehicles, Avie found herself nodding off. She was with her darling dad and could relax now. She was on her way home to Kent.

The children were delighted with their presents. Robert loved his cuckoo clock and Matthew adored his lion. Avie had told her parents what a beautiful area it was, and they were already planning to visit Switzerland next year.

Avie had gone over on the bus to see Betsy and Herbie in the village of Hampton Copse, admiring the autumn colours of the trees on the way. She was determined to be more independent now, after her sojourn in Switzerland. She felt she had come of age and was confident to achieve anything she chose.

On the journey back to England she and Rachel had read their reports by Mme Corbeau and overall were quite pleased with them. She had said that each girl had gained confidence and their French had improved. They had thoroughly enjoyed their time at the Institut and were sad when it ended. But they had made many friends and the course would stand them in good stead, when they came to apply for situations in the workplace. Hopefully it would be an Open Sesame to a brilliant career.

Betsy and Herbie were delighted with their presents and Janey too. Her sister was quite grown-up now at sixteen and loved her pretty jewellery. They all wanted to hear about everything and were wide-eyed when she told them how Rachel's brother had treated them to dinner at a first-class hotel. Avie noticed that Betsy was more forgetful now. She seemed to get side-tracked. She said she would make them a cup of tea and then Avie saw her feeding the chickens. Well, *she is sixty-five now,* she thought.

Herbie was just as active as ever and he was ten years older. He was still working as a carpenter in the village, but just taking on jobs that appealed to him now. He was at last receiving the Government pension, which helped their finances a little. Harriet now owned their cottage and had installed an inside bathroom, which had made their lives easier.

Back at The Laurels, Avie tried to broach the subject of the Norland Nannies. But Jeremy was insistent they wouldn't even talk about it until after Christmas. To Avie her aim of becoming a Norland Nanny was fast becoming a dream. It seemed an age ago since she had met up with Penelope Cartwright at the dentist. She was impatient to go ahead with it.

Avie was enjoying being back with her parents, but noticed that Harriet seemed rather unsettled. She was forever in her study, scanning through her accounts and papers.

'She doesn't seem very relaxed', she said privately to Jeremy. 'Is she all right? She's always looking through her account ledgers. Is there a problem?'

Jeremy's face dropped. 'Oh, you've noticed. Yes, she does seem to be worried about something, but she won't open up and tell me about it.' He shrugged. 'I suppose she'll tell me in her own good time...' He looked directly at Avie. 'There's no problem with the accounts here. I deal with those. But it's the Stour Tollway account that I think is the trouble...'

Avie looked concerned. 'Oh? I didn't realise she still dealt with that.'

Jeremy nodded. 'She told James she would be happy to carry on with it after our marriage. She likes to keep an eye on things over there, to keep her hand in.'

Land belonging to Pelham Hall had been a tollway for centuries, where it met the bridge over the River Stour near the Pilgrim's Way. Farmers herding their sheep and cattle over the bridge paid a small fee to the tollkeeper. These fees helped with the maintenance of the bridge and the road. The toll-way was in a remote part of the estate and not easily accessible. The tollkeeper had died a few months ago and Harriet had appointed a new man, Ernest Wilcox. A small cottage also came with the job, so it was a prized post.

'I suspect Harriet is regretting appointing this man', said Jeremy confidentially. 'He's not being very straight with her and I reckon he's fiddling the books...'

Avie was shocked. 'So where did this man come from? Was he recommended to her as an honest person?'

Jeremy looked a little uncomfortable. '*Ay, there's the rub*', to quote our friend Shakespeare.

Harriet chose him herself. She came across him during a charity visit to the workhouse and was impressed by his attitude. He seemed to want to better himself. So she gave him the opportunity and appointed him. It was a bit controversial, I can tell you.' Jeremy met Avie's eyes. 'So, there's the problem in a nutshell. She doesn't want to admit that he's a wrong 'un. And yet I'm sure she suspects it. It must be him. No-one else deals with it.'

'Have you faced her with it – told her you're suspicious?'

Jeremy sighed. 'I've tried to, but you know what she's like. She can be very stubborn. If she would only admit there is a problem, I could help her, go through the books. But she has got so much pride, your mother.'

'Could I help at all? Have a word with her?'

Jeremy shook his head. 'She wouldn't like that. No, I think I've got to go through the books when she's out, speak to some of the farmers and then face her with it. It's obviously worrying her. We need to sort it out.'

Then he turned to Avie with a bright smile. 'But I don't want you worrying your little head about this, Avie. Now, I believe we've all been invited over to Pelham Hall tomorrow for a nice family lunch, should be good, eh? See your cousins, they're growing up fast...'

'...and we've got the Harvest Festival service first at St. Cuthbert's, I believe,' Avie said. 'Do we need to take anything for that? Fruit or vegetables?'

'Good idea, let's go down to the orchard and we can pick a few apples – we've got quite a glut this year...' He patted Rufus, the cocker spaniel, at his feet. 'Let's take Rufus with us. Come on, boy.'

Chapter 11

Avie had been home for a few weeks now and was already missing the school in Montreux. She realised with a jolt that she would probably never see most of the girls again, despite their fervent declarations to keep in touch. She had exchanged addresses with Claire, Rachel and Amy and to her surprise had already heard from Ruby. She sounded very happy to be home and said her marriage had 'turned a corner'. So Avie was pleased for her and hoped that they might be able to see each other sometime, despite their crosses in the past.

Avie was still waiting to hear from Rachel. She wondered whether she would be going to Paris to work in Tom's hotel or whether she had chosen another path. She had received a letter from Claire, and it sounded as if her career was already taking off. She had recently been offered a post at the British Embassy in Geneva, which she was considering. Avie knew Claire was bound to be successful in whatever sphere she chose. She admired her so much. She was a brilliant student, but somehow managed to disguise this fact and be one of the girls.

It was then that Avie thought of Roberto. She had felt really attracted to him and he was such a lovely young man. But when they kissed there was no spark, no connection. She had sent him a short letter, but in her heart she didn't think she would ever see him again, when you added the tyranny of distance to the mix. And as for William, she hadn't heard from him and didn't want to make the first move. She did feel rather mixed up about their relationship.

Meanwhile Avie felt she was kicking her heels rather, waiting around until after Christmas, when Jeremy had said they would contact the Norland Nannies. She had been playing tennis with her cousins at Pelham Hall - albeit with a jumper and scarf on against the cold -and enjoying playing board games with Robert and Matthew when the rain came down.

But although she loved amusing the children, she had to admit she was becoming increasingly restless. She was itching to do a proper job and earn some money! So, when over dinner one night Harriet casually announced that she had found Avie a post, Avie's eyes lit up.

'Hey, where is it and what is it?' she enquired breathlessly.

'Don't get too excited, Avie. The post is for a Classroom Assistant at the local primary school in Avenue Road. They would like to interview you, but as far as I can gather the job is yours for as long as you wish. I happened to meet up with the Headmistress at a function I was at...'

'Wonderful!' Avie was quite chuffed, and her mind began whirring with ideas and the joy of dealing with young children.

Education had moved on considerably since Edwardian times. Dame Schools had been abolished and a new Department for Education set up by the Government. It was now of course compulsory for children to attend school. The Education Department set the syllabuses and standards required by law and this strict discipline ensured that most children could read and write by the time they were seven. Pupils were medically examined regularly and the school leaving age had been increased to fifteen. Brighter pupils were offered college places until they went to university at eighteen.

So it was with some trepidation that Avie found herself neatly attired and entering Avenue Road Primary School two days later. It reminded her of the interview with Mme. Corbeau when she first arrived at the Institut, very nerve-wracking. It was late afternoon and all the pupils had already departed, when she entered the building, set in the centre of the village of St. Peters, named after the church. A lady dressed in a neat blouse and skirt came forward as she entered the class-room, where rows of desks faced the blackboard and a desk. Avie noticed a large picture of the King and Queen on the wall, along with the Union Jack.

'Miss Spicer?' She nodded. 'The Headmistress will see you now. Come this way.' And Avie was shown into a smaller room, where a tall lady with grey hair rose from her desk and smiled as she shook hands.

'Good afternoon, Miss Spicer. Please take a seat. Now I have spoken to your mother, and I believe that you have just returned from Switzerland, is that right?'

'Yes, ma'am. I was at a finishing school for six months.'

'And did you enjoy the experience?'

'Very much, thank you, ma'am. It was an excellent school.'

'And what was the syllabus?'

'Mainly social etiquette, but we had flower arranging classes, Keep Fit classes and tennis lessons. We also studied French and

Art Appreciation. And we went on outings in the neighbourhood to various points of interest.'

'And tell me, do you have any experience of dealing with young children?'

Avie was happy to inform the Headmistress that she had worked at a Mother and Baby home and as a nanny and was hoping to become a Norland Nanny eventually. She also had a First Aid Certificate, which could be useful. The Headmistress took a paper from her desk and studied it. 'Your mother has shown me this essay which I believe you wrote while at the school.' Her eyes scanned the words quickly. 'It certainly seems to be an excellent essay on Monet, I commend you for it. Your handwriting is very good. Now tell me, would you be interested in working at this school?'

'Yes, ma'am, but what would my duties be?'

'You would be helping the teacher, so handing out exercise books, pencils, etc., fetching things where needed, filling the inkwells. We did have the children as ink monitors, but it got out of hand. The boys were very clumsy and spilt ink all over the place, so we decided it was better this way. And, oh yes, you will be required to supervise the children, when they are on a break or having lunch, or in the temporary absence of Miss Palmer.'

Avie's eyes brightened. 'I would like that, ma'am. I love children and would be very happy to help the teacher.'

'But I understand you can only work up to Christmas, is that right?'

'As far as I know…'

The Headmistress stood up and smiled at Avie. 'Very nice to have met you, Miss Spicer. You will receive a letter from us very soon offering the post and hopefully you can start with us here in a couple of weeks... I will give you back your essay, which I notice was Highly Commended, well done.'

'Thank you, ma'am. I look forward to it.'

* * *

Avie had just finished her first day at Avenue Road school. She felt stimulated and happy as she left the building, waving to some of the children who were being collected by their parents. She had enjoyed the experience and loved engaging with the pupils, some of whom were very amusing in the things they said. Avie heard everything about their pets at home. Little Dorothy had a rabbit and Johnnie tried to describe their cat, like a tortoise! *Tortoiseshell, he must mean,* thought Avie. Sometimes they gave a little too much information about their parents. 'Dad gets drunk every night', or 'Mum stole some apples from the orchard'.

Avie was quite enchanted with the classroom, which was decorated with the children's paintings and jam jars full of flowers from their gardens.

The teacher, Miss Palmer, was in her late twenties and they had got on well overall. But Avie did feel she was always trying to exert her authority over her new assistant. And she didn't like the way she shouted at the boys and girls at times. She also snapped at her, if she dared to joke with the children during the mid-morning break. It was Avie's nature to be friendly with people and she was most at ease with young children. But Miss Palmer couldn't stop her smiling at them and giving the occasional wink now and then.

The teacher was very strict in the classroom and insisted on complete silence while she was at the blackboard. One of the pupils, Dan, an untidy boy, big for his age, had been flicking ink pellets at some of the girls behind the teacher's back. Miss Palmer happened to turn round unexpectedly and caught him in the act.

He was immediately despatched to the corner of the room, where he had to stand with his arms out straight for half an hour. Avie thought this was rather cruel, but she kept quiet, as she collected up the exercise books, before the bell rang for the mid-morning break. In addition, Dan had to write fifty lines saying: 'I must not misbehave in class.'

There were thirty children in the class, the girls all wearing white smocks over their dresses and the boys in white shirts, grey pullovers and short grey trousers. At the lunch break Avie had to keep an eye on the children, as they ate their packed lunches and had fun in the playground. Some of them were bowling hoops, others playing singing games or hopscotch and the boys kicking a football around. So there was much hilarity and squeals of laughter, as the pupils let off steam.

Avie gave a sigh of satisfaction, as she wheeled her bicycle onto the road. It had been a good first day and she felt at ease at the school. *Nice to be doing a proper job*, she thought. She rode the short journey into Canterbury and tied her bicycle to some railings nearby. She had offered to buy some linen napkins for Harriet and was making for Debenhams department store.

The city was quite busy with traffic, both motorised and horse-drawn, with plenty of people milling about, either shopping or relaxing at a café. There was a demonstration in progress, by Suffragettes, marching through the streets and waving their banners, closely watched by several policemen. Only a few months ago, a Suffragette, Emily Davison, had been killed, when she threw herself in front of a horse in the Derby at Epsom. She had become a martyr as a result, so the police were now very vigilant when the Suffragettes were demonstrating. Avie was glad to see they were still active, as she believed in the Cause passionately. The town was a draw for Christians, with its magnificent twelfth-century cathedral. The Precincts area was quite crowded with visitors clutching their guidebooks, as they admired the many fine timber-framed houses.

There were a few beggars in the city, who chose their pitches carefully, aiming at the tourists who might be more generous with their money. Avie often saw one old chap with a toothless grin and she gave him a copper or two now and then. She sometimes engaged him in a little chat. He had been injured in the Boer War and had only one arm, so Avie felt pity for him. But this time when she spotted him at the corner of an alleyway, to her surprise he was standing up. And he seemed rather agitated about something as she approached him.

'What's up, Jack, you all right?'

He shook his head. 'It's me dog, Trinny. He's got himself stuck in the kitchen back home. Can you come and 'elp me? Poor thing, he's that upset…'

Avie was doubtful. She had shopping to do and it was nearly four o'clock now. 'I don't know', she began, thinking to herself that she had never seen this old chap with a dog before.

'It's just up the alley, not far, won't take a minute. I can't do it on me own, y' see, 'cos of me arm…' And he touched his flapping sleeve. 'I went to a neighbour, but 'e was out...' He looked quite tearful.

Avie softened her heart. 'All right, I'll just come and take a look...' And she followed Jack up the dingy alleyway. Away from the main thoroughfare, there was rubbish strewn about and weeds sprouting between the worn and cracked paving slabs. The alleyway ended at a group of dilapidated hovels and a row of shabby cottages. Jack made for one of the hovels and pushed open the door.

'Come this way, miss. It's very good of ye. I'll just see 'ow 'e is.'

Avie was cautious and began to feel she had made the wrong decision. But she followed Jack into the small room, peering through the gloom and trying to see the dog. Dirty dishes littered the stone sink and there was a putrid smell in the air.

Then as her eyes adjusted to the dim light, all at once Jack hobbled past her and slammed the door, shooting the rusty bolt. Avie suddenly felt very alarmed. There was no dog in the room, that was evident, and she was alone with this old beggar. He had tricked her into entering his dirty hovel. How could she have been so stupid?

'Where's the dog then, Jack? I don't see any dog.'

Jack came up to her and gave a gappy grin, his face lined and gaunt. 'I just wanted a bit o' company, y'see? You're a lovely young lady - how about a kiss? And where's your purse?' And he drew closer, pulling at her jacket and bag with his blue-veined hand.

Avie was horrified, her heart pounding. But she kept her head. She had been in a similar situation like this once before, though the perpetrator had been a titled gentleman, not a beggar.

'Get off me – I shall report you for this.' And she gave him a swift kick in the groin with her sturdy leather shoe. Jack doubled up in pain and nearly lost his balance. 'Ooh, you bugger, you!'

Avie ran to the door and struggled to shoot the rusty bolt. She wiggled it in desperation, injuring her fingers, and finally it was unbolted. She managed to unlatch the ancient timber door and escape from the cottage. Free at last!

She ran up the alley-way, sobbing with relief and realising she had had a narrow escape. As she reached the busy environment of the High Street, she tried to smooth her dress down and wiped her bleeding fingers on it. *Must look respectable, I'm a teaching assistant now*, she thought. But the experience had shocked and frightened her and she started sobbing again, as she stumbled along the pavement, breathing heavily.

'Annie-Violet, is that you? Are you all right?'

The deep voice penetrated her tortured thoughts, and she looked up. It was Ted, a schoolfriend from years ago. He had worked as a gardener when she was at Craven Manor. She felt such relief to see a friend when she was feeling so wretched. Avie flung herself into his arms and sobbed again, tears running down her cheeks.

Ted steered her into a small café and ordered some hot strong tea. 'This young lady is upset. Bring it quickly, please!'

Avie tried to compose herself as she sat at the table. Other customers were casting curious glances at her dishevelled appearance and tear-stained face. Ted took her hand and gripped it firmly. 'Now tell me what happened,' he commanded.

Avie felt foolish now, but she recounted the story of how the old beggar had tricked her into going into his hovel and then tried to kiss her and steal her purse. 'Oh Ted, thank goodness you were here. It's so lovely to see a friendly face.' And Avie looked at Ted, his honest gaze, his sunburnt hands holding hers. He seemed to have changed. He'd matured from the shy young gardener into a confident young man.

The tea arrived and Avie sipped at it gratefully. It was hot and sweet and certainly seemed to calm her and give her strength. 'So do you think I should report it to the police?' she asked Ted.

He nodded. 'I reckon, but see what your parents say...'

Once they had finished their tea, Avie gathered her thoughts. 'Now I was supposed to be going to Debenhams to get something for Harriet, but...'

Ted shook his head. 'I think it might be best if I took you straight home, young lady. You've had a nasty shock. I've got my van here. Where is it you live now?'

Avie had previously lived at Craven Manor when she was a scullery maid. 'It's quite close, St. Peters, near the church, off the Sturry Road. But oh,' she suddenly thought, 'my bike, I've got my bike here. Can we pick it up, please?'

'Of course, let's do that right now.' And they set off together to the van, Ted still firmly holding her arm.

Chapter 12

'What *were* you thinking of, darling?' Harriet rounded on her daughter on hearing of her escapade. She shook her head. 'To put yourself at risk like that - it doesn't bear thinking of!'

Avie shrugged. 'I sort of trusted him. I'd spoken to him before - he seemed a nice old chap… And I suppose I felt sorry for him, because of his disability.'

Jeremy put his arm around Avie. 'Anyway, thank God you're safe now, that's the main thing. And it was a miracle you happened to meet Ted and he could bring you home. He looks a fine young man, I must say.'

Harriet and Jeremy had been so shocked when they heard Avie's news. They thanked Ted profusely for bringing Avie home and wanted him to come in for a cup of tea and a chat. But he said he had work to do. He was working for a big landscaping firm that undertook various jobs around the neighbourhood.

'So, the thing is, are we going to report it to the police or not?' Harriet said, turning to Jeremy. 'It really was reprehensible behaviour, not to mention abduction.'

'Personally, I think not. You've just started working at the school, Avie. I don't think it would be a good idea to have your name splashed all over the papers in a situation like that, involving an old tramp.'

Harriet looked reflective. 'M'm, perhaps you could ask the local vicar to have a word with the wretched man. Give him a warning. I don't see why he should get away with it scot-free. The vicar could set him some work to do perhaps in recompense. Clearing the graveyard or something.'

'Good idea, Hattie. I'll find out who the local vicar is and speak to him myself. I'm sure he'll understand and make the old chap see the error of his ways.' He turned to Avie with a sober look on his face. And you, young lady, must watch your step. You're too trusting with people. So, don't go off with old tramps anymore, all right? Learn a lesson from this.'

'Yes, Dad.' Avie's eyes were twinkling, despite her grim experience. She had recovered from her ordeal and felt so relieved to be home.

Harriet lifted the teapot. 'More tea, darling?' Avie shook her head. 'Tell us all about your first day at the school then. How did you find it?'

'Yes, I enjoyed it. But I had to be careful with the teacher, Miss Palmer. She was eager to point out that she was in charge all the time. I wanted to have a chat and a laugh with the children, but she didn't encourage that, even at playtime. And she made one of the boys stand in a corner with his arms out straight for half an hour, which I thought was so unkind...'

'What had the boy been doing?' asked Jeremy.

'Flicking ink pellets at the girls, only a bit of fun...'

'Well, you are only a junior, so you have to respect her authority, I'm sure,' said Jeremy.

'You'd better *try* to like the teacher, even if you don't', Harriet said, as she rang the bell for the parlourmaid. 'It sounds an ideal job for you.'

But then there was a scuffle at the door and all at once the housekeeper, Mrs. Salisbury, entered the room, accompanied by a red-faced gentleman in a peaked cap. Everyone was rather startled, and Jeremy stood up, looking annoyed at the intrusion. Mrs. Salisbury appeared decidedly flustered and Rufus started growling.

'Beg pardon, ma'am, sir, but this 'ere gentleman insists on seeing you. He says he won't leave until he does...'

Jeremy approached the man, who had taken off his cap and was standing in an aggressive stance, feet apart and chin raised.

'Jackson? Is it Farmer Jackson? What is this about, man? This is quite an intrusion. Explain yourself!'

Farmer Jackson's face was serious, but he offered his hand to Jeremy. 'Beg pardon, sir, forgive the intrusion. But I 'ave come quite a way to see you. I 'ad to find out, y'see...'

'Find out, find out what?' Jeremy looked puzzled.

'Whether you be putting the prices up on the Stour Tollway. The tollkeeper says you are and there's going to be a new sign erected. Is that right, sir?'

Jeremy turned to Harriet. 'We haven't put the prices up, have we? My wife deals with this. Anyway, sit down, man and Mrs. Salisbury, fetch Mr. Jackson a cup of tea. I'm sure you'd like one? Let's be civilised about this.'

'Thank 'ee, sir. I 'ave come representing quite a few farmers, sir.'

'It must be a misunderstanding,' Harriet said. 'No, we haven't raised the price of the toll for over five years. Why, does Mr. Wilcox tell you otherwise, may I ask?'

Farmer Jackson looked down at his cap, gripped tightly in his hands. 'Not only tells us otherwise, ma'am, but is already charging the new amount. He says it be one penny for each sheep now and two pennies for each cow. Well, I can tell you that mounts up when you've got twenty sheep and fifteen cows.'

Jeremy and Harriet both looked startled. But to Jeremy's relief Harriet kept her cool and shook her head. 'No, that's not right. There's something amiss here.' She hesitated. 'We did feel there was a problem at the Stour, didn't we, Jeremy? But we couldn't quite put our finger on it. We were about to investigate it, weren't we, Jeremy?'

Jeremy nodded, amazed at Harriet's audacity, but silently praising her panache in dealing with the situation so smoothly. He gave a sly wink to Avie, who was all ears and gazing at her mother with admiration in her eyes.

But Harriet continued. 'I'm so sorry to hear this news... Ah, here comes Mrs. Salisbury with the tea. Now, let me pour you a cup, you poor man, you must be parched...'

'We'll get to the bottom of this trouble, Jackson, don't you worry. And you did well to come and see us about it,' Jeremy added.

'And we'll see everyone is reimbursed if they've been overcharged', Harriet said, as she handed Farmer Jackson a welcome cup of tea.

Mr Jackson nodded. 'Thank 'ee, ma'am. No, I'm afraid Mr. Ernest Wilcox is not very popular in the Stour Valley. We all thought it were a bit queer, prices going up and not being told in advance, but we all trusted him at first. But now, we're not so sure. He's an old lag, I believe, and can't forget his former ways. 'ard to teach an old dog new tricks, y'see, sir.'

'Avie, offer Mr. Jackson some cake and let's have a chat.'

And so Farmer Jackson's visit became quite amicable, as Harriet and Jeremy engaged him in some talk on farming methods and milk yields. Avie was feeling rather tired and wondered how she could leave the room quietly and seek the sanctuary of her bedroom. But before she could do so, Mrs. Salisbury appeared again in the doorway. 'Excuse me, madam, but there is a visitor to see Miss Avie.'

All at once Avie forgot her tiredness and her eyes became alert. 'Oh, who is it, Mrs. Salisbury?'

The housekeeper smiled a secret smile. 'The young woman said you don't know her, miss, but she is sure you'll want to see her...'

'Oh, how mysterious!'

'Show her into the dining room, Mrs. Salisbury.' Harriet said.

'Excuse me, everyone...' Avie said and got up to leave the room. But Harriet rose and came with her. 'I think I'll just see who this mysterious person is who won't give her name, before I allow you to see her, darling. Excuse me a moment...'

Mother and daughter entered the dining room and Avie gasped.

A young woman was standing there, admiring some of the paintings on the walls. But it was the smart uniform she was wearing that had made Avie gasp. For she was a Norland Nanny.

* * *

The young lady turned, as they entered the room and came towards them, smiling and assured. 'How do you do? My name is Felicity Trenton - Mrs. Grainger gave me your name.'

Harriet shook hands with the young woman. 'Harriet Spicer. Oh yes, I believe you worked for the Graingers, is that right? I remember now, they said they had employed a Norland Nanny. Now, may I introduce my daughter, Avie?'

Avie gazed at Felicity as she shook hands, admiration shining in her eyes. 'How do you do? Lovely to meet you!'

'Avie is interested in becoming a Norland Nanny...' Harriet murmured. 'Please sit down.'

'Please forgive my intrusion, calling unannounced. But I was in the neighbourhood and thought I would just see if you were at home...'

'My daughter has recently returned from Switzerland...'

'...I was at the Institut Pierre Philippe in Montreux. It was great, I had a wonderful time. Did you go there?'

Felicity shook her head. 'No, I was in Geneva, but we visited Montreux, lovely town. Now, I've brought a few leaflets with me, which give lots of information about the organisation. So, you must apply, filling in a form about yourself and then after an interview, if you are selected, you will be offered a post.' She hesitated. 'You must state if you are prepared to go abroad with the family, but I should mention that if you don't wish to do so, this would severely restrict your chances of being offered a post. Many of the families do spend time abroad, I have to say.'

Avie and Harriet nodded but kept quiet.

'But the main point you should realise is that you are essentially on probation for the first year. It will be eleven months before you are allowed any leave...'

Avie and Harriet exchanged gloomy glances and Avie pulled a face.

'...it is a big commitment to take on and one which you should think about carefully before agreeing to accept a post.'

Harriet nodded, looking rather concerned. But Avie seemed undeterred and asked: 'And there's a period of training, I presume, before one takes on a post?'

'Yes, there is a training programme in London which lasts about a month and then you accompany a fully qualified nanny for two to three weeks to gain more experience.'

'Well, we have a lot to think about,' murmured Harriet, 'but it has been so good to meet you and thank you for the information...'

She looked at her watch, as she stood up and offered her hand again. 'Thank you for coming today, Felicity, but I should add that Avie has just started another position nearby, working as a classroom assistant at the local primary school. So even if she did want to apply, she wouldn't be available until well after Christmas.'

'But we can certainly make some enquiries...' put in Avie.

Miss Trenton smiled warmly back at them. 'Well, I hope the information I have given you will help you come to a decision. I love the job, but it's not for everyone. And it does depend very much on the family you join, and the different personalities involved.'

'So nice to have met you, Felicity and thank you for coming.' Avie paused, then said impulsively, 'I don't suppose you know Penelope Cartwright, do you?'

Felicity's eyes lit up. 'Oh yes, I know Penny, lovely girl.'

'I happened to meet her in Montreux, purely by chance. She looked so smart in her uniform, I just had to speak to her.'

Harriet led the way out to the hall, and they waved, as the young woman walked away from the house and hurried down the drive.

'Well, this has been quite a day', murmured Harriet as they returned to the house. 'So many visitors! And of course for you, Avie, are you sure you're fully recovered from your ordeal –let alone your first day at the school?'

Avie nodded and gave Harriet a hug. 'Yes, I'm fine now, thank you, Mum. But I am a bit tired, it's been a lot to take in. I might just go up to my room for a while now before dinner.'

Her mind was spinning with plans and thoughts, and she wanted to digest them all quietly, before she changed for dinner. She felt thrilled to have met another real live Norland Nanny and was itching to look through all the leaflets she had left and make further enquiries.

Then she realised with a start she had a job to go to in the morning. So much had happened that day, she had almost forgotten. She would see the children again, not to mention the dreaded teacher, Miss Palmer. *So one step at a time*, Avie, she thought to herself. *Calm down and don't get overexcited.*

But the thought of herself in that brown uniform kept returning to her again and again, as she rested on the bed. It was mid-October now, so with any luck if she applied soon, she might be starting the position next year. Yes, 1914 could well be her special year…

Chapter 13

March, 1914

Avie stood in front of the long mirror and surveyed herself critically. She had arranged her hair into a neat bun and then set her new hat on top, pulling it down firmly. She had fixed her stud earrings, the only ones allowed. Tightening the belt on her brown dress, she then tried the cape on, giving it a swish. M'm, very stylish indeed! Avie was a vision in brown - at last! She might need it to-day, as the March wind was still fresh.

Today was the day Avie started her first post as a Norland Nanny! She had sailed through the training period and shadowed a qualified Norland Nanny. She had ticked the box, stating she would be happy to go abroad with the family. Avie had been dreaming about this moment for many months and was so excited it had finally arrived.

She had been assigned to a family called Williams. There were two children, a boy aged eight and a girl of five. Mr. Williams was a banker, she had been told, and their main residence was in Surrey. But they regularly went to France or Italy during the children's school holidays. Mrs. Williams was an artist and did some local charity work.

The children were at a private school fairly near their home and Avie would be expected to take them to and from school. She had to look after their welfare and encourage their hobbies.

Jeremy was taking her up to Notting Hill in London, the Headquarters of Norland Nannies, and Mr. Williams had agreed to meet her there and take her to his home in Esher.

Jeremy loaded Avie's big case into the boot of the car. 'Now, are you sure you've got everything?'

Avie nodded, as she hugged Harriet tightly. 'Bye, Mum, I'll be in touch...'

Harriet looked a bit tearful, as she watched her daughter enter the car, clutching her handbag. 'Best of luck, darling, I hope it all goes well. Write, won't you? Let us know what's going on. It only seems like yesterday when you were coming back from Montreux...'

Avie looked aggrieved. 'Mu-m, I've been home for six months! Bye!'

Avie looked back at the house as they went down the driveway. She'd had a good few months and so enjoyed seeing the family. Christmas was wonderful, the children over the moon with excitement as they helped to decorate the tree and then open their presents on Christmas morning. They had gone to the Boxing Day Hunt at Pelham Hall, where they had a bracing time in the snow. Her job at the school had been amazing, she had so engaged with the children and loved helping the teacher, who had mellowed somewhat over the months, because of Avie's enthusiastic response to everything.

She had caught up with Clara and Isabel and they had gone to concerts locally and in London. It was great to see her friends and she hoped to meet up with Isabel sometime, as she worked in London.

But now at last she was on her way to London and there was a family awaiting her. It would be so exciting, getting to know the children and the parents. She hoped they would all get on. It was essential to have a good rapport with the mother, particularly, everyone said. So she had vowed to make sure this happened.

'We're coming into Notting Hill now,' Jeremy murmured, as they began to meet more traffic. 'Now I think it's this street here, I did look it up on the map...' He turned into a side street and Avie began looking for house numbers; she soon spotted the substantial terraced house with the plaque on the door, 'Norland Nannies'. Avie's tummy turned over. The moment had come; she was excited, yet nervous, at the same time.

She got out of the car and Jeremy took her case from the boot. 'I'll just take it up the steps for you, it's quite heavy...' At the top of the steps, Jeremy turned to his daughter and gave her a big hug. Bye, darling, best of luck! Keep in touch, won't you?'

'Bye, Dad, thanks for everything. Bye!'

Avie watched, as her father walked back to the car, giving a wave. She drew her breath in and rang the doorbell. The door opened and a fresh-faced young woman stood there. She beamed when she saw Avie and opened the door wider. 'Come in, are you Avie Spicer? I'm Deborah Cox, Miss Taylor's assistant. Mr. Williams has arrived and is awaiting you, so come this way...'

Avie nodded and followed the young woman into the hall and then into a front room. A gentleman of medium height dressed in a suit was sitting by the table and he rose when he saw Avie. He had a balding head and a little goatee beard, and he gave a smile and put out his hand.

'Mr. Williams, meet Avie Spicer, your new Norland Nanny!' Mr. Williams had been told that Annie-Violet preferred to be called 'Avie'.

'How do you do, Avie, Ernest Williams. Have you come far today, may I ask?'

'My father has just brought me up from Kent, Canterbury. It's a pleasure to meet you, sir.'

Deborah went to the table, where there were some papers in a folder. 'Now if you could both sign these forms, here and here... I think you can be on your way... Thank you. Lovely to see you both, good morning!'

They were soon leaving the building and driving away in Mr. Williams' Mercedes. He seemed a quiet gentleman and so conversation was rather sporadic, as they progressed along the streets and out of London. 'It shouldn't take long,' he said breezily, 'we'll probably be there in half an hour.'

'So you were at a finishing school in Switzerland, I hear,' he said, as he negotiated the traffic. 'Tell me all about it, where was it?'

And Avie was happy to talk about Montreux and the school. Mr. Williams was interested, as he had travelled in Europe extensively and knew the country.

'You have some French then,' he said.

'Yes, sir. I'm not exactly fluent, but I can get by...' Avie murmured.

'That could be useful, we go to France quite a bit. And do you ride, may I ask?'

'Oh yes, sir, of course. I've been riding for several years. So do the children enjoy riding?'

The gentleman nodded. 'Henry does, but the little one is not so keen. She had a tumble from her pony once and that scared her...'

They were soon passing open fields and the leafy lanes of Surrey, and a signpost for Esher appeared. After a few more minutes, they drove down a tree-lined road and through some imposing entrance gates, engraved with the name 'Claremont House'.

The house came into view – it was an impressive Georgian country house, almost as grand as the house Avie had worked at as a scullery-maid all those years ago. But she didn't think this was the time or place to mention that. As the car stopped outside the front door, a liveried chauffeur appeared, offering to put the car away. But Mr. Williams shook his head and said he would need him, as he was going elsewhere almost immediately. The chauffeur opened the boot and took Avie's case into the house.

'Now, my dear, come this way and meet my wife. The children are both at school at the moment, you will meet them later.'

He led the way into the wide entrance hall, calling her name. 'Prudence, we're back'. A slim lady appeared from the sitting-room, her fair hair wild and dishevelled. She had a bemused look on her face and the air of someone who was rather distracted. She was wearing a floaty dress made of chiffon and had a ribbon in her hair.

'Hallo, my dear, this is Avie, our new nanny. Her name is Annie-Violet, but she likes to be known as 'Avie.''

Mrs Williams offered her hand to Avie, who felt it was like shaking hands with a will-o-the-wisp, she was so fragile. 'How do you do, I hope you had a good journey?' She was quietly spoken and didn't quite meet Avie's eyes as she greeted her.

Avie smiled, as she surveyed this frail person and was amazed she had managed to produce two children. 'Yes, thank you, madam, we met up and have driven down here in very quick time, thank you.'

'Now I expect you will want to see your room, so our housekeeper, Mrs. Pearson, will show you up. You are on the second floor, near the children's bedrooms.' She rang a bell pull by the fireplace. A middle-aged lady appeared in the doorway, wearing a printed overall over a grey dress.

'Ah, Pearson, this is our new nanny, Miss – um, what is the surname?'

'Spicer, the name is Spicer', put in Mr. Williams rather impatiently. 'My dear, I must be off again now - going to see the accountants at Reading. I'll be back for dinner later...' He left the room and a moment later they heard the front door close.

Mrs. Williams waved a pale arm towards Mrs. Pearson. 'I will leave you in the capable hands of Mrs. Pearson. Excuse me, I have – um, other things to do...' And she disappeared into the next room and closed the door.

Mrs. Pearson stared at Avie's capacious suitcase. 'I'll get Thomas to shift that, I'm not taking that up the stairs.' She led the way up the wide, shallow staircase, with its fine curved banisters. 'Come far 'ave you?'

'Kent, Canterbury', Avie murmured

'Oh, nice, my 'usband used to watch the cricket there. Now, 'ere we are. This is your room, and the children are either side of you, so 'andy...'

She led the way into a spacious, sunlit bedroom, with its own en suite bathroom. Pretty flower-strewn curtains were at the windows, matching the bedspread and pillow shams. There was a triple-mirror dressing-table in one corner and a small desk in another. A comfortable armchair was set by the window. A large mahogany wardrobe dominated the space of one wall.

'Oh, what a charming room,' said Avie.

'Ope you'll be comfortable, miss. Now, would you like me to send up some tea and sandwiches? It's nearly lunchtime by my reckoning. And I'll get Thomas to bring your case up. If you want anything ironed, leave it out and one of the maids can do it. Orl right? I'll leave you now and you can 'ave a bit of a rest, before the little buggers come back, excuse my French, only joking, miss, they're nice children really.'

And as she left the room, Avie felt rather lost. Here she was, amongst all these new people, and for some reason she felt deflated. She had built it up in her mind so much, being a nanny, that now she was here she didn't quite know what to make of it… She worried it might be difficult to build up a rapport with Mrs. Williams, as she seemed so distant. But then, of course, she realised. The missing element was the children. Once she met the children she would feel differently.

When her case arrived, she was able to sort her clothes out and hang them up. Some of them needed ironing, so she left these on the bed.

She arranged her silver-backed brushes and mirror on the dressing-table, together with a couple of framed photographs. Avie had also brought her little model chalet house, to remind her of Montreux and the school. She placed this on the windowsill. There, it looked more like home now!

There was a timid knock on the door and a maid arrived,

bringing a tray with tea and sandwiches. She was wearing a black dress, with white apron and mob cap.

'Hallo, and what's your name?'

The parlourmaid bobbed and smiled at her. 'Elsie, miss.'

'And have you been here long, Elsie?'

'Only a few months, miss, but I'm getting used to it - it's my first job, see, since I left school...'

This remark took Avie back to when she was a scullery maid, then a parlourmaid, at Craven Manor. She had been run off her feet with duties and felt quite exhausted by the time she fell into bed every night. That had been *her* first job, too, after leaving school.

'Busy, I'm sure,' Avie smiled. 'Well, thank you for bringing this. Now could you ask Mrs. Pearson what time we have to collect the children?'

'I'll ask her, miss.' And the maid bobbed again and left the room.

Avie wolfed down the sandwiches and took her cup of tea to the window to look at the view. There was a lovely vista over the garden, where she could see immaculate lawns surrounded by flower beds, with a riot of spring flowers nodding their heads in the breeze. And a small copse of trees was visible further down the garden.

A tap on the door, so Avie called out 'Come in!' and Mrs. Pearson entered the room. 'You wanted me, miss?'

Avie smiled. 'I just wondered what time we have to pick up the children, that's all...'

'Don't you worry about that, miss, someone else is bringing them back today, as it's your first day. They should be back here by four o'clock or so.'

'Oh, who is bringing them, may I ask?'

'You'll be pleased to hear that there is another Norland Nanny living just down the road. So, she offered to bring the children back, just for today. Her charges go to the same school.'

Avie's heart lifted. That was great news. She felt she would have an ally living nearby. 'And is the school far, do we have to drive there or can we walk?'

'They can walk, fortunately, miss. It's only about ten minutes away. They're at Templeton School, so it's handy.'

Avie realised she knew nothing about the children, except their ages.

'What are the children's names?'

Mrs. Pearson nodded. 'Henry is eight, and a real knock-about child, into everything, loves his cricket. And little Cynthia is five - and just like her mother, very dainty and airy-fairy, if you know what I mean.'

'Oh, lovely, I am looking forward to meeting them,' murmured Avie. 'And Mrs. Williams is an artist, I believe…'

'That's right, miss. I shouldn't say it, but she's away with the fairies most of the time, very into her art she is. And I should warn you, never go near her when she's painting - she's in another world and doesn't like any interruptions.'

'And where is her studio, where does she paint?'

'It's an area off the sitting-room - I think it was a conservatory once. But the light is good there, plenty of big windows, so it's ideal for a studio…'

'And Mr. Williams is a banker?' Avie said. 'Is that in London or locally?'

'Oh, London, of course. He's a big noise in the Westminster

Bank – Head of International Finance or some such, so he travels to Europe quite a bit. Again, treat him with caution - he's busy all the time, so he gets a bit impatient now and then. But he's got his secretary here - he arranges all the travel and accommodation and day-to-day appointments. Mr. Eric, he's called, if you should encounter him.'

'Oh, so he lives here, yes?' Avie was surprised.

Mrs. Pearson gave Avie a strange look. 'Yes, he lives here all right… funny old world, isn't it?' And all at once she began to gather the tea-things hurriedly onto the tray and made her way to the door.

Before she left she turned and said: 'I should mention their routine, the children's supper is at five o'clock, then they see their parents for an hour at six, have their baths and go to bed at about half past seven. The main dinner is served at eight o'clock. But if you get peckish, tea is laid out at four o'clock in the garden room.'

'Thank you, Mrs. Pearson, that's very helpful.'

'I hope you'll be very happy here, Miss.'

Chapter 14

'Hallo, old chum, I'm Phoebe! How are you getting on?'

Avie had been sitting in the garden room, as Elsie brought in the tea-things, when she heard a voice calling and then suddenly found herself surrounded by children. And another Norland Nanny with a mass of curly fair hair appeared by her side, offering her hand. The children immediately went off in all directions chattering away and Avie was looking into the smiling face of Phoebe Danvers-Smythe. It was four o'clock and they were back from school.

Avie gave a grin and felt an immediate affinity with this lovely girl and wished she could spend some time with her. 'Oh, hallo there!' she laughed. 'I'm Avie Spicer. Thanks so much for bringing the children back, it's very good of you...'

'Not at all, my charges go to the same school, so it's no trouble.'

'So, how long have you been a Norland Nanny?'

'Only a year, so I'm just out of probation,' smiled Phoebe. 'And you've just started today, have you?'

Avie gave a chuckle. 'Yes, I haven't even met the children yet, just the parents. So how are you liking the post, Phoebe?'

'Oh, call me Feebs,' the young woman answered, 'Yes, it's a good job - but it does depend on the family you're placed with...

How are you liking it so far, or is it too early to say?'

Avie rolled her eyes. 'Too early, but I'm sure it will be fine.' She looked out to the garden where the children were racing about. 'Well, I'd better take charge of the children - if I can find them! Thanks so much again, Feebs - are you sure it's all right to call you that?' she giggled.

'Yes, of course. Now, I'd better gather my charges up as well and take them back home. Shall we go out in the garden and give them a shout?'

'Perhaps we could meet up at the weekend,' suggested Avie, as they made their way into the garden. 'We get Sundays off, don't we?'

'Yes, and it's very relaxed on a Saturday too. Why don't you come to me and we can decide what to do. I'm at The Firs down the road – you can't miss it, it's a really ugly house, though I wouldn't tell my employers that!'

Phoebe waved her arms at her charges and called out to them. 'Come, children, we're going back now...'

Avie watched as the children ran towards their nanny, laughing and happy, a boy and a girl about the same age as Henry, she reckoned. She smiled at Feebs and nodded her head. 'So shall we say half past ten on Sunday morning, or is that too early for you?'

'No, that's fine, perhaps we could go on a walk by the river or something and then have some coffee somewhere - how does that sound?'

'That'll be fine, so see you then... Bye, then, and thanks once again!'

'Bye, and best of luck!' Phoebe gathered up her charges and

they departed through the garden room, waving goodbye. Avie felt heartened to have met this new friend. She seemed a nice girl. It would be comforting to have someone she could have a chat with and maybe confide in if necessary. And she was just down the road!

Now, I'd better make myself acquainted with my charges, thought Avie and she called out to the children, who were playing on the swings near the copse of trees.

'Come on, Henry, come Cynthia, let's go and have a drink now...'

The children came running over and stood in front of her, breathless from their exercise. Henry was a sturdy, confident lad, with a ready smile and untidy brown hair. He was the opposite of his sister, who was a slight figure with wispy fair hair. Her big brown eyes surveyed Avie, with a serious look.

'Hallo there, now we must introduce ourselves, mustn't we? I'm Miss Avie and I believe you are Henry, is that right? And you must be Cynthia... How do you do?' And they all shook hands solemnly.

She turned to the small girl. 'So, how was it at school to-day? What did you do?'

'We went on a nature walk in the woods', said the little girl. 'I liked it...'

'And what did you see there, any flowers?'

Cynthia nodded. 'Lots of primroses and a few violets - oh, and we saw a rabbit too and some horses and sheep in the fields when we were walking there.'

'And did you pick any flowers?' Avie asked.

Cynthia smiled a tiny secret smile. 'I picked some special

flowers - just for you – I'll show you when we go back...' She looked up at Avie from lowered lashes. 'We knew you were coming today, didn't we, Henry?'

Henry shrugged nonchalantly.

Avie smiled and put her arm around the girl. 'That was very sweet of you to think of me, thank you.' Then she turned to Henry, who was standing with his hands on his hips, looking a little truculent.

'Can we have a drink now, please, I am parched!' he croaked, clutching his throat – and promptly fell on the grass in a mock collapse, to Cynthia's amusement. She gave a shriek of laughter.

Avie put her head back and laughed. 'Yes, of course, let's go in now and find a drink...'

The children helped themselves to some orange squash in the garden room and Avie poured herself a cup of tea. She felt a few pangs of hunger, so took one of the cakes on offer and the children did the same. They would be having their supper soon, so she restricted them to one cake each.

'Now, what did you do at school today, Henry?' she asked.

'Oh, it was boring, maths, then science, but we had cricket practice after which was good.'

'And are you a batsman or a bowler?'

'We have to be both in our team, we all take a turn, but I do prefer batting...'

'And what's the most runs you have ever scored?' Avie asked, knowing this was important.

Henry nodded. 'I was on forty-eight once, and hoping to get my fifty, but then I was out, caught in the slips...'

'Oh, that was disappointing! But I'm sure you will get fifty soon,' Avie said. 'And do you like playing sport, Cynthia?'

The small child shook her head. 'No, I hate sport, but I do like drawing...'

Avie wasn't surprised at this news, as the little girl looked so much like her mother in her appearance and her mannerisms. 'You'll have to show me some of your drawings,' she said. And to her surprise the child ran off immediately to her room. She came back with a pile of sketches, a mixed bag of flowers, faces, animals and birds.

Avie looked through them and was very impressed. She had obviously inherited her mother's talent - not that she had seen any of Mrs. Williams' work, but for one so young they were excellent sketches, so it was evident she was a gifted child. 'These are lovely...'

Little Cynthia suddenly looked distraught, and her brown eyes widened. 'Oh, bother! Forgot to bring your flowers - I'll get them now...' And she ran off again and returned with a rather crumpled bunch of primroses which she presented to Avie.

'These are for you', she said in a rather dramatic fashion, almost bowing as she gave them to her.

Avie smiled. 'That is very kind of you, Cynthia - a real touch of spring. I shall put them in my room.'

'Now, I've got some homework to do,' said Henry, picking up his satchel. He looked at the clock on the wall. Half past four. 'Might just get it done before supper...'

And he ran off up the stairs to his bedroom.

'I will play with my dolls,' Cynthia announced to Avie. 'Would you like to see them?'

'I'd love to,' murmured Avie and the child ran off to the playroom to fetch them.

Avie was beginning to realise that this little child was desperate for some attention. And it pained her to realise that since the children had come home, not once had either of them asked for their mother. She had a feeling that Mrs. Williams was so immersed in her painting that her children were the last thing on her mind.

Cynthia returned clutching several dolls of every description. There were china dolls with beautiful clothes and wigs, there was a golliwog, a rather worn teddy bear and a small soft, fabric doll dressed in just its underclothes.

'Oh, you've got a lovely collection!' exclaimed Avie. 'Now can you tell me what their names are?'

Cynthia went through each doll, explaining their names and telling Avie who had given them to her.

'And what about this little doll in her vest and pants - where are *her* clothes?' asked Avie. 'She looks a bit sad…'

Cynthia gave Avie a scornful look. 'She's my favourite. I've got lots of clothes for her, so I dress her differently each day, 'cos she likes it,' murmured the small child, as she pulled out some tiny clothes from her pocket and began dressing the doll.

'And what's her name?'

'Petunia', said Cynthia, as she pulled a dress over the doll and found a hat for her. 'Mummy told me that name, pretty, isn't it, like the flower…'

That was the first time Avie had heard her mention her mother and she was glad. 'So will you see mummy soon?' she asked.

Again, another scornful look. 'We see our parents at six o'clock every night, for an hour,' she said patiently, as much to say - I'm surprised you didn't know that!

Avie knew this was often the case in well-to-do or aristocratic families. The children were virtually being brought up by their nannies and often grew to love them more than their parents, sadly.

Mrs. Pearson appeared in the doorway. 'Cook says children's supper is ready, miss, so could they come now.'

'Thank you, Mrs. Pearson, I'll call Henry, he's upstairs…'

The children disappeared to have their supper and Avie had some time to herself. She wrote a quick letter to her parents and filled in her diary. She had decided to keep a diary of events, now she had started her new job.

Then it was bath time for the children. She supervised them, but obviously they were old enough now to wash themselves. Henry preferred a shower anyway, and little Cynthia seemed to splash around with the ducks and fish in the bath, while singing away to herself. So, although she seemed a serious little child, Avie felt she was quite self-disciplined and happy enough in her own skin.

As the clock in her bedroom chimed six o'clock, Avie tidied herself up and changed out of her uniform into a smarter dress, in readiness for dinner with the parents and Mr. Eric. She hadn't met him yet, but had heard from Mrs. Pearson that he had his own suite of rooms, at the front of the property. He was obviously a busy man, but Mrs. P. had also said he liked a game of golf. So, when he had some spare time, this is where he could be found, as he was a member at Esher Golf Club nearby.

She knew the children were seeing their parents at this time, so she wandered down to the sitting room and relaxed in a comfortable armchair by the window.

It was a light-filled room, overlooking the front terrace. Bronze figurines adorned fine Sheraton furniture, and Persian rugs were scattered before the sofa, which was upholstered in a rich, blue damask brocade, matching the elegant curtains at the windows. There were paintings on the walls, some of them very modernistic. Avie wondered whether these were the work of Prudence Williams. Stunning flower arrangements in crystal vases were set about the room. Who had crafted these? Avie mused.

She had picked up a magazine and was flicking through it, when a gentleman appeared in the doorway. He was clad in a sports jacket and plus fours and carrying a set of golf clubs. *This must be Eric*, she thought, and turned with a smile, as he spotted her. He was quite tall and slim and Avie reckoned he was in his mid-thirties. A slick of blonde hair fell over his forehead as he moved. He was a good-looking man.

'Ah, you must be the new nanny, yes?' he said, smiling as he put down his golf clubs. He came over and shook hands with her. 'How do you do? I'm Eric Chapman, Mr. Williams' private secretary.'

Avie stood up and gave him a smile. 'How do you do? I'm Avie Spicer and yes, I'm the new nanny...'

'And have they kept you busy today?' he asked. But Avie shook her head. 'No, not really, I arrived today, so I only met them once they came back from school. But yes, charming children, I'm sure we will get on just fine.'

Mr. Eric went to the drinks cabinet and poured himself a drink. 'Can I get you one, a sherry perhaps?'

'I'll wait till Mr. and Mrs. Williams are here, sir, thank you. I see you have been playing golf - did you have an enjoyable game?'

Mr. Eric leaned against the antique wall cabinet. His voice was a soft, sardonic drawl. 'It was passable. I try to fit it in when I can. As you can imagine, Mr. Williams keeps me fully occupied. He's such a busy man.' He tossed back his whisky and picked up his golf clubs again. 'Now, I must go and get out of these clothes. I'll see you later...' And he disappeared into the hall and up the stairs.

Avie took a wander in the garden, admiring the many beautiful mature trees and flowering bushes coming into bud now spring was here. It was a lovely private garden, not overlooked by any other house. She ventured further down towards the copse, where she could see a gardener still working. He was raking up twigs and branches and turned as she approached and touched his cap.

'Evening, miss...'

'Hallo there, you're working late, the light is fading.'

The man shrugged and continued filling his wheelbarrow with spent branches and twigs. ''Tis useful kindling, miss. Still gets cold in the even time.'

'And what's your name, may I ask?'

'I'm Jake, miss, live down yonder...' And he pointed over the boundary wall towards the village.

'Been working here long, Jake?'

'Five year now, give or take...'

'Good employers?'

'Don't see much of 'em, to be honest. It's mainly the estate manager I deal with, he's all right.'

Avie looked at her watch and saw it was gone seven. She felt she must get back and see the children into bed.

'Nice to have met you, Jake. Bye for now!' And Avie turned and made her way back to the house, Jake touching his cap once more.

Back in the house, Avie went to the sitting room and found Mr. and Mrs. Williams and Mr. Eric all seated there, relaxing with a drink. Mrs. Williams seemed more animated and had changed into a smarter, more conventional outfit.

'Hallo, Avie!' cried Mr. Williams. 'We thought we'd lost you – where have you been?'

Avie smiled. 'Just having a walk in the garden, sir, it's so pretty.'

'Would you like a drink, m'dear?'

'I'll just pop up and see the children and then I'll be back.' She had felt uncertain about whether to sit and socialise with the parents or not, but decided that it might be better to wait until the children were tucked up in bed. When she saw the children, they both looked a bit sleepy and were already in their pyjamas in their bedrooms. Henry was finishing off some homework and Cynthia was doing some drawing at a table.

Cynthia looked up as Avie came into the room. 'Miss Avie! We didn't know where you were!' She sounded quite indignant. But then she said: 'We have decided we like you. So come and read me a story...'

Chapter 15

Dinner was an awkward affair. Ernest Williams led the conversation, with Mr. Eric chipping in now and then. But Prudence was very quiet and Avie felt she should keep her own counsel, as she had only just arrived.

But then the conversation turned to Easter, only a month away now. The family would be going to Paris, as Mr. Williams had business there, in the Paris branch of the Westminster. As it was the school holidays, the parents felt it would be a suitable break for the children as well. Both children were already learning French, as Ernest felt it was essential for them to start learning a new language - and the sooner the better.

It did cross Avie's mind that it might be an opportunity to see William. But it had been nearly a year now since that fateful day when she visited him. She couldn't believe how time had flown. So *perhaps not,* she thought, reluctantly. Part of her was wanting to see him again. After all, he had written a sincere letter, apologising for his behaviour. But then Avie dismissed the idea. She was bound to be very occupied, looking after the children.

'So where do you stay when you're in Paris?' she asked, as the footman took away some dishes.

'Oh, the Ritz,' Ernest replied. 'It's the best hotel in Paris, so central - and most times we can book our usual suite…'

'I'll check out availability, sir,' put in Eric, 'it should be fine, I'm sure.'

Ernest turned to Avie, as the footman brought in the coffee. 'If you could let me have your passport, Avie. I will put it in the safe.'

Avie nodded but felt slightly uneasy at this arrangement. She would have preferred to keep her passport in her own possession.

Prudence served the coffee to everyone, and Eric helped himself to milk. 'We have to hope this Balkan situation doesn't get any worse…' he said quietly. Avie didn't get the opportunity to read many newspapers and she was unaware of any problems in Europe. But she thought she would stay quiet and just listen to what was being said.

Ernest nodded. 'That's true, there's a lot of unrest, following the Balkan wars, Germany getting involved now. We'll have to keep an eye on the situation.'

'But meanwhile, it will be lovely to go to Paris next month,' Prudence said, her eyes sparkling. 'I need some more clothes, so it will be an ideal opportunity.'

Ernest gave a laugh and shook his head. 'I could have sworn you already have plenty of clothes, my dear! But we all know what women are like.'

'I was in Paris last Easter,' Avie said, 'it was such a lovely time of year to be there. The Bois de Boulogne was looking spectacular.'

'Have you got friends there?' enquired Eric. He was obviously curious, as to how a humble nanny could afford to stay in such an expensive city.

'I did stay with friends, as it happened,' Avie replied. 'One of my friends at the school has a brother who runs a hotel there...'

'Not the Ritz, I presume!' Ernest laughed and Avie shook her head, smiling.

'No, just a small hotel, but in a very good central position, near the Arc de Triomphe.' As Avie said these words, she remembered dancing with Tom at the Summer Ball. He was such a nice man, with a good sense of humour. She also thought of Rachel and wondered how she was getting on. Perhaps she could catch up with her... She had heard from her some weeks ago. She sounded so busy in her new post at the hotel, she hadn't had time to write before.

'I could help the children with their French, perhaps, sir?' Avie suggested. 'Go through some of the phrases and words with them. Obviously, I'm not a teacher, but I could have a session with them doing conversational French - what do you think?'

Ernest looked interested in her suggestion. 'Good idea, Avie. Just a few of the phrases they might need there, it would help, I'm sure.'

And so the evening ended on a positive note and as Avie made her way up to her room, she felt happy in her new situation. They seemed a nice family, even if Prudence was a little eccentric.

And she was seeing her new friend, Feebs, at the weekend. Now that sounded an excellent idea to her!

* * *

After a couple of days looking after the children and taking them to school, Avie began to feel quite at home at Claremont House. Henry and Cynthia were well-behaved children and, maybe because of their mother's seeming indifference to them, they seemed to be growing up with an independent outlook. Once they got home from school, they both set about either doing their homework or occupying themselves in their own pursuits, without being told to do so.

Avie was growing quite fond of little Cynthia. She was a little madam and knew what she liked and wasn't afraid to let you know. Avie had once or twice called her 'Cindy', as she felt it suited her. And after an initial hesitation, the child seemed to like her new name. But unfortunately, her mother got to hear about it and called Avie into the study one afternoon.

When Avie entered the room, she could see Prudence was angry. She was pacing about, with a pinched look on her face. And she turned on Avie as soon as the door was closed, her face set in a stern expression and her eyes flashing.

'I hear you have decided to give my daughter a new name – yes?' Prudence was breathing heavily and obviously very annoyed.

Avie quaked in her boots, fearing the worst. 'I'm sorry, madam, I just called her Cindy once or twice, I do apologise.'

Prudence came up to Avie and glared at her. 'How dare you! How dare you call my daughter by another name! Her name is Cynthia - after my mother, no less. And it is not your place to go around giving my children different names, do you hear?'

Avie couldn't believe this was the same fragile creature she had met earlier in the week. Her eyes seemed to be full of hatred. She was obviously a very protective mother hen, despite her indifferent attitude. Avie's heart sank. She knew she had to apologise profusely and just hope she would be forgiven.

'I am so sorry, madam. I don't know what came over me. I

won't do it again, I promise. Please forgive me.' She had to appear extremely contrite and so did her best to beg her employer's forgiveness, without grovelling.

'Promise me you will never call my little girl that silly name again, promise me...'

'I promise, madam, I promise.'

There was a pause, while Prudence caught her breath and seemed to calm down a little. 'I realise you are new to this profession, Avie, but you must abide by the rules while you are living in this house - do you understand? I don't want to complain to Norland Nannies about your behaviour, so I will give you one more chance. One more chance, that is all you have, or you will be sent packing back to - wherever it is you came from. I have mentioned this incident to my husband, and he agrees with me. So I hope I can rely on you to behave yourself in future, understood?'

Avie stood in front of her mistress, head down, feeling utterly ashamed that it had come to this. This was the last thing she had expected, to be reprimanded only a few days after she had arrived. She thought she had been falling over backwards to please everyone and do the right thing.

'Yes, madam, I will behave and I'm so sorry once again, madam, and I do apologise.'

'You may go now, Avie.'

Avie scuttled into the hall and fled to her room, feeling on the verge of tears.

* * *

'Silly old bat - bit of an over-reaction, wasn't it?' Phoebe voiced her thoughts when they met on Sunday.

Avie shrugged. 'I understand her anger, but I only called her that name once or twice... But I have to accept it and try to conform, don't I?' She turned to Phoebe, as they walked along the banks of the River Mole, with overhanging willow-trees budding profusely overhead. 'Have you ever had anything like this happen to you - did you ever do anything wrong?'

'Plenty of things, old chum, but I was lucky enough not to get caught out, that's the difference.' She gave a laugh. 'I swore in front of the children once, that's the kiss of death! Then another time I criticized a mother to her son – told him I thought she was a nosey old devil! But fortunately, the boy agreed with me, and it never came to light.' She put her arm round Avie. 'So don't worry about it, sunshine, perhaps she was in a bad mood 'cos one of her paintings didn't work out. She'll forget about it, you see. Meanwhile–' Feebs waved an arm towards the tree-lined path they were following by the river. 'Isn't this the loveliest spot? I love it round here, it's the most beautiful countryside and so quiet and peaceful.'

Avie gazed about her. The path was leading to a little bridge over the river and other walkers were striding purposefully along, as they took advantage of the mild spring weather. *Yes, she thought, it is beautiful and I seem to have found a new pal. I must forget all about grumpy Mrs. Williams and enjoy myself.*

They sat down on a bench nearby and Avie and Phoebe carried on chatting, while admiring the sunlit, tranquil scene about them.

'So do you go abroad with your family much?' Avie asked.

'Yes, we went to Italy last summer, Sorrento and round there. The family took a villa, and we had local help. It was idyllic, the most amazing climate and such an interesting area, with Vesuvius nearby, Pompeii and Herculaneum, and the Isle of Capri. And are you likely to go away at Easter?'

'Yes, we're all going to Paris. Mr. Williams has some business there and Mrs. Williams wants to buy some clothes. So they decided we would all go and have a little break during the holidays.'

'Oh, that should be nice, I love Paris - and Paris in the spring is the ultimate!'

' I'm trying to teach the children a few French phrases – silly really, I don't know much French myself, but I do know a few phrases, which might be useful to them. And I've got a friend there - her brother runs a small hotel and so I might be able to see her, if I have time...'

'Oh great, sounds ideal. Now, shall we press on? There's a little café further on which I think is open on Sundays, we can get a coffee or something...'

And the two girls carried on walking into the village, chatting away and laughing together.

* * *

'Avie! How lovely to see you again! How are you, old girl?'

Avie was up in London a couple of weeks later and meeting up with Isabel, her friend from her Suffragette days. They had decided to go to the theatre together and see 'The Belle of New York', a musical now on in the West End. They were on their way to the Aldwych Theatre in the Strand, which was abuzz with smartly dressed people, going on a night out. Avie had her hair loose tonight, with an Alice band. It was nice to abandon the neat bun for once...

'Great to see you, Isabel! Where are you working now, same place?'

Isabel nodded and linked arms with Avie, as the girls made their way along the crowded pavement towards the theatre. 'Yes, I'm still here in the Strand. It's only a small company making cardboard boxes and office stuff. But I find it very handy to work there and the people are nice. It's so convenient for the shops, or Charing Cross or the theatres, so I'm staying put now... how about you?'

'Yes, I've started working with the Norland Nannies, for a family in Surrey, so I'm enjoying it. Oh, here we are, here's the theatre.' 'The Belle of New York' was illuminated in fluorescent lighting, for all to see.

The girls entered the brightly lit foyer, carpeted with thick plush pile and produced their tickets for a smart, uniformed gentleman. The area was crowded with people chattering and laughing. The walls were lined with colourful posters of forthcoming shows and attractions at the theatre. Verdant palms in brass planters were adorning every corner and a resplendent gentleman was standing nearby, selling programmes. They were soon directed to their seats up in the gallery, by a smiling usherette.

'I've heard this is a very good show,' murmured Isabel, as they took their seats in the auditorium. 'Everyone in the office has seen it and loved it.'

The orchestra struck up with the theme tune from the show and there was a welcoming atmosphere over the whole theatre, as everyone relaxed in their seats and settled down to enjoy the music. Then the heavily swagged velvet curtains opened with a flourish and the show began, with a troupe of attractive young women performing their opening routine. The backdrop was of the spectacular Manhattan skyline with its tall buildings. Avie and Isabel were whisked away into another world of glamorous American singers and tough-looking gangsters in sharp suits.

Avie looked around the theatre, with its ornate boxes with velvet curtains just below them. She was enjoying her night out with her chum. Isabel produced a box of chocolates and the girls munched on these happily, while singing along to the well-known tunes. At the interval they both left their seats and mingled with the other patrons, as they bought some ice-cream.

'So, tell me about your new job. How is it working out?' Isabel asked.

Avie nodded. 'Yes, it's good, I'm enjoying it, though I have to be careful with the mother - she's a bit temperamental. She's an artist and if she's had a bad day, everyone knows about it.'

'But of course I haven't seen you since you went to Switzerland, have I? So how was that?'

Avie's eyes sparkled. 'Excellent, I really enjoyed it - and I learnt a lot there. It was very worthwhile. I'm sure it helped me obtain my post with the Norland Nannies. Yes, I'm going with the family to Paris at Easter, so that will be great.'

'Oh, I say, good for you. Have you been there before?'

'Yep, I was there last year, and I've been before with my parents. One of the girls has a brother there and I also had a boyfriend who lived there - well, you met him at my eighteenth, I think, William.'

Isabel nodded and smiled. 'I seem to remember he was *so good-looking*. So what happened to him - are you still seeing him?'

'No, sadly, we had a falling out, but, hey,' Avie gestured, 'plenty more fish in the sea, eh?'

Isabel laughed, as the bell rang for the audience to return to their seats. They began to file into the auditorium again.

The girls enjoyed the show very much and had a quick drink at a nearby hotel, once it ended. It had been quite a fast journey for Avie by train from Esher, so she felt they could perhaps meet up again before she went away to Paris.

They kissed and hugged each other, as they parted company at Charing Cross Station. And they vowed to meet up more often, perhaps to go to an art gallery or round the shops.

It was great for Avie to have some time to herself and enjoy her friend's company. She was obviously dedicated to the children during the week, but the weekend was an opportunity to do other things. *Must go home and see the family, before I go to Paris*, she thought, as the train chugged into Esher station. She had been trying to write to them every week, but it would be nice to see them.

Chapter 16

Paris, Easter, 1914

The family were on their way to Paris. The Easter holidays had arrived! The Channel crossing had been rather squally, as sadly the weather had turned somewhat rainy and unsettled. But fortunately, the children were good sailors and had no ill-effects from the rough crossing. In fact, they thought it was exciting. Cynthia was clutching her favourite doll, Petunia and both were thrilled to be going to the Continent.

Avie had been coaching them in some conversational French. They now both knew a lot of useful phrases: 'My name is Henry/Cynthia. I am eight/five. I am here on holiday with my family. Thank you, sir/madam. This is my doll, Petunia. I would like an ice-cream, please. Good morning/Good evening.'

But Cynthia's favourite phrase was: 'Pleased to meet you', or: '*Enchantée de vous voir*'. And this she said with great style, almost curtseying, as she uttered the words.

So Avie felt the children at least knew some French and could answer politely, if they were spoken to.

On arrival at Calais, they had transferred to the train which took them to Paris. It was all very exciting for the children, but to the adults it seemed a long and tedious journey and very tiring. The weather had now improved slightly and by the time they arrived in Paris a few weak rays of sunshine were penetrating the leaden clouds.

They settled into their rooms at the luxurious Ritz Hotel in Place Vendome. Avie had never seen such an amazing bedroom. The furniture was exquisite, and the walls were hung with silk draperies, in a dainty floral pattern. She had her own bathroom and, of course, every room was now connected to electricity. There were stylish Art Nouveau table lamps beside the bed and on the antique armoire.

The hotel was so refined and elegant, Avie wished she had brought more smart clothes with her. She felt distinctly under-dressed, when she walked about the public rooms. However, most of the time she was in her Norland Nanny uniform. Avie always felt so proud to wear her uniform, but at times longed to wear a pretty dress. She knew, too, in the evenings she would be restricted to either having dinner in her room or the dining room, as she had to take care of the children.

As soon as they arrived, Mr. Williams had asked for her passport. And when Avie protested, he informed her there were sometimes thefts at the hotel. It would be more sensible to keep the passport in the safe in his bedroom, he advised. So Avie was persuaded it might be the wise thing to do.

The next day at breakfast the family were discussing their plans for the day ahead. Prudence immediately said she wanted to visit the Modern Art Museum and make an appointment with one of the fashion designers, Chanel, Dior, Balmain or Givenchy. Ernest said he had a business appointment with the bank and would be accompanied by Eric.

Avie had enquired at the reception desk about entertainments for children. She was told that the best place to visit would be the Tuileries Gardens. They had all kinds of delights available to amuse young children - acrobats, jugglers, donkey rides, carousels – and there was also a boating lake. It sounded ideal. A lemonade stall was mentioned and a stall selling toys. The children's eyes lit up at this news – they were so excited.

Cynthia held up her doll. 'There we are, Petunia, I told you it would be good. We can do all sorts of lovely things here.'

Before they all went their separate ways, the children ran into the sitting room to kiss their parents goodbye and tell them their plans for the day. The adults departed. But as Avie was dressing little Cynthia ready to go out and putting a scarf around her neck, the child suddenly realised her special doll was missing. So, a frantic search ensued.

'Now, where did you last have her?' asked Avie.

'I had her when I was saying goodbye to mummy and daddy,' she said, looking quite tearful. A frown was on her face, and she shook her head. 'Can't go without 'tunia.' She began to sob.

They were all downstairs in the foyer about to leave, so the kindly concierge offered to keep an eye on the children, while Avie dashed back upstairs. She entered the elaborately furnished sitting room and began to search. She scoured the whole room without success, but then thought it might have fallen behind the sofa against a wall. She peered over and saw it. 'Ah, there it is!'

She climbed behind the heavy sofa to retrieve it. As she did so, Avie heard the door open and the sound of men's voices entering the room. Ernest and Eric. What were *they* doing there?

Why weren't they at the bank meeting? Then there was a silence and Avie heard heavy breathing and sighs. She peered cautiously round the corner of the sofa. And saw to her horror that Ernest and Eric were engaged in a passionate kiss. A chill of shock and disbelief went through her. The embrace went on for a long time and Avie realised she was in a desperate situation here, if she was discovered.

She had vaguely heard about males who preferred men over women, but had never encountered any herself. Pansies, people called them, nancy boys. But she also knew it was against the law to have a homosexual relationship. Avie went hot and cold, as she crouched down and hoped she wouldn't be discovered.

Unfortunately, as she moved her position, her shoe came up against a brass floor lamp and made a squeaking sound. She held her breath. But the men had heard the noise and came over to investigate.

'What is that - is someone there?' Ernest crossed the room and pulled back the sofa. He gave an exasperated gasp.

'What on earth are *you* doing here, girl?'

Avie felt she could ask him the same question. But she drew herself up and held out Cynthia's doll. 'I was retrieving this, sir. Cynthia mislaid it. Refused to leave without it.' Avie looked Ernest in the eye in a challenging manner and glanced across at Eric. He was clearly flushed, angry and embarrassed. But then he moved away and left the room, head down, without saying a word.

Ernest grabbed hold of Avie's coat and pulled her to him. He was shaking and furious. 'If this gets out, it will end my career,' he stuttered. 'Don't you dare say a word to a soul about this, do you understand?' He shook her shoulders. 'If I find you have reported this, you will be done for. In fact, I forbid you from going out today. You will stay in your bedroom and not speak to anyone, do you hear?'

'Take your hands off me!' Avie's ire was up, and her eyes were flashing. But she kept her cool. 'The children are waiting downstairs, Mr. Williams. We're going to the Tuileries Gardens. They've been looking forward to it - there is special entertainment there for them. They wouldn't understand if we cancelled it now. They would be heartbroken.' She suddenly felt angry about the situation. 'Don't your children mean anything to you?'

Ernest was silent for a moment, then ran his fingers through his hair, looking troubled. 'I don't know, I just don't know...' He gave her a despairing look.

'What happened to your bank appointment?' Avie asked, coolly.

'It was cancelled,' he mumbled. 'Now, let me think...' He hesitated, then said in a more conciliatory tone. 'I'll allow you to go with the children, providing - providing - you *promise me* you will go there and return immediately and not get in touch with anyone. If I hear you have contacted a person in authority, I warn you, you will lose your job with Norland Nannies. I will concoct a tale about you, and your career will be finished before it's started. And don't forget, I have your passport in my safe, so you can't go running back to England...'

Avie was shaking inside, her heart racing at this horrific turn of events. But she still felt she had the upper hand. The law was on her side. She would go along with his plan, for the moment. But once she left the hotel safely, she would re-consider it. Her mind began spinning with ideas. She knew Tom was quite nearby in his Hotel du Parc, a few streets away. If she could only contact him, he would help her, she knew. He would know what to do.

With relief Avie rejoined the children in the foyer and they left the hotel. She had decided she would call in at Tom's hotel and hope he would be there. Failing that, she could ask for Rachel, and she could give a message to Tom.

'I've just got to pop into a hotel near here, children, for a minute, to see someone. Won't take long. Then we can go on to the Tuileries Gardens - it will be such fun, won't it?'

The children accepted this news quite happily, with little Cynthia skipping along the pavement and Henry taking note of the different cars he could see on the street. They turned into the Rue d'Eglise and the Hotel du Parc came into sight. Avie led the children into the lobby and sat them down opposite the reception area. 'I've just got to speak to someone here,' she said. In a moment of inspiration, she gathered up a handful of sweets, which were freely available on the reception desk, and gave them to the children. 'Now, don't move from this spot, all right?'

She approached the reception desk. 'I'm a friend of the manager, Mr. Reynolds. Would he be free, by any chance?'

'What name, madam?'

'Avie Spicer. But if he's not there, could I speak to his sister, Rachel? It's rather urgent', she added.

The receptionist went to the telephone and made a call. 'Mr. Reynolds is free, madam. So would you like to follow me?'

Avie felt an enormous rush of relief at this news. Thank goodness, now she could get some advice...'Tom!' Avie had to restrain herself not to fall into his arms at the sight of him. It was so good to see a friend, when she felt so agitated. He looked surprised to see her, but grinned and said: 'Well, this is a turn-up, I must say, I didn't know you were in Paris. Take a seat. Like your smart uniform.'

Avie had to force herself to smile back, but then said immediately: I'm afraid this isn't a social call, Tom. I'm in trouble and want some advice…'

Tom's face became serious and grave. 'My dear girl, whatever is it? Tell me all about it.'

'Before I start to divulge my problem, I have two children sitting out in Reception. Is there anywhere else they could go, so that I know they are safe? I'm responsible for them, you see. I'm a Norland Nanny now, as you can see.'

Tom nodded and at once lifted the telephone and called a staff member. 'They can go to the staff common room, they will be looked after there all right–the girls all adore children. They will be spoilt rotten!' He spoke in rapid French to someone for a minute and a young girl appeared at the door.

'If you could go with Renée here, Avie, and tell the children what's happening, then we can sit down and have a little chat, all right?'

Avie nodded and within minutes was back again and sitting opposite Tom. She didn't know where to begin. But then it all came pouring out and she ended by saying: 'So you see, I'm not sure what to do…'

Tom shook his head and started by saying: 'First, let me say how unlucky you are to encounter such an unpleasant situation in your first post as a nanny. But now, the question is, if I report his behaviour to the police, they will want evidence. And they will only have your word on this, for the gentlemen concerned are bound to deny it.

'But if we could bring another charge against him, a more minor infringement of the law, just to bring him into custody, then we might be able to gather some more evidence of this, um, homosexual behaviour.' Tom was quiet for a moment and was obviously thinking of something, for then he said: 'Now can you describe these gentlemen to me, Avie, or I don't suppose you've got a photograph of them?'

Avie shook her head. 'Well, Mr. Williams is in his late fifties, I suppose, of average height, with a balding head and a little goatee beard. And Mr. Chapman is quite tall and slim, with blonde hair and is about thirty, I think.'

Tom nodded and then said: 'As a small hotel we have quite a few people staying here who, shall we say, don't want to get noticed? We are always on the lookout for potential homosexuals, but sometimes they can slip through the net. I'm thinking of a couple we had staying a few months ago. They might fit the description you gave me. They said they were father and son and happy to share a room. I happened to be on duty that night. We were nearly full, so although the receptionist was slightly doubtful about the booking, she agreed for them to take the room.'

'No good checking the register? ' said Avie. 'I suppose they would always give false names…?'

'Spot on, Avie, you're right,' smiled Tom. 'You're in the wrong business!'

But Tom continued. 'Now we do always take a secret photograph of our visitors - not many of them realise that, but it's a record for just such an occasion as this, if, say, they had provided a false name.'

'So you would be able to prove they were here,' Avie said. 'M'm, interesting. Now, if you wanted some minor infringement evidence to bring against him, I've just thought of something. He's been keeping my passport in the safe in his bedroom, against my wishes. He refuses to let me have it, until the last minute we are travelling. I don't think that is quite right - what do you think? And when this all came up, he said I had to stay in my bedroom, not leave all day and not contact anyone. He was threatening me, and manhandling me, he shook my shoulders. He also said if I reported it, he would concoct some story to Norland Nannies and ruin my career.'

'That's intimidation, he sounds a nasty character. But I'm glad you've told me this, Avie, it will be useful to bring a case against him.' He was writing notes on a pad as she spoke. 'But meanwhile,' Tom turned in his chair and gazed directly at Avie. 'What are you going to do now? Will you stay with the family, until things get too difficult, or what?'

Avie smiled at him. 'I was hoping you could advise me about that. The trouble is, I love those children and I would hate to upset them by just disappearing.'

'How about steeling yourself and staying with them while you are all in Paris, but then once you get back to England, invent some family crisis that you have to go home for, how about that?'

Avie looked doubtful. 'I don't know whether I could bear to remain with the family, knowing what I know now. Maybe, you could tell the police about the passport situation, so that I could return to England, and then once they've gathered more evidence on the homosexual question, the police could bring more charges...'

'I think you must forget about upsetting the children, Avie. This is a serious incident that can't be ignored. Now if you want us to help in any way, I'm sure Rachel would be happy to do anything - she happens to be in England now. She could send you a telegram, purporting to say there is a family crisis that you must return to immediately, how about that?'

'Hey,' Avie's eyes lit up, 'that sounds like a good idea. Then the children would believe it and not feel I'm deserting them. Yes, I like that!' She leant forward. 'Please thank Rachel for me, won't you? How is she? I haven't seen her for so long.'

Tom stretched his arms. 'She's been working her socks off here the last six months, so I told her to go back to England and take a proper break.'

'Hope I can see her while she's in England', murmured Avie.

'Now, just to get it straight', Tom said, looking at his notepad, 'I will contact the police about the passport issue, and ring Rachel. I will also inform the police that we have a potential homosexual infringement here that needs to be investigated. They needn't mention that when they speak to Mr Williams. He will just think it's about the passport.'

Avie sat back in her chair and gave a sigh. 'Tom, you're such a brick!' Suddenly, she felt happier about this awful business. She had *hoped* he could resolve the problem, and he had.

Chapter 17

'Sorry about that, children, it took longer than I thought. But anyway, we can go off now to the Tuileries Gardens and enjoy ourselves! Did you have fun with the girls back there?'

Henry and Cynthia nodded, as they hurried along the pavement leading to the Gardens. 'It was great - they gave us some little cakes the cook had just made...'

'... m'm, they were lovely, made of chocolate', put in Cynthia. 'Oh, and we had some Easter eggs! The girls were making little baskets for the *Pâques vacances,* Easter weekend, so pretty... then we felt sick', she added.

'And we spoke some French,' added Henry, 'I *think* they understood us.'

'And I said '*Enchantée de vous voir*' to a lot of people', giggled Cynthia, 'and I gave a curtsey as well, they liked it. And they loved Petunia, they thought she was the best doll ever...'

When Avie had collected the children from the common room, the staff had been enchanted with the children: little Cynthia doing her curtsey, looking so pretty with her winsome features and fair hair, and both the children trying so hard to speak French. Avie had thanked the staff profusely for looking after the children. She had felt happier, knowing they had been cared for so well.

They arrived at the Gardens and there was so much to see! Avie didn't quite know where to take the children first. She could see jugglers tossing their balls in the air, she could see acrobats performing in another area. But the colourful carousel, with its catchy music, had caught the attention of the children and they both wanted to go for a ride on that.

The Tuileries Gardens was a huge area – it had been used for fencing events at the Summer Olympics in 1900 – and so it was very popular with young families and visitors. There was so much going on, there was even a small zoo. But the children were enjoying riding on the carousel. Cynthia was clutching Petunia tightly to her chest. 'Isn't this fun, Petunia? Round and round we go…' She was really enjoying herself, with a big grin on her face.

Once the music had ended and the carousel came to a stop, they made for the puppet theatre.

'Let's get a drink first,' suggested Avie and they joined the queue at the lemonade stand. She suddenly realised that she herself was thirsty, as she and Tom had been so busily engaged talking, there hadn't been time for a drink. There were also Easter eggs on display, so Avie bought a couple for the children as a treat.

But on the way to the puppet theatre, they had to pass the boating lake and Henry changed his mind. He wanted to go in one of the small boats.

'Now you have to sit still,' Avie said, as they all clambered aboard the small craft. 'You don't want to fall in now, do you?' But then they lost an oar and, as Avie tried to row with just one, they soon ended up going round in circles. So Avie decided this wasn't a good idea. But Cynthia had spotted something. 'Hey,' she cried, 'look, donkey rides! Can we have a ride?'

The children were soon trotting along the grassy area on the donkeys, but to Henry it was child's play. He felt he was too big for a donkey; he was used to riding a pony. So although Cynthia wanted another ride, Henry declined, with all the dignity an eight-year-old could muster.

'Now, let's all have an ice-cream and a little rest', suggested Avie, who felt exhausted after trailing round with the children for over two hours. All the events of the day had suddenly caught up with her. She felt so sad when she looked at the happy faces of the children enjoying themselves, entirely unaware of their father's unsavoury behaviour. So Avie thought she would like to treat them to something, knowing that she might be called away back to England within a day or so.

After they had gobbled up an ice-cream and had a rest, she pointed to the toy stall. 'Look over there, children, a toy stall! Now would you both like to go and choose a present? It will be my treat.'

'Thank you, Miss Avie, thank you!' And the children raced over to the toy stall and tried to decide what to buy. They both looked over the array of tempting toys on display. Henry chose a model aeroplane and Cynthia found some dolls' clothes to add to Petunia's wardrobe. They both went up on tiptoe to give Avie a kiss and say thank you, which she thought was very touching, particularly in the sad circumstances that only she knew about.

'Now I suppose we'd better think about getting back to the hotel,' she said reluctantly. She had a leaden feeling in the pit of her stomach, at the prospect of meeting up again with Mr.

Williams and Eric. She looked at her watch. 'It's four o'clock, yes, I think we should go back now.'

She knew Mr. and Mrs. Williams were due to go to the Ballet that night. She had to bath the children and have their meal sent up to the room. Avie wanted dinner in her room tonight. Once the children were in bed, she would try to put all these horrible events in some kind of perspective. Yes, she had to return to England. There was no other option. She couldn't stay here, that was obvious. She couldn't even bear to look at Mr. Williams, after today's revelations.

Well, she would await Rachel's telegram. And once it arrived, she would try to compose her face into some resemblance of shock at the news, whatever that would be.

Back at the Ritz they were told that Mr Eric had been called away unexpectedly to the South of France, where his parents lived. *Well, surprise, surprise*, thought Avie, but she was relieved that he had gone. She never wanted to see him again. When she thought about it, he had been a slimy individual, with an inflated opinion of himself and his place in society. And no doubt now, with the prospect of a possible court case looming, he was hoping to disappear without trace. If Ernest was expecting some support from his lover, it wouldn't be forthcoming, Avie suspected.

She supervised the children's baths and ordered their meal and one for herself for later. The children were quite fatigued after their energetic day at the Gardens and so were more than ready for bed by seven thirty. Mr. and Mrs. Williams were busy getting ready to go out for the evening. The *Ballet Russes* was visiting Paris and performing at the Opera House. Fortunately,

Ernest seemed to be avoiding Avie, which suited her fine. He was the last person she wanted to see.

Prudence was quite animated. She'd had a wonderful day, she told Avie. She had spent the morning at the Modern Art Museum, had lunch with a friend and then enjoyed a lazy afternoon with dress designers from the House of Givenchy. They were preparing a whole new wardrobe for her. 'My idea of the perfect day!' she had exclaimed. Little did she know of the revelations about to break. Her whole world would come tumbling down. For Avie had a feeling that Mrs. Prudence Williams would be completely lost without her husband. She was a woman of contrasts, Avie felt. One minute the vulnerable, frail artist, the next the selfish socialite.

'Enjoy your evening!' Avie called, as Prudence and Ernest waved goodbye, clad in their stylish evening clothes. *Let's hope it's a good one*, she thought. *It might be the last one together for a while.*

* * *

The next day the family were slow to rise. Everyone seemed to be extraordinarily tired, after their pursuits the previous day. Breakfast was a scrappy affair, with the children yawning and loath to leave their beds and the Williams still asleep at ten o'clock. Avie seemed to be the only one who was up, washed and dressed and in a reasonable state of alertness.

This was just as well, for she was alone when there was a knock on the door and Avie opened it to find a jaunty young telegram boy standing there, in his smart blue uniform and pillbox hat.

'*Mam'selle* Spicer? *Telegramme ici, pour vous. Merci.*'

And he handed her the yellow envelope. Even though Avie knew it wasn't a real emergency, just the sight of the telegram gave her a shock, and she was glad she was alone. For now she could read it and work out what to say, without being stared at by the family, who were bound to be curious.

The boy still waited there, so Avie ripped it open and quickly read the words. Trying to disguise her feelings, she said to the boy with a straight face - '*Pas de réponse, merci.*' 'No reply.' And he disappeared.

Once alone, Avie read the words again:

'PLEASE   RETURN   IMMEDIATELY.   RUFUS SERIOUSLY   INJURED   IN   ROAD   ACCIDENT. HARRIET DEVASTATED AND NEEDS YOU. JEREMY.

And she had to smile. For Rufus was, of course, the family's elderly cocker spaniel. But she then decided that Rufus would now become her mythical 'brother', age ten.

At that point Avie heard the door open and the children started wandering into the room in their dressing-gowns. 'Did we hear a knock on the door?'

Henry quickly noticed that Avie was holding a telegram and he came up to her at once. 'What is it, Miss Avie, is something wrong?'

Avie immediately felt guilty at the deception, but she had to assume a shocked face and sat down on a chair. 'I'm afraid it's my brother, Rufus, Henry. He's had an accident. The family needs me there. I must return to England.'

Henry's face dropped, but being a polite and caring child, he put his arm around her. 'Oh, I'm so sorry, Miss Avie, what happened? Is he very badly hurt?'

Little Cynthia also came over and Avie could see there were tears in her big brown eyes. 'Don't cry, Miss Avie. He will get better soon.'

'They say he's seriously injured; I don't know to what extent.'

Henry immediately ran out of the room. 'I must tell father; you will need to go back home. Father will make a booking for you for the Channel crossing.'

Avie was feeling so uncomfortable to be deceiving everyone, but when she thought about it, she had had nothing to do with this situation. It was entirely the fault of Ernest Williams.

Henry returned and went to the breakfast tray, which had been delivered. He poured Avie a cup of tea and handed it to her, piling it with sugar. 'Father said to give you hot, sweet tea, so here you are. Now sit down and drink it quietly.' He was an amazing young child, so mature for his age. Avie felt devastated that she was going to lose these dear children.

The door opened once more, and Ernest entered the room in his dressing-gown. He looked rather bleary-eyed. He went up to Avie and lightly touched her on the shoulder. 'I'm so sorry to hear you've received bad news. This is terrible for you. But once you have had your breakfast, you must pack up your things. I will arrange for you to travel back to England as soon as possible. The hotel here is very good. I'm sure they will make all the necessary arrangements. Now, this accident, it's your brother, I believe? So how old is he, may I ask?'

Avie sniffed and tried to look suitably upset. 'Ten, sir, he's only ten. I don't know the circumstances, but they say he's been seriously injured. My mother needs me there, I must return at once.'

Ernest nodded. 'Of course, of course. And I will retrieve your passport from the safe immediately.' *How ironic*, Avie thought, *that he was now volunteering to give her the passport*. He didn't seem to be at all suspicious of her sudden return to England.

'I'm so sorry about this, sir, leaving you in the lurch. Now shall I contact Norland Nannies for them to send a replacement nanny, or will you manage on your own for the rest of the time?' Even as she said this, she doubted that Norland Nannies would agree to a replacement, when they heard the circumstances of Avie's departure.

Ernest turned to Prudence, who had now appeared in the doorway. She was clutching her head and looking like a small wraith in her diaphanous robe. 'What do you think, my dear? Shall we look after the children ourselves for the rest of the week?'

'I expect we could manage for a few days,' Prudence said doubtfully, ' and then perhaps arrange for another nanny once we get back to Surrey.' She clearly didn't relish the prospect of caring for her own children for too long. She glanced at Avie. 'So sorry about your, um, trouble.' She didn't sound too upset.

'I don't quite know how long I will be required at home,' murmured Avie. 'I could keep you informed perhaps.'

'You *will* come back again, won't you?' pleaded Cynthia in her high voice.

Avie nodded to pacify the child, but in her heart she knew it wouldn't happen. It was too serious a situation to ignore.

And so the wheels were set in motion for her rapid return to England. It had been a dramatic few days here in Paris. Avie knew she would be happier back home, despite being desperately sad to leave the children. She had grown quite fond of them in a short time. But as she stepped into the taxi later, her lasting memory was of Henry, ever stalwart and calm, his arm around his sister. She was holding her beloved doll and trying to brush away the tears, bottom lip trembling.

Avie was almost in tears herself, as she waved goodbye.

Chapter 18

Avie had arrived at Calais. She needed to send some telegrams. While on the train she'd had time to reflect on what she should do. Before she left, she had spoken briefly to Tom to keep him informed of her movements. She also asked him to thank Rachel for sending the vital telegram to the Ritz; Rachel had spoken to Jeremy before sending the telegram, and they had agreed on the wording. She hadn't informed Jeremy of the reasons for Avie's sudden departure, though at least they knew she was on her way home now. But Avie thought she would send a brief telegram to them, to let them know roughly what time she would be arriving.

The other telegram she sent to Mrs. Pearson, the housekeeper at Claremont House. Avie had realised that she needed to have her clothes and personal effects sent back to her home in Kent. She didn't need to explain herself or give a reason for this. The telegram merely said: FAMILY CRISIS, NEED TO RETURN HOME URGENTLY. PLEASE PACK UP MY BELONGINGS AND SEND TO: THE LAURELS, FIVE OAKS LANE, ST. PETERS, CANTERBURY, KENT. THANKS. AVIE SPICER.

Mrs. Pearson could make of this what she wished. And Mr. Williams could pick up the bill from Carter Paterson. That was the least he could do!

As Avie boarded the cross-Channel ferry and settled herself down in an inside cabin, she felt a great sense of relief. Yes, it was sad that her first post with the Norland Nannies had ended so abruptly. But in the circumstances, she felt it was the right thing to do. Hopefully, when she explained the situation to the powers-that-be at Norland Nannies, they would agree with her. And hopefully, too, after a discreet pause, she would be placed with a more agreeable employer.

Now Avie knew why the Nannies she had spoken to before were all careful to give the proviso: yes, this is a wonderful job, *but* it depends very much on the family you are placed with. Most families would be honest, reliable people, Avie thought, as she rested on the bunk. But obviously there were a few bad apples in the crop.

And she had been unlucky enough to encounter one.

* * *

'Welcome home, darling!' Harriet welcomed Avie, as she and Jeremy arrived back from the station. 'You must be so tired, come in and we'll have a cup of tea.'

It was late evening by this time. Avie had had a very tiring day travelling and was glad to be home. She sank into the comfortable sofa in the sitting room, and took off her ankle boots, as Jeremy brought her luggage into the hall.

'Great to be back!' she sighed. She looked around the familiar room with its books and ornaments on the shelves, and the pictures on the walls. She felt safe now. Rufus, the spaniel came up to her, licking her hand, as she petted him. 'Glad to see Rufus is in rude health, she laughed to Harriet. 'Whose idea was it to use his name in the telegram?'

'I think it was mine,' Harriet smiled. 'We didn't want to alarm you, we just wanted to get you back home! Now, can I get you a sandwich or something, darling?' asked Harriet, as Jeremy entered the room. 'We've had dinner, but we can always rustle you something up…'

Avie shook her head. 'No, I'm all right, thank you, Mother. I'm just very weary, but a cup of tea would be lovely.' She had told Jeremy of the surprising revelations about her employer on the journey back from the station. He had been shocked to the core. But he was adamant that she had done the right thing in returning to England as quickly as possible.

'Now, Avie, darling,' he said. 'I don't want you going all through this nasty business again to Harriet, so you just relax, and I will tell her all about it later.'

Avie nodded. 'Thanks, Dad, good idea. I don't want to re-live it all again just now, I must admit. I just need a cup of tea and then I'll retire to bed, I'm rather tired.'

Harriet looked worriedly at Jeremy when she heard the words 'nasty business', but she kept quiet, realising that Avie had had a long journey and was ready for her bed. 'It's good to have you back again, darling. But I'm sorry if there was some trouble there by the sound of it.'

Mrs. Salisbury entered the room with a tray of tea and nodded to Avie. 'Nice to see you, miss.'

'Lovely to be back,' murmured Avie. 'Children all right, Mum?' It would be good to see Robert and Matthew again, she thought sleepily.

'Fine, fine. We took them to the zoo the other day, they loved the monkeys. And we're taking them to a show in London next week - *Alice in Wonderland*... they love going on the train, it's quite an adventure for them. You might like to come with us? I expect you'll need to go up there again, won't you, to see Norland Nannies?'

But when Harriet looked across at her daughter, she was asleep.

* * *

Central London, The Next Week.

'Hey, boys, look at the boats on the river!' Avie pointed at the busy scene on the River Thames to the children, as they walked along the Embankment in London the following week.

The family had come up on the train to see the children's show, '*Alice in Wonderland*', which was on at a theatre nearby. Robert and Matthew were so excited about the outing. They had loved the journey on the train and were now skipping along the wide pavement, eyes agog at the hustle and bustle of London, with its big red buses and so much traffic. They could see the river was thronged with boats and ships of all kinds. It was such a new spectacle for the children, they were transfixed. Harriet was holding Matthew's hand very tightly. There were so many people about, she was fearful he would disappear in the crowds. And Jeremy was striding along with Robert, who was six and could look after himself, now he was a big boy - or so he thought!

Harriet had taken the children to Hyde Park, while Avie and Jeremy had had a sober interview with Miss Taylor, senior executive of Norland Nannies in Notting Hill. She had been utterly shocked when she heard of the events Avie had to report. And she endorsed wholeheartedly Avie's actions in leaving the family as quickly as possible and returning to England. 'It's feasible you may be required to give evidence in court or have to make a statement,' she warned. 'But we will do our utmost to avoid this, if we have any say in it. And as for the family concerned wanting a replacement nanny, I'm afraid that is out of the question. They will have to go elsewhere.'

'I must say, Miss Spicer, I regret so much that your first posting with us has ended in this, um, unsavoury manner. It is unfortunate, to say the least. You are very unlucky. But we will do our best to place you next with a tried and trusted family. I'm sure you won't have any more problems.'

Jeremy had insisted on coming with her to the interview. Avie needed the support of a parent, he thought. She was only nineteen, after all. He felt as a solicitor with years of legal experience behind him, he wanted to be there to offer advice, if necessary.

Avie was glad he was there. She felt more confident with Jeremy beside her. But she was happy that Miss Taylor had immediately backed her decision to leave the family in Paris and return home. And she was hopeful that within a few weeks, she might be placed with a new family, with happier consequences.

'Now,' said Harriet, as they neared the theatre. 'Shall we have a cup of tea before we go in? I'm parched, I don't know about you, Avie.'

Jeremy looked at his watch. 'We've got time. It doesn't start until half past two and it's only two o'clock now.'

'Ah, here's a little café,' said Harriet. 'Let's go in …'

They went into the cafe, just off the Embankment, and sat

down at a table near the window. A waitress came up and took their order, tea for the adults and hot chocolate for the two boys.

But Avie's gaze had suddenly moved outside the window. She had spotted someone passing by and stood up, her eyes alert. 'Excuse me,' she murmured, 'I've just seen someone, I have to speak to him...'

Harriet protested at her sudden departure, but nothing was stopping Avie. She almost ran out of the café. She was hurrying after a tall, dark-haired young man walking along the pavement. Avie just knew she had to speak to him.

She caught up with him and tapped him on the shoulder. 'William!'

He turned and when he recognised Avie, he gasped and held out his arms. 'Avie! I don't believe it!'

Avie ran into his arms, and they hugged each other rapturously. They both started speaking at once. 'What are you doing in London?' 'I can't believe we've met like this!' They were both laughing and joyous at this unexpected meeting. William steered her to a low wall, where they both sat. They held hands and gazed at each other.

'So, what are you doing in London?' Avie asked, admiring William's thick, wavy hair and longing to run her fingers through it.

'I'm visiting the London office, we're doing a joint project with an Italian architect. And you? What 'ave you been doing?'

'You know I was in Switzerland, well, that finished and now I have joined Norland Nannies...'

'...enjoying it?'

'Well, I've just come back from Paris...' She didn't want to elaborate.

William scanned her face, his dancing eyes locked with hers. Then he dropped his gaze. 'I 'ave to say, I was bitterly disappointed when I didn't 'ear from you. I missed you, missed you terribly.'

Avie shook her head and sighed. People were passing by, but the couple saw no-one.

'I'm sorry, I was caught up in the school, it was so busy there. But, she paused, remembering her acute shock at finding him with another young woman. 'I was very mixed up, I didn't know what to believe. That girl in Paris. Was she really your cousin? I didn't know and I was very hurt...'

William came closer and put his arm around her. 'I'm sorry, darling. Yes, she *was* my cousin. It was quite true what I said. But when I didn't 'ear from you in the autumn, I was uncertain about your feelings.'

Avie looked at her watch. 'Can we meet tonight? I'm taking the children to the theatre soon, I must go...'

But William shook his head. 'I'm off to Italy tonight, it's this project, it's so urgent, I'm so sorry. But perhaps when I come back? Look, give me your telephone number, I'll get in touch on my return, promise.' He stood up, and they hugged again, his lips seeking hers. A rush of desire swept her body as they kissed, and she knew how foolish she had been. 'I must go, William. *Au revoir...*' She searched in her bag for a pencil and scribbled the phone number down and gave it to him.

William began to turn away, then stepped back and kissed her again. 'You 'ave captured my 'eart, *ma petite*. And you are even more beautiful than I remember. Until we meet again, Annie.' His deep voice with his broken accent resonated within her – he had certainly captured *her* heart.

Chapter 19

London, June, 1914

It was now the middle of June. Avie had been working at her new posting for a couple of weeks now. To say it was chalk and cheese from her first posting would be an understatement. She had been placed with a family called Duckett, who lived in a solid terraced house in Islington. They were a happy couple, if somewhat disorganised. Derek Duckett was an engineer and he and his wife were both great supporters of their local church. They were also the proud parents of James and Luke, nine-year-old twins who attended the local school.

When Avie had arrived, she had been astounded at the state of the house. Every room seemed to be in disarray. Piles of clothes and toys were left on beds, books were piled up in corners. The only room to pass muster was the kitchen, which was the domain of Mrs. Herbert, the cook/housekeeper.

But the Ducketts were quite happy in this untidy environment. They had lived there for several years and didn't seem to see the chaos. Freda, the young maid, did her best to clean the place and tidy up every day. But Avie was glad that at least it was a very happy household. She had been greeted with such warmth and affection from the start and shown to her room, where a comfy bed, piled high with cushions and soft toys, awaited her.

'Welcome, my dear!' Derek's face shone with good-natured bonhomie and his eyes twinkled as he spoke. 'So you've come from Kent, I believe? Well, when I heard this, I said to Elsie, 'now that is such a lovely county.' Oh, the orchards, the fruit, the hops, and beautiful countryside - nothing like it. How you could leave it and come here to smoky old London, I don't know.'

'But we're glad you did,' put in Elsie. 'I love my boys, but they're little terrors at times and so I need a bit of help.' She held her back, wincing as she did so. 'The good Lord has struck me down for my sins, so I'm not as able as I was. But we manage, don't we, Derek? We manage...'

The poor maid, Freda, had to look after the family pets, in addition to her other duties. Karl was a dachshund and Mac was a Scottie dog. The twins loved playing with their pets and were also in charge of feeding them once a day. Mr. Duckett firmly believed it was essential to give children tasks to do. 'It gives them a sense of responsibility', he said. And Avie had to agree. But the children weren't allowed to take the dogs out for a walk on their own. This was Freda's job, on top of everything else the young girl had to do.

Avie would sometimes take the boys to the park, giving Karl and Mac some exercise as well. The boys loved walking them and Avie felt she was helping young Freda at the same time. She well remembered how exhausted she had felt when she was working as a maid.

The parents went regularly to church, Mr. Duckett pushing his wife in a wheelchair, and they were both involved in plenty of voluntary work. Derek Duckett ran the local Scouts group and Elsie helped in the Women's Club, despite her disability.

So Avie was enjoying her posting. She felt very relaxed there and it was also easy to see her friend, Isabel, on her days off. Handy to pop back to Canterbury on the train, too, to see Harriet and Jeremy and the boys for the weekend now and then.

Avie had seen William one more time after that amazing encounter by the Thames. She had been in a daze after seeing him and kept reprimanding herself. How could she have doubted him, when he wrote the letter about his cousin? They met in London again and he took Avie to a swish restaurant in Regent Street. She wore a new black dress with discreet beading on the shoulders and bodice. Her auburn hair was styled on top of her head in a loose chignon. 'Stunning!' was William's verdict.

They had talked and laughed so much during the evening, but then came the moment Avie had been half-expecting. Before they parted, William had again asked her to come back with him to his hotel. She had been sorely tempted, it was true, when William's fingers caressed her breast. But Avie knew only too well what would happen if she agreed. She loved him and was enormously attracted to him, but she wasn't prepared to chance falling pregnant. It was a big risk, she knew, and one which would jeopardise her whole life and career. Avie had heard about contraception, of course, but was doubtful as to its reliability. So once again she had to say no to him, when part of her was aching to say yes.

But he seemed more understanding now, she felt. He realised her dilemma. He was also caught up in a busy career, with numerous demands on his time.

He was returning to Paris after this outing, so Avie hadn't seen him now for over a month. But this time they kept in touch by telephone and so were able to exchange news about their lives. William had now moved into the apartment he had inherited from his uncle, in the coveted St. Cloud area of Paris, near the golf course. He longed to show it to her and had had it re-decorated and refurbished to his own taste.

Avie stopped her dreaming and brought herself back to the present. She was due to pick the boys up from school soon and so tidied herself up and fetched her jacket. It was only ten minutes away, so she set off walking. The day was clear and sunny, and she enjoyed the exercise.

Once outside the school she waited, joining the group of other mothers and Norland Nannies who were meeting their charges.

'Avie, is that you?' She heard a voice nearby and turned around. And couldn't believe her eyes. For there was Phoebe, her friend from Esher, also dressed in the nanny uniform and smiling broadly at her.

'Feebs, I can't believe it's you! How are you? Are you living nearby?' She was amazed.

The two girls hugged each other and were both so excited to meet up again. Phoebe held Avie's arm, looking concerned. 'But what happened in Surrey? You disappeared and no-one would tell me what was going on.'

'I can't tell you now, I'll tell you later. But anyway, I'm here now and my family are lovely, nine-year-old twin boys. How about you?'

'My family moved up here, the father was promoted to a post in the City. Oh, here they come!'

The children started emerging from the school, running to their parents and nannies as they saw them, waving and calling out.

Avie spotted James and Luke. 'Hallo, boys, good day?' The young boys were identical twins and at first Avie had difficulty in telling them apart. They both had curly brown hair like their father and brown eyes like their mother. A very lively pair, they just loved playing practical jokes on people. Elsie tried to help Avie by dressing the boys in different-coloured jumpers, but then they would swap these when she wasn't looking. They would pretend to be each other and confuse poor Avie by saying: 'But I just *had* my breakfast, I don't want any more.' Or: 'You know I don't like peaches, Miss Avie, don't make me eat one!' But Avie reckoned she had sorted them out now. She knew Luke was naughtier than James, so she would watch out for his antics.

The girls sat for a moment on a nearby bench with the children. 'So where are you living, Feebs? Is it nearby?'

She nodded. 'I'm in Pulbright Street, where are you?'

'Cadogan Crescent, so that's quite close, I think. But can I phone you there, is it allowed?'

Phoebe grinned. 'Oh yes, they're very easy-going, my family. Here, I'll give you the phone number and the address. We can get together at the weekend, perhaps.' She reached in her bag and scribbled a few lines on a piece of paper.

Avie shook her head, as the girls stood up and began walking down the road with the children. 'Amazing coincidence we should be so near each other again - it must be fate!' The girls both laughed.

'We're destined to be friends, I can see!'

Avie turned to Feebs with a knowing look. 'I'm back with my

French boyfriend again...' Her heart was beating faster at the thought.

'Oh, great, how did that happen?'

'We just met by chance when I was up in London with my family. He was over here on business and our paths crossed on the Embankment...'

'Oh, very romantic! Are you just as smitten?' asked Feebs, as the children spotted some swings in a nearby park and went running off.

Avie nodded and as she spoke, she knew it was true. 'He's the One, I know it now. He is just so, so - wonderful!'

Feebs started pushing the swing for the youngest of her charges. 'That's great, Avie. Pity he's not over here, though. Must be difficult, conducting a relationship at such a distance.'

'Might be able to go over there and see him soon, perhaps...'

'Could be a bit tricky, with this trouble in the Balkans - things aren't looking good, have you heard?' She shook her head. 'I wouldn't be going over there if I were you. There's a lot of unrest, I believe.'

Avie was never one to read the papers much, but she had vaguely heard that there was a situation developing in Europe which sounded rather ominous. 'But surely it wouldn't affect us, would it?' she said, as the children raced about the playground between the slide and the swings.

'Not sure...' Feebs murmured. 'We'll have to see what develops. If I were you, I would keep an eye on the papers, before you go making any arrangements to visit your boyfriend. But I'm sure your employer could advise you.'

Avie nodded, feeling rather uncertain and worried suddenly.

'Anyway,' she said cheerfully, 'I'd better take these two boys back home to have a drink or something. I'm sure they're hungry.' She laughed. 'They're always hungry! Come on, boys, let's go!

I'll give you a ring before the weekend - we can go off somewhere together...'

Feebs gathered up her charges and the girls parted with a cheery wave.

* * *

Central London, End Of June, 1914

Avie and Phoebe were having a day out in London. It was the weekend, so great to have some time to themselves. Phoebe hadn't visited London much before, so they were going round the tourist spots. They had seen Buckingham Palace, they had 'done' the Tower of London, they had been to Trafalgar Square. They were now trailing round the National Gallery, looking at the artwork. Amazing pictures, they both agreed. They particularly liked the National Portrait Gallery.

In truth they were both getting rather tired, but were determined to see the sights. As they moved from one place to another, they couldn't help but notice the headlines on the paperboys' pitches. 'WAR RUMOURS GROW' they shouted, to the alarm of the public. But Phoebe tried to play it down. 'I expect it's a bit exaggerated', she said, 'they probably sell more papers that way...'

They were both aware there had been some trouble in Europe, but were so busy in their respective jobs, neither of them had given it much thought. As far as they knew, it was nothing to do with England. Avie had, however, taken Feebs' advice and

decided not to visit William in France. She had also spoken to
Mr. Duckett, who had advised her it would not be a good time
for her to visit Paris.

'How about a nice cup of tea?' Avie suggested, as they left the
gallery.

'Good idea, let's go over there, I can see a little café.'

'I'm parched, don't know about you...'

They settled themselves down in the café, choosing a corner
table, and ordered some tea and buns. It was quite crowded with
shoppers, visitors and tourists, so the smiling waitresses were
kept busy, dashing about taking orders, and coming back with
loaded trays.

'So where are your family, Feebs?' Avie asked, as she helped
herself to milk and sugar.

'They're in Devon,' smiled Feebs, 'so it's a great spot to go
back to when I've got some leave. It's near Sidmouth, lovely area.
I miss it at times - especially when I'm in the middle of a big city
like this. I long to go back to those tranquil little villages and
those lovely hills...'

At that point, there was a commotion in the doorway. A
young man rushed in, waving an evening paper. 'Bad news,' he
shouted. 'Some bloke's been murdered in Europe - they reckon
it's going to start a war...' And he ran out again.

Everyone in the café looked rather startled, but carried
on drinking their tea and nibbling their cakes. Most people
shrugged. 'Nothing to do with us,' the lady on the next table said
to the girls.

And another man put in mournfully. 'There's always someone
being murdered somewhere...'

But Phoebe reckoned they should get a newspaper and see what it was all about. She drew back her chair and left the café, returning a minute later with a newspaper. The girls spread it out over the table and tried to absorb the story. They ran their eyes quickly over the front-page article. It had a big headline:

'HEIR TO AUSTRIAN THRONE MURDERED

'Archduke Franz Ferdinand, heir to the Austro-Hungarian throne, and his wife were both assassinated today in Sarajevo. This could be the trigger for the conflict which has been threatening to erupt for several months.'

'Sounds bad,' murmured Avie. 'Let's just hope it doesn't come to war...'

'Doesn't sound good,' said Feebs, looking grim. Other people in the café had also decided to buy papers and soon everyone was passing them around and shaking their heads, as they took in the sensational news.

The girls finished their tea and buns rather more quickly than they would have liked. Somehow, in the light of this rather dramatic news, they felt they should return home at once. It was an instinctive reaction, but they both agreed and so started to make their way to the Underground. On the train there was an atmosphere of foreboding, as people read the papers with sombre faces. There was a growing realisation that yes, there could be a war. Men would be called upon to fight.

It was then that Avie thought of William...

Chapter 20

Weymouth, Dorset, a week later.

'Now, let's all have an ice-cream!' beamed Elsie Duckett, as they settled themselves down on the sandy beach, while Derek tried manfully to erect the deckchairs. But the twins were already racing towards the sparkling sea, followed by Karl and Mac, barking at the waves excitedly.

Much to Avie's surprise, Mr. Duckett's reaction to the news of trouble in Europe had been very mild. 'Yes,' he nodded, as they sat listening to the wireless in the sitting room. 'I thought as much. It's been threatening for a while. But don't worry', he surveyed the boys' faces, looking up expectantly at him, 'there's no need to panic. We're still going on holiday...' The boys had just broken up from school, so the long summer holidays stretched ahead.

At this the boys let out a cheer. 'Hurrah! Thank you, Father. Can we start packing?' And they ran from the room chattering to each other, closely followed by the two dogs, trying to climb the stairs quickly with their little legs.

The weather promised to be kind to them the next week, so Avie helped pack the boys' cases, with their swimming trunks and beach towels. She also made sure they included boring things like toothbrushes and face-flannels and a few clothes. Luke and James adored going on holiday and were over the moon with excitement as the day approached.

'Now, we must take our bats and balls to play cricket on the sands - remember last year we forgot, and it was humongous!'

'And I suppose we have to take some board games, in case it rains,' muttered James gloomily.

'No, it won't rain, it's always lovely in Weymouth. Don't you remember, one year we got so sunburnt on the beach, Mum thought it was sunstroke?'

'And how about the year we got locked out of the house and you had to climb through the window?'

They both thought this was hilarious and giggled at the memory.

The family had been going to the same holiday house for many years. It was a big Victorian house right on the sea-front. It had four bedrooms and a sunny living room, as well as a balcony which overlooked the sea. There was a wide garden at the back, where the dogs could run about.

They always took Freda along, but Elsie tried to make it easy for her, so that she had a bit of a holiday as well. They had simple meals and sometimes ate out or bought fish and chips. And Elsie helped with the washing-up now and then and tried to keep the laundry under control. The boys were expected to do a few jobs as well, taking out the rubbish and feeding the dogs.

As a Norland Nanny, Avie was never expected to help with the housework. Her duties were solely confined to the welfare of the children. But she did bring her summer clothes. Derek had been so sweet and said he didn't want to see her brown uniform. 'You can do your duties just as well with a summer dress on, my dear', he had said. So Avie had hung up her uniform in the wardrobe and was happy to pack her summer dresses.

The Ducketts knew the Jurassic Coast very well. They'd had outings to various beauty spots and local points of interest over the years. They had been to Abbotsbury Gardens and Chesil Beach, with its steep pebbly beach. The boys had wanted to swim there, but were warned there were dangerous currents. Lulworth Castle was another top spot and they often had picnics at Lyme Regis.

The twins were intrigued by the names of the villages of Piddlehinton and Piddletrenthide. And when they heard about the River Piddle, they had gone into fits of uncontrollable giggles and were spoken to sternly by their father. But he did have a faint smile hovering on his lips as he admonished them.

The Ducketts were so gregarious, they chatted to everyone on the beach and in cafés. They had sometimes brought complete strangers back to the house for a game of 'Snakes and Ladders' with the children, if the weather turned against them. But Elsie had now stopped this practice. One of the visiting children had eaten all the biscuits, much to the boys' chagrin. They particularly liked custard creams and this greedy boy had eaten six! 'Love thy neighbour', joked Derek, 'but not if he is greedy!'

Mr. Duckett is the eternal optimist, thought Avie, as she lay back on the deckchair. *He seems so calm, in the face of all this trouble in Europe. He's a good man to have around at a time like this.* She adjusted her hat and relaxed, as she watched the children enjoying themselves in the sea. *I'm so lucky to have been placed with this jolly family. They are so happy and content with their lot. They jog along and just take life as it comes.*

Avie had tried to contact William by phone, but there was no reply. She just had to hope that France wouldn't be involved in this conflict, if it came to that.

Harriet and Jeremy had phoned up. They sounded very worried and wanted her to come home. But Avie had a job to do and now her duty was to stay with the Ducketts and their boys. The twins were good boys, if very mischievous, so they kept her busy. She had to have her wits about her, to keep abreast of their various antics.

The boys came running back with the dogs, who proceeded to shake themselves over everyone. Avie gave them towels to dry themselves.

'Hallo, boys, did you have fun?'

Luke grinned, as he towelled himself off. 'It was smashing!'

'...we saw a jellyfish,' James said, 'but we steered clear of it. Now can we have an ice-cream, please?'

'Yes,' said Luke, sounding quite indignant, 'we've been here for a whole hour now and we haven't had an ice-cream yet!'

Avie got to her feet, grabbing her purse. 'Come with me, boys, and we'll see what we can find...' And they made their way to the ice-cream kiosk.

* * *

The next two weeks seemed to fly by, in a blur of cream teas in pretty villages, energetic walks (minus Elsie) along the Southwest Coastal Path and a visit to Charmouth, searching for fossils on the beach at low tide. They even stumbled on a Summer Fayre in Charminster, where the boys made for the swing boats and the helter-skelter slide. Nearer to home they visited the Pleasure Pier at Weymouth. They laughed at the Pierrots and went on the coconut shy.

Travelling through the New Forest, the twins were fascinated by the ponies running wild -and then eating flowers in people's gardens! They also loved the Cerne Giant, the huge figure etched out on the hillside near one of the villages. And as they wended their way home, Avie noticed a sign for Sidmouth, reminding her of Feebs and her family connection there. What a lovely area it was! She could understand her friend felt homesick now and then living in London, coming as she did from this tranquil and beautiful county, with its green hills and sheltered coves. She wondered if Feebs was away with her family during the summer.

But the holiday was ending. Derek had announced that it was Elsie's birthday the next day and the boys wanted to stop off at some shops, to find a suitable present for their mother.

Avie decided she would give Elsie some flowers and Derek said he had already brought a present with him.

In the gift shop, the boys wandered about searching for something. Luke suddenly spotted a huge plush pink rabbit, three feet tall.

'She would love that!' he exclaimed, and James agreed. They asked the shopkeeper to get it down from the shelf and they inspected it.

'What do you think, Dad, would she like it?'

Derek looked a bit bemused, but then nodded and they decided to buy it.

'She likes rabbits,' nodded James. 'Especially pink ones,' giggled Luke.

'Now, we have to find a cake shop,' said Derek. 'We want a big birthday cake, with cream and jam and strawberries, she loves those. Oh, and some cards.'

Elsie loved the pink rabbit the next day. She unwrapped it cautiously. 'What can it be, boys?' And then laughed and laughed, once she saw the huge rabbit emerging from the tissue paper, with its long ears. 'Thank you, boys, I love it,' she cried, wiping the tears of joy from her eyes. After a final game of cricket on the sands, they all gathered for a special birthday tea. The birthday cake took pride of place on the table.

And they all sang 'Happy Birthday' as Elsie blew out the candles and they munched the delicious cake with cream and strawberries. Then the twins insisted on doing the Hokey Cokey, so they all linked arms and began to sing the song, while dancing the steps. How the boys loved this dance!

'Ooh, Hokey-Cokey-Cokey! Oh, Hokey-Cokey-Cokey! Put your left arm in, left arm out, in, out, in, out, shake it all about, you do the Hokey Cokey and you turn around, That's what it's all about! Whoa! Hokey-Cokey-Cokey. Knees bend, arms stretch, Ra! Ra! Ra!'

Then they pulled Freda into the line, and she joined in, everyone laughing.

Oh, it was such fun, Avie thought. Everyone so happy! The best birthday party she'd ever been to!

It had been a wonderful holiday, and Avie suddenly realised she had really needed it. What with the sordid happenings in Paris and now the threat of war, it was a real break away, some light relief. But now, sadly, it was coming to an end, as they would be returning to London the next day.

Chapter 21

Back in Islington, Avie was supervising the boys doing their homework. She was surprised that the school had set homework for the holidays. But it was only a few sums and an essay on 'What I did in the Summer Holidays', so it wasn't too arduous. And the twins had a lot to write about, as they had been so busy on their holiday in Weymouth, as well as other activities.

The boys were both Cub Scouts and so an outing had been arranged for them to visit Brownsea Island, near Poole. There was a big Scout camp there and Derek had been involved in organising the transport of the boys and their tents and other essential items. It was a big event to cater for, as over a hundred boys would be staying there. However, the Cubs were going for a one-night stay only.

It was a haven for nature there, apparently, and famous for its red squirrels and Sika deer. So the boys would have a wonderful time, mixing with boys of their own age with similar interests. There was a big lagoon there, as well as lakes and beaches, a peaceful and tranquil spot.

Luke and James loved being Cub Scouts and couldn't wait until they were fully-fledged Scouts. They adored all the events, from long hikes to crossing rivers in a dug-out canoe. And they were passionate about camping, but their father had insisted they had to know exactly how to pitch a tent. So often in the summer, the boys would erect a tent in the garden and spend a night there - their idea of great fun! They had Karl and Mac for company and Mum and Dad were only a stone's throw away, so Elsie was quite happy for them to do it. The first time they had pitched a tent, it had collapsed on them, causing much hilarity. But their father got to the root of the problem by discovering they hadn't tied the guy ropes correctly, a very important factor.

Avie wasn't involved in the outing to Brownsea Island, as it was already very well supervised, but she accompanied Derek, when he took the boys down to Poole a few days later. They had to hire a local boatman to transfer them to the island.

'Have fun, boys! Don't fall in the sea and be careful when you climb trees, all right?' She was discovering she was as anxious about the boys as Elsie and had grown to love them both in the few months she had known them.

They left the boys in the capable hands of Mr. Beamish, the jovial Scoutmaster at the camp, who soon introduced them to the other boys in the small group.

As she and Derek returned to London, Derek opened up about the war situation. 'It sounds pretty bad,' he admitted privately to her. 'There's been a naval arms race going on between Britain and Germany which is causing alarm. Britain has negotiated agreements with France and Russia, but it remains to be seen what Germany's reaction will be. We must just wait and see... Meanwhile,' he turned to her in the car, as they drove into London, 'we don't want to worry the boys, so as far as they're concerned, the summer holidays are still a lot of fun, all right?'

'Of course, sir.'

Once back in Cadogan Crescent, Elsie greeted Avie with the news that there had been a telephone call for her.

'Oh, who was it?'

'A young lady called Rachel, and she said she would ring again. She and her brother are in London and would like to see you.'

Avie's eyes brightened. 'Oh, great, I haven't seen her for ages...'

But as she returned to her room, Avie was puzzled. How come Rachel *and* Tom were both here in London? Who was looking after the hotel in Paris?

After lunch the telephone in the hall rang and Avie answered it, as she happened to be passing through. It was Rachel and so after a few minutes' chat, they made plans to see each other in central London.

* * *

Will be good to see them both, Avie thought, as she made her way to the Underground station. It was now early August and a stifling hot day, so she was just wearing a light summer dress.

They met outside the Savoy Hotel in the Strand and found the Little Gems Tea-room nearby, where Tom had said he would join them soon. When Avie saw her friend, she thought she looked very tired and strained. She also noticed she was wearing a black jacket over her dress, which looked rather odd for such a hot day.

As it was so warm, they ordered an orange squash drink, instead of tea. Avie grasped her friend's hand. 'How are you, Rachel? I feel I haven't seen you for ages...'

Rachel smiled, but then her face dropped. 'I'm afraid Tom and

I are over here on a very sad mission, Avie. Our father has died suddenly and so Tom has had to engage a temporary manager at the hotel in Paris. We are here for at least a week or so. Naturally, we want to stay until the funeral has been arranged to support our mother. We're up in London today to see the solicitor about the will.'

Avie's eyes registered her shock. 'I'm so sorry to hear that news, Rachel. Please accept my condolences. Had he been ill before or was it very sudden?'

'Very sudden, I'm afraid. A heart attack. So mother is beside herself with grief and we both feel terrible that we're not in the country. We might have to re-think our plans, we're not sure yet...'

'That's a big problem for you. And you don't have any other siblings who can help?'

Rachel shook her head. 'It's just us two.' Her eyes were distraught with grief, as she continued. 'So poor mother doesn't know what to do about the farm, we employ a lot of people and there are five hundred acres, some arable, the rest grazing land for two hundred head of cattle. It's quite a dilemma. He was only sixty-one as well, too young, too young...'

'Did he have any brothers or sisters?' Avie asked.

'He's got a brother, Uncle Dick, who's a widower, but I don't think he could help. He's already retired, and he wasn't in farming, he was an accountant.'

'Ah, here comes Tom.' Avie spotted him, as he entered the tearoom and came over to them.

He gave Avie a brief hug and sat down at the table. 'So sorry to hear the news, Tom,' Avie murmured, 'please accept my sympathy.' He nodded, and gave his order to the waitress. Avie thought he looked quite drawn and harassed, understandably.

'How was it at the solicitors?' asked Rachel. 'Pretty routine?'

Tom sighed. 'He's a good man, but these things take time. I expect it will all take weeks to come through.'

'It's so difficult with you not living here, I expect...' Avie said, sipping at her drink.

'I've been thinking about that,' Tom said gravely, turning to Rachel. 'What I reckon we should do, old girl, is for you to go back to Paris with me after the funeral, pack up your things and then return here to live with Mother. She needs your support and with the situation in Europe now, it's not a good time for you to be over there, anyway.'

'But will you stay over there yourself?' Rachel said. 'I don't like to think of you in Paris, when they're talking of things erupting any day now...'

'I might see how this temporary manager gets on. If he wants to stay on - and he is a Frenchman - it might be best for me to return here. There's going to be so much to sort out with the farm, I need to be on the spot to get things done.'

Tom finished his tea and looked at his watch. 'Well, I'm sorry to rush you both, but we need to get back now, Rachel. That fast train to Cambridge leaves at four o'clock.' He smiled at Avie. 'Sorry we can't spend more time with you, but we did want to see you briefly. How are you? How's the new posting?'

'Absolutely fine, I love the family, nine-year-old twins, and it's working out well. Any news of you-know-who?' she enquired, as Tom stood up.

Tom nodded. 'The police are on to him and gathering

evidence. Several hotels have picked him up on their recordings. Nasty business.'

Avie hugged Rachel and Tom and they all left the café together. 'Forgive us for dashing away,' murmured Rachel, as Tom hailed a taxi.

'Lovely to see you both, and let me know when you come back, won't you?'

Avie waved and her friends stepped into the taxi on the busy London street and were swept away to St. Pancras.

Oh, glory be! She suddenly felt deflated and alone. And began to make her way to the Underground station, her mind abuzz with worrying thoughts.

* * *

The next morning Avie rose early and went downstairs to breakfast. To her surprise she found Derek already down there and fully dressed, sitting listening to the wireless. He looked up as she entered the room, a troubled frown on his forehead, most unlike himself. He had a distracted air about him.

'Good morning, sir...' Avie said cautiously, sensing something was amiss.

'Morning, Avie.' He shook his head. 'It's happened, my dear girl, it's happened. Britain is at war with Germany...'

Avie clapped her hand to her mouth. 'Oh, no, when did you hear the news?'

'Last night on the wireless. I was up quite late and they made the announcement at eleven p.m. There were crowds of people milling in front of the Palace, apparently. And when they heard the news from the Prime Minister, they all cheered and threw their hats into the air, I believe - extraordinary!'

'So did something occur for it to happen now?' Avie asked.

'Germany had invaded Belgium and refused to remove their troops. Britain has always sworn to defend Belgium's neutrality and so we declared war, Avie, we declared war...' His eyes were tired from lack of sleep and there were dark circles beneath them. 'I haven't told Elsie yet. She went to bed early, like you, and was asleep when the announcement was made. I thought it best to let her rest. I'll tell her once she wakes up.' He stood up and began pacing the room. 'These are troubled times, Avie, troubled times.'

'And of course, the boys are away - Elsie will be worried...' put in Avie.

'She's bound to be. She won't be happy until they're back here again. But I was going to pick them up this afternoon anyway, so I'll just go down this morning instead - make it earlier. I'm hearing on the wireless that Recruiting Offices are already being set up - and young men are flocking to enlist – amazing patriotism, quite amazing. We shall always remember this date, the fourth of August, 1914.'

'And do the staff know about this, sir?' Avie asked. It was essential that everyone in the house was aware of the critical situation.

'Yes, I saw Mrs. Herbert this morning and she has told Freda the news. A lot of people still don't read, you know, Avie, incredible though that is. I don't think Freda knew about it. They will be worried about their relatives, if they are enlisting. 'Still', Derek lifted his chin and forced a smile, 'it may only be a short scrap - let's hope so. Some commentators are already saying it could be over by Christmas. Now, I've had my breakfast, so I'd better get myself ready to go down to Poole to pick up the boys, once I've broken the news to Elsie, that is,' he added.

As Derek left the room, Avie began to think about Tom and Rachel. They had just lost their father and were in the middle of a dire personal situation themselves - and now this! Surely Rachel wouldn't go back to Paris at this time? She was suddenly worried for her friend and Tom, of course.

She had some breakfast and was upstairs cleaning her teeth, when she heard an anguished cry from the Ducketts' bedroom. Derek had obviously just told Elsie the terrible news about the outbreak of war. And she knew what her reaction would be. She sounded quite hysterical and Avie could hear Derek trying to pacify her.

'My boys, my boys are not here, and war has been declared!' Avie heard her cry. 'We must get them back at once. I'll not rest till they are back here again.' More sobs and cries came from the bedroom. Avie could hear Derek trying to tell her he was going down to pick them up very soon. But Elsie was quite inconsolable in her grief.

She heard him say: 'Avie is here, she'll look after you, they'll soon be back - they will probably be back this afternoon, if I step on the accelerator.'

Avie felt she could intervene, as it was such a desperate time. So, she tapped on the bedroom door, which was open and next to hers. 'Come in,' she heard Derek call out.

Poor Elsie was sitting on the bed in her dressing-gown, her eyes red with grief. Her hair was still in her curling rags, and she dabbed at her face with a handkerchief. Avie stepped forward and put her arms around Elsie, whose shoulders heaved as she sobbed. 'Don't upset yourself, madam, the boys will soon be back with you again.'

Derek was brushing his hair in front of the mirror and looked quite relieved to see someone else try to comfort his wife. He had done his best, but his wife was so upset, it was impossible to placate her. He took a jacket from the wardrobe and put it on.

'Well, I'll be off now. I'll see you later. Goodbye, my dear - and when you next see me, I'll have the boys with me, so don't you worry.' He kissed his wife and turned to leave the room.

'Hope you have a good journey, sir. We'll see you later. Bye.'

And they heard Derek descend the stairs and slam the front door.

Avie turned to Elsie. 'Now, let me fetch you a nice cup of tea, madam, I'm sure you could do with that.'

Elsie sniffed and tried to compose herself. 'That would be very nice, dear, thank you.' She lay back on the pillow and Avie ran downstairs to fetch her tea.

And on the doormat was the daily newspaper, with its dramatic headlines:

'BRITAIN AT WAR WITH GERMANY'.

Chapter 22

Avie decided it would be best to distract Elsie from the current situation. So she suggested a 'walk' to the park, pushing her in the wheelchair. The nearest park was fairly close and was a pretty haven, with banks of flower beds, grassy areas and lovely trees. They would provide some shade from the sun, too, as the temperature was rising yet again. She decided against taking the dogs, as she felt it would complicate things, with the wheelchair to push.

What she hadn't envisaged, however, was that there would be numerous families with children there, as it was the holidays. Children running around, children playing on the swings and children calling happily to each other.

So, although it was a pleasant stroll, as they traversed the park, Avie noticed that Elsie was becoming quieter and quieter. They passed nannies with children, children on their own playing ball on the grass. And above all, children's voices chattering, as they enjoyed themselves.

And then she saw that Elsie was beginning to dab her eyes with her hankie. *Oh dear*, she thought. *This is a disaster. We never should have come.* So, after a leisurely perambulation around the fountain and back, Avie decided they would return to the house.

'Might go back now,' she said in a cheerful voice. 'No doubt Mrs. Herbert wants some instructions about dinner...?'

She wheeled Elsie as fast as she could out through the park gates. Then they trundled back along the road. Fortunately, it wasn't far. As they approached No.12 Cadogan Crescent, a slight, untidy figure came into view, running towards them. It was Freda in her cap and apron, and she appeared rather alarmed, as she waved at them.

'Freda! Whatever is it? What are you doing here?' Elsie said, as the girl stopped beside them, panting and breathless.

'Sorry, madam, I be coming to find you. We didn't know what to do, you see, when it arrived, what with the master gone away and you gone out, we didn't know, you see...'

Avie took charge. 'When what arrived, Freda? Slow down, you're not making much sense...'

Freda's eyes were round with shock, as she spoke. 'A telegram, madam, a telegram arrived for the master, just after you'd gone out...'

Elsie clasped her breast, and she gave a gasp. 'A telegram? Oh, I knew it, I knew it - I knew we should never have let them go...' And she began to weep copious tears into her handkerchief once more.

'I'm sure it's nothing to worry about', soothed Avie, 'but anyway, we're nearly home now, so let's press on.' And she began pushing the wheelchair even faster. Poor Avie was feeling quite breathless in the heat, but she was a strong lass.

Once they were home, Mrs. Herbert appeared in the sitting room, where Elsie had collapsed onto the sofa and was fanning herself with a magazine. The cook had taken charge of the telegram, which she now solemnly handed to her mistress, in the absence of the master, to whom it was addressed.

But Elsie couldn't cope with this. 'Oh, no, no, I can't read it. It must be bad news, it's one of the boys, I know it...' And she turned away from it, refusing to handle it, as if it had a bad smell.

Again, Avie decided to take charge of the situation. 'Give it to me, Mrs. Herbert, I'll read it -I'm sure it's nothing too drastic.' And she ripped it open.

'DUE TO WAR, AM BRINGING TWINS BACK EARLY. AWAIT ARRIVAL MID-AFTERNOON. MR. BEAMISH, SCOUTMASTER.' she read aloud. A broad smile crossed Avie's face and she put her arm around Elsie's shoulders.

'There you are, madam! Nothing to worry about! The twins are being brought back early! They will be here soon, in fact - ', she looked at the grandfather clock, 'they should be here in a few hours, how about that?'

Elsie's face dissolved into a beaming smile. 'Is that right? Oh, happy days!'

Everyone started laughing and smiling, but at the same time, Avie suddenly realised that Derek didn't know about this, of course. He was on his way down there to pick the twins up. Oh dear, he wouldn't be too pleased. What a wasted journey. They might well have passed each other on the same road.

But anyway, it was a good outcome, and the main thing was that the boys were on their way back at this very moment and would soon be reunited with their down-hearted mother.

* * *

It was great to have the boys back. It suddenly got very noisy in the house – and untidy. The boys' knapsacks slung on the floor, toffee papers and apple cores falling out, dirty underwear stuffed in shoes - it was a bit chaotic! They arrived about three o'clock, having been delayed by army trucks blocking the road near Salisbury. Mr. Beamish, the Scoutmaster, explained that on hearing the news of the outbreak of war, the powers-that-be had decided to take all the Cubs back home at once. They quite understood parents would be worried about their children and want them brought back. When he heard Mr. Duckett had driven down to Poole that morning, he shook his head. 'Unfortunate, but I'm afraid I didn't know that.'

Elsie was over the moon with excitement to see her boys again. She kissed and hugged them so tightly, they could hardly breathe. They had only been away for twenty-four hours, but to her it seemed an eternity.

Despite their long journey, the boys were exuberant. They never stopped talking, one boy finishing his brother's sentences for him, as they recounted all their activities at Brownsea Island.

'We learnt how to shake hands with the left hand...' Luke began.

'...because it's nearest the heart', explained James earnestly.

'Then we went tracking in the hills and learnt how to do signalling with a torch.'

'And after that we went on the lagoon in a canoe!' exclaimed James.

'...it was such fun, we nearly fell in!'

'And we saw some owls swooping about...'

'...and saw one catch a mouse!'

'Oh, and we learnt some new knots – and we saw loads of red squirrels.'

'And we're going to get badges, - 'cos we did so well'. Luke said proudly.

After they had wolfed down a huge late lunch of corned beef sandwiches and apple pie, they had wanted to play with the dogs in the garden. They had missed them while away. Karl and Mac went berserk at the sight of the twins, barking incessantly and jumping up.

Derek had telephoned from Poole, while the boys were in the garden. Understandably he was rather annoyed that he had driven all that way, only to find that the boys had already been taken home. But he just wanted to check they had got home safely. He said he should be back at about five o'clock. But he had heard there could be a hold-up at Salisbury, due to troop movements, so it might be later.

* * *

The news on the wireless was now listened to avidly by everyone in the household. Even Mrs. Herbert had it on in the kitchen, replacing her usual popular tunes, such as 'Aba daba Honeymoon'. The Recruitment Offices had been overwhelmed with young men wanting to enlist, some as young as fifteen, lying about their ages. There was a real sense of patriotism sweeping Britain, following Lord Kitchener's call to arms. All the young men wanted to 'give the Germans a good hiding' and serve King and Country. The young soldiers were sent to army camps in Wiltshire for a training period, then sent to France. This was a volunteer army who were champing at the bit to Do Their Bit.

Crowds of people had got wind of troop-train departure times and were gathering at the stations to cheer the men on. It was a poignant sight. Mothers and girlfriends, sisters and younger brothers, all waving Union Jack flags and singing patriotic songs as the trains left. 'Rule Britannia' was sung lustily and of course, the National Anthem. And as the trains began to pull away, the womenfolk were sobbing and crying out - and waving until the train was out of sight.

Avie had received a telegram herself from William, which took her by surprise. It was very brief. It merely said:

'FRANCE AT WAR, AM ENLISTING. LOVE YOU. WILLIAM'

It sent a pang through her heart, and she prayed to God that he would be kept safe. She would sleep with it under her pillow, she vowed.

She had also heard from Rachel. Her friend had rung up just before the boys arrived back. 'I'm not going back to France, Avie,' she said. 'Tom said I must stay here and look after Mother, now we're at war, and I agree. And he's hoping he can return here too, if this temporary manager agrees to stay on.'

Avie was relieved her friend had made this decision. She felt much happier knowing she was in England and hoped that Tom would be able to return as well. Indeed, of course, he might want to enlist himself, anyway.

Mrs. Herbert appeared unexpectedly in the sitting room one afternoon. She began speaking in strident tones to Elsie, her face grim. 'I've heard there's going to be shortages, madam -shortages of everything. We need to stock up on our supplies. Hope you don't mind me saying, like. We must buy extra of everything - we don't want to run out of stuff. We've got mouths to feed here, madam.'

Elsie looked a little bewildered by the cook's demands. She didn't like being spoken to in this direct manner. 'I'll see what Mr. Duckett says when he gets home, but I expect he will agree,' she said cautiously. 'Perhaps tomorrow we could order a few extra things. We'll see.' Elsie wasn't used to making decisions herself and was dubious about ordering extra supplies, until it had been sanctioned by her husband. But Derek had to agree to this request - it was the only sensible option.

A few days later Avie noticed there were long queues at the shops. Everyone was panicking and wanting to buy extra supplies. Consequently, the shops had now started to ration everything. Supplies of basic commodities such as sugar, flour, candles, wicks, oil, tea and petrol were now in short supply.

On arriving home Derek had, of course, agreed to Elsie's request to order more supplies and Mrs. Herbert had now stocked up on necessities. So the family were happy they had plenty of food in the house.

They heard on the wireless that Mrs. Pankhurst had spoken to the Government and agreed to their request. The Suffragettes would now scale down their demands, in this emergency, and work with the Government to recruit women to do jobs formerly held by men. And within a few weeks women were working as bus conductresses, as guards on the trains, and doing farm work. And young women were taken on in hospitals in a voluntary capacity -known as the Voluntary Aid Detachment or VAD, doing all sorts of menial jobs to assist qualified nurses.

* * *

The next weekend, Avie had been planning to ring up Isabel and arrange to meet her. The weather was still pleasantly warm, and she thought they could visit one of the London parks and have a picnic perhaps. But before she could do this, the doorbell rang and Avie opened the door, expecting to see the boys back from visiting their friends.

To her surprise she found Phoebe standing there. And she had a jauntiness about her and a confident air. She looked different.

'Hey, Feebs, long time no see! Will you come in?'

Feebs hesitated and then shook her head. 'Forgive me, I won't come in. But could you spare some time? I've got something to tell you.'

Her voice sounded strange, as if she was hugging a secret. So Avie agreed and, after calling out to Elsie that she was going out, she joined her friend.

The two girls walked a short way down Cadogan Crescent, then Feebs made an odd suggestion. 'How about we go to the graveyard instead of the park - the church is just round the corner. It will be quieter there.'

It was true that, as it was still the school holidays and continuing good weather, the parks were rapidly becoming quite crowded with noisy children playing games. So Avie agreed, thinking Feebs must have something on her mind and wanted a quiet chat.

They entered the small graveyard surrounding the Church of St. Mary. The only other person was a gardener, clipping the grass edges, who tipped his cap as they passed him. They found a seat in front of a grimy-looking stone angel, guarding one of the ornate Victorian gravestones.

'Now, what's up, Feebs? What's this all about? You're being very mysterious!' Avie gave an amused glance to her friend, as she sat back in the seat.

'I wanted you to know, Aves. I've resigned from the Nannies.'

Avie was quite shocked. 'Really? Is this because of the war, or are you unhappy there?'

'The war was the catalyst,' Feebs explained. 'And when I received the Notice from Notting Hill, I knew I had to do it...'

Avie was puzzled. 'What Notice was this? I haven't received anything...'

'Oh, well I'm sure you will do soon. They're sending them out to everyone, now we're at war. It's a Special Dispensation Notice from Norland Nannies.'

'And what does that mean exactly?' Avie asked, still rather mystified.

'It means we can break our contract with our employers, if we wish to help in the war effort, or go home to support family, things like that. All parties must agree, but if they don't, then the mob at Notting Hill will find a replacement or something.'

Avie was intrigued. 'And what is it you wish to do instead then, Feebs? I'm all ears...'

Phoebe lifted her chin and gazed at her friend directly. 'I'm going to be an ambulance driver.'

'Crikey! That's a bit of a change from being a nanny. I didn't know you could drive.'

'Oh yes, I've been learning on the private estate at home for several months. Now I just have to get my special licence to drive an ambulance.' She looked decidedly chipper about it.

Avie put her hands together and gave a little clap. 'Well, well done to you! You sly old dog, you. You never mentioned it. So, who's been teaching you, may I ask? Is he tall and handsome?' She gave her friend a bemused smile. 'And how are the employers taking it?'

Feebs gave a shrug of her shoulders. 'I just presented them with a fait accompli – take it or leave it. They're not that happy, but they understand it's what I want to do, and I've got the Government backing to do it.'

'You didn't fancy being a VAD then, I take it?' Avie said.

'Come off it! Rolling bandages and dealing with slops? No thank you! I had a spell in the hospital doing training for this job, children's ward, I expect you did too?'

'Well, no, I didn't. It was supposed to happen, but then it was cancelled...'

'Well, anyway, I decided I didn't want hospital work after that. Now', Phoebe looked at the fob watch on her jacket. 'I've got to get back. I'm taking the little horrors out to tea for a final treat...'

She got to her feet and the girls made their way out of the quiet graveyard, and into the street again, busy with traffic.

'Well, best of luck with it, Feebs, hope it goes really well.' The two friends hugged and Avie felt rather emotional. She would miss her, and who knew when she would see her again?

Feebs turned to her friend. 'And what about you, are you making a change - or are you happy where you are?'

'Not sure yet. I love my family, so I'm staying put at the moment.'

And the two girls parted at the corner of the street, going their separate ways. It was only when Avie turned into Cadogan

Crescent that she realised Feebs had never told her who had taught her to drive.

Chapter 23

It was now September, and the boys were back at school. But Avie somehow found herself even busier than usual. Derek had suggested to her that, if she had time, the church was desperate for someone to organise a Soup Kitchen or at least help out there a couple of times a week.

Avie had now received the Dispensation Notice from Norland Nannies. So she felt she could help the war effort, without compromising her care for the boys.

She had immediately admitted that she wasn't the best cook in the world, but said she would be happy to assist someone and dole out the soup, providing she could be back in time to meet the boys from school. It was emerging that there were numerous families locally, who were feeling the strain of being without a bread-winner, as many men had been recruited to go to war. Although the Government was issuing a Separation Allowance, most people admitted it was not enough to feed a family of four or six. And often the allowance was slow in coming through, so there was a real necessity for some help in the community.

The whole atmosphere in London had changed since war had been declared. People's lives had been turned upside down and many of them were now doing jobs unfamiliar to them, to help the war effort. Freda had astonished everyone by handing in her notice. She was going to work in a munitions factory at the Woolwich Arsenal, she announced. She had heard it was much better pay and her auntie lived nearby and could put her up.

'Hope she knows what she's doing', Avie chatted to Elsie. 'It's dangerous work and it's also a risk to health, to be exposed to chemicals, filling shells and all that.'

Elsie nodded. 'It might be better pay, but I've heard that it can turn your skin yellow - they call the workers 'canaries', I believe… Oh, and I read today that the Women's Peace League is organising a big rally in Trafalgar Square this weekend. I'm sure the Suffragettes will be there too …'

'Good for them. And what's this Derek was saying about the Belgian refugees? You're collecting for a fund for them, is that right?'

'Yes, that's right. These poor devils were turfed out of their homes in Ghent and came over here, with just the clothes on their backs. Mrs. Lacey at the church is organising a Sale of Work to bring in some funds for them.' Elsie shook her head. 'War is a terrible business, young Avie, it disrupts so many lives…' She added some more soda crystals to the water in the big stone sink.

The two women were in the kitchen washing up, after Freda's sudden departure. Mrs Herbert was busy at the stove, cooking the dinner. They had tried to find someone else, but so far, no luck.

At that point the doorbell rang, so Avie went to the door. Rachel was standing there, to her delight.

'Rachel! This is a nice surprise, come in.' Avie ushered her friend into the sitting room, where they both sat down. Rachel sat back in the chair, placing her bag at her feet.

'I was in London, so had to look you up. I was going to ring you, but there was a queue at the telephone box. I decided I would just turn up, hope you don't mind.'

'No, no, lovely to see you. Would you like a cup of tea or coffee?'

'Tea would be topping, thanks.'

Avie called out to Mrs. Herbert.

' What's happening in your family then?' asked Avie. 'Is Tom back here yet?'

Rachel gave a hollow laugh. 'You'll never guess what happened. Tom came back and decided to enlist. But as soon as he was interviewed, they picked up on his fluent French and have placed him in the Special Ops division and he's back in France...'

Avie's jaw dropped. 'Wow, well done to him. But no doubt you're a bit uneasy at that?'

'Well, obviously he's not on the front line,' Rachel gestured with her hands, 'but yes, it is a bit of a worry, but you know Tom, he's very calm. He takes things as they come, nothing much fazes him.'

'But how's your mother now? How is she coping?'

'She's doing well, thank you. And we've had a bit of a breakthrough at the farm since we last spoke...'

'Oh?'

'Uncle Dick has come forward. He was obviously very shocked at losing his brother so young. But once he got himself together, he could see Mother needed some help there. So he's come to live at the farm, and he's appointed a farm manager - one of the men who has worked there for years. And he's also sorted out all the finances. We feel very relieved - and very grateful to him, as we were in a bit of a pickle.'

Mrs. Herbert entered the room, bringing a tray of tea and biscuits.

'Oh, thanks Mrs. H. - this is my friend, Rachel, who I met in Switzerland...'

'Seems a long time ago now, doesn't it?' Rachel laughed.

'Well, it is a year, I suppose...'

Elsie entered the room and Avie introduced her to Rachel. 'We're looking for a kitchen maid - I don't suppose you know of anyone, do you?' she asked Rachel.

'Rachel's from Suffolk, madam, so she probably doesn't know anyone round here, do you, Rachel?'

Rachel shook her head. 'You could try an agency,' she suggested. 'They might be a bit dearer, but they've got access to a lot of people.'

'That's an idea, we could try one perhaps', nodded Elsie.

'If not, we'll just have to manage with Mrs. Herbert. I'm sure we could cope.'

'Yes,' laughed Avie, 'we'll rope the boys in to help...'

'That would be a disaster!' Elsie said darkly.

Avie glanced at the grandfather clock in the corner. 'Crikey, it's ten to three, I must go and meet the boys...'

Rachel stood up and the two girls left the house together. 'I'll walk with you on my way to the Tube', said Rachel. 'I'm catching the four o'clock back to Cambridge.'

' Are you involved with war work in Clare?' Avie asked.

'Well, I help in a Soup Kitchen once a week.'

'Oh, I might be doing that soon. How does it work? Do you give them bread rolls as well, or any sandwiches? And do you charge people anything?'

Rachel shrugged, as the girls approached the school gates. 'We ask for a halfpenny, but sometimes they can't even give that, it's very sad. But we are given all sorts of stuff by farmers, a few chickens, free vegetables, some fruit, and sometimes the bakers give us rolls or bread they haven't sold that day. It works out quite cheap to produce. You'll find that the Red Cross can provide a few huge pots and pans as well.

'It's a pity you're not nearer,' mused Avie. 'We could do with someone like you to sort out our Soup Kitchen.'

'I'm sure you'll be fine, once you get started on it. But I find you must be quite strict and make them queue and be orderly. If not, you'll get people pushing in front, or coming back for more, when other people haven't had a first helping.'

The girls stood outside the school, waiting for the children to emerge.

'A friend of mine has just left the Nannies to become an ambulance driver,' she told Rachel. 'Have you tried driving yet?'

'Oh yes,' Rachel said breezily, 'but it was a tractor, so not quite the same!'

'Could be useful', Avie nodded. She was beginning to think she should learn to drive. A lot of women were doing that now.

'Well, old sport, I'd better be off now to catch that train,' Rachel said, as the children came running out of the school building. 'I'll leave you with your little charges...'

'Well, thanks for coming and give my best to Tom when you next speak or write. Bye!' The two girls hugged and Avie waved, as her friend darted across the road to the Tube station. *M'm, nice to see her. Such a pity she's so far away.*

* * *

The new kitchen-maid had arrived. Elsie had taken Rachel's advice and gone to an agency. Her name was Matilda and she was a tall, lanky girl with soulful dark eyes. She was very quiet, but was familiar with all the domestic duties required of her. She soon picked up the daily routine from Mrs. Herbert and they seemed to get on reasonably well. So Elsie was relieved and happy once more.

But Derek had just returned from his engineering works a few miles away. And he *wasn't* very happy. He was complaining how prices were rising – from train fares to food. 'People are finding it difficult to make ends meet'. He shook his head. 'And now this', and he waved the evening paper. 'People have started targeting Germans and German shops here.'

He showed Elsie an article in the paper. 'A jewellery shop in the East End owned by a German family for years has been vandalised. Red paint poured over the windows. And the words 'GERMANS OUT' scrawled on the door. Nasty business.'

Elsie gasped as she read the report, with its photo of the damage. 'Oh, my goodness, look at that. How wicked! I hope they've arrested the culprits.'

'It was young lads, apparently. Senseless vandalism. But the worse thing is the German couple were taken away by the police for questioning. They're aliens, you see. And of course, they may have been removed for their own protection. They've now set up detention camps for aliens in Wiltshire, I've heard.'

'Dear me, dear me', murmured Elsie, looking very troubled. 'It's come to a sorry pass.'

'Anyway,' said Derek, his eyes brightening as Elsie poured him a dry sherry, 'what's for dinner, my love? I'm starving.' He smiled round at everyone. 'Now what have you all been doing to-day?'

And half an hour later they all sat down to a delicious dinner - yet another wholesome meal produced by the stalwart Mrs. Herbert. It was lamb chops with mint sauce and vegetables, Derek's favourite, followed by rice pudding.

The twins chattered about their day at school and Avie was telling them about the Soup Kitchen being set up in the church hall.

The next day once the boys had come home from school, Avie decided she would take them to the park, along with the dogs. The weather was still sunny, though with a distinct autumnal chill now. The boys loved walking the dogs and they ran ahead, once they reached the park and let Karl and Mac off their leads for them to have some freedom. The leaves on the trees were turning from green to russet and yellow, a lovely sight.

Avie watched from a seat, as the boys played on the swings and the dogs ran about, following scents and making snuffling noises.

Then all at once she heard a high-pitched yelping noise from one of the dogs and looked up in alarm. Two teenage boys had appeared from the bushes and were pelting Karl with stones. She couldn't believe her eyes! She stood up and ran over to the spot where Karl was cowering, as the boys continued to hurl stones at the poor defenceless creature. Mac the Scottie was nearby and getting very agitated, barking non-stop.

Avie yelled at the boys, waving her arms as she approached. 'What do you think you are doing? Get off my dogs! Or I shall call a policeman.'

As Avie drew nearer, the young lads dropped their stones and ran off, shouting 'Germans Out!' She went over to poor Karl, who was lying battered, bruised and bleeding on the ground. James and Luke left the swings and ran over, looking horrified.

Avie took off her shawl and wrapped up the poor animal in her arms.

'Oh no, Karl, Karl!' cried James, stroking him and on the verge of tears. 'Why would anyone attack our dear little dog?'

But for one so young, Luke was amazingly aware of the current war situation. He looked at his brother scornfully.

'Because he's a *German* dog, silly, don't you realise?'

And a chill went through Avie's heart, as she knew it was true.

Chapter 24

Avie was at the church hall, where the Soup Kitchen had now been set up.

The person in charge was a formidable lady called Mrs. Philbert. She never smiled, had no small talk and her buxom figure was heavily corseted. But those that knew her said she was ruthlessly efficient and would get things done. So Avie was hoping that in time she would at least come to respect her.

The soup had been made in batches, courtesy of the ladies of the parish (or their cooks) and was now piping hot in huge tureens. It was a chunky vegetable soup with pearl barley and was being kept hot by oil burners underneath the tureens. Cutlery and bowls were placed on a table nearby, along with baskets of bread rolls and thick slices of bread. Long trestle tables and benches had been placed at the other end of the room.

They were awaiting their first recipients and a straggly queue was forming outside the hall. 'I'll just deal with that queue,' muttered Mrs. Philbert and she stomped off in a determined fashion, wearing her sensible hat.

God help the queue, thought Avie to herself. *She'll have them saluting next time.*

People started entering the hall in an orderly fashion,

accompanied by Mrs. Philbert, waving her arm in the direction of the soup tureens. She had no doubt spoken to them sternly before they entered.

There was no choice, it was just vegetable soup, take it or leave it. But there were mugs of Bovril or Oxo on offer as well, so Avie thought it represented pretty good value for one halfpenny. A tin had been placed hopefully at one end of the table, labelled 'Donations -suggested One Halfpenny.'

Avie started dishing out the soup, two ladles full for each bowl, and she tried to smile at each person and look them in the eye as she gave it to them. It was her nature to be friendly to people and Mrs. Philbert wasn't going to change that. 'Help yourself to bread', she said, with a smile.

As Rachel had mentioned, some greedy people wolfed down their bowl of soup and came back for more. But Mrs. Philbert soon put a stop to that. Her eagle eye missed nothing, and she ordered them back to the tables again.

'If there's any left over after half past one,' she said, eyeing them keenly, 'you might be able to have some more. But we are serving this soup between one o'clock and half past one, so there may be more people coming. We must be fair.' Her expression brooked no argument and she never, ever smiled. She reminded Avie of Madame Corbeau at the Swiss school, she was the same - very formidable.

Mrs. Philbert turned to Avie, during a slight lull in the proceedings. 'And are you helping out at the Sale of Work?' she asked.

'Not at the moment, madam. I'm a Norland Nanny, so my first duty is to my boys. But I'm happy to deliver handbills to advertise it, anything like that. When is it taking place?'

'Next Saturday at half past two. To support the Belgian refugees, as you no doubt are aware. I hope you will be there.' She sounded so strict; it was more of an order than a request. 'And who are you with?' she asked curtly.

'The Ducketts in Cadogan Crescent. Very nice people.' She knew they were pillars of the church, so hoped this would please the lady, who merely grunted.

'I believe my employer is offering some items for sale, so we'll see what we can do.' Avie gave an encouraging smile to the lady, but then another group of people came through the door and approached the table eagerly.

'I think we need more bread cut, Miss Spicer. Can you deal with that? I'll see to these people.'

Avie willingly left the company of Mrs. Philbert and went through to the kitchen. There she found two women engaged in washing up, laughing and joking with each other.

They smiled at her as she entered the room and raised their eyes to heaven. 'How are you finding Mrs. Philbert?'

'I call her SNN', laughed Avie. 'Strictly No Nonsense.'

The two ladies giggled. 'That's a good one - but you 'ave to 'and it to her, she's a real trouper. Now, what's your name, love?'

'I'm Avie, I look after Mrs. Duckett's boys - I'm a nanny... and you are...?'

They both nodded and smiled. 'Oh, we know Mrs. Duckett and 'er boys - full of mischief they are! I'm Polly and this is Jude. So 'ow's it going out there - quite a few people 'ave turned up then?'

'Yes, I think there's quite a need for it,' Avie replied.

She thought of telling them about the incident with the dog in the park the other day, but then wondered whether it would inflame the situation, so decided to keep quiet. Derek had reported the unfortunate event to the police and they had taken a statement from Avie. It had upset the whole family, but particularly the boys. They loved their little dogs and to see one of them injured like this was devastating to them. They had taken Karl to the vet to have him checked over, but fortunately there was no lasting damage, and the dog was recovering slowly. Elsie had been horrified when she heard about it, so Avie was glad she hadn't been there when it happened.

Avie cut up the bread and replenished the baskets. The time was approaching half past one now and the crowds had dwindled. She peered into the tureens - there was still some left. She turned to Mrs. Philbert. 'It's nearly half past now, madam, shall we offer the rest to the people that are here?'

The dignified matron looked at her fob-watch, pinned to her ample bosom. 'We'll wait until exactly half past one I think, Miss Spicer, then they can have the rest if they wish.'

The clock ticked over to half past and Mrs. Philbert gave the green light for people to have seconds. There was quite a rush. But this time they rationed it to one ladle full, to be fair to everyone. Once everyone had finished eating, the ladies from the kitchen came out and began clearing the tables.

'You've got a lot of washing-up there,' smiled Avie, as she took off her apron and fetched her coat.

'We don't mind, ducks, we're 'appy to 'elp out, aren't we, Jude?' They were real Londoners and so very friendly.

'Well, I might see you later in the week or next week perhaps?'

Avie smiled and she made her way to the door.

To her surprise, Mrs. Philbert called out to her as she left, raising a hand. 'Goodbye, Miss Spicer and thank you!' And was that a ghost of a smile hovering on her lips?

Well, what a surprise, the lady was human after all!

* * *

Avie arrived back at Cadogan Crescent, feeling pleasantly satisfied. She had at last made a start on helping with the war effort. It was the least she could do, she felt. So many other people were doing so much more.

As she entered the hall and took her coat off, she could hear Elsie talking to someone in the sitting room, and then Elsie came out to the hall, closing the sitting-room door behind her. She looked rather flummoxed, as she often did when an unexpected situation cropped up.

Avie's eyes flicked up at her. 'What is it, madam, is anything wrong?'

Elsie lowered her eyes, and her cheeks flushed a little. 'You have a visitor, Miss Avie. It's your father...'

'Oh, I hope nothing's wrong at home...?' Avie had a feeling of dread in her stomach. It was unusual for Jeremy just to turn up like this. It had never happened before. She started towards the sitting room.

Jeremy was sitting on the sofa, and he rose when he saw his daughter, his face tense and anxious.

'Dad! This is a surprise - but I hope nothing's wrong?'

They both embraced and then sat together on the sofa. 'Is

everything all right?' Avie asked, her heart in her mouth.

Jeremy nodded and gave a weak smile. 'Everyone's fine in Canterbury, but', he hesitated, then said slowly, 'We've had some news about your young man, William, so I thought I should let you know.'

Avie gave a gasp. She knew William was engaged in the war in France. She had been worrying about him and praying for him every night. 'Oh no, is he all right, has something happened?' Her heart was racing in alarm.

'Now calm down, dear, but let me explain the situation to you. He was leading his men in the Battle of the Marne - a fierce battle which resulted in a French victory, but with horrendous losses. William was badly injured and treated initially at a field hospital.'

Avie's eyes had been fixed on her father, as he told her this news. 'So, what happened, will he be all right?' She knew the soldiers often suffered horrific injuries, losing their limbs or their sight. She was fearful of what Jeremy had to say.

'They are confident he will make a good recovery. His left leg was shattered by a shell landing very close to him. They thought they might have to amputate at one stage. But he's now been transferred to a military hospital in Paris and seems to be doing quite well.'

Avie gave a sigh of relief. 'Oh, thank God for that, I'm so glad. But who gave you this news -was it Pierre?'

Jeremy shook his head. 'Pierre is in another regiment. It was Sylvie. She heard the news from Pierre and he asked her to let you know. James gave her our telephone number when she rang Pelham Hall.'

Miss Sylvie was a French lady's maid at Craven Manor, when Avie worked there as a young girl. She had met Pierre, the chauffeur, and they fell in love instantly. And it was through Pierre that Avie had met William, so she was forever grateful to him.

Avie hugged her father - it was so good of him to travel all this way to tell her this news in person, rather than ringing up. 'Thanks so much, Dad, for letting me know all this. I've been worrying about him, but it's so difficult – there's not much news in the paper about the French campaigns, obviously. But everyone's quite well at home – Harriet and the boys?'

'Yes, fine, everyone's doing well. But when are we going to see you for a weekend?' he asked. 'It's been ages since you came back.'

Yes, Avie felt guilty that she hadn't been back to see her parents for several weeks. She still wrote to them when she could, but she seemed so busy with other duties, that it had slipped her mind.

'Let's look at the diary,' she said, as Matilda brought a tray of tea and sandwiches into the room. She flicked through it and together they found a mutually convenient date when she could go back to Canterbury.

They decided on a weekend in October. 'It will be really good to see everyone', she said. Avie then turned to the tea-tray and poured a cup for Jeremy and offered him a sandwich.

'So, you've been helping out at a Soup Kitchen today,' Jeremy said, as he tucked into his sandwich. 'Many turn up?'

'There must have been twenty or so,' Avie said. 'It's difficult to gauge how much soup to prepare, when you have no idea how many are going to come.'

'Harriet's finding that as well - oh and she's started a Knitting Circle, don't laugh!'

Avie nearly choked on her sandwich. 'I didn't know Mother could knit?'

'She can't,' laughed Jeremy, 'but she had a crash course from Mrs. Salisbury...' They both giggled, as they sipped their tea.

'And how are Granny and Grandad?' asked Avie.

Jeremy waggled his hand. 'Not the best, frankly, they've both got ailments, but they are in their eighties now.'

'And are both the boys fighting fit?'

'Robert is showing signs of some artistic talent,' Jeremy said, raising his eyebrows. Robert was his child from a previous marriage and his late wife had been an artist, so he would be pleased if her talent had been passed on.

'Oh?'

'He won a Junior Art Prize at school for his picture of a horse. And I must admit it was pretty good - he got the proportions just right. Quite a difficult subject for a child of seven. And little Matthew has just started nursery school and is causing mayhem...'

Avie laughed. 'Well done to Robert. Give them all my love, won't you? Goodness, he's seven now, I can't believe that. He would get on well with my boys here, Luke and James. They're nine and they're into everything. They've recently come back from Brownsea Island, near Poole, where the Scouts have a camp.'

Avie suddenly looked at the grandfather clock. She'd forgotten all about her charges. It was already a quarter to three. 'Help, I must go and pick them up soon.'

Jeremy finished his tea and patted his mouth with a napkin.

'Thank Mrs. Duckett for the tea and sandwiches, but I must go now anyway. I'll come with you.'

They said goodbye to Elsie on the way out and left the house together.

'Let me know if you have any more news about William, won't you?' said Avie.

'Of course, straight away. And we look forward to seeing you next month, my love. It will be so good to see you properly.'

Father and daughter embraced, and they went their separate ways at the end of the road.

Chapter 25

The Sale of Work was in full swing at the church hall. There was a huge banner outside, saying 'Support the Belgian Refugees. Sale of Work Here Today.' Stalls had been set up all round the room and these were piled high with intriguing goods on display.

Avie had helped by dropping handbills in the nearby houses and there was a good crowd of people coming through the door. There was quite a buzz in the room, as everyone chattered and inspected the items, armed with capacious bags. Elsie had donated quite a few items – there were knitted garments, tapestries, small vases and lots of pictures and trinkets.

She had to admit, frankly, she had agreed to help mainly to take her mind off William. He was constantly in her thoughts, and she prayed to God he would recover from his injuries. It sounded so serious. But thank goodness the medical team had managed to avoid amputation. The very thought of that possibility made Avie cringe in horror.

As soon as the public had heard of the plight of the Belgian people, they had responded immediately, raising funds for them and offering accommodation. Forced to evacuate their homes in Ghent when the Germans invaded their country, these poor people had fled across the Channel to England.

There were already some Belgians living in Islington and you could easily identify them, Avie thought sadly. They had left their homes with only the clothes on their backs. Now they had arrived, they had to resort to searching in second-hand shops. The Red Cross had provided them with some essentials, but they had very few possessions.

There was also a free second-hand clothes stall in the hall, and this was proving very popular. Mrs. Lacey, from the church, a smiling lady with grey hair, seemed to be overseeing the proceedings. Avie had also seen her friends Polly and Jude in the kitchen, filling up several tea urns. And the trestle tables and benches were in use again for a well-needed sit-down.

'Anyone here speak French?' Mrs. Lacey called out, amidst the general hubbub, from her clothes stall.

Avie went over and offered her services. 'I'm not brilliant, but I might be able to help,' she said.

Mrs. Lacey gave a relieved smile as she approached. She waved her hand towards two middle-aged ladies standing nearby, looking a bit lost. 'These ladies are from Belgium and can't speak English. They also don't know about our currency. They only arrived here yesterday. Can you help them?'

Avie went up to the ladies and gave a smile, shaking hands with them. She introduced herself in French, then asked their names. 'Ah, so it's Esmeralde, is it and Margarethe, oui? *Bienvenu à Angleterre!*' Welcome to England! *Enchantée de vous voir!* Nice to meet you. *Qu'est ce que vous cherchez? Une robe, peut-etre?* What are you looking for - a dress, perhaps?

Quel taille?' What size? The ladies seemed very happy to hear French being spoken and began smiling, as Avie showed them some dresses on a stand. '*Il y a beaucoup des robes ici...*' There are plenty of frocks here. '*Regardez ici...*' Have a look.'

The ladies began searching through the frocks and picked out one or two. And then Avie led them to another stall which had underwear, socks and shoes on offer. This was being managed by the redoubtable Mrs. Philbert and she gave Avie an encouraging nod, when she saw she was helping the strangers. Once they had chosen a few things, she helped the ladies by explaining the currency. 'This is a pound note, worth twenty shillings, this is a shilling, here is a half-a-crown, this one is a sixpence, this one a florin.'

She stayed with them for ten minutes or so and brought them a cup of tea, trying desperately to remember her French. She was surprised; she had retained quite a bit of knowledge, but didn't know how grammatical it was!

Once they had finished their tea, the two ladies picked up their bags full of their precious things and stood up. 'We go now', Margarethe said, '*nous partons maintenant. Merci beaucoup.*'

'*Au revoir!*' called Avie, giving a wave.

And they left the hall, clutching their bags and looking a lot happier than when they came in.

'Thanks for doing that', smiled Mrs. Lacey. 'Where did you learn your French?'

'I was in Switzerland for a while', murmured Avie, 'so I picked it up a bit there. So where are these poor souls living now?' she asked.

'They're in a hostel I believe - it must be so confusing for them, in a strange country...'

Before Avie left the stall, she noticed that the two ladies had left two newspapers behind on the bench and went to pick them up to discard them. But then she saw one was in French. It was *Le Matin*, the popular French newspaper. She picked it up and sat down again, trying to make sense of some of the headlines. She happened to see the Marne was mentioned - that was the place where William had been injured - he was sure Jeremy had said the Battle of the Marne. She popped it in her bag – she would try to read it later, with the aid of a French dictionary. It seemed to be a report of the battle.

The other paper there was in English and was called the Wipers Times. Avie had heard vaguely about this paper, which was roughly produced in the rest camps. It was an attempt to boost the soldiers' morale. It was full of dark humour, much needed in the trenches. 'Wipers' was what most British soldiers called 'Ypres' which she knew was a battleground in Belgium. A lot of these were passed around in the *estaminets*, where the men went for some social life.

Jeremy or Derek might like to see that as well, she thought, and so put it in her bag, as she left the hall.

Elsie greeted Avie with a welcome cup of tea, when she arrived back. She and Derek were quite happy for Avie to support the war effort and were doing more to look after the boys themselves now. This was very generous of them, considering they were still paying the Norland Nanny fees.

Avie showed Derek the French newspaper *Le Matin* and he was immediately interested. Together they pored over the paper and, with the aid of a French dictionary, between them got the general gist of the article. It was indeed a report on the Battle of the Marne, an area on the outskirts of Paris. And although the French had gained a significant victory, it was far from sweet. The report estimated that as many as 80,000 men had been killed in the bloody skirmishes, with hundreds of casualties like William.

Derek ran his eyes over the foreign words. He could read French reasonably well, but was not fluent speaking it. 'The regiment is called the First Infantry Regiment,' he said. 'And it seems to me they are also saying that their uniform is controversial. I think I remember reading about that somewhere. Their coats are blue and their trousers are red, so they stand out on the battlefield.' He shook his head. 'Not good.'

'Oh, here comes the postman!' Elsie called out, as she glanced out of the window. 'We don't often get a second post on a Saturday. Can you fetch it, Matilda?' The young girl had come in to collect the tea-tray.

The maid brought back a clutch of letters, but also there was a special postcard amongst them. 'Oh, what's this we have here?' Elsie said, picking it out from the letters. She held it up. 'Well, look at that - how pretty!' It was an embroidered card with scalloped edges. A floral design on the front had been worked in silk, in vivid colours of red, blue and white, the colours of the French flag. There were beautiful roses and lilies and a dove of peace at the top.

'Oh, it's for you, Miss Avie! Perhaps it's from your sweetheart?'

Avie's heart skipped a beat. Could it be from William? Was he in a fit state to write a postcard to her? She took it from Elsie and read the few words, written in a shaky hand. But yes, it was indeed from William, her love, her first love.

She was surprised to see it was in French, but Derek explained that the French Censor probably didn't allow foreign languages. Avie translated it as:

'I send you my best love, *ma petite*. But my duty is to defend *La Belle France*, so I will return to the battlefield as soon as I am fully recovered. All my love, William. xxx'

Avie loved the card and hugged it to her chest. She would keep it forever. But the thought of her sweetheart going back to the fray was chilling. And it took the edge off her happiness.

Chapter 26

'Hallo there - my name is Betty Chambers. We're canvassing people to-day to see if they can give any time to Queen Mary's Relief Clothing Guild.'

When Avie was approached by this earnest-looking lady at the church hall, she was fully prepared. She was already working at the Soup Kitchen twice a week, but that only took about an hour, so she had decided that, to be fair to Elsie and Derek, she would only devote two days a week to her war effort work - and that one of those days would be at the weekend.

Queen Mary had made an urgent plea on the wireless for people to donate used clothing. It was to help ex-soldiers, disabled men and the unemployed. The Queen was a popular figure; she was so dignified and gracious and always so interested in the causes she supported. Some of the men had returned from the Front to find women were now doing jobs they had formerly held. And they were reduced to begging in the street or selling matches or buttons. It was a pitiful sight, particularly if the men were disabled. A lot of them were living ten to a room and in terrible conditions.

'So what's involved?' asked Avie cheerfully. 'I can only give one day a week - I'm a Norland Nanny and I have a duty to my employers.'

The lady's face brightened. 'One day would be absolutely topping, my dear, whenever you can manage it. The work is in central London and it's dealing with used clothing - sorting and packing it up to send to other depots. Nothing too onerous. We pay your fares to and from the depot if you wish. It's in Pimlico, so central, near the Tube station.'

Avie smiled and nodded at Betty. 'All right, count me in. But I can only do one day in the week or possibly a Saturday.'

'Oh, wonderful. May I put your name down? That is so kind of you. Now, it's Miss…?' And she took Avie's personal details. Another volunteer ticked off.

Before she left the church hall, Avie popped in to see Polly and Jude in the kitchen for a quick cup of tea. But she found they had a young man with them. He was of slim build and looked very tired and anxious. And then she noticed his limbs were shaking.

'Oh, hallo, ducks,' Polly cried when she saw Avie. 'Nice to see you. Now this is my son, Peter. Peter, this is our friend, Avie.'

The young man immediately looked distressed at meeting a stranger and turned away. And Avie began to realise here was a case of shell-shock; she had heard about it, but never seen it before.

Avie shook hands with Peter, then turned to Polly, murmuring: 'How about we go for a little walk in the park? It's so noisy in here - it's probably upsetting him…'

The three of them left the babble of the church hall and wandered next door to the park, Polly holding Peter's hand. It was a tranquil spot and there were only a few people taking the air and enjoying the late autumn sunshine. Avie squeezed Polly's hand, as they walked along, and they exchanged glances.

'Just come back from the Front, Mons,' Polly said in a low voice. 'It nearly finished 'im off. He's only twenty. He was a bright, confident lad before 'e went. Now look at 'im.' She cursed aloud. 'Bloody war, I 'ate it.'

'I'm sure he'll recover in time', said Avie. 'Can the doctors give him anything to help?'

'He's taking some medicine, but it's not doing much good. He doesn't sleep well - wakes up screaming with nightmares about the shelling and the rats - it's awful to see!'

'I'm so sorry', she murmured, but then looked at her watch. 'I'm afraid I have to leave you here', she said. 'I've got to pick up my charges from school…'

'You're a good girl, Avie.' Polly put her arm on Avie's shoulders. 'Most people don't want nothin' to do with 'im.'

'We could meet sometime perhaps; he might get used to me. Oh look, he's gone over to the swings. Do you think he'd like a swing?'

'He might, now that's a thought.' His mother sounded surprised, but went over to her son and started giving him a push, reminding him how to push himself. Polly gave Avie a wave as she left the park and Peter looked up, too, and just stared at her. It was a start, she felt.

Polly is a brave woman, she mused. *She keeps so cheerful and yet she has all this trouble at home.*

* * *

Next morning at breakfast Derek seemed very quiet. 'All right, sir?' she asked. She knew he had a busy, responsible job in his engineering firm, and he also worried about Elsie and her problems.

He shrugged. 'I'm all right. It's just that - um, yesterday I had a bit of an unnerving experience...'

'Oh, what happened?'

'I was walking along Millbank, minding my own business, when this well-dressed woman came up to me and handed me a white feather. And then she said, as bold as you like, 'You know where you should be!'

'I was flabbergasted! 'I'm fifty-two, madam', I told her. 'I did my bit in the Boer War. 'It shook me up rather, I can tell you.'

Avie was incensed. To accuse a stranger of cowardice in public was so insensitive. 'Bloomin' nerve!' she said. She could see the incident had upset Derek. He looked much younger than his age and the woman must have thought he was in his forties. The recruiting age was from eighteen to forty-five, she believed.

'If I were you, sir, I'd take it as a compliment - she thought you were young enough to serve!'

Derek gave a chuckle. 'You're a tonic, Avie!'

Avie was going to Pimlico today to start her charity work. She went on the Tube and then walked to the address nearby, Ebury House, Ebury Street. It was a crumbling old mansion, standing in its own grounds and quite impressive.

The building had been requisitioned by the Government to house Queen Mary's Relief Clothing Guild. Boxes of used clothing were conveyed to the centre and all the garments were then washed and sorted, before being sent to other depots around London. With winter coming on, there was a real need for coats, trousers, sweaters, scarves and hats, so these were being given priority now. It was mainly men's clothing, but there were a few women's things as well.

She entered the main hall, which was a huge area. Must have been the ballroom, she reckoned, admiring the panelled walls and beamed ceiling, albeit now covered in cobwebs. Avie was relieved to see there were already four other people there, busily sorting items. And she was seized upon as soon as she entered by a young man, with a cut-glass accent, a raucous laugh and a clipboard.

'Hallo there, first day? And the name, madam?' He found her name on a list and ticked it off. 'I'm Rupert, by the way. Now, if you could join that group over there. They're looking for sweaters and jumpers. And then once you're done there, move on to the next table - all right? They're doing trousers and underwear.' He gave a chortle. 'In case you're wondering, these things have all been washed, but feel free to wear gloves, if you don't want contact, all right? Any problems, see me.'

He looked Avie up and down. 'Like your flaming hair - do they call you Carrots?' He seemed to think this was hilariously funny, but to Avie, it wasn't very original. She was wearing her hair shorter now and loose with an Alice band, to be more practical.

She joined the group, and they exchanged names. But they were all so busy, sorting and tossing things into boxes, there wasn't much time for chat. 'Can I just ask you', Avie said to the nearest person, Mary, a young woman about her age. 'If we notice some item is beyond repair or in need of repair, do we toss it out? Or put it somewhere else?'

Mary pointed towards yet another huge box labelled 'NOT WANTED'. 'In there', she said with a shrug. 'It takes too long to repair them. Still, never know, we might get a visit from the Queen. She often comes to these depots.' Avie raised her eyebrows. A lady came trundling in with a tea-trolley, during the afternoon, which was very welcome, so they had a little break.

'How come Rupert isn't at the Front?' Avie asked Mary, sotto voce. Most young men had enlisted and there was a noticeable lack of them in the population now.

Mary sniffed. 'Flat feet, apparently.' But her look to Avie disputed this.

Two hours later, Avie was still laboriously plodding along. She found the work very monotonous. It was so repetitive and hard on the back, bending over to retrieve the items and then sorting them.

By four o'clock she decided she'd had enough. 'I have to go now', she told Rupert, 'I'm due back home.'

Rupert nodded. 'That's fine. Hope to see you next week perhaps? Well, thanks for your time, Miss Spicer, much appreciated. We can put you on packing next time, if you'd rather.'

Avie felt so weary, as she left the room. But hopefully she had been useful to someone, she thought.

She was mightily relieved once she reached No.12 Cadogan Crescent.

Everything seemed very calm and ordered at the house. Mrs. Herbert greeted her with a smile and Matilda gave a nod. There was music playing on the wireless. Elsie and Derek were as usual very congenial and having a glass of sherry, which they also offered to Avie. They were happy to hear about her day.

The boys were in their rooms, doing their homework; they had walked home on their own to-day and found it quite liberating. The dogs were snoozing by the fire... And a delicious smell was coming from the kitchen. It was a peaceful, domestic scene.

Just before dinner, the doorbell rang and Matilda went to answer it. 'There's a young lady outside, asking for you, Miss Avie.'

'Did she give a name?'

Matilda shook her head.

Avie stood up and went into the hall, where the front door was half open. She opened the door wider. And was surprised to see Phoebe standing there, wearing a capacious, flowing cape.

'Oh, Feebs!' began Avie, taken aback. But Feebs looked distraught and interrupted her.

'Oh, Avie, I've been a bloody fool. Can I come in?'

Chapter 27

'Now, what's this all about?' Avie had hugged her friend and decided to go to her room, to be more private. She was shocked at the change in Feebs since she last saw her, at the start of the war. She had been vivacious, happy and confident then. Now she seemed anxious and agitated. Whatever had happened to cause this?

Avie had spoken briefly to Elsie and asked if her friend could stay the night. 'She's in trouble, Elsie. And could Mrs. Herbert make the meal stretch to one more?'

Elsie nodded. 'Matilda can bring it up on a tray. And I'll tell her to make up a bed in the boxroom.'

Avie squeezed her hand. 'You are so kind, madam, I do appreciate it. She seems very upset about something. I don't know the full story yet.'

Back in her room, Avie faced Feebs with a direct look from her blue eyes. 'Are you in some kind of trouble, Feebs? Tell me all about it.'

'Sorry to barge in like this, Aves. But I'm a bit desperate. And now I've lost my job.'

Avie gasped. 'What, your job as an ambulance driver? What on earth happened?'

Feebs took off her voluminous cape and stood before her. 'I'm up the duff, that's what happened. And as soon as they found out, I got the sack.'

Avie caught her breath, as she surveyed Phoebe's now rather rounded figure. She was shocked and speechless. 'Um, how far gone are you?' she managed to stutter.

'Nearly six months. I was able to hide it for several months, but now I can't get away with it any more...' Feebs shook her head. 'I'm a fool, I loved that job. It was so busy all the time, lovely people.' Her eyes began to fill with tears. 'I've really stuffed it up.'

'And what of the gentleman in question?'

Feebs struggled to keep her composure. Her lips were trembling. Beads of perspiration appeared on her forehead. 'I've just heard to-day - he was killed at Messines last week...'

'Oh my God – Phoebe!' And Avie came over to her friend and embraced her, as she sobbed her heart out on her shoulder.

'I loved him, really loved him. He was called Charlie and yes, in case you're wondering, he was the one who taught me to drive. I fell for him in a big way. He was just working temporarily at the farm, but as soon as we met, I knew I couldn't resist him. It was like a story in a cheap novelette...'

'And does your family know about all this?' Avie asked gravely.

'Well, they know I'm pregnant. But they don't know I've lost my job, yet.'

'Do they know about Charlie?'

'Oh yes, they were the ones who told me... they heard from Charlie's father.'

'Are they going to stand by you, do you think?' Avie knew a lot of families rejected their daughters in similar cases, because of prejudice and bigotry towards unmarried mothers.

'They were totally shocked at first and kept saying I'd brought shame on the family and all that. But in her last letter my mother said they would welcome me back and look after me. She'd had a change of heart.'

'Oh, thank goodness', murmured Avie. There was a knock on the door and Matilda came in with a tray of food.

'Thanks, Matilda. And you're making up a bed, I believe?'

'That's right, miss.'

'Thanks so much.'

Feebs managed a relieved smile. 'Oh, thank you. That's very kind. I'm sorry to be disrupting the entire household like this.'

The two girls sat on the bed and ate their meals, sharing a tray. It was a beef casserole with dumplings. And Avie suddenly remembered those halcyon days in Montreux, when the girls had cooked the same meal with dog's meat, to much hilarity. It seemed a long time ago now.

When they had finished their meal, Feebs turned to Avie cautiously. 'There's one other thing', she said. Avie looked rather alarmed. What more was coming?

Phoebe gave a wry smile. 'Don't worry, no more revelations. It's just that I wanted to sound you out. Now this is only an idea, but when the baby is born, I wondered whether you would look after him (or her) during the day? I would pay you, of course. Then I could return to the Ambulance Service… As I say, it's only an idea. If you feel you couldn't do it, I would quite understand.'

Avie looked doubtful. 'Well, trouble is, it wouldn't be just my decision. It would need the family's consent here - they may not like it. They're avid churchgoers and the idea of having a baby out of wedlock is completely anathema to them. And, of course, they're paying big fees to Norland Nannies for me to look after their boys…'

'They don't need to know I'm not married, do they?' interrupted Feebs. 'We could just say my husband was killed at Messines?'

Avie ignored this comment. 'The Ducketts may also feel it's not fair on the boys. Can we leave that idea open for the moment? Let me think about it.'

'If not,' Feebs said, looking grim, 'Mother might conceivably agree to take care of the baby, but of course I wouldn't see much of him (or her), as they're in Devon.'

'Are you booked in at a hospital for the birth?'

Feebs nodded. 'I've got a friend who's a nurse and she said I must have regular checks and give birth in safe conditions. I'm booked in at a hospital in Sidmouth, quite near my parents. I'm going back home for the next few months.'

'And what's your due date?'

'January the twentieth.'

'Not long to wait…' It was now 19th October, so three months to go.

The girls fell silent, and Phoebe began to yawn. It had been a traumatic, emotional revelation for her and dramatic news for Avie to absorb, after her busy day. Avie was very doubtful about looking after the baby. She had the boys to care for and now she also had her various activities to support the war effort. *Who knows how long the conflict will last?* she wondered. *I don't think it would work*, she thought. *And I can't start telling lies to the Ducketts. They've been so kind to me. They're such lovely people with high principles.* As much as she would love to help Feebs, it was a step too far, she felt.

But before she took Phoebe to her bedroom, Avie had a thought suddenly. And she put it to Feebs before they said goodnight. 'You're assuming that you would get a job in the Ambulance Service in London, once the baby is born, aren't you?' Feebs nodded.

'Well', Avie shrugged, 'they have Ambulance Services everywhere – there would be one in Sidmouth or then there's Exeter, a bigger city. So why don't you think of joining the Service down there? Then perhaps your mother could look after the baby during the day, but you could come home at night and see to him?'

Feebs looked interested. 'Why didn't I think of that? My brain is made of cotton wool at the moment! It's a thought', she murmured. 'It wouldn't be as busy as in London, but that might not be a bad thing… Good thinking, Aves.'

And the two girls hugged each other, both feeling utterly exhausted.

'Sleep well, goodnight!'

Chapter 28

'The Laurels', Canterbury, Kent

'Darling, lovely to see you!' Avie was back in Canterbury and her father had come to the station to meet her. She had been looking forward to this weekend with her parents and spending time with the children.

Once they reached The Laurels, Harriet greeted her warmly - and the boys ran headlong into her arms, exclaiming with delight. She searched in her bag and found the two toffee apples she had bought for them, to whoops of delight.

'Now, you must ask Mummy if it's all right to eat those now. Don't want to spoil your appetite for lunch.'

But Harriet nodded good-naturedly, and the boys ran off to their playroom. 'Will you come and see my toy cars?' Matthew asked in his high voice.

'I'll be there in a minute, Matthew...'

'They've both grown so much!' Avie said, as they relaxed in the sitting room. She looked fondly around the familiar room. There were family photographs on the sideboard. One of Harriet and Jeremy on their wedding day. Another of Avie at her eighteenth party. And a lovely smiling one of the two boys.

Rufus the spaniel came up and nuzzled her. It was good to be back.

'And I hear that Robert won a prize for Art - wonderful news! May I see it?'

'I'll fetch it,' said Jeremy, leaving the room.

'We're thinking of having it framed,' murmured Harriet. 'It's really very good for his age. He's obviously inherited his mother's talent.' There were other framed pictures around the house painted by Mary, Jeremy's first wife, who had tragically died, giving birth to Robert. They were mainly landscapes, but a few flower studies and still life pictures.

Jeremy came into the room holding the picture, drawn on art paper, and showed it to Avie. She caught her breath. It was amazingly good. The proportions of the legs were perfect and the eyes very alert. The horse's dark brown coat was shiny and sleek, and he was pawing the ground, as if wanting to be off on a canter.

'It's extremely good,' Avie said in admiration, gazing at the picture. 'Did he copy it from a book, or did he study the horses in the stables?'

'He used to go down to the stables and take a sketch book, didn't he, Hattie?' Jeremy was obviously so proud of his son's achievement. 'We're thinking we might send him to a private tutor who specialises in art. His teacher at school says he has exceptional talent, for one so young.'

Harriet nodded, then turned to Avie. 'Now, is there any more news of William? You must be so worried.'

Avie put her head on one side. 'Well, I did receive a special postcard from him the other day which he had written himself, so he must be improving. But I'm afraid he's going back to the trenches, once he's better...'

'I'm sure he is highly regarded as an officer. Anyway, Sylvie has our number now,' Harriet said, 'so if she has any news, I'm sure she will get in touch...'

A small figure appeared in the doorway. It was Matthew, tousle-haired, one sock adrift from the other.

'Are you coming?' he said in a plaintive voice, looking accusingly at Avie.

Avie stood to attention and saluted, making Matthew laugh. 'At once, sir, your word is my command.' And she left the room with the child, and they ran along the corridor together, Rufus following them, wagging his tail.

Harriet exchanged glances with Jeremy. 'Lovely to have her back!'

*   *   *

Next day the family were due to go to Pelham Hall for lunch, so the boys were left to their own devices, as the adults dressed.

When Avie was presentable, she came downstairs and heard an anguished cry from Robert, so ran to see if she could help. Robert was standing on the terrace, and he turned when she came out. 'Look, Avie, see what my brother's done now!'

Avie followed his gaze and saw that Matthew had been riding his tricycle on the terrace and then decided to try the lawn. Unfortunately, it had rained heavily overnight and so now the lawn was churned up with tyre marks - and Matthew's tricycle was covered in mud.

Avie shook her head but laughed. 'He's a pickle, isn't he? And look at him now...' The tricycle had got bogged down in the turf and so Matthew had decided to hop off it and return to the house. His soggy, disconsolate figure stomped onto the terrace, leaving muddy footprints everywhere he walked. He was about to go into the house, but Avie reached him just in time and removed his wellington boots, covered in mud. Phew!

'Mr. Lonsdale won't be very happy', said Robert, but he had to laugh at the sight of his little brother, with mud all over his clothes and face. Mr. Lonsdale was the gardener and took great pride in his immaculate lawn.

'I think you'd better come with me, young man', said Avie and picked him up and carried the boy through the sitting room to the stairs. 'I think you need a bath, sunshine, come this way!'

She called out to Harriet and Jeremy to tell them what had happened, and they came out of their bedroom to see their muddy son. They had to laugh at the sight of the small boy, and Harriet shook her head. 'Trust Matthew to decide to do something like that, just before we're going out...'

Jeremy gave a chuckle, as he knotted his tie. 'He's always in scrapes, that one.'

'I don't think it will make us too late,' murmured Harriet, looking at her watch. 'Just give him a quick bath and I'll find him some more clothes...'

By midday the small boy was freshened up and wearing a pristine set of clothes. 'Now don't go near any muddy grass, all right?' Avie warned him.

'Only wanted to ride my bike,' Matthew grumbled, looking rather grumpy.

Robert was dressed very tidily and neatly and he jumped into the car and sat next to Avie. He was a quiet child, but quite self-contained and confident. Avie had praised him for his special picture and asked to see some more of his sketches. She had been amazed at the variety of subjects - he had drawn faces, animals, birds and flowers. So she hoped that Harriet and Jeremy would be able to find a suitable tutor, as the child obviously had talent.

* * *

The family gathering at Pelham Hall was now in full swing and the grandparents had been very amused, when told of Matthew's escapade. The three cousins, Thomas, Paul and Benjamin, declared it to be hilarious and were soon chasing about the corridors with the two boys. Although their cousins were slightly older than Robert and Matthew, they got on very well. Before long they were having fun sliding down the banisters into the hall below, until Jeremy stopped them and told them that lunch was ready.

Avie was soon telling everyone about her war-effort duties and mentioned Ebury House, the mansion in Pimlico. At this Lady Edith's eyes brightened and she turned to the Earl. 'I'm sure we went there years ago, to some function...'

The Earl nodded. 'I think you're right, my dear. Wasn't it the seat of Lord and Lady Galbraith, back in the nineties?'

'I expect it was a beautiful house then,' murmured Avie. But she thought privately it was just as well they couldn't see it now, in its present dilapidated state.

Harriet responded by recounting her experiences in the

community, with her Knitting Circle and Soup Kitchen. Not to be outdone, Amelia chipped in with news of her voluntary work at the hospital, doing bandage rolling or engaging with recuperating patients. Avie also mentioned William, as they had all met him at her eighteenth birthday party.

'And have you had any Belgian refugees here yet?' she asked, changing the subject.

'Oh yes, and people have been so kind, inviting them to stay in their homes and setting up Funds to help them financially.' Harriet laughed suddenly. 'Most people are grateful for some help, but there are a few who are rather sniffy. One woman refused to accept a couple's offer of a room, when she saw it. The cottage was small and obviously not as spacious as they were used to.'

'Beggars can't be choosers,' Jeremy commented, with a shrug.

'And have you come across any 'conchies',' Avie asked. Conscientious objectors were people who objected to war on moral grounds and refused to fight.

'There are one or two, mainly from the church,' James said. 'But on the whole most people are passionate about defending their country in time of war.'

'I wonder if they will bring in conscription', the Earl said, as the footman brought in the coffee.

'If it goes on much longer, they might have to - the figures are horrendous for the war dead.'

'And are you going off soon, James?' Jeremy ventured. Avie had wondered whether her uncle was going to enlist, but hadn't liked to ask.

James nodded. 'Oh yes, I'm due in the next wave. I tried to

enlist when it started, but then they closed the Recruiting Office. But now I've heard they're opening it up again next week.'

'Well, the best of luck to you, sir! Which regiment?'

'Oh, the Buffs - what else?' James laughed heartily. 'Father's old regiment, The Royal East Kent, can't wait.' He looked around the table. 'Let's give the Germans what for - they certainly need it…'

'Well done, son, you give 'em hell!' said the Earl, raising his glass.

'Here's to victory by Christmas - you never know, it could happen!'

'Steady the Buffs!'

Everyone raised their glasses - and Avie thought of William.

The weekend had ended on a patriotic note.

Chapter 29

Clare, Suffolk, a month later..

'Rachel! At last we meet!' Avie threw her arms around her friend. She had just arrived at Cambridge station and was looking forward to spending a few days with her.

Derek had said she was overdue for some leave. And he lectured her that she had been devoting too much time to her war efforts. It was now the end of November. 'You need to get out and see your friends', he said. 'You've been stuck inside looking after the boys or slaving away at that Pimlico place for too long. So, I order you to go and have some time off! Have some fun for a change!'

How could she refuse? Derek was so magnanimous. Avie felt she had been dealt a generous hand, when she landed this posting.

Rachel linked arms with her friend and the girls left the station and found her trusty vehicle parked nearby. They were soon heading out of the amazing city, with its prestigious university buildings, and entering the open countryside. The stark trees were a reminder they were now in winter, and it was bitterly cold. There were small farms dotted about and churches, with just a few cottages grouped together here and there.

'And how is your mother now?' Avie asked.

'Tons better, thank you. She improved rapidly once Uncle Dick arrived. I think initially she was worried that, with father gone, she would be shouldering all the responsibility, for the farm and for her life in general. Uncle Dick has been a godsend. He's taken over and reorganised everything. Appointed a farm manager - Herbie Cox, who's been here for years and knows the place backwards.'

'But you said your uncle knew nothing about farming, I believe...?'

'Nor does he, but he's surrounded by experienced people here and he's a fast learner... Here we are, here's our place, Home Farm.' And Rachel swung through the farm gates, scattering the chickens, and brought the vehicle to a stop in front of the old farmhouse.

It was a traditional timbered building with a thatched roof, and several outbuildings faced a central courtyard. Avie could see stables nearby and cattle in the field, munching the grass. She took a deep breath and inhaled the fresh country air. It was lovely to be in the countryside like this, after the smoky atmosphere of London.

'Oh, it's so good to feel the fresh air on my face!' she exclaimed.

Rachel linked arms with her again, her face wreathed in smiles. 'Great to have you here after all this time, Avie! Now, come and meet Mother.'

Dora, her mother, was at the stone sink in the big farmhouse kitchen, with its flagstone floor. She turned as they entered and wiped her hands on her apron.

'Mother, this is Avie, my friend from Switzerland. Avie, meet my mother, Dora.'

Dora put out her hand and gave a smile, as they shook hands. 'Hallo, Avie. We meet at last! Rachel's been talking about you so much, I feel I know you already.' Her grey eyes twinkled as she spoke. Avie could see the likeness between them.

'I've been telling Mum about all our escapades in Montreux...'

Avie giggled. 'Does she know about Bonzo the dog?' Rachel nodded and Avie shook her head. 'Can't believe we got away with that.'

'Now I'm sure you'd like a cup of tea after your travels, Avie?'

'Oh, thanks so much Dora - may I call you that?'

'Yes, of course.' And she put the kettle on the range and took the big floral teapot and some china from the dresser.

'Let's go into the sitting room,' Rachel said, 'and you can tell me what you've been doing lately. Are you involved with any war work?'

They both relaxed onto a plumpy couch with comfy, worn cushions. A big inglenook fireplace faced them, with a blazing log fire burning in the hearth.

'I'm helping in a Soup Kitchen twice a week and I give some time to a Clothing Fund sponsored by the Queen. It's frightfully dull, but it's to help disabled servicemen, so it's a good cause. How about you?'

Rachel shrugged. 'I also help in a Soup Kitchen in the village, but I'm here to help Mother, so I drive her to places if she needs to go anywhere or do any other jobs she wants. I often do the housework. We're trying to economise at the moment and do without a scullery maid.'

Dora came in carrying the tea and a plate of cakes and biscuits on a tray, then left, closing the door. 'I'll leave you girls to chat.'

'Now, what's the news of Tom?' Avie asked. 'Is he still in France?'

Rachel nodded. 'We only get limited updates on him. Most of his letters are blanked out by the Censor, all over the page. We don't quite know what he's up to. But he's signed the Official Secrets Act, so he can't tell us much anyway. We have heard through a friend; he was sent behind enemy lines at one stage and working undercover with the French Resistance. And what's the news of your French boyfriend? I think you said you happened to meet him in London?'

'Yes, that's right, purely by chance.' Avie's eyes shone at the memory. 'We saw each other once, but then of course war was declared and it all changed. And now he's enlisted, but he was badly injured and is in hospital recovering now...'

Rachel looked concerned. 'Oh, I'm sorry. Hope he recovers well.'

Avie looked across at her friend, as she sipped her tea. 'And what's happening in *your* love life, may I ask? Anything exciting?'

Rachel's cheeks developed a pink flush. 'Well, as you know, farming is a protected industry, so the young men don't tend to enlist. So yes, as a matter of fact, I have met someone rather special...'

'Oh, bravo! What's he like?'

'Well, he's quite tall, with dark hair and wears a moustache - and he's President of the Young Farmers Association.'

'So where is his farm - or I suppose it's his father's farm, is it?'

'Fairly close, a few miles away and yes, he helps his father. But they've got a thousand acres, so he certainly needs his help.'

'And what's the gentleman's name?'

'Arthur, but I call him Art', Rachel smiled a secret smile. 'He's really nice...

'And will I have the pleasure of meeting him?' Avie smiled.

Rachel nodded. 'Well, we do have the Young Farmers' Ball in Lavenham tomorrow night. So, if you'd like to, we could all go together...?'

'Oh great, but I haven't brought anything suitable to wear!' exclaimed Avie. But then she remembered. 'I do have my long black dress with the beading, perhaps I could dress it up a bit?'

'Hey, yes - I've got plenty of jewellery you can borrow – and what size shoe are you?' And the girls hurried to Rachel's bedroom to find some accessories. They spent the rest of the day chatting and laughing.

Later Rachel found some wellies for her and showed her round the farm. But it was just a cursory visit, as the light was fading, and a chill wind was blowing across the fields.

Before dinner Avie was introduced to Uncle Dick and she could see that Dora had a close affinity to her brother-in-law. He was a quiet man but seemed very confident and sociable. He was interested to hear all about Avie's experiences in London, helping the war effort and her post with Norland Nannies. She did, however, keep quiet about her unfortunate time in Paris and glossed over it, merely saying how delightful the children were.

After a delicious dinner, the girls retired to bed early, knowing they had a late night the next day. And Avie snuggled down in her warm, comfortable bed, her feet hugging the hot water bottle. It was somehow comforting to know that her friend was right next door. So lovely to see her again. She and Rachel had been through a lot together and she felt they were soul mates.

Saturday dawned and when Avie drew back the curtains, she could see there had been a heavy frost overnight. The fields were glistening with it, glinting and sparkling in the pale early-morning sunshine.

At breakfast Rachel outlined her plans for the day.

'I have to go into Lavenham this morning to buy something for Mother. Would you like to come with me? It's a pretty market town, with so many timbered buildings that date back to the fifteenth century. I'd like you to see it in the daylight - and we could have coffee there perhaps. Tonight when we go to the Ball, it will be dark, of course.'

'Oh, great, I'd like to. Where's the Ball being held?'

'At The Swan in Lavenham. It's a medieval former Priory and Weavers' House and is now a hotel. It's an amazing building - you'll love it.'

Avie felt slightly miffed that Rachel hadn't mentioned this Ball before she came. She could have brought something dressier to wear - her pink silk, perhaps – if she'd known about it. But anyway, her black crêpe de Chine dress was very smart, and Rachel had lent her a pretty shawl to wear over it.

It was a fine wool in pale pink and had iridescent thread running through it at the edges. She also had lent her a pearl necklace, which went well with her own pearl earrings. To complete the outfit Avie was borrowing some gold evening sandals, as fortunately they were the same size. And also, she had found a small black evening bag. So, all in all, Avie was happy. It would be fun to go on a night out. She hadn't done that for a long time.

The drive into Lavenham only took about twenty minutes and when they arrived the market town was quite crowded with shoppers. Christmas was only a few weeks away now and so people were already buying gifts. Some of the shops were already displaying Christmas decorations and there was a Christmas tree outside the Town Hall, so it looked quite festive.

Rachel went off to buy some special flour for her mother and Avie wandered along the main street, admiring the many half-timbered houses. Then she spotted the Swan Hotel on the opposite side of the road. It had a wide frontage and was heavily timbered in black and white, very impressive. She looked forward to seeing the interior tonight at the Ball - and could well imagine huge, inglenook fireplaces and exposed beams. There was quite a buzz in the town, and she did some window shopping, warmly wrapped up against the cold in her wool coat, hat and scarf. There were many attractive buildings, now converted into shops selling a variety of goods.

Rachel had pointed out a small café where they could meet for coffee and so Avie went in and sat down. It was warm and cosy inside and the room was adorned with palms and potted plants. A collection of pottery items had been arranged in the window. On the spur of the moment Avie bought a little pottery jug for Rachel's mother, then thought she would buy two and give one to Elsie, who had been so good to her.

Rachel arrived and the girls ordered coffee, as the café began to fill up.

'So, what do you think of Lavenham?' Rachel asked.

'Lovely. The old buildings are amazing - and the Swan looks such an historic place,' Avie replied, 'it will be good to go there tonight and see inside.'

Rachel nodded. 'It's even better inside. What did you buy,

I see you've got a package?...' But her words were interrupted by a tall young man with a fine moustache tapping her on the shoulder. *This must be Arthur*, thought Avie.

'Hallo there, Rachel!' Rachel turned and her eyes lit up. 'Oh, hallo, Art, this is my friend Avie, who's staying with me.'

Arthur's eyes swept over Avie quickly and he gave her a friendly grin. 'Hallo, Avie, how do you do? Are you coming tonight?'

They shook hands, as the coffee arrived.

'Yes, I am – looking forward to it.'

'Can you join us for coffee?' Rachel asked. But the young man shook his head. 'I'm here with Mother, helping her with the shopping. She's injured her hand. But I'll see you both tonight! I'll pick you up about half past seven, all right? Excuse me dashing off, Bye!'

And he left the café as quickly as he had arrived.

'That was Arthur,' laughed Rachel.

'He looks nice,' Avie murmured, 'will he be bringing a friend?'

Chapter 30

Lavenham, the Young Farmers' Ball.

Avie and Rachel had returned from Lavenham, had a quick sandwich lunch and were now in the serious business of getting themselves ready for the Young Farmers' Ball.

'So how many people are attending?' Avie asked.

'Oh, it's a big occasion locally, so there will be about a hundred and fifty, I think it is,' Rachel said, as she looked through her jewellery box and selected some earrings.

Her eyes sparkled, as she went to her wardrobe and pulled out her dress. 'Here it is! What do you think?' She held it up. It was a proper ball gown, with a fitted, boned bodice and full skirt and was in a striking turquoise-blue colour, which suited her fair hair admirably.

Avie caught her breath. It was a beautiful taffeta gown, with sparkly diamante decorating the bodice and short sleeves and more diamante edging the hem. 'Oh, it's lovely', she gasped. 'You'll be the belle of the Ball!'

Rachel shrugged. She was a quiet, modest girl, but you could see she had chosen a rather special dress, for a rather special occasion. 'I thought I'd buy something extra smart', she said quietly. 'Arthur *is* the President, so I thought I should make an extra effort. Of course, the men will be in black tie, so they will look so smart as well. After seeing them all the year in corduroy trousers and sweaters, it will make a nice change to see them dressed up,' she added.

'Now, is Arthur bringing a close friend with him, do you know,' Avie asked, 'or will I be at the mercy of any spare men around?'

Rachel laughed. 'Oh, there will be plenty of spare men around, don't worry about that. He has got a friend he goes around with sometimes, so I expect he will be there...'

'Oh, what's his name?' asked Avie.

'Charles – he's the local livestock agent. Bit of a dark horse,' she added.

Avie nodded. 'Now, I'd better go and wash my hair and have a bath,' she said and went off to the bathroom.

Three hours later the girls had changed into their dresses and were in Rachel's bedroom, arranging their hair. Rachel was putting hers up in a chignon, whereas Avie had decided to wear her hair loose, with a pink, sparkly Alice band.

She had taken care with her make-up and accentuated her eyes a little, a touch of lipstick and her complexion was shining with a healthy glow. She was quite excited at the thought of going out and meeting some new people. It was true, as Derek had said, she hadn't been out to enjoy herself with her friends a lot lately. She felt comfortable in her black dress. Decorated with discreet beading on the shoulders and bodice, it was a perfect fit. The deep V-neck gave just a glimpse of Avie's décolletage. She had last worn this dress when she had seen William in London. She remembered the evening well. It was etched on her memory.

It was a smart, expensive frock, purchased quite extravagantly from Harrods and so she felt very confident in it. It was plain, but very stylish. And her pearl earrings and Rachel's pearl necklace enhanced her appearance.

'Now, have you brought some scent with you - or do you want to borrow some of mine?' Rachel asked.

Avie shook her head. She had brought a small bottle of 'Soir de Paris' with her, which was her favourite perfume.

'I think we're just about ready', Rachel smiled, and looked at her watch. 'Art will be here soon, let's have a quick glass of sherry before he comes!'

An hour later they were arriving at The Swan in Lavenham, after a fast ride in Arthur's motor. Art seemed to be in high spirits, laughing and joking with the girls, as he negotiated the twisty country lanes. The little town was looking very festive, with Christmas lights festooned over some buildings and The Swan had a welcoming air, as they entered the old building.

They made their way to the vast hall in the centre of the building. Exposed beams dominated the ceiling, with a inglenook fireplace at one end, with a Bressumer beam across it. The log fire was blazing fiercely, and the warmth was very welcome. A poster of the King and Queen was displayed on the wall near the dais, with the Union Jack placed nearby. The room had been decorated with streamers and balloons. A huge Christmas tree stood near the fireplace, twinkling with coloured lights and decorations. And at the other end of the room a band was seated on a dais, playing popular tunes. An atmosphere of conviviality greeted them as they entered.

They were immediately surrounded by a circle of friends, all hailing each other as they met. Uniformed waiters circulated amongst the crowd of people with trays of drinks, which were happily accepted. Maids in black dresses were offering canapés.

All the ladies were complimenting each other on their outfits and there was admiration in the gentlemen's eyes, as they surveyed the ladies in their finery. But Avie was thinking how nice it was to see the gentlemen so smartly attired. She remembered when William had come to her eighteenth birthday party, looking so handsome in his dinner jacket and bow tie. She prayed to God he would make a good recovery from his wounds and return home safely.

But her thoughts were interrupted by Rachel introducing her to a dark, rather swarthy-looking gentleman, who had appeared by her side. He had an incipient moustache and a trace of stubble on his chin. Impeccably dressed in evening attire, he had a foulard knotted at his neck, instead of a bow tie. This gave him the look of a Romany, Avie thought.

'Avie, this is Charles - Charles, meet Avie, my friend from London who is staying with me at the moment.'

Charles' eyes locked with hers, as he offered his hand. 'How do you do?' he murmured in a low voice.

And as Avie took his hand, a strong frisson of sexual attraction ran through her body, most unexpectedly. She tried to pull herself together. 'Hallo, Charles, um, so you're a friend of Arthur's?' Suddenly her heart was beating faster, and she didn't quite know what to say, most unlike herself. Charles continued to stare quite unashamedly at her and not once did he smile. 'That's right. I've known Arthur for quite a while. You work in London, I believe?' he said, as the waiter re-filled their glasses. 'Which part?'

'I'm in Islington - I'm a nanny, so I'm looking after nine-year-old twins - a very busy post!' Avie felt on safer ground now, talking about the twins. And she started to gabble on about their school, their scouting activities and the family in general.

'And have you always lived in this area?' she asked.

He shrugged. 'I tend to travel around quite a bit, inspecting the cattle, going to auctions. I was down in Devon recently, near Exeter...'

'So, what is it you do, may I ask?' Avie said, knowing full well what it was.

'I'm a livestock agent, buying and selling cattle for clients, dealing with transportation and all that.'

Avie nodded. She was then able to mention she knew someone who lived in Devon and what a lovely county it was. Also, the holiday they had had in Weymouth before war broke out.

'Are you able to fit in any war work in your busy schedule?' Charles asked, as Arthur left their group to address everyone.

'Tell you in a minute,' Avie whispered, as Arthur took the microphone and spoke to the assembled company from the dais, Rachel standing beside him in her stunning gown.

'Good evening, everyone and welcome to the Young Farmers' Ball, 1914. This is a very special occasion tonight. The first time we have gathered together like this, with the country in a state of war. As you know the Government is reliant on our farming community to provide the country with fresh fruit and vegetables and other crops, at this critical time when imports are banned. We have a very important role to play. But the enemy must be faced and conquered and I'm sure we are all doing our best to support the war effort in these dark days. For that reason, I would like to announce we are donating ten per cent of our ticket sales tonight to the SSFA, the Soldiers, Sailors & Families Association, that fine organisation, who do so much to support the servicemen returning to our shores injured or disabled. And God willing, we will emerge victorious from this conflict.'

A big cheer erupted at this, but Arthur continued: 'I thank you for coming tonight to support the Young Farmers. We are grateful for your patronage and hope you will enjoy yourselves into the bargain. Have a good night – oh, and if it's not too early, a Happy Christmas to one and all! Thank you and goodnight. Now we can start the dancing…!'

And he offered his hand to Rachel, and the couple took to the dance floor. The band began to play some popular music and several couples soon joined them.

Charles turned to Avie. 'Would you like to dance?'

'I'd love to,' she smiled. The music was the popular song, 'Aba Daba Honeymoon', and soon everyone was joining in, singing the words.

'Now, you were going to tell me about your war work…' prompted Charles, as they moved around the floor.

'Oh yes,' Avie shrugged, 'I'm not able to do too much, as I have my post as a Norland Nanny, but I do fit in some work in a local Soup Kitchen, and go to, um, a place in Pimlico which deals with used clothing, to help the unemployed and um, disabled servicemen. Queen Mary has set up this scheme…' she trailed off. Avie was finding it difficult to maintain a normal level of conversation with Charles, while dancing with him. She found him a disturbing presence and the frisson she had experienced earlier had only increased, now they were so close. She began looking at his lips and imagining kissing him - to her amazement. What was she thinking of?

'So how do you know Rachel then?' Charles asked, placing his arm more tightly around her waist.

Avie smiled. 'We met in Switzerland, when we were at finishing school…'

'Oh! I'm impressed.' He raised an eyebrow. 'And was it a valuable experience?'

'It was great, we had such fun there.' Her eyes sparkled. 'And we learnt a lot, as well as improving our French.'

'And where were you in Switzerland?'

'Montreux, beautiful place.'

The music finished and they returned to their seats. Rachel came up to them, accompanied by another young man, very fresh-faced and smiling, like an eager puppy. 'Avie, this is James, James, meet Avie, my friend from London.'

She wagged her finger at Charles. 'You're monopolising my friend, you naughty man,' she laughed, 'come and dance with me. This is the Ladies Excuse Me dance.' And on cue the band started up again.

Later in the evening, Rachel caught up with Avie. 'I hope you didn't mind my stepping in like that. I thought you needed rescuing! How did you find him? A lot of girls won't go in a taxi with him…' she added.

'Now you tell me!' Avie grimaced.

'No, truly, what *did* you think of Charles?'

Avie flicked her blue eyes up at Rachel. 'I think he's dangerous…'

But what she didn't tell Rachel - she also found Charles rather fascinating…

Chapter 31

Avie was slow to wake the next morning, after the Ball. She was just stirring, when Rachel came in with a welcome cup of tea. She was still looking sleepy herself and Avie sat up, stretching her arms.

'Sleep well?'

'Like a log, oh, thanks, Rach. Good morning!' She smiled. 'Good night, wasn't it? A lot of fun.'

Avie had really enjoyed the evening and had ended up dancing with quite a few different young farmers. She had also danced with Charles again - and he was the one she remembered. He was quite an intriguing character, she thought.

She had surprised herself when she was drawn to him physically. But in the cold light of day, she realised he was not her kind of person. He was too intense and brooding. Now she had come to her senses, she reproved herself. How could she be unfaithful to William, even in her thoughts? *Please forgive me, William*, she begged.

Rachel nodded. 'Glad you enjoyed it. Yes, it was good - I think it went splendidly!'

'Arthur spoke very well, I thought,' Avie said, sipping her tea. 'He's a confident speaker and very popular with all the farmers he deals with.' She smiled at Avie. 'No rush today, we'll just take it easy. Oh, by the way,' Rachel said, as she turned to leave the room. 'Your mother phoned last night, apparently, and wants you to phone her back.'

'Oh!' Avie was slightly taken aback. 'I didn't realise she knew this number…' Alarm bells began to ring in her head.

'Mum said she rang the Ducketts first, and they gave her this number.'

'Oh, I'd better ring her right away. May I use your phone?' Suddenly Avie felt anxious. Not more bad news, surely. It was unlike mother to telephone her while she was away like this.

'Of course, I'll show you where it is.'

Avie pulled on her dressing-gown and followed Rachel downstairs to the hall, where the telephone was located. Within a few minutes she was connected to The Laurels and speaking to Harriet. 'I believe you rang me, Mother? Nothing wrong, is there?' she said cautiously.

There was a pause and then her mother came back on the line. 'We've heard from Sylvie again, darling. About William. Now, is it possible for you to come here to-day for me to tell you the news?'

'No, sorry, Mother, I can't possibly do that – it would take me all day to reach you. I'm in Suffolk, staying with Rachel. If you've got some news, tell it to me now, please…'

She heard her mother sigh and then she said, 'All right, I understand. The thing is, darling, I'm afraid William's back in hospital again. He had recovered well from his leg injuries and gone back to the trenches. But then there was fierce fighting – somewhere, I forget where it was - and he was injured again, the same leg. And he's now contracted dysentery. So again, he was treated in the field hospital, but then transferred to the big military hospital in Paris, where he was before. I'm sorry to be the bearer of bad news, my love, but that's what's happened – and we thought you should know...'

Avie felt distraught. She had been hoping and praying that William would recover and soon be back to his old self again - but now this, another injury, plus the dysentery. She had heard that dysentery was a big problem in the trenches, due to the poor diet and insanitary conditions, but at least one felt that could be cured.

'Oh God, that's awful,' she said to her mother. 'He's having such a terrible time, poor man. But, um, I'm sure he will pull through - he was very fit and healthy when he joined up...' she said bravely. 'But thanks for letting me know, Mother. I feel frustrated that I can't send a message to him, to support him.'

'I think one can send messages to loved ones through the Red Cross at times like these, but it's only relatives who are allowed to send them, I believe,' Harriet said. 'You could speak to Sylvie perhaps and send a message through her...?'

'I'll think about it, Mum, but let me have Sylvie's telephone number anyway, if you could...'

'Certainly, darling. I'll look it up and let you have it. Now, are you enjoying your time up there with Rachel?'

'Yes, thank you. It's lovely to see her again. We went to the Young Farmers Ball last night in Lavenham - that was great fun.'

'I'm glad to hear that – you need a bit of enjoyment. You've been working far too hard at these war effort events.'

'But everyone there is all right, Mum? You and Jeremy and the children?'

'Yes, we're fine - all soldiering on, as they say! Now you will be back here for Christmas, darling, won't you? It wouldn't be the same without you. The boys are getting so excited about it. They've already sent their letters up the chimney, telling Santa what they want!'

'You'll have to tell me what they asked for - I might be able to buy it for them,' laughed Avie. 'Now I'd better go – I'm using their phone here, mustn't clock up too much! As I say, thanks for letting me know the news, Mum, and I'll look forward to seeing you all at Christmas, not long to go now! Give my love to everyone, won't you? Bye!'

And Avie rang off, feeling so upset to hear the news about William, but thinking it was good of Harriet to let her know.

She went to find Rachel, who was now in the kitchen, setting out the breakfast table.

'Bad news again, old chum?' Her face was anxious as she waited for Avie's reply.

Avie nodded. ''Fraid so, William's back in hospital again – he injured the same leg again and has now contracted dysentery, poor chap.' She shook her head. 'I just wish I could send a message to support him, it's very frustrating…'

'I'm sorry - but he's getting good treatment over there, is he?'

'Oh yes, sounds like it. He's been taken to the big military hospital in Paris, so he should receive good care.'

'Now,' Rachel donned her apron, 'who's for bacon and eggs? Can you take it, after last night's festivities?'

'I might just be able to manage it,' laughed Avie.

Rachel began preparing the bacon and reached for the frying pan. 'Now, come on, Avie Spicer, tell me about your dances with

Charles - have you arranged a secret assignation?' she laughed. 'You looked pretty cosy there...'

Avie shook her head, laughing, putting up her hands defensively. 'Not me - not guilty! I found him a bit intimidating, to be honest. You know, I don't think he smiled at me once!'

Rachel shrugged, as she cracked some eggs. 'It's just his manner - but yes, he's a bit of a loner. He doesn't have many girlfriends, as far as I know. And yet he gets on very well with the chaps, all men together and all that, curious.'

'Though, I must admit, I did find him attractive, in a weird sort of way,' Avie said slowly.

'But Arthur's seen another side to him. He's very good with disabled children, he said. They met up with some people once, who had a child wearing callipers. And this poor child also had a cleft palate. But Charles was so sensitive and kind to him, surprising.'

After a hearty breakfast, the girls decided they would wrap up warm and go for a brisk walk. Rachel said she had something to deliver to a nearby farm, so it was a bracing walk in the cold conditions. But they both agreed it helped to blow the cobwebs away, after last night's excesses.

Avie had decided to return to London later that afternoon, so that she was there the next day to take the boys to school. There was a Nativity Play in the afternoon at the school, so she had said she would take Elsie. The boys had been cast as shepherds – but they were looking for ways to stand out from the crowd, apparently – so goodness knows what they had planned!

Dora insisted on cooking some delicious roast lamb for them all at lunchtime, which was more than acceptable, so the girls were able to have a final chinwag before lunch.

Avie had so enjoyed seeing Rachel at home with her mother - and she was glad that her friend seemed to have found a young man that she really liked. And the Young Farmers' Ball was a highlight for Avie to remember, as she boarded the train at Cambridge and waved goodbye to her friend.

* * *

Once back in London, Avie was in a hurry to return to No.12. She felt stimulated by her weekend away - it had been so good to see Rachel again. And as she turned into Cadogan Crescent, she really felt she was coming home. She was so happy with her family here - they were really kind and thoughtful to her. And the boys were an absolute delight - such characters! She would have to think of something to give them for Christmas, now rapidly approaching.

Avie let herself into the house with the key she had been given – and found Derek and Elsie both in the sitting-room. She had telephoned to let them know roughly what time she would be back. But they were both sitting rather formally together on the sofa, as she came into the room. Their manner was not their usual relaxed style. Their faces looked rather tense, and Derek gave a nervous smile when he saw her.

'Hallo!' she said cautiously, 'hope you are both well?' She immediately sensed that something was wrong, but waited for them to reply.

'Yes, fine,' Derek replied, 'and did you have a good weekend away?'

'Oh, lovely, thank you! It was great seeing my friend and we went to a Young Farmers Ball last night - such fun!'

Derek cleared his throat and asked Avie to sit down. She wondered what was coming.

'I'm sorry, my dear, we have something to say to you. It's not easy for us. You've been such a marvellous nanny to the boys, and we have come to think of you as part of the family over the months...'

Avie stared at the couple, feeling her heart beating faster. They were both looking very straight-faced, and Elsie had started to avoid her eyes and look embarrassed.

'I'm afraid we have to tell you that we can no longer keep you on as a nanny. The financial constraints since war broke out have been very difficult and the fees are getting beyond us, I regret to say. But we thank you from the bottom of our hearts for everything you have done for the boys and the family. We appreciate all your efforts and will, of course, give you a first-class character reference, should you require it...'

Avie gasped and she shook her head. She had not been expecting this. It was a total shock and she just felt so sad, so very sad, that her association with this lovely family was going to come to an end.

'Oh, I'm so sorry, sir!' She went over to them and hugged them both. Elsie was in tears and Avie was on the verge. She felt distraught inside and was struggling to control her emotions. 'I've enjoyed working here so much', she said, in a tremulous voice. 'You've both been so kind to me. I'm going to miss you all so much!'

The two boys then appeared in the doorway and ran up to her. She held them close and couldn't speak for a moment.

Derek kept repeating: 'I'm so sorry, Avie, I'm so sorry, we didn't want to do it,' as he shook his head.

Elsie was patting her eyes and sniffing. 'We've loved having you, pet, I'm so sorry.'

There were tears in the boys' eyes as they clung to her. 'You *will* come back and see us, won't you, Miss Avie?' James pleaded.

'And you will still take us to the play tomorrow, won't you?' Luke's eyes widened as he spoke. 'We've got such a good wheeze planned! You mustn't miss it!'

At these words, Avie came to her senses, and she laughed through her tears. 'Of course I will, Luke - wouldn't miss it, I'll be there!' She looked around at everyone. 'Now I think we all need a nice cup of tea, don't we?' she suggested. 'I'll go and ask Mrs. H.' And she left the room to organise it.

Later, over tea, Avie had a heart-to-heart with Derek, trying to keep it business-like. 'So, when would you like me to leave, sir? When is it convenient for you?'

'Well, as it's so near Christmas, could you stay on this week and then perhaps depart on Friday? The boys finish school then and it would be a natural break, as it were.'

Her heart was torn apart, but Avie nodded bravely. 'That sounds fine, sir.' She hesitated. 'I quite understand your dilemma, sir - a lot of families are in a similar situation. This war has caused so many problems... But I'd like to say, sir, that working for you has been a privilege, I've enjoyed every minute of it. And your boys are both such a delight. You must be very proud of them.'

Derek placed his hand on hers. 'Avie, I shall recommend you to anyone I meet who requires a nanny - and of course I will praise you to the rafters to Norland Nannies.'

'Thank you, sir, much appreciated.' And they had a brief hug.

Chapter 32

It was the afternoon of the Nativity Play and Avie was taking Elsie along. She was quite excited about her boys appearing as shepherds. 'They've never been in a play before,' she said proudly. She had helped prepare their costumes, some cloaks and a tea-towel head-dress arrangement. Avie didn't like to remind her that they were entirely non-speaking roles. They just had to walk on stage with two other boys and sit down in a circle, while a narrator said the famous words: 'And lo, an Angel of the Lord appeared, and they were sore afraid.'

But Avie was sore afraid when she remembered Luke's words - 'We've planned such a good wheeze, you mustn't miss it!' She just had to cross her fingers and hope that they weren't going to disgrace themselves. They might be planning to pull off some stunt in front of the audience of parents and friends. Elsie seemed blissfully unaware of any of this - and Avie certainly didn't want to enlighten her! If something happened, well, it happened and everyone would have to make the best of it.

But as she had left the boys that morning at the school gates, Luke had given her a big wink as he said: 'See you later, Miss Avie!' Her heart was in her mouth, as she and Elsie entered those same school gates at half past two and took their seats in the school hall.

There was quite a buzz in the audience, as the hall began to fill up with parents, jostling for the best position to see their children. Sitting in the front two rows was a restive group of schoolchildren, who weren't appearing in the play. Their role was merely to cheer on these brave souls, who were the chosen ones. They were fidgeting and whispering amongst themselves until the play began.

The Headmistress appeared on stage and said a few words, welcoming the audience to 'our little play' and without more ado, she declared 'Let the Play Begin!'

The stage curtains were drawn back to reveal the four shepherds sitting in a circle, holding staffs, against a backdrop of fields and mountains. A large shining star was depicted in the dark night sky. The familiar carol, 'While Shepherds Watched their Flocks by Night' was sung by an unseen choir and then the narrator began telling the story of the Nativity.

Avie looked keenly at the boys in their costumes. They seemed to be more bulky than usual in the chest area, under those cloaks. She was immediately suspicious and continued to watch them, fearing the worst. And when the Angel of the Lord appeared, being pushed on stage, standing on top of what appeared to be a cupboard, there was suddenly a loud bleating noise. And out of the boys' cloaks appeared two live lambs, struggling to move.

Everyone in the audience gave a gasp and some of the children in the front rows began to titter.

But the young girl playing the Angel of the Lord, clad in a white, diaphanous costume and wearing wings bigger than she was, gamely carried on regardless. She declared loudly 'Fear not, for I bring you tidings of great joy! For unto us is born a Saviour, whom ye shall call Christ the Lord, in the town of Bethlehem. And you will find Him in a manger, wrapped in swaddling clothes, there being no room at the inn.'

At that point, the lambs broke free of the boys' hands and started to totter about the stage, bleating loudly.

The Headmistress, Miss Clarkson, initially looked extremely annoyed, but seemed to have decided to let things happen and deal with the consequences later, for after a whispered word with her deputy, she smiled bravely and continued to watch uneasily, as the drama unfolded on stage.

The four shepherds were now cowering in fear, as the Angel continued her amazing story of the birth of Jesus. They certainly looked 'sore afraid' at this Heavenly Being appearing to them, their acting skills being put to the test.

Avie had to admit the stunt had caused a stir, and the boys were now trying to rescue the lambs, before they disappeared into the audience. There was quite a buzz in the crowd. Everyone seemed to think it was a genuine portrayal of the shepherds' story, and an original one at that. The boys managed to grab the animals and put them back inside their cloaks again, with just a hint of a smirk on their faces. The shepherds then whispered together, and all stood up and said: 'Let us go now to Bethlehem.' And they left the stage.

She was completely mystified as to how they had obtained two live lambs. There were no farms near Islington, as far as she was aware. They must have had help from a friendly adult, but who? Most of the parents were law-abiding folk who were very conservative and wouldn't dream of upsetting the applecart in this way.

Avie turned to Elsie, who had been watching with amusement at the antics of the lambs. 'Did you know anything about this?' she asked her.

Elsie shook her head. 'No, they kept it quiet, God bless 'em,' she said. 'Novel idea, I must say - never seen it done like that before!' She seemed to think it was an entirely intended turn of events. 'Such a pity Derek has missed this,' she murmured.

'But where did they get the lambs from?' Avie said, shaking her head. 'Do they know anyone with a farm near here?'

'Not many farms in Islington!' Elsie said. But then she seemed to think about that. 'Unless…'

'Unless what?'

'When I come to think about it, they do have a friend whose father owns a small-holding in Essex - he could have provided the animals for them, but', she shrugged, 'that's only a guess, I don't know whether that's what happened…'

The stage curtains had now been swept back again and then after a pause, scene two of the play began, now set in Bethlehem - a tranquil scene of a cattle shed, with an inn nearby. The Virgin Mary and Joseph were sitting on bales of hay by the side of the manger, in which the Baby Jesus was sleeping.

The narrator continued her Nativity story, as the choir began to sing 'Away in a Manger' in the background.

The Three Wise Men then appeared, bearing gifts for the Baby Jesus, gold, frankincense and myrrh – and the four shepherds also entered the cattle shed, this time minus their lambs.

The carol 'We Three Kings of Orient Are' then came wafting over the audience, with the unseen narrator speaking all five verses of the carol, explaining the significance of the precious gifts.

The Nativity Play ended with a final rendition of 'O Come All Ye Faithful', with all the cast assembled on stage, as the curtains closed.

The audience heartily applauded the performers and James and Luke experienced the joys of appearing on stage, for the first time. Elsie clapped incessantly and Avie really felt that the boys had somehow pulled off a stunt, which had been wildly successful.

The Headmistress appeared on stage and thanked 'our cast of performers' and now seemed to be taking the credit for the unusual turn of events with the live animals. 'Our shepherds wanted to do something a little different,' she smiled indulgently, 'and although we were a little sceptical at first, we gave them the chance to recreate a genuine scenario. I hope you all enjoyed our little Nativity Play. And well-done, boys and girls, all credit to you! I would like to wish you all a very Happy Christmas and a safe and prosperous New Year. Thank you and good luck to you all!'

Avie was amazed - the boys had somehow got away with it. And as she left the hall, a reporter from the local newspaper appeared and wanted to know who the boys were, who had produced two live lambs out of nowhere. Word had got around about the unusual Nativity Play and sent him to investigate. The Duckett twins were soon being applauded for their amazing stunt - *just wait until Derek hears about this! thought Avie.*

Once home, the boys were cock-a-hoop about the success of their stunt. It could not have gone any better. But they had been spoken to quietly by the Headmistress, before they left the school. She had gently reminded them that they should have spoken to her first, before deciding to include live animals in the performance. However, she couldn't be too angry with them, as the audience had obviously loved seeing the lambs and moreover, thought it was a genuine part of the play. Indeed, it was a wild success, according to the local paper, who claimed it was the best Nativity Play ever produced in Islington. The newspaper had wanted a photograph of the boys with the lambs, but the Headmistress quickly scotched that idea. This was mainly because the lambs had been whisked promptly back to their home turf again by their owner, who wished to remain anonymous.

So the identity of the co-operative adult remained a mystery – and the boys' lips were firmly buttoned up.

But it had given Avie an idea for a Christmas present for the twins. And the next day, once she had taken the boys to school again, she went shopping in Oxford Street. She made for Selfridges, the department store, where Florrie had worked all those years ago. She remembered visiting the Toys Department there - they had the most amazing selection of soft toys and furry animals. They were bound to have two lambs, she was sure. And indeed, they did, and she purchased two identical woolly lambs, with cute bells around their necks. She also bought them a huge tin of chocolates which she knew they loved.

While in Selfridges Avie bought some presents for Matthew and Robert. A train set for Robert and a jigsaw puzzle with large pieces for Matthew. She would have to buy the rest of her presents in Canterbury, she decided, as she was overloaded already.

London was looking very festive, with bright decorations festooned in all the streets and buildings. A huge Christmas tree had pride of place in Trafalgar Square and there was an atmosphere of gaiety and joy, despite grim reminders of the war now and then. Disabled men were selling buttons and matches at street corners or busking, playing a violin, with a hopeful cap set before them on the ground.

The troops at the Front had all been sent a special festive tin for Christmas from Princess Mary. The tin contained tobacco and cigarettes, a picture of Princess Mary and Christmas cards from her and the King and Queen. The soldiers treasured this and many of them never even opened it.

Avie had wandered into Hatchards, the bookshop, in Piccadilly and was looking through the amazing variety of books on offer. Then she spotted a bound copy of the 'Wipers Times' which included several editions in one. It was full of humour and a few cartoons and so she decided to buy it for Derek. He would love it, she knew. She was keeping the pottery jug for Elsie, bought in Lavenham. She had loved working for this family so much and wanted to give them a few Christmas presents before she left.

Avie had decided not to tell Harriet and Jeremy that she had lost her job, just yet. She thought it best to turn up unannounced and then reveal the situation once she had arrived. She had sadly started doing her packing and was amazed how emotional she felt about it. They were such a jolly family and she had formed a close relationship with the boys. but she had to accept that the war had changed a lot of things. Many families were finding they couldn't afford the extra niceties of life and had to make do with the bare essentials.

Once back at No.12 Avie wrapped up all her presents and then before she knew it, Friday had arrived. She had said her goodbyes to the boys when they went to school and Derek, before he went to work. It had been difficult for her, so she kept it brief. 'Keep in touch, won't you? Let me know how you get on...' Though in her heart she doubted they would. Children just accepted things and never looked back.

She had placed her Christmas gifts under the Christmas tree, decorated by the boys with energy and verve the previous night. And said a quick farewell to Mrs. H. and Matilda.

So it was just Elsie there, when the taxi arrived, and the driver took her huge suitcase and stowed it away.

Avie hugged her, as she sat in her wheelchair. 'Thank you so much for everything, madam.' Elsie's eyes were looking moist, so again she kept the farewell short.

'Oh, nearly forgot,' she said, 'we'd like you to have this from us all - and the boys have wrapped something up, I don't know what it is...' And she thrust three gifts into her hands. 'Thanks a million for all your help, Avie, you've been a treasure!'

Avie embraced her one more time. 'Have a great Christmas! Bye!'

And she ran down the steps and into the taxi, to be whisked away to Charing Cross.

Chapter 33

Canterbury, 'The Laurels'

'This is a surprise, darling!' Avie had arrived at The Laurels by taxi from the station. The driver was a cheery chap, taking her heavy case and leaving it by the front door, then departing with a wave.

Harriet was slightly taken aback to see her. They knew she was coming back for Christmas, of course, but she hadn't set a date for her arrival.

'Come in, come in, lovely to see you!' Then Harriet spotted her daughter's large suitcase. 'Oh, you've come for quite a stay, oh, good...'

Avie hugged her mother as she entered the house, pulling off her long scarf and hat.

'I've got a lot to tell you, Mum...'

'Everything all right, darling?'

'Sort of...' Avie couldn't hide anything from her mother for too long.

'I'm sure you'd like a cup of tea?' And Harriet scurried away to the kitchen to see Mrs. Salisbury. She was soon back. 'Everyone's out, I'm afraid. Jeremy's gone into Canterbury again and he's taken the boys to see Father Christmas at Debenhams. Now, what's happened? Come on, tell your old mum all about it.'

Avie looked her mother in the eye. 'I've lost my job, Mum...'

Harriet's face fell and she came over to Avie on the sofa. 'Oh, darling, I *am* sorry. What happened? I know you loved it there.' She put her arm around her and embraced her.

When she heard her mother's sympathetic voice and saw the concern in her eyes, Avie suddenly succumbed to the sadness which had been building up inside her since Monday. She hadn't cried at the news at No.12. She had been keeping her pride intact and shielding herself. But now the floodgates opened, and she burst into tears. Yes, she *was* sad to lose this job. It had been ideal for her. She had loved the Ducketts and adored the twins. She would miss them terribly.

Mrs Salisbury entered the room and placed a tray of tea-things on the coffee table. She nodded amiably to Avie, but quickly left when she saw she was sobbing.

Harriet held her close and murmured words of comfort. 'Don't get upset, darling. I'm sure you'll find another good posting soon.'

'I don't think so, Mum. It's the war. People can't afford the fees now. Everyone's having to make sacrifices, even the Ducketts. Anyway,' she tried to pull herself together. 'I don't want the children to see me upset like this.' She found a handkerchief, blew her nose and patted her eyes. 'I'll get over it.'

She raised her eyebrows at Harriet. 'Not having much luck with Norland Nannies, am I?'

Harriet nodded and squeezed her arm. 'Think positive, darling. You're a strong young woman, Avie. And we've got

Christmas coming up. The children are *so* excited about it all. Anyway,' she turned to the tea-tray. 'Let's have a nice cup of tea, that cures everything.' And she began to pour it from the pretty, floral china tea-pot.

Avie then realised she hadn't told her mother about the boys' Nativity Play. So she embarked on the story of the lambs and the local press getting involved.

Harriet laughed at the story. 'Amazing, how did they do it? The boys will like that one. They never told you who had helped them?'

'I think they had sworn never to reveal his name, Scout's honour...'

As Avie said this she suddenly had a thought. Could it have been Derek, their own father, who had helped them? It was a possibility. He knew a lot of people locally. And when they had recounted the happenings at the Nativity Play to him, it had crossed her mind that his reaction was not as spontaneous as it usually was... She would never know, but anyway, the stunt had gone off remarkably well, which is all that mattered.

As she sipped her tea, Avie looked around contentedly. Christmas cards displayed on every surface. Paper chains hung across the room, hand-made by the boys that very week. The Christmas tree by the fireplace, sparkling with decorations. It was good to be home again.

So Avie was all smiles again by the time Jeremy and the boys returned from Canterbury. They were all delighted to see her so unexpectedly and the boys were soon regaling her with news of their visit to see Father Christmas in Debenhams. 'He was very kind', Matthew said earnestly, 'but he looked *very* old.'

The next week was a blur of shopping trips to Canterbury

and visiting Betsy and Herbie at Hampton Copse. She gave them their presents and brought news of Florrie, whom she had seen recently in London. Florrie was expecting a happy event in the spring and Avie was glad to tell them she was looking absolutely radiant.

They were very sad to hear about her job, but certain she would soon find another one. Avie was hoping to see them over Christmas and Janey too. Her sister had left school and was working in the village shop. She looked quite the young lady now.

* * *

Avie was in her room at The Laurels wrapping presents, when she was given the terrible news. It was a few days before Christmas.

Jeremy tapped on the door, and she could see Harriet hovering behind him. She looked up and could see immediately from his tense manner that something was wrong. 'Dad?'

'Darling', he began slowly, 'I'm afraid, um, we've just received some bad news… It's William…'

Avie stared at him, her eyes locked with his. But Jeremy continued. 'I'm so sorry, my love - his condition suddenly deteriorated, he passed away two days ago in the hospital in Paris…'

Her blue eyes widened in shock. 'Passed away? No, no, that can't be right. What did he die of?' Suddenly, all the breath had left her body.

Harriet came forward and held her hand. 'He died of dysentery, I'm afraid.'

'I didn't know you could die of that…' she faltered, now thoroughly bewildered.

Jeremy sat beside her and put his arm around her. 'It was amoebic dysentery, which affects the liver. It's quite rare, but it's usually caused by drinking contaminated water. Conditions in the trenches are quite horrendous.'

Avie began to breathe heavily, then clutched her head and let out an anguished cry. 'No, no, I can't believe it, my beautiful William, gone!'

Tears ran down her cheeks and she started to pace the room. The presents she had been wrapping lay abandoned on the bed, the gift paper now crumpled and forgotten.

'I'll fetch her something', Jeremy said tersely and left the room.

Harriet tried to console her, but the realisation began to sink in - she would never see her beloved William again. Avie slumped on the bed and buried her head in the pillow, her lovely auburn hair tousled.

She tortured herself with thoughts. She had never sent a message to him through Sylvie and now she regretted that. William had always seemed so healthy and fit; she had always thought he would come through the war. And for him to die from dysentery was the final insult. He was a dedicated soldier. Why couldn't he have died from injuries sustained in battle? Somehow it would have been more noble. But in her grief, she wasn't thinking rationally.

Harriet sat for a while with her, stroking her head, as Avie lay sobbing, her shoulders heaving. Jeremy came back with a tot of whisky, which he insisted she drank. Harriet tidied the presents and paper and put them in a pile on a chair. But then they realised she needed to be alone in her grief. So, they left her there clutching the pillow, and quietly closed the bedroom door.

* * *

Christmas passed in a fog of mixed emotions for Avie. For the sake of the children, she tried to retain some modicum of jollity, although they had been told she had lost a dear friend in the war. Little Robert had come up to her and squeezed her hand. 'Sorry about your fwiend', he said, his eyes looking moist as he spoke.

And when she had opened her presents on Christmas morning, Avie was seized afresh by another sadness, as one was from the Ducketts. It was a framed photograph of them all, the boys smiling gamely at the camera, looking unusually neat and tidy, and Derek and Elsie straight-faced. But she gritted her teeth and tried to think of the good times she had enjoyed with them all.

The gifts from the boys were sadly in poor shape, as they were chocolate bars and had been affected by the warmth of the room, under the tree. But it was chocolate she loved – Fry's Chocolate Cream and Fry's Turkish Delight - and after they had been placed in the refrigerator for a little while, they were delicious to eat. So sweet of them, she thought.

Avie had written a note to Sylvie, asking her to pass on her condolences to Pierre, still at the Front. She also asked him to convey her sympathy to William's mother. She had met her a couple of times and found her very cold and aloof, but felt she should at least be polite and sympathetic to the woman, who might well have been her mother-in-law, if times had been different.

Avie found again the lovely, embroidered postcard, which William had sent her all those months ago. She would keep it until her dying day, with its delicate silk flowers on the front and William's shaky hand-writing on the back, telling her he loved her. She would also treasure the amazing Cartier jewellery he had given her for her eighteenth birthday, now in the safe here at The Laurels. They had both had such hopes then for their relationship. Avie had been certain they would soon become engaged. But it had never happened - due mainly to the misunderstanding on her part when she visited him in Paris that ill-fated Easter. She cursed herself when she thought about that.

She suddenly thought, too, of Phoebe. They had both lost their loved ones now and both lost their jobs. Avie even began to wish she had allowed William to seduce her that night in London - she might be carrying his baby now.

She snapped out of her reverie. *Don't be silly, Avie*, she lectured herself, *have some sense.*

Avie hadn't spoken to Feebs for months. She was due to give birth in a few weeks' time. *I must get in touch with her*, she thought, *see how she is and tell her my sad news*. And it entered her mind for the first time that in her changed circumstances, she might be able to help her friend. If Phoebe wanted to go back to her job as an ambulance driver, once she had recovered from the birth, of course, maybe Avie could take care of the baby for a few weeks at least.

She must write as well to Rachel and Tom. They had been good friends to her over the years and a tower of strength during her difficult time in Paris, particularly Tom.

The family were due to go to Pelham Hall for the weekend to celebrate New Year's Eve, but Avie had declined this offer and decided to stay at home. She didn't feel like socialising at the moment. She would write these letters to her friends and have a quiet, reflective time on her own, go out for some bracing walks.

And during those walks, the memories of William kept flooding back. They had known each other for four years. And considering they were separated by such a distance, they had managed to see each other several times.

Avie cast her mind back to their first meeting at Pelham Hall and their walk in the garden, accompanied by a chaperone - for she was only fifteen. Then she recalled William showing her the sights of Paris the following year, along with Harriet and Jeremy. William was busy studying at the Sorbonne after this, for his architecture degree. And Avie was caught up at the Mother and Baby home, then looking after Katherine's baby. But she well remembered showing him round the magnificent Canterbury Cathedral, when he came over on a flying visit. He was so impressed with the ancient building.

Her fondest memories were reserved for her eighteenth birthday party. She felt they were becoming very attached and had eagerly anticipated becoming engaged to him. But after that, of course, she was whisked away to Switzerland and her new life in Montreux, so didn't have the chance to meet up with him.

Her biggest regret was the meeting in Paris during the Easter weekend. She had jumped to all the wrong conclusions, when she had found him with his cousin, Amelie. And even when he had apologised in a sincere letter and explained the circumstances, she had doubted him. Avie regretted that now.

Those doubts had led to a whole year without them seeing each other, until that chance meeting on the Embankment in London. Avie thought back to their last meeting, when William had taken her to dinner in Regent Street. She had worn her special black crêpe de Chine dress. They had laughed and chatted, never wanting the evening to end. And before they parted William had tried to persuade her to come back with him to his hotel. All her instincts were saying 'Yes, yes, go with him', but again she had said no, being sensible. Despite this Avie had had high hopes for their relationship - until war broke out and everything changed.

But she would always remember William murmuring as he left her for the last time: 'You 'ave captured my 'eart, *ma petite.*' It was a phrase he had used the first time they met, and it still resonated within her today.

Chapter 34

Sidmouth, Devon, end of February, 1915.

Avie was on her way to Devon on the train to stay with Phoebe for a few weeks. She had spent a reflective time at home over the past month or so, recovering from the shock of William's death. To celebrate her 20th birthday, they had enjoyed a quiet family meal at Pelham Hall. But she had now decided it was high time she joined the real world again.

Phoebe's baby had been born on 21st January and Emily-Jane was now six weeks old. She had been named after Charlie's mother. Feebs had formed quite a bond with the family since Charlie's death and she regarded it as her second home. They lived in the quaintly-named village of Newton Poppleford, quite near to Sidmouth, where her own family had a dairy farm.

They had been so kind to her, and Emily Senior had been an enormous help, giving her tips about breast-feeding and how to hold the baby, if she developed colic.

Feebs had applied to join the Exeter Ambulance Service and been accepted on a part-time contract, which suited her very well. Avie was coming down to Devon on an experimental basis, to see how she liked looking after a young baby. She had previous experience from years ago, when she had worked in a Mother and Baby home and looked after the baby daughter of Katherine, a titled lady. So she felt she was well qualified to do the job. Avie had visited Debenhams and bought a pretty baby gown with matching bootees, as a gift for Emily-Jane, in a pale pink colour. Feebs would love it, she knew.

* * *

'Avie, at last we meet up! Great to see you!'

'Feebs!'

The two girls hugged each other when they met at Honiton station. It had been a long and tiring journey from Kent, but when she saw her dear friend again, she knew it was worth it.

Avie looked around the forecourt. The air seemed sweeter, milder here. Early daffodils were already blooming. The trees were bursting with new leaves. She could hear birds twittering in the trees. She glanced at Phoebe as they made their way to the car - 'You look terrific - motherhood obviously suits you!'

Phoebe seemed so much more relaxed now, back to her old self again. Her eyes were sparkling, her complexion was clear and fresh, and her hair was glossy, tied back in a ponytail.

Before she opened the car door, Feebs gripped Avie's hand. 'So sorry about William, Aves.'

Avie nodded. 'We're both in the same boat now?'

Feebs grinned, as she started the engine. 'But we have to carry on, eh?'

'So how is the little one?' Avie asked, as Phoebe drove out onto the main road.

'She's thriving. I'm still breast-feeding at the moment, but I'll have to stop that once I start work.'

'And when is that?'

'Couple of weeks - I thought I'd ease you in gradually,' she said with a chuckle.

They arrived at the old farmhouse on the outskirts of Sidmouth. It was in an isolated position, with fields stretching in every direction and the green hills rising in the distance. Cows were munching on the grass, and she could see horses in the stables nearby. The door opened and Phoebe's mother, Maggie, emerged, as they drew up. She was a plump, smiling woman and she shook Avie's hand, her eyes crinkling up as she spoke.

'Good to meet you, Avie. Phoebe has told me so much about you.' Her face softened. 'My sympathy to you, my dear. This war is a real horror story. Come in, I'm sure you need a cup of tea after that long journey.' She led the way into the big, farmhouse kitchen and asked Katie, the kitchen-maid, to put the kettle on. Benny the Labrador came up to them, wagging his tail enthusiastically. Avie met Brian, Phoebe's father, briefly, as he dashed in between jobs and gave a friendly greeting.

Meanwhile Feebs had disappeared from the room and soon returned, carrying baby Emily-Jane in her arms, wrapped in a white shawl.

'Here's my pride and joy.' And her pride was certainly evident, as she brought the infant closer to Avie. The baby was now stirring from a daytime nap and opening her big, brown eyes. 'Meet my little Emily-Jane.'

Avie looked at the child and put out her hand, for her to grip her finger. The baby stared at Avie with an unflinching gaze on her sweet, chubby face. 'May I hold her?'

'Of course.' Feebs carefully passed her precious bundle to Avie and for a moment Avie wished - oh, how she wished - that *she* had a little baby - William's baby - to look after. But she was in fantasy land and the moment soon passed.

Feebs was delighted with Avie's gift: the outfit was a good fit for the little one, with room to grow. 'I don't have that many clothes for her, so I can really do with this,' she admitted.

Over the next two weeks Avie enjoyed helping Feebs care for baby Emily-Jane and bathed her and dressed her, like a real-life doll. She changed her nappy and once Feebs had stopped breast-feeding, she learnt how to prepare the baby's bottle from the powdered formula.

All her previous experience gradually came back to her and she gained confidence every day. She was prepared to wash the nappies, as well, until Maggie told her in no uncertain terms that Katie, the kitchen maid, would deal with this rather unpleasant task.

Soon little Emily began to recognise her and was starting to smile. The girls enjoyed taking her out in her perambulator for a walk, when the weather was kind.

Avie also met Charlie's parents and got on well with Emily, the mother. There was a bus service to Newton Poppleford, so she would be able to reach her, once Feebs started work. But Avie was beginning to realise that it would be essential to learn to drive in this country area. Distances were quite great between villages and if you didn't drive, you would be stuck at home. She knew now why Feebs had wanted to learn.

However, it wasn't possible here and now. She vowed to make it a priority once she returned to Kent. It would be so useful to her, if she ever returned to nanny work. Jeremy might be persuaded to teach her, she thought. He had more spare time these days, as he had engaged a new younger solicitor, who now worked in his practice in Canterbury.

* * *

Phoebe had started work and had to drive into Exeter, a journey of about thirty minutes, borrowing her father's car. Fortunately, as she had already worked as an ambulance driver in London, she didn't have to pass any more tests. She just had to familiarise herself with the various streets and areas in Exeter, quite a big city. She studied maps and soon got to know the different place names, and the other crew members were very welcoming.

Avie missed her friend at first, but Phoebe was only working three days a week, so they had time together in between. But Avie was loving looking after baby Emily-Jane and soon developed quite an affinity with her. She loved bathing her and dressing her and taking her out for walks. However, because of the isolated position of the farmhouse, the routes for the walks were very limited. And pushing a perambulator along rutted farm tracks was not ideal, with the nearest village several miles away.

There was a bus service which passed nearby, going to Sidmouth in one direction and Newton Poppleford in the other. So Avie soon found out the bus times and began planning a visit to take the baby to see Emily, Charlie's mother, in Newton Poppleford. Then she realised, of course, she was faced with a big difficulty. There was no room for the perambulator on the bus. She had occasionally seen women holding their young babies in shawls and carrying them about. Or once or twice she had even noticed mothers carrying young infants in a sling across their bodies. But when she thought about it, those mothers seemed to be either working-class or of Romany extraction. Avie doubted whether Feebs would approve of her daughter being carried in this way.

But she thought she would sound out Phoebe's mother, all the same. She constructed a strong sling made from heavy cotton material and knotted it firmly around her neck, placing baby Emily carefully inside. Then she approached Maggie, who was sitting quietly doing some sewing in the sitting room. 'What do you think of this?' she asked.

Maggie looked up and her face, normally so good-natured and pleasant, changed instantly, when she saw her precious granddaughter ensconced in the sling. Her eyes flashed. 'What on earth are you doing? Stop that at once. I don't like it...' And she gave a shudder of disgust and shook her head.

Avie immediately removed baby Emily from the sling and placed her in the bassinet. 'Oh, I'm sorry, I just thought...'

'Only Romanies carry their children like that. Phoebe wouldn't like it. It looks - very primitive, somehow...'

'I'm sorry', Avie apologised again. 'I was just trying to think of a way of going on the bus with the baby...'

Maggie's face remained very disapproving. 'I'm afraid you will just have to wait until Phoebe can take you in the car.'

'Yes, of course, I will, it was probably a silly idea.'

'Yes, it was.'

Phoebe had hinted once or twice before that her mother had a temper, but this was the first time Avie had encountered it.

In truth, Avie was really missing living in a village. At The

Laurels she only had to walk down the road a short distance and there would be a few shops to visit or a bus into Canterbury. And at Pelham Hall, it was only a hop, skip and a jump to reach a village shop or café. Avie was beginning to feel unusually restless and bored. She was fine when looking after the baby, but babies of that age sleep a lot and she was finding it difficult to occupy herself in between feeds.

She was looking idly out of the window, which overlooked the central courtyard of the farm. It was late afternoon now and a herd of cows was being brought back from the fields to be milked. At that point, Phoebe's father appeared, accompanied by another younger man - and Avie did a double take. For it was Charles, her friend from the Young Farmers' Ball, she was sure it was him.

Avie's interest was immediately alerted, but the two men disappeared into the milking shed before she could take another look. She had to make sure.

'Oh, um, I've just seen someone I know', she muttered to Maggie, 'excuse me for a moment…'

'Oh?' Maggie looked up absently and glanced out of the window. 'Oh yes, I believe Brian was having a visit from our livestock agent today - is that who you mean?' And she returned to her sewing.

But Avie was already pulling on her warm coat and some boots and opening the door. If Charles was out there in the farmyard, she wanted to see him. He still intrigued her. She remembered now. He had said he had visited Devon before and travelled around the country. It must be him.

As she was going out of the door, Maggie called after her. 'Tell them to come in for a cup of tea when they're done, it must be pretty cold out there now...'

Avie gave a relieved sigh. That would give her the perfect excuse to speak to them. And she hurried across the chilly courtyard to the milking shed. Once in the doorway she could see the two men inspecting the cows, as they herded them together for the milkmaids. Yes, it definitely was Charles, but dressed so differently now.

'Hallo there, Brian', she called, and the two men looked up, startled by the sudden intrusion. 'Maggie said to come in for a cup of tea when you're done, all right?'

Charles was staring at Avie in disbelief, unable to believe his eyes. 'Oh, it's you!'

Brian gave a grin, looking from one to the other. 'Oh, you two know each other, do you?' The two young people were still gazing at each other. A slow smile crossed Charles' face. 'Yes, we met up in Suffolk a few months ago'. He was still mesmerised by Avie and seemingly dumbstruck.

'Hallo, Charles! Fancy seeing you!' She grinned back at him. 'Well, come in for some tea when you're finished, all right?'

'We will,' said Brian, 'we've earned it, I think. 'We've been trekking about in the cold for too long, eh, Charles?'

Charles ended up staying for dinner. He seemed to know Brian and Maggie quite well, having visited the farm many times over the years. To Avie, he seemed a different person tonight, from the mysterious man she had met in Suffolk in November. He seemed more approachable, somehow.

They were all in fits of laughter when he recounted an episode with a drunken farmer and a bull. He could imitate the West Country accent to a T.

After coffee Brian and Maggie had pleaded fatigue and disappeared to their room. Phoebe went off to give the baby her ten o'clock feed, leaving Charles and Avie alone.

'Come and sit next to me, Avie'. And he patted the sofa. Avie felt very relaxed in his company, after the friendly banter during the evening, so she joined him, with Benny the dog at their feet. The fire in the inglenook fireplace was dying down now, but still gave out plenty of warmth.

'Now, come on, Miss Spicer, tell me your life story', he urged. 'Rachel was saying you were adopted, is that right?'

Before she knew it, Avie was telling him all about Betsy and Herbie and her job at Craven Manor as a kitchen maid. Then the astounding news when she had discovered she was a Foundling. And her mixed emotions when she found out Lady Harriet was her real mother.

Charles was a good listener and very understanding. Avie felt she could talk to him. She found herself telling him all sorts of things she had never told anyone before. How she had resented Harriet at first, coming into her life, and how it had taken her several months to accept the fact, even though she had wanted to find her.

'And what about Switzerland?' he asked, taking her hand and edging closer.

Avie had been anticipating this physical contact with him, but when it came it seemed entirely natural. The powerful sexual frisson now sweeping her body was stirring her soul and she felt alive for the first time since William had died.

'I think we'd better leave Switzerland until another time', she murmured, 'there's so much to tell. But what about you?' She turned to him and suddenly he was very close. Charles pulled her to him and brought his lips down on hers in a deep kiss, which took her breath away. But then he quickly drew back.

'Forgive me, I couldn't resist you. You captivate me, Avie and now, your amazing story. I hope it's not too soon...' His dark eyes scanned her face gravely. 'I believe you have recently lost someone close to you?'

She nodded dumbly. 'I can't talk about him yet...'

'I'm so sorry', Charles murmured. At that point the grandfather clock struck eleven and Charles released his hand. 'I must go, or my landlady will lock me out.' He stretched his arms and stood up.

Avie also rose and he clasped her hand again. 'It was such a surprise to see you here - I can't tell you.'

'And for me. Where are you staying?' She wanted to know all about this fascinating man.

'Fairly close by, a family in the village. Now, I'd love to take you out to dinner. There are some good restaurants in Exeter. How about Friday, are you free?'

Avie gazed at him, feeling slightly uncertain as she spoke. 'That would be nice,' she began cautiously. But then to her own surprise she found herself inviting Phoebe along as well.

'Would you mind if Phoebe came too?' she asked politely. 'She needs a break from the baby.' She suddenly felt Charles was rushing things rather. Feebs would love it, I know', she burbled on, 'she hardly ever goes out.'

When she thought about it, if Feebs was there, it would all be more casual, not so personal. She liked Charles and found him attractive, but didn't feel quite ready for the closer relationship he was perhaps expecting. It was too soon after William's passing. Charles looked rather surprised at her suggestion. He pulled on his jacket rather hurriedly and made for the door. Inviting Phoebe had obviously not been part of his plan. But he was in her parents' house, having just had dinner with them all, so it was rather difficult for him to refuse.

'Hey, yes, good idea, um, has she got a special friend, so we could make it a foursome?'

Avie shook her head. 'She hasn't mentioned anyone, she's still getting over Charlie.' She gave a grin, as she followed him into the hall and opened the door. 'We're a couple, aren't we?! You're stuck with us, I'm afraid. Two ladies for the price of one!'

Charles gave an awkward guffaw, feeling no doubt he'd been manipulated. 'Well, I'll say goodnight, Miss Spicer. And I shall look forward to seeing you on Friday'. He gave her a brotherly peck on the cheek and went off into the blustery night.

Chapter 35

May, 1915, The Laurels, Canterbury

The war had almost receded into the background, while Avie had been staying with Phoebe. Her parents rarely listened to the wireless and didn't take a newspaper. They had few visitors. They seemed only concerned with running their dairy farm, in its isolated position.

It was quite a rude awakening when Avie returned to Kent. Harriet and Jeremy were always on top of current events and they soon informed her of the latest happenings in the war situation.

'You heard about the *'Lusitania'* last week, I imagine?' Harriet asked her, briskly, as they welcomed her back with a cuppa in the sitting room, Rufus sitting at her feet.

'No, what is that, what happened?'

Harriet clicked her tongue in exasperation. 'I can't believe you didn't hear about it. The 'Lusitania' was a Cunard liner travelling across the Atlantic from America to Liverpool. But off the Irish coast she was hit by a German torpedo and sunk, with the loss of twelve hundred lives, men, women and children…'

Avie gasped. 'Oh, my God, how terrible!'

'There have been protests all over the country about the

barbarity of it all.'

'And did you hear about the Zeppelin raids in London?' put in Jeremy.

'No, that sounds bad …' She was somewhat alarmed.

'Good job you're not working there any more', he said darkly. 'Terrible raids - this ominous dark shape appears in the sky, making a humming sound, and moves on, then finally drops bombs over the town, killing people and destroying homes. People have been sheltering in basements and Tube stations.'

Avie was shocked beyond belief. She just had to hope that the Ducketts were safe and her friend, Isabel, as well as other people she had met. She must ring them to check they were all right.

She looked back on her time in Devon as a brief respite. Looking after baby Emily-Jane, who had been an absolute joy, spending time with Feebs on her days off, and seeing Charles so unexpectedly there. She felt they had developed quite a good rapport in a short time. But he was a busy man. After their three-some dinner out, he had moved on to the Cotswolds the next day.

The dinner had been very enjoyable, at a smart restaurant in Exeter, overlooking the River Exe estuary. They had all chatted away very amicably during the evening, Charles being very entertaining. Feebs regaled them with stories from her ambulance experiences. Not to be outdone, Avie had made them laugh with the Bonzo story from the school in Montreux.

Avie and Phoebe had worn their most elegant dresses, Avie in her pink silk and Feebs in black. Charles was in conventional evening clothes, looking very smart. Avie had asked Phoebe to stay with her when they reached home; she wanted this friendship to develop slowly and naturally. She was becoming increasingly fond of Charles, as well as finding him extremely attractive. He seemed to find an excuse to call at the farmhouse several more times after this and Avie began eagerly anticipating his visits. They had even walked round a muddy field in the rain once, for a private chat. And another time when he discovered Avie could ride, they had saddled up some horses and gone for a short ride together.

However, Avie was realising that caring for a young baby was not the most stimulating job in the world. And she had found time to reassess her career plans. The one that she found most appealing was teaching, so she had decided to apply to a teacher-training school in London and take a course. She loved children and had really enjoyed her time as a classroom assistant last year. Harriet had made some enquiries and they thought Goldsmiths College in New Cross would be ideal for her. It was a two-year course and they provided basic accommodation in a hostel. So Avie was going for an interview next week and crossing her fingers she would be accepted. She realised that the London area was a more dangerous place these days, but she would take her chances with that, along with most other people.

Life had to go on, despite the war.

* * *

Clare, Suffolk.
Rachel had invited her up to Clare for the next weekend, so Avie was soon packing her case again. She felt she knew the area quite well, after her previous visit. And of course, now it was May, warm, sunny weather greeted her as she met her friend at Cambridge

station. Rachel seemed in very good form and the two girls were soon spinning along the leafy lanes in the family motor.

After seeing the countryside in winter, it was a revelation to see it in early summer. All the trees were now in full leaf by the roadside and the cottage gardens were a riot of colour. It was quite enchanting. 'I'll take you the scenic route back home,' smiled Rachel and they went past woods carpeted in bluebells and gardens full of flowering bushes, as they drove through pretty villages with thatched cottages.

To Avie, Rachel had seemed especially elated when they had met. Then she suddenly noticed a sparkling diamond ring was adorning the third finger of her left hand, as it rested on the steering wheel.

'Why, you sly old dog! You didn't tell me! You're engaged - congratulations, old bean! That's lovely news!' And she hugged her friend as she drove along, nearly causing her to swerve into a hedge.

'Arthur is the lucky man, I imagine?'

Rachel blushed and gave a radiant smile. 'Yes, of course.'

'And how is he?'

'Yes, very well, very busy of course, this time of year...'

'And have you set a date for the wedding yet?' Avie asked.

'Not sure yet, maybe next year...'

Avie's blue eyes sparkled. 'How exciting! Can I be your bridesmaid?'

'Of course, of course, I was going to ask you. We'll have to decide on some colours... But first we have another wedding...' Rachel smiled.

'Oh?' Avie gave a querying look. It couldn't be Tom; he was heavily engaged at the Front.

'My mother and Uncle Dick are getting married!'

'Oh, wonderful - and when is that?'

'In September - just a quiet Registry Office affair, but it will be so good for her...'

Avie remembered how happy the couple had seemed together. 'That's marvellous news -I'm so pleased for her. And what's happening with Tom - is he all right out there in France?'

Rachel waggled her hand. 'As far as we know. He came home on leave last month. But of course, he can't tell us much.'

'But he looked well?'

'Not too bad - he'd lost some weight, but he seemed fine in his spirits.'

Avie nodded. Tom's sangfroid was legendary.

They were now passing an impressive Georgian mansion in its own grounds, as they left the small village of Stoke-by-Clare. And Rachel waved an arm towards the house with a smile. 'That's Charles' place', she announced casually.

Avie turned her head to look again at the fine country house. 'Really? That's where Charles lives?' Her jaw had dropped.

'Well, yes, his parents own it, but he has a whole wing to himself. He's the son and heir, of course...'

Avie gasped and shook her head. 'I had no idea he lived in such splendour.'

'His father was Liberal M.P. for Sudbury, but Charles is not interested in politics.'

She was amazed. Charles had omitted to mention where he lived here in Suffolk - and she had never asked him. He was a man who rarely spoke about himself. He was very modest.

Avie turned to her friend, her eyes shining, as she thought of him. 'Did I tell you I happened to meet up with him in Devon?'

'No, I don't think you did...'

'He was in the area and came to the farm where I was staying, to inspect the cattle. We met, purely by chance - amazing coincidence. Then he kept popping back again after that', she laughed, 'He couldn't seem to stay away...'

Rachel chuckled, as they neared Home Farm and she changed gear. 'Arthur mentioned he seemed to be spending a lot of time in the West Country. Now we know why! And are you falling under his spell?' she asked mischievously.

Avie gave her friend a curious look. 'Do you know, Rachel, I think I am...'

And as she said those words, Avie realised it was true. She *was* falling under Charles' spell, and that filled her with excitement.

'That's wonderful, old chum - he's a lovely fellow. And what's happening about Goldsmiths College? I know you said you were applying...'

'I'm going for an interview next week - so wish me luck.'

'I can see you as a teacher, bossing those children about!' Rachel laughed.

Avie could picture it, too. She gave a happy sigh. There were so many things coming up! Training to be a teacher. Being a bridesmaid to her dearest friend. And then, there was Charles ...

THE END